LYDIA HARTE'S REVENGE

BY

TED KOZAK

Why wait for justice?

Published 2020 by Midnight Star Press

MIDNIGHT
STAR PRESS.

Print Edition ISBN: 978-1-7339231-2-5
Electronic Edition ISBN: 978-1-7339231-3-2

ALSO BY TED KOZAK

Alex and Christina—Saving Lumenaria
The Messiah's Spy
Teresa—The Snake Witch
Charlie Wolf's Revenge
Charlie Wolf's Justice
Lydia Harte

Special thanks to Jim Kerr, and Virginia Kozak who made suggestions for improvement of the manuscript that led to this book.

All errors in the manuscript, unfortunately, are mine alone.

Malibu Beach Post

March 20, 2006

Oceania Manor Fire Victims Identified

Police have identified four persons who have died from a suspected arson fire at Oceania Manor in Malibu in the early morning hours of Saturday. They are Sophia Benedetto age 79, her son Jonathan Benedict age 53, his son, Milo Benedict age 29, and Carlos Aldana, who is believed to be an employee of Mr. Benedict. Jonathan Benedict was the owner of Pacific Coast Conversions in Culver City and Benedict Armory in Greenville, N.C. Milo Benedict worked in the Culver City business for his father and was an L.A.P.D. reserve officer assigned to Century Division.

Lieutenant Marilyn Shepherd of L.A.S.O. Homicide has stated that the case is being investigated as a murder-suicide but would give no further details. She requests that anyone having any information about the case should contact her at . . .

CHAPTER ONE

March 21, 2006. Tuesday

LYDIA HARTE had driven no more than three blocks from her condo near Century City when the driver of a black sedan that had been following her began honking the horn. Lydia had spotted the car within minutes after she had driven out of the underground garage of her condo onto Pico Boulevard. There were two people in the car behind her, a man driving and a woman with blonde hair in the passenger seat.

When Lydia didn't pull over, the man behind the wheel laid a hand on the horn and kept it there, letting out a continuous blaring sound. Lydia looked in her rear-view mirror. The blonde was now holding up a red spotlight and waving it. Lydia knew that almost anybody could get hold of a red spotlight and use it to pull over an unsuspecting person who thought he or she was being pulled over by the police. When she was a newly-appointed police officer at the Police Academy last summer, a detective from Robbery-Homicide Division spoke to her class about a case he handled where a rapist-killer had stopped his victims by using such a technique.

Taking no chances, Lydia reached into the belly band holster that fitted snugly on her hip and pulled out her off-duty weapon, a .45 Springfield XDS semi-automatic pistol that was fully loaded with match grade ammo. Over the past couple of weeks, she had become an expert shot, courtesy of her friend, Jeremy Morgan, who owned a tactical pistol range.

Lydia wasn't sure she should pull over to the curb in response to the red light until a siren came on from the car behind her. Sirens were a lot harder to get hold of, but Lydia was taking no chances, particularly after the strange phone calls she had been getting. Some of them were innocent, like the female lieutenant from Sheriff's Homicide who wanted to talk to her. Others were not, like the calls from a man with a gravelly voice who kept calling her about some property he thought she owned. The only problem was that the property was not hers. It was held in a trust set up by her stepfather, Jonathan Benedict, and Lydia wanted no part of any property controlled by that trust.

But the phone calls from the man with the gravelly voice had piqued her curiosity. There was an implicit threat in the way the man talked, and Lydia didn't like being threatened by anybody. She wanted to find out who was making those phone calls, and why he was talking about property that didn't belong to her.

Lydia was sure that the blonde in the car behind her had no connection with the man with the gravelly voice, but she was not about to take any unnecessary chances. She had been shot once while on duty, and someone on another occasion tried to ambush her.

She pulled her BMW into a small shopping center and parked in the fire lane next to a drugstore. The black sedan stopped behind her car, and the blonde got out. Lydia kept an eye on the woman as she approached the open passenger window of her car.

The woman wore a black linen pantsuit and was wearing a semi-automatic pistol in a hip holster. For some unknown reason, she kept her hand on the butt of the gun as she walked toward Lydia's car, seemingly unaware that people on the sidewalk stopped to stare at her.

When the blonde thrust her face into the car window, she got a big surprise.

The barrel of Lydia's Springfield XDS was pointed at her face.

"What the fuck?" the woman said, as she backed away, her hands raising so fast that her boobs jiggled like a bowl of gelatin. "Don't you recognize me? Put the fucking gun down! Now!"

It was Lieutenant Marilyn Shepherd from the Los Angeles Sheriff's Homicide Unit, a woman whose lack of intellect was disguised by her astonishingly good looks.

Lydia lowered the gun to her lap.

Shepherd looked in the direction of her car and nodded at the driver.

Lydia looked in the rearview mirror. The man in the black sedan got out. It was Shepherd's partner, Sergeant Simeon.

"What do you want, Lieutenant?" Lydia asked Shepherd.

"Put the gun away."

"What do you want?"

Shepherd leaned on the windowsill of the car door, her eyes on the gun in Lydia's lap. Her breath smelled like a mixture of garlic and peppermint.

"Why won't you cooperate with us, Lydia?"

"Cooperation is a two-way street, Lieutenant. And don't call me by my first name. We're not friends."

"Can we talk?"

"I guess you didn't hear me. Talking is a two-way street, Lieutenant. You don't seem to understand that."

"What in hell is that supposed to mean? You're a police officer. You have a duty to cooperate."

"And if you wanted to interview me," Lydia said, "you should have called my Commanding Officer, and he would have set up a time for us to meet."

Shepherd began mechanically nodding her head up and down, and Lydia didn't know whether to interpret it as a sign of acknowledgement or a nervous tic.

"I need some information," Lydia added.

"Maybe, if you're a good girl, I might be able to help you. It depends on what kind of information you want."

Lydia's face flamed red. She started her car. "Watch your toes, Lieutenant. I wouldn't want to run over them."

"Wait a minute, Harte. Let's talk about this. I can't give you any information about the case that's confidential."

"I don't want confidential information, Shepherd," Lydia said emphasizing the woman's last name without acknowledging her rank.

"Okay. Shall we go back to your condo and talk?"

"We can talk in the restaurant across the street."

Lydia had met Lieutenant Shepherd last Sunday along with her partner, whose full name was Sam Simeon, so named by parents with a weird sense of humor, or more likely by parents who were ignorant of California place names.

Shepherd was investigating the deaths of four people who were related to Lydia by her mother's marriage to Jonathan Benedict. The bodies were discovered in a fire at Jonathan's estate in Malibu just last Saturday morning and included Jonathan, his son Milo Benedict, his bodyguard Carlos Aldana, and Jonathan's mother Sophia Benedetto.

Even though Shepherd worked for the Sheriff's Department, the interview had taken place in the office of Captain Thomas Kemper, the Commanding Officer of LAPD's Century Division. When Lydia entered his conference room after being called in from home, she was surprised to see the room was full. Present at the long conference table were Lieutenant Robert Hardeman, the Officer-in-Charge of Century Detectives, Sergeant Hector Maldonado from Intelligence Division, and two detectives from Robbery-Homicide.

Shepherd had informed Lydia that the purpose of the interview was to find out what knowledge Lydia had of Jonathan Benedict's connections with organized crime. Shepherd had heard that Lydia believed that Benedict had killed her mother and staged the death to look like a traffic accident. So, in Shepherd's mind, Lydia was a suspect in the death of Jonathan Benedict. After obtaining some background information on the family, Shepherd began questioning Lydia as if she were personally involved in the deaths.

When it was pointed out that Lydia had a solid alibi for the night the murders took place, Shepherd continued to question Lydia in an accusatory manner.

Captain Kemper had enough. He peremptorily ordered Shepherd out of the police station.

After that experience, Lydia was not optimistic that her interaction with this bimbo was going to be a pleasant one, particularly since she decided to conduct the interview with Lydia away from the police station.

"So," Lydia said when they were seated in a corner booth of the restaurant, "what do you want?"

"I want to ask you some questions about what happened at Oceania Manor on the morning of March 18."

Lydia shook her head. "I wasn't there. I don't know what happened at Oceania Manor on March 18th. I was in bed . . . in my condo."

Lie number one. Lydia was at Oceania Manor, and she knew exactly what had happened there.

"And that was verified by Robbery-Homicide?"

"I believe so. The conversation regarding my alibi took place outside of my hearing."

"How is it that Robbery-Homicide was able to give you an alibi?"

"I have no idea."

Lie number two. Lieutenant Grayson at Robbery-Homicide believed that Lydia had killed several police officers. In fact, his detectives came to her apartment a few weeks ago in the middle of the night and questioned her regarding her whereabouts earlier that evening

"Were they following you?"

"I don't know that they did."

Lie number three. Lydia knew that Robbery-Homicide had been following her.

Lydia leaned forward. "Listen, Lieutenant, I need to know if this is going to be a mutual exchange of information."

"What are you talking about? Mutual exchange of what kind of information?"

"I thought I made it clear when you stopped me. I need information. I need to know who was at Oceana Manor the night before Jonathan was killed. And I need access to the property as soon as possible."

"Oceania Manor is still a crime scene. No one is allowed access. And what makes you think that you own the property?"

"The property was owned by Sophia Benedetto. I have been told I was a joint tenant."

"So?"

"So, that means when she died, I became the sole owner of the property."

Shepherd brushed a golden lock of hair off her forehead. "I don't know if that's true or not," she said in a sulk.

Lydia stood up. "Can't say it's been nice seeing your again, Lieutenant."

"Sit down!"

"Screw you!" Lydia started for the door. Before she got there, someone touched her arm gently. Lydia turned, expecting to find Shepherd behind her. It turned out to be Sergeant Simeon.

"Officer Harte, I apologize for what happened back there, but we really could use your help."

"I already told you guys what I want. Why should I cooperate with you?"

"Listen, the entire property is a crime scene. We can't let you in until we're done. But I promise we'll get you in there as soon as possible. Now, what do you need?"

"I want the names of the people who attended the poker party the night before the murders. I'm talking about last Friday night."

"What poker party?"

Lydia found out what she wanted to know. They didn't know that Jonathan had a poker party with his hoodlum friends every Friday night. Therefore, they didn't have a clue as to who was at Oceania Manor just before the fire broke out, and they didn't know that the gatehouse at the entrance of the estate had a CCTV system that recorded everyone entering and leaving the property.

Lydia looked back at the booth where they had been seated. Shepherd was standing beside the table, looking as if she were about to burst into flames.

"If I can calm her down, would you let us ask you some questions about that poker party?" Simeon asked.

Lydia nodded.

Five minutes later, Lydia was back at the booth with Shepherd and Simeon. It took that amount of time for Simeon to calm his boss down, but there was still evidence that she had not recovered from her emotional explosion by the persistence of a pink glow on her face.

"Okay, Officer Harte," Simeon began, "can you tell my boss what you told me about the poker party that Jonathan had every Friday night?"

Lydia kept her gaze focused on Simeon when she spoke. "Jonathan had a poker party every Friday night at Oceania Manor with his pals."

"How come you didn't tell us this before?" Shepherd asked.

"I don't know. Maybe, you didn't ask the right question."

"Listen, babe—"

"I'm not your babe, Lieutenant, and I resent being called that. Ask your next question."

"Who were these people you say attended a poker party at Jonathan's mansion every Friday night?" Shepherd asked.

Lydia looked at Shepherd. That pink was not going to go away for some time. "I was hoping that you already knew that, Lieutenant. I was hoping you could tell me who they were. But to answer your question, I don't know who attended those parties. I left Oceania when I was sixteen. I was never around when Jonathan had a poker game even when I lived there."

"Why not?"

"Because my mother always took me somewhere on Friday night."

"How do you know he still had a poker game every Friday night?"

"Because grandma . . . I mean, Sophia told me."

Shepherd took a quick look at Simeon before looking back at Lydia. "Did you just call Sophia Benedetto 'grandma'?"

Lydia sighed. "I did. She really wasn't my grandmother, but she treated me like I was her granddaughter. So, I got in the habit of calling her grandma."

"Did she ever tell you who attend the poker games?"

"No."

"What about you mother?"

"She never told me either."

"Do you know who might be able to tell us who attended those games?"

Lydia paused for a moment. She had her own idea about where she could get hold of that information. It was in the CCTV system in the gatehouse. If she told Shepherd about its existence, she would lose any chance of finding out what was on that system.

"Have you talked to Sergeant Maldonado? He might know."

"I have. He told us a lot about Jonathan's activities, but he never mentioned any poker games."

Lydia knew Intelligence Division had a twenty-four-hour surveillance on Jonathan's estate, and they knew who was coming and going into the mansion. The only reason Maldonado didn't tell Shepherd about the Friday night poker games was because he didn't trust her. That was not unusual. He also refused to share any information with Lydia.

"Okay," Shepherd said, looking down at her notebook and also looking very confused.

Simeon cut in. "Officer Harte, one of the reasons we wanted to talk to you was to find out how Sophia Benedetto got along with her son and grandson. Do you have any knowledge of any animosity between them?"

"Well," Lydia said, "they seemed to get along. After all, she owned Oceania Manor, and she let Jonathan and Milo live there."

Lie number four. Lydia knew that Sophia was disgusted with the way Jonathan had treated Lydia's mother. Sophia had also believed that Jonathan had ordered Lydia's mother killed.

"Do you know of any reason why Sophia Benedetto would kill her son and grandson?" Shepherd suddenly asked.

Lydia saw Simeon stiffen at the question.

"I don't," Lydia said. She leaned forward. "Why would you ask something like that unless you think Sophia killed Jonathan?"

"We found a .357 Magnum next to her body. We think she killed Milo."

Simeon quickly put a hand on Shepherd's shoulder to stop her from saying anything more, but she continued, "Jonathan ran, hid behind his desk, and came up with a gun and shot her. It looks like she killed him before she died."

Lydia was absolutely stunned by the statement. How in hell did they come up with that conclusion? She knew it didn't happen that way. She was there and knew what really happened.

After Lydia left, Sophia must have staged the scene to make it look as if she had killed Jonathan and Milo.

"Anyway, that's just one theory," Simeon quickly added, shooting a disgusted look at his boss. "Then again, it may have been Martians who did it and framed the old lady."

"Then, we have a problem with Aldana," Shepherd said, ignoring Simeon's sarcasm. "We don't know who shot him. Would you have any idea why he was shot?"

"I have no idea," Lydia said.

Lie number five. Lydia had shot Aldana right after Jonathan had ordered him to take her out to the desert and kill her.

"He was Jonathan's bodyguard," Lydia continued. "Maybe, he was trying to protect him."

"So, under your theory there had to be another person who was in the room?"

"I have no idea who was there, Lieutenant."

Lie number six.

"I notice you carry a Springfield XDS."

Shepherd was back to her old habit of making a statement when she wanted an answer to a question.

"I carry a Springfield XDS," Lydia responded listlessly. She was rapidly getting tired of Shepherd. "You saw it when you stuck your face into my car."

"Do you like that gun?"

"I do."

"It uses a .45 ACP cartridge."

Lydia realized where this was going. They had discovered that the bullets used to kill Aldana and Milo were from a gun using a .45 ACP cartridge.

"Yes, it does."

"Can we test your gun for ballistics?"

No worries, Lydia thought. The gun that killed Aldana was in Jonathan's gun vault in the basement. Lydia had put it there before the house caught fire. But she wasn't going to let Shepherd have her off duty gun.

"No. I won't let you test my gun for ballistics," Lydia said.

"Why not?"

"Listen, Lieutenant. You told me last Sunday that I wasn't a suspect in what happened at Oceania Manor. Why are you treating me like I am?"

"I seem to forget you're still a rookie and don't know anything about homicide investigations. I'm just trying to cover all bases. It's what we do."

"Well, let me tell you this, Lieutenant. I bought the Springfield XDS you saw today at Tactical Gun and Supply yesterday afternoon. If you really want to tie up loose ends, maybe you ought to haul everyone at the store in for questioning."

"I don't appreciate the sarcasm, Officer Harte."

"I don't like the implication you think I had anything to do with what happened at Oceania Manor."

"I'm going to ask you again. Will you let us test your gun?"

Lydia got up. The only way she let the interview get this far was that she wanted to find out what Shepherd knew about what happened at Oceania Manor. She had learned enough. It appeared that Shepherd was convinced Sophia Benedetto had shot Jonathan and Milo because a .357 Magnum was found near her body, and it matched the bullets found in the bodies of the two men. Shepherd also believed that Jonathan had shot Sophia, but she had no clue who shot Aldana. And it was also apparent they had not discovered the massive gun vault in Jonathan's basement that contained over a thousand revolvers and semi-automatic pistols.

"I'll be talking to your supervisors about your lack of cooperation, Officer Harte," Shepherd said, trying to get off a parting shot.

Lydia stopped at the door of the restaurant. Making up her mind, she turned and walked back to the table where Shepherd and Simeon were sitting.

"Did you take notes when you interviewed me the other day?"

Shepherd glared at her.

Lydia turned to Simeon. "During the interview last Sunday, I mentioned that Jonathan had a gun vault. It's located in the basement, and it contains close to a thousand guns. You might want to check it out."

CHAPTER TWO

SERGEANT MALDONADO walked into his boss's office on the fifth floor of police headquarters and dropped a typewritten report on his desk.

Captain Malcolm Smith, the Commanding Officer of LAPD's Intelligence Division, looked up at him. "So, what's next, Hector?"

Maldonado shrugged. "I need to get Officer Harte to cooperate."

"What's her problem?"

"She's hardheaded," Maldonado said. He paused for a moment. "She wants information about Benedict's known associates, and I won't give it to her. And before you ask, there's two reasons why. One is that it's confidential, and secondly, I'm afraid of what she might do with it."

Smith laughed. "She's just a girl, Hector. What are you afraid she might do?"

"She's not a girl, Captain. She's a young woman and a tough one at that."

"Sounds like you admire her."

"I do, Captain. Why don't you read my report and then we can talk?"

Smith agreed. He waved Maldonado off, picked up the report, and began reading.

Confidential Memorandum

To Captain Malcolm Smith
March 21, 2006
Subject: Jonathan Benedict

The investigation into the deaths of Jonathan Benedict, his son Milo, his mother Sophia Benedetto, and his bodyguard Carlos Aldana is being handled by L.A.S.O. Homicide. Lieutenant Marilyn Shepherd and Sergeant Samuel Simeon are in charge of the investigation. Lieutenant Shepherd has been uncooperative in sharing information with this Department. However, the majority of information contained in this report about the homicides that occurred last Saturday morning at Oceania Manor was obtained from our friends in L.A.S.O.'s Organized Crime Unit.

Our surveillance team reported that Jonathan Benedict conducted his usual Friday night poker game at Oceania Manor in Malibu on the night of March 17, 2006. The last person to leave was Jacob Nilsson who was seen driving south on Pacific Coast Highway at 12:15 a.m. on the morning of the 18th.

L.A.C.F.D. Station No. 4 in Malibu received a telephone call from an elderly woman in distress reporting a fire at Oceania Manor at 1:13 a.m. The call came from a private number listed to Jonathan Benedict.

Fire units arrived on scene at 1:24 a.m. and forced their way through a locked front gate. On arrival, they found that the first floor of Oceania Manor was engulfed in flames. The firefighters were successful in extinguishing the fire, which was confined to the first floor.

At 5:53 a.m., firefighters discovered four bodies in the library of the mansion. They notified arson investigators who then notified L.A.S.O. Homicide.

The following is a summary of the Sheriff's homicide report:

The body of Jonathan Benedict was found behind a desk. The bullet that killed Benedict hit him in the forehead, passed through the skull, and into the wall behind the desk. The fragments that have been recovered are believed to have come from a .357 Magnum. On the floor next to Benedict's body was a 9mm. Glock 17. Three rounds had been fired from the weapon.

The body of Milo Benedict was found next to an end table that was located ten feet from his father's body. He had been shot in the face and the damage to the skull was extensive. The bullet was recovered and determined to be a .45 ACP. Milo was also shot in the scrotum while he was lying on the floor. That bullet was recovered and was determined to be a .357 Magnum. Next to his body was a Glock 17. That weapon had not been fired.

The body of Carlos Aldana was found next to the ruins of a poker table believed to be custom made. He had been shot in the abdomen. The bullet was recovered and determined to be a .45 ACP. While he was lying on the floor, he was shot in the chest. That bullet was recovered and determined to be a .357 Magnum. Next to his body was a 9mm. Glock 17. It had not been fired.

The body of Sophia Benedetto was found next to the fireplace which was located on the north side of the library. She had been shot in the left clavicle and the bullet was recovered. L.A.S.O. Forensics has determined the bullet was matched to the Glock 17 that was found next to Jonathan Benedict's body. Mrs. Benedetto had what appeared to be a self-inflicted wound. The entry wound was under the chin. It angled upward into the brain pan. The bullet recovered was from a .357 Magnum and matched a Smith and Wesson .357 Magnum that was lying at her side. Ballistics determined the .357 Magnum found next to Mrs. Benedetto's body was used to shoot Carlos Aldana in the chest and Milo Benedict in the scrotum. It probably was used to kill Jonathan Benedict, but there weren't enough fragments left to make a match.

Lieutenant Shepherd was puzzled by the fact that Carlos Aldana and Milo Benedict had evidently been first shot with a gun using a .45 ACP cartridge. No gun in that caliber had been found on site. She speculates it might be possible that a third person used that gun, or that it was taken from the scene by one of the first responders.

Shepherd made some astonishing conclusions from this evidence. She concluded that Sophia Benedict killed her son, Jonathan Benedict, shot grandson Milo Benedict in the scrotum while he was lying on the floor, and Carlos Aldana while he was also lying on the floor. In my opinion, this was a remarkable achievement by a 79-year-old woman who on occasion had to use a walker.

s/s Sergeant Hector Maldonado

Captain Smith looked up when Maldonado returned to the room with a cup of coffee in his hand. "I don't understand this, Hector. Someone shoots this Aldana fellow in the stomach and Milo Benedict in the face with a gun using a .45 bullet. They turn around and shoot Aldana in the chest and Milo in the scrotum with a .357 Magnum. The evidence would seem to suggest there were two shooters. The old lady and someone else."

"It would," Maldonado replied. "The gun that fired the .45 ACP was not recovered. It would suggest there was another shooter."

When it came to lies, Maldonado was in the same league with Lydia Harte. He knew who did the shooting. It was one person, and it sure as hell wasn't Sophia Benedetto. He even knew how Lydia went to extraordinary lengths in fashioning an alibi. But he wasn't going to tell his boss what he knew. If he did, he would probably lose the most resourceful asset he had.

"So, who in hell is this Shepherd?" Smith asked.

Maldonado shook his head. "Hate to say this in this day and age, Captain, but the fact that she has been promoted to lieutenant so young does not set well with me. I believe she has impressed promotional boards by her good looks. I saw her in action when she interviewed Officer Harte last Sunday, and she doesn't know what the hell she's doing. She makes a statement instead of asking a question and then expects an answer. Her partner, Simeon, is an experienced investigator. I could tell from his face that he was unhappy with the way his boss handled the interview."

"I noticed you didn't make any conclusions in this report about this case."

"If it weren't for the evidence that suggests this was the monster of all family disputes, I'd say it was a mob hit." Maldonado felt a cringe in his gut when he realized what he had said. This was no mob hit, but when you really took a look at it, it really was one colossal family dispute that started when Lydia's mother, Vivienne Benedict, was murdered.

Maldonado continued. "The fact that evidence suggests that grandma shot grandson in the balls would certainly suggest she was pissed at him, but I don't believe it for a second."

Smith looked puzzled. "But why would Benedict shoot his mother?"

"Maybe, he wasn't aiming at his mother."

Smith leaned back in his chair. "You have been trying to bring down Jonathan Benedict for nearly ten years, Hector. That's how long it's been since your brother was murdered. You probably know more about the Benedict family than anyone on this Department. So, what do you really think happened up there, Hector?"

"I think there was another shooter, Captain."

"So, you think it might have been a mob hit?"

Maldonado shrugged and didn't answer. He didn't want Smith to know what he was thinking. He was certain that Lydia Harte had killed Jonathan and Milo Benedict and Carlos Aldana, but he had no idea how she managed to pull it off and make it look like Sophia Benedetto did it.

"Is there any way we can get Harte to cooperate with us?" Smith asked. He was looking out the window towards the Federal Building.

Maldonado sighed. "She won't, Captain. Not without significant pressure."

"Have you explained to her why we need to know who wants title to Benedict's property."

"I have. She says it's not her problem. She doesn't want anything to do with Benedict's estate."

"Why not?"

"She knows what Benedict did to her mother. I think she'd rather forget all about Jonathan Benedict and his estate."

"Benedict's holdings are worth millions, maybe as much as a billion dollars. Why should she pass that up?"

"She doesn't care."

"Money's not a problem for her?"

"No, sir. She has lots of it. Over five-hundred million by my reckoning."

"Where did she get that kind of money?"

"A trust established by her mother."

"Does she intend to remain on the job?"

"I talked to Richard Hagerty this morning, Captain. He works with her and believes she plans to stay with the Department for quite some time. She seems to like police work."

"You said something about her not cooperating unless there was significant pressure placed on her."

Maldonado nodded.

"Well then," Smith continued, "I've got an idea about how to apply that pressure."

CHAPTER THREE

LYDIA HARTE didn't give a damn about Jonathan Benedict and his estate, but the fact she was being threatened by someone who had called her several times and demanded that she sign off on the estate aroused her curiosity. She was not happy about being threatened on the phone by an unknown person with a menacing voice, but she was even more displeased when she received a phone call from the secretary of a law firm who handled a modification to her mother's trust and who wanted her to come in for an appointment to discuss Jonathan Benedict's estate. Her first response was to say no, but curiosity got the best of her. So, when she entered the law offices of Johnson and Landry on the fifteen floor of the Trinity Building in Van Nuys, she did so with the intent of learning as much as she could about who was pestering her to give up her rights to an estate she didn't want.

After a five-minute wait in the lobby, the receptionist answered a phone, listened for a few seconds, and then turned to Lydia.

"Mr. Landry is ready to meet you. Are you sure you don't want any coffee?"

"I'm sure," Lydia said for the third time in the past five minutes.

The receptionist led Lydia down a hall to a conference room where two men were waiting. The tall one, a redhead, stood up from his seat at the head of the table and introduced himself as Bill Landry. He moved quickly toward Lydia, shook her hand, and pulled a chair out for her to be seated.

The first words out of his mouth were, "Would you like something to drink? Coffee perhaps?"

Lydia shook her head. "Mr. Landry, how long will this take? I have to be at work by three o'clock."

Landry smiled. "About a half hour should do it." He pointed to the man seated across the table from Lydia. "This is Vince Moretti. He is the trustee of the estate."

Moretti didn't rise from his seat when Lydia entered the room, nor did he offer to shake hands. He didn't look Italian despite the name. His face was pale, and his blonde hair was so thin that the whiteness of his scalp shone through.

"Do you know what a trustee does?" Moretti asked.

Lydia noticed that the man had a high-pitched voice. She was expecting a voice that sounded like the one she had recently heard over the telephone, the one that sounded like the crunching sound made by walking over gravel.

"I know it's like an executor of a probate estate," Lydia said. "Were you related in any way to Jonathan? Most trustees are usually family members of the person who set up the trust."

"I'm not related," Moretti said. "I'm just a businessman who specializes in doing this sort of thing."

"Who do you work for? A bank, perhaps?"

"I work alone. A sole proprietorship. But I do have people working for me. People who know how to manage businesses while estates are being settled."

"Do you have a business card?"

"Sorry. I don't have one with me."

Lydia stared at him for a moment.

Moretti was wearing a lemon-colored linen suit with a white shirt and blue tie. For some reason, Lydia had taken an instant dislike to this man, and she didn't know why.

He reached down below the table and brought up a file that he laid on the desk. He opened it and slid it around so that Lydia could see the top document. It looked like a formal agreement with a line for a signature.

"Miss Harte, I have a buyer for Mr. Benedict's entire estate. He is willing to pay you five million dollars if you assign the estate over to him."

Lydia glanced at the document. She thought back to the phone calls she had been receiving. It would be tempting to sign that document and get rid of something she didn't want. But five million for an estate that was probably worth more than a half billion dollars was ridiculous.

"You must take me for an idiot, Mr. Moretti."

Moretti shook his head. "I don't, Miss Harte. Surely, you recognize your claim to Jonathan's estate is tenuous. You aren't even mentioned as a beneficiary of the trust."

"I don't know much about property law, Mr. Moretti, but I do believe I inherit Mr. Benedict's estate because I'm his only living relative."

"An adopted one at that," Moretti replied. He glanced at Landry who had leaned back in his chair and was staring at Lydia with a look of puzzlement. Moretti turned back to Lydia. "Okay, so you know a little bit about property law. But what if there are alternate beneficiaries who have a claim on the estate?"

Lydia turned to Landry. "Are there alternate beneficiaries?"

Landry shook his head slowly and then said, "No."

"What happens if I don't sign that document?" Lydia asked Landry. "As a matter of fact, what happens to the estate if I do nothing at all?"

She sensed that Moretti had shifted uncomfortably in his chair.

"Then it escheats to the state," Landry said. "And that means . . ."

"The state of California gets it all," Lydia interrupted.

"That's right."

"So, let me guess. Whoever Mr. Moretti represents wouldn't like that to happen, would he?"

"Look here," Moretti began, "I . . ."

"I'm talking to Mr. Landry, sir," Lydia cut in without looking at him.

Landry leaned forward and placed his hands on the table. "Miss Harte, if I may. Maybe I can negotiate a better deal for you."

"And how would that work, Mr. Landry? You're the attorney for the trust and you want to represent me as well? That would be a conflict of interest, wouldn't it?"

"I'm sorry, Miss Harte. I didn't mean it that way. What I meant was maybe Mr. Moretti and I can see if we can get you a better offer."

"Can I see exactly what we are talking about?"

"What do you mean?" Landry asked.

"What properties are included in Jonathan's estate?"

"I can't tell you that, Miss Harte. You're not a beneficiary."

Lydia stood up. "Do you know what I think, Mr. Landry? I think I need my own attorney to handle this for me."

"Mr. Milburn doesn't have the personnel to handle an estate like this, Miss Harte. He wouldn't even come with you to this meeting."

"I know he doesn't want to handle this case, Mr. Landry. But he can recommend someone who can."

"If you want a recommendation, Miss Harte, I can do that for you. I have in the past worked with a firm in Century City called Mayes, Murphy and McBride. They have the resources to help with an estate as large as this one, and they have a good reputation. Mr. Murphy is running for mayor. He is also a skilled litigator."

"Thank you," Lydia said, thinking it would be a cold day in hell before she would follow the advice of Landry. She turned to Moretti. "A counteroffer, Mr. Moretti. Tell whoever you represent, I want five hundred million dollars for my signature on that document."

Lydia didn't immediately leave the premises. She stood next to her silver BMW in the parking lot on the east side of the Trinity Building. From that position, she could see the side entrance of the building without being easily spotted by someone coming out.

Moretti came out fifteen minutes later, casually swinging his briefcase as he walked. He headed toward the back of the lot.

Lydia stood on her tiptoes, trying to keep him in view. He got into a silver Mercedes.

A few minutes later, Moretti was driving out of the lot toward the street. Lydia hurriedly got in her car and tried to catch up with him.

One block later, she pulled up behind him while he was stopped for a red light. When she finished writing the license number of his car on a notepad, she looked up.

Moretti was staring at her in his rearview mirror, and his pale eyes showed that he didn't look happy.

CHAPTER FOUR

LYDIA HAD gotten used to the glares and the quiet hissing she received from some of the officers when she entered the roll call room at Century Division. Her consolation was that only a minority of officers treated her that way when she walked down the aisle to take her place in the front row.

Even though Lydia was scheduled to work with Dick Hagerty that night, she couldn't sit with him. Since she was still a rookie or a boot as the officers called newly minted police officers, she had to sit in the front row with the other rookies who were still on probation.

Lydia's problems at work began with a series of unfortunate incidents that involved a group of officers who called themselves the Wrecking Crew. It started four months ago when she had graduated from the Police Academy. Both of her partners back then, Mosby and Cruz, had taken a day off, and Lydia found that she had been assigned to work with Jim Searles who was not only a member of the Wrecking Crew but also a misogynist. Five hours later, she and Searles were shot under mysterious circumstances while investigating a burglary in a warehouse. When she returned to work under strict instructions not to discuss the shooting with anyone, Lydia found herself confronting a small group of officers who believed she had shot Searles. That was when Hagerty stepped in and volunteered to work with her.

But Lydia's problems didn't end there. She had been singled out by at least a quarter of the officers on the P.M. Watch for having betrayed her fellow officers when she interviewed a prisoner and learned that the

Wrecking Crew had been involved in a conspiracy with her stepbrother, Milo Benedict, to burglarize warehouses that stored electronics and household appliances. While the majority of officers assigned to Century Division approved of what Lydia had done, there was a significant number of others who didn't think that any police officer should rat out another police officer under any circumstances.

When roll call was over, the officers went out to the parking lot in the rear of the station to relieve the officers who were coming off shift. It was the custom that rookies carry their helmet and their partner's helmet as well as the shotgun out to the police car. But Hagerty had a different practice. He carried his own helmet. And when he let Lydia drive the police car, he carried the shotgun.

Lydia liked working with Hagerty as well as their relief partner, Kenny Ferris, who was on a day off. Both men took their jobs seriously and didn't allow the backbiting of the politicians or the negativity of the press dampen their enthusiasm for doing aggressive police work.

She had met many people who were highly motivated when she studied computer hardware design at U.C.L.A., but Hagerty was in a class by himself. He was respected by nearly everyone in the Division and was acquiring a reputation as an officer who was extremely proficient in police work. It was he who convinced Lydia that the Department's monthly qualification requirement was not enough to maintain proficiency with firearms, and that she needed to improve her shooting skills by practicing at least once a week on a range. He also convinced her to get rid of the Glock semi-automatic she had been issued and replace it with a .357 Magnum revolver, a gun that he personally carried. Lydia thought that the powerful weapon was the reason why Hagerty was called Gunsmoke by other officers behind his back. But she didn't know then just how deadly Hagerty was with a gun.

A half hour into the shift, Lydia remembered she had not run the license number of the car driven by the man who had tried to convince her to sign over her interest in the Benedict estate. She took out her notebook, found the license number, and typed it into the police computer.

Hagerty looked at the notebook in her hand. "Where did you get that number?"

"It's something I need to check out."

"Personal?"

"Yes."

"Jesus Christ, Lydia. You're still on probation. They can fire you for doing something like that. Didn't they tell you that at the Academy?"

Hagerty pulled the police car to the curb.

"Let me see what you got." He swiveled the monitor toward him. He studied the computer screen for a moment.

"Who is he?" Hagerty asked.

Lydia explained what she had been doing that afternoon, and how the man had tried to get her to sign over her interest into Jonathan's estate.

"What did you say his name was?"

"I didn't. He told me his name was Vince Moretti."

Hagerty swiveled the monitor back toward her. "Well, the car he's driving isn't registered to him."

Lydia looked at the monitor. The name listed as the registered owner of the car was Roberto Moreno who had an address on Stone Canyon Drive in Bel Air.

Lydia felt her face turn hot with anger. "He lied!" Lydia blurted out. "I knew it. I knew he was lying."

"He might not have been lying," Hagerty said. "Maybe, he borrowed the car."

Hagerty watched her for a few seconds before saying anything else. "Okay, let's say he didn't borrow the car. Let's say it's his. Since he seems connected with the Benedict estate, you should give Intelligence Division a call."

"I won't do that."

"Why not?"

"Because when I ask them for information, all I get is a runaround. They didn't tell me a goddamn thing about how my mother was killed. I had to find out on my own."

Hagerty reacted by drawing back from her. "What are you talking about? I thought she was killed in a traffic accident."

"She was murdered!"

Hagerty cocked his head. "She was murdered?"

"Yes." Lydia was still staring at the computer screen.

"Knowing you," Hagerty said, "I would have expected you would have done something about it."

Lydia realized she had said too much. She also realized that Hagerty was expecting her to comment on what he had just said. She didn't take the bait.

"So, who did you talk to down there?" Hagerty asked. "At Intelligence?"

"Maldonado. In the Organized Crime Unit."

"Maldonado is one of the good ones. He must have his reasons for not giving you any information."

Lydia stared straight ahead, looking at nothing.

"Okay," Hagerty said. "I'm all in. If you're in trouble, so am I. Let's see if this guy has a criminal record." He began typing Roberto Moreno's name into the criminal records system.

A minute later, the result came back.

Roberto Moreno had been arrested eight times including assault with a deadly weapon, battery, and rape, but he had never been convicted.

It was a quiet night until 8:23 p.m. when the radio toned three sharp beeps that broke the silence in the police car. A second later, the calm and measured voice of a female dispatcher came on the line.

"Five-Adam-99, and all units in the vicinity, shots fired inside the grocery store at 3600 Lyon Street. Five-Adam-99, handle the call Code Three."

Hagerty checked to make sure Lydia's seatbelt was hooked up. He reached down, turned on the siren and emergency lights, and hit the accelerator.

Lydia, taken by surprise, was driven back into her seat by the sudden acceleration.

Hagerty yelled at her over the siren and the high-pitched roar of the engine. "Lydia, roger the call with a five-minute e.t.a."

"Lydia leaned forward and grabbed the mike. "Five-Adam-99, roger the call, five-minute e.t.a."

Seconds later, another voice came on the radio from a female police officer. "Five-Adam-45 will back-up with a five-minute e.t.a."

The dispatcher came back on the line. "Five-Adam-99, P.R. reports shots are still being fired inside the store."

Lydia keyed the mike, acknowledging the update.

"This is going to be bad," Hagerty said calmly as he slowed the car and made a right turn on Pico Boulevard against a red light. "Get on the air and ask Adam-45 to cover the rear of the store."

Lydia did so.

"We'll be coming in from a bad angle," Hagerty said. "The store is on a corner and the entrance faces the intersection. When I stop, jump out of the car, and use the door for cover. Do you hear what I'm saying?"

"Yes, sir."

Three minutes later, they reached Lyon Street.

Hagerty skidded the car to a stop facing the entrance of the grocery store. Lydia threw open the car door. She got out and knelt on her right knee. Using the car door for cover, she aimed her revolver at the entrance of the grocery store.

Just inside the doorway, Lydia could see part of a long counter with an old-fashioned cash register sitting on it. She couldn't see anyone moving inside the store.

On the radio, Five-Adam-45 reported they were arriving in the alley behind the store.

Then a voice broke the silence.

"They're gone!"

Lydia looked behind her. A young black man wearing a U.C.L.A. sweatshirt was standing on the sidewalk. He was giant-sized. Lydia recognized him from when she ran track for U.C.L.A. He was a defensive lineman on the football team.

"Where did they go?" Hagerty asked.

"The motherfuckers shot at me!"

"Are you hurt?"

"No!"

"Where did they go?" Hagerty repeated.

The young man stepped off the sidewalk and pointed south. "That way. They got into a blue car and took off three minutes ago."

"How many were there?"

"Two. Maybe a third in the car. Looked like Mexicans."

"Are there any more inside?"

"I don't know."

"Don't go away. We'll need to talk to you."

Lydia picked up the mike. "Witness reports two male suspects described as Hispanic left the scene southbound on Lyon in a blue car."

"Get the shotgun," Hagerty said calmly to Lydia. "We're going inside. Stay alert. We don't know what's in there."

CHAPTER FIVE

HAGERTY FOUND the first body, a male Japanese, behind the counter. His last name was Hamada, and he worked the store with his wife. Mr. Hamada had been shot in the face. The cash register was open and had been emptied. Brass cartridge casings lay scattered on the floor.

Lydia had met the man and his wife a few weeks ago when she and Ferris handled a call at the store about a drunk who was pestering customers for a handout. Hamada was a pleasant man in his seventies who spoke in heavily accented English. Lydia could not imagine why anyone would kill him.

Lydia heard a scraping noise coming from the back of the store. Hagerty motioned her to take the next aisle over. Lydia entered the aisle and cautiously moved forward. At the rear of the store, she found a short hallway leading to what looked like a storeroom. To the left of the hallway was a small office, and to the right was the entrance to a walk-in refrigeration unit.

Lydia entered the office. She held back a gasp when she saw the owner's wife lying on the floor next to a safe. Lydia remembered Mrs. Hamada as a gentle little woman who spoke with a lisp. But now, she lay there on the office floor, like an obscene caricature, her dress pulled up to her loose-fitting bloomers. A pattern of five bullet wounds was stitched in a rough line from her right knee up to the thigh. A sixth bullet had burned a hole in the middle of her forehead. A dark pool of blood had flowed around her head and thighs.

The smell of burnt gunpowder and blood made Lydia gag. She doubled up, cupping her mouth with a hand.

"You don't want to do that in here," Hagerty said. "Take it outside."

"I'm all right," Lydia said. She straightened up, holding her stomach with her left hand, not realizing that was exactly the same place where she had been shot four months ago.

"They were trying to get the combination to the safe," Hagerty observed. He was standing behind Lydia. "Come on, we need to get out of here. I'll secure the scene. You grab ahold of the witness across the street and get a description of the suspects."

"What about the scraping sound we heard?" Lydia asked. "There must be someone else in the store."

Hagerty backed out of the office and looked down the hallway before replying. "You're right. Let's check out the storeroom."

They started cautiously down the hallway toward the storeroom when they heard a faint scraping sound behind them.

They both stopped and turned.

"It came from the cooler," Lydia said. She was fully alert, having shaken off the nausea she had felt in her stomach. "I think someone is in there."

Hagerty took up a position to the right of the cooler entrance, Lydia to the left, their guns at the ready. Hagerty signaled she should open the door and he would go in first.

Lydia lifted the latch and pulled open the heavy door. Hagerty entered the cooler and Lydia stepped in behind him.

Crates of soft drinks and beer lined the left wall. To the right was the display case that opened out into the store. Placed against the far wall was a cardboard barrel that was papered with advertising that made it look like a giant can of Japanese beer.

"I know you're back there!" Hagerty yelled, pointing his gun at the barrel. "Come out with your hands up."

There was silence for just a moment, and then an object came arcing over the top of the barrel. Hagerty hastily stepped back, bumping into Lydia.

The object broke into pieces on the concrete floor in front of him. Liquid splashed on his shoes and trousers. It was a bottle of Sapporo beer.

"Go away," said a tiny voice. It came from behind the barrel.

Hagerty looked at Lydia. "It sounded like a Munchkin." Hagerty sounded serious, he was not making a joke.

Lydia put the gun in her holster and made her way toward the cardboard display. A little girl, wearing a pink sleeveless shirt and powder blue shorts, was crouching behind the display. She was holding a bottle of Sapporo beer in her tiny hands, ready to throw it, like a grenade. She looked up at Lydia, a terrified look in her eyes.

Lydia scooted down, so that she was eye level with the little girl. "What is your name?"

The little girl drew back, clutching the bottle like a teddy bear.

"You're going to be all right," Lydia said. "My name is Lydia. I'm your friend. What's your name?"

Hagerty came up behind Lydia, his revolver still in his hand. "Stay with her. I'll handle the witness and secure the scene."

"Hagerrie." It was the little girl speaking. The look of terror in her face was gone. She stood up.

Hagerty scooted down. "Tamiko, this is Lydia. She will take care of you."

"Baba."

"Baba not here, Tamiko. Stay with Lydia. She good girl. Okey dokey?"

The little girl smiled. "Okey dokey, Hagerrie."

Hagerty turned his attention to Lydia. "She doesn't speak much English. I'll be outside."

It took two minutes before Lydia was able to connect on a personal level with Tamiko. She was unable to get much out of her except for the word "baba" which Lydia understood was her word for grandma. Lydia finally persuaded Tamiko to come to her. She picked her up. The little girl was violently trembling.

Lydia didn't want the little girl to see her grandmother's body, so she pressed her face to her shoulder and walked out of the cooler and into the store.

Once outside, Lydia was astonished at the pandemonium that lay before her. Their police car was still in the position where Hagerty had parked it, but there were numerous other police cars parked in the street. The intersection in front of the store was blocked off. Across the street, a large crowd had gathered. A police sergeant on a bullhorn was asking the crowd to leave. Two officers were trying to move curious bystanders out of the intersection.

Suddenly, a brilliant light lit up from the other side of the intersection. The little girl turned in Lydia's arms to see what was happening. They were being filmed by a television news camera.

Sergeant Joanna Watson, the Assistant Watch Commander, appeared at Lydia's side. "Take her to the station. Be careful. Don't step on the cartridge casings."

Watson was pointing to the ground. Two 9mm. cartridge casings were lying on the sidewalk.

Lydia saw Hagerty in a little huddle in the middle of the street. He was standing next to Lieutenant Robert Hardeman, the officer in charge of Century Detective Division, and a homicide cop whose name Lydia didn't know. They were talking to the U.C.L.A. football player who was a witness to the shooting.

She started to take the little girl to their police car, but Watson stopped her. "We need to leave your car where it is for now. You and Hagerty will use my car to take the girl to the station."

"Did you know those people very well?" Lydia asked Hagerty. They were sitting at the report writing table that was used by uniform officers in the detective squad room. Lydia was watching Tamiko, who was sitting in a chair next to a female detective from the Juvenile Unit. The little girl was drinking from a cardboard container containing chocolate milk.

"I did." Hagerty sighed and lay down his pen.

They had been writing up their statements on a Department form called a 15.7.

"The old man and his wife came here from Japan about a dozen years ago and bought that shop. They slowly began converting the shop to Asian foods only and were doing quite well. They brought a grandson with them who married a student from U.C.L.A. They were killed in a traffic accident a year after they were married."

"Do you know if Tamiko has any other relatives?"

"I don't think so. Not in the U.S. anyway."

"What will happen to her?"

"They'll put her in a foster home with a Japanese family. Maybe try to locate relatives in Japan who will take her."

"Do you think she saw who did it?"

"I don't know." Hagerty was sounding a little exasperated. "Listen, Lydia, we need to get these statements done if we want to get out of here by the time the sun comes up."

"Sorry." Lydia picked up her pen and looked down at her statement. She had written only one paragraph. It described their arrival at the scene and the brief comment made by the U.C.L.A. football player. She leaned forward on the desk and propped up her forehead with her left fist.

Hagerty looked up, concerned. "What's wrong?"

"Nothing."

Hagerty lay his pen on the table and stared at Lydia until she looked up at him.

"What's wrong?" Hagerty repeated. "Spit it out."

"Have you seen anything like this before?"

Hagerty leaned back in his chair. "I've been to quite a few homicide scenes in my eight years on the job. You never get used to it."

"But have you seen anything like what was in that store? They tortured that woman. Trying to get her to open the safe."

"It's the worst one I've ever seen. Like I said, you can never get used to it." Hagerty looked at the little girl who was smiling at something the juvenile officer had said. When he spoke again, his voice was softer, but it had a menacing edge to it. "We got two sadistic bastards out there on the street. If we don't catch them, they'll do it again."

"But why murder two people just to steal a couple of bucks from the cash register?"

"They were after the safe. It's where the old man kept his money. He didn't trust the banks."

"But how would anyone know that unless . . .?"

"Whoever did it knew they kept their money in the safe." Hagerty paused for a moment. "Look, I know this is bothering you, Lydia. I don't mean to be insensitive, but we have a job to do. Right now, that means writing up what we saw."

The U.C.L.A. football player was brought in the station by a homicide detective and taken to one of the interview rooms. Shortly after that, patrol officers brought in an elderly lady and took her into the other interview room.

A homicide detective by the name of Fentress came into the room and walked over to the report table. He looked at the little girl who was still seated next to the juvenile officer, and then turned to Hagerty. "Did they get anything out of the little girl yet?"

"I don't think so. She doesn't speak much English."

"Have you finished your statements?"

Hagerty nodded.

Fentress waved Lydia to move across the table and sit next to Hagerty. He took her seat and began reading their statements carefully. After reading them for a second time, he looked across the table at Hagerty. "Did you touch anything while in the store?"

"I didn't, but . . ." Hagerty looked at Lydia.

"I opened the cooler door," Lydia said.

"And that was it?"

They both nodded.

"What did the witness say when you got there."

"The little girl?" Hagerty asked.

"I meant the football player."

"It's in my report," Hagerty said.

"Well, yes," Fentress said. "Did he say anything else?"

"No."

"And the little girl?"

"Her name is Tamiko. I remember her saying two words and they had nothing to do with the shooting."

Fentress scratched his chin, looking thoughtfully at Hagerty's report. "You didn't mention the bottle. Why would they break the bottle?"

"What bottle?" Hagerty asked.

Fentress looked up. "There was a broken bottle of beer in the cooler. We're having it fingerprinted."

Lydia began quietly laughing and Fentress, clearly annoyed, looked at her.

"The little girl," Lydia said, "threw it at us."

Hagerty and Lydia got off work on time. Before she left the detective squad room, Lydia took one last look at Tamiko. The little girl was still sitting on the chair next to the juvenile officer. Fentress was seated on the floor, cross-legged, and showing Tamiko a teddy bear.

Lydia caught up to Hagerty as he was walking to his car in the parking lot behind the station. "Do you think there is anything we can do for that little girl."

Hagerty shrugged. "They'll find a foster home for her. Don't worry about it. They'll take good care of her." Hagerty looked out at the street. "We need to keep doing our jobs. Keep working like we do. Maybe, we'll get lucky and catch the bastards."

Lydia wiped a tear from her eye. "I better go home." She began walking toward her car.

Hagerty stopped her. "Lydia, this is what we do for a living. We clean up after people's messes. Never forget that."

"I know that," Lydia said. "I'm going home tonight with no one there. You have a family to keep your mind preoccupied."

The instant Lydia said that, she wished she hadn't said it. It made her feel like she was feeling sorry for herself.

"Then you need to come home with me," Hagerty replied. "My wife can make up a cot in the den."

"I can't do that to your wife, Dick. She's got you and three kids to worry about without having a stranger in the house."

"Have you got someone to come over and spend the night with you?"

"I'll be okay."

"Alone?"

"Yes."

"You need someone to talk to. Want to go out and get a drink and talk about it?"

"You've got court tomorrow morning," Lydia said, as she turned toward her car again. "I'll be okay."

Hagerty watched her as she walked away. He pulled out his cell phone and made a call.

Lydia sat in her car for a few minutes, staring at her cell phone, thinking she needed to talk to someone. The obvious choice was her friend, Jenny Hamilton, but she was handling a crisis of her own. Jenny's fiancé had broken up with her because he found out that she was bisexual and had a relationship with another woman.

Lydia had friends from her days at U.C.L.A. but had lost touch with them once she had joined LAPD. Putting her cell phone away, she started her BMW, backed out of her parking spot, and drove the car onto the street. Her cellphone rang a minute later. She pulled her car over and answered the call, expecting it to be from Hagerty.

It wasn't Hagerty. It was her newest friend, Jeremy Morgan, who owned the Rivercreek Range near Santa Clarita and who ran an intensive combat shooting seminar called 'The Gunfighter's Combat Course'.

"Hey Lydia, what's going on?"

Lydia paused for a moment. She smiled for the first time that night.

"Let me guess. Hagerty called you and said I needed help."

"Yes, he did call me, but so what? I wanted to talk to you anyway. When will I see you again?"

"What are you doing right now?"

"I have company. We're playing cards."

"At midnight?"

"Of course, we'll be playing at least until three before we sack out in the barn."

"In the barn. With the horses?"

"We haven't got the tents set up yet, so we'll be sleeping in the barn. The horses are in the corral. They're roughing it tonight."

"Why sleep in the barn? You have a house. It even has two bedrooms." Lydia said this, knowing that Jeremy's house was a rustic cabin set on a ranch in a small canyon located off San Francisco Canyon Drive at the edge of the Sierra Pelona mountains. The cabin was so small she doubted whether there was any room in the house that could host a card game.

"That's what we do when we get together."

"Don't you have to work tomorrow?"

"I do, but I also have people who can open the range for me."

Lydia recalled that when she attended her first session in Jeremy's combat course, he had three employees who he claimed were all named Jose.

"Why don't you come up. It's only an hour's drive, and you can have the bedroom all to yourself. I'll even put on clean sheets for you."

"I can't."

"Yes, you can."

"No, I can't."

CHAPTER SIX

March 22, 2006. Wednesday.

LYDIA TURNED onto the dirt road leading to Jeremy Morgan's ranch less than an hour after she had gotten off the phone. The road was graded and followed a small stream up the canyon to a 35-acre hollow where the ranch was located. Lights were on in the barn. Five Jeep Wranglers in different shades of green camo were lined up in an orderly row next to the barn.

Lydia stepped out of her BMW and looked around. A breeze blew down the canyon, bringing with it the mixed scent of desert jasmine and pinyon pine. The moon had not yet cleared the mountain to the east, and the stars were sprinkled across the sky like powdered sugar on gingerbread. One hundred yards up the canyon from the barn, the porch lights of Jeremy's cabin were on. For a moment, Lydia thought she saw something slinking off to the left of the cabin, but when she looked harder, it was gone.

She looked back up at the stars. The night sky was just like this when she had attended a preparatory school on the edge of a vineyard in the Napa Valley. Views like this were virtually impossible to see in Los Angeles.

Her enchantment with the beauty of the canyon at night was interrupted when loud laughter came from inside the barn. Bracing herself for the reaction when she entered the barn, she walked toward the huge sliding door that was partially pulled back.

A huge cable spool about the size of a small car was in the center of the barn. Five men, all of them around thirty years of age, all wearing black ball caps with an insignia in silver that looked like two falling bombs, were seated around the makeshift table. They were playing cards. One of the men was Jeremy. Another man, red hair with no ball cap, stood behind Jeremy looking over his shoulder.

The only light in the barn was a crude chandelier made of several bare lightbulbs that hung over the card table and cast eerie dancing shadows on the walls as it swung back and forth. Lydia entered the barn and moved left, keeping her back to the wall, trying not to be noticed in the semi-darkness. She wanted to hear what men talked about when a woman was not present.

There were no surprises. The men were talking about what hands they were playing and making cracks about each other's lack of adeptness at playing cards.

Most of the men had a bottle of beer next to their chips, one of them had a pint of expensive whiskey next to his cards. After watching them for a while, Lydia realized that even though they were boisterous, they were all sober, a group of men who were friends, having a good time mocking each other. Over a period of five minutes, she did not see one of them take a drink of beer or whiskey.

The man who was standing behind Jeremy looked up and paused for a moment when he saw Lydia. "Jesus!"

"What?" a man to the left of Jeremy said. "Have you finally seen the light?"

"Look what the mountain lion dragged in," the man said, pointing at Lydia.

They all looked in her direction.

"This can't be the girl that Jeremy was raving about," another man at the table said. "She's got two legs, two eyes, and isn't even smoking a corncob pipe."

Jeremy, smiling, stood up. "Gentlemen, this is my friend, Lydia. Lydia, come over and meet the worst card players on the planet."

Lydia took a few steps into the light.

Jeremy walked over to her. He led her to the wooden spool where the men were now standing with their caps off.

He introduced each of the men to Lydia one by one. Lydia was so bewildered by the attention focused on her that she forgot most of the names the second Jeremy introduced them, except for the guy with a beard named Marcum, and the bald guy next to him who was named Beard. To Lydia's surprise, they all acted like gentlemen.

"So, this is what an LAPD copper looks like nowadays," said one of the men. He had a shock of reddish-orange hair that almost looked as if his head was starting to catch fire under the unfiltered light.

"Don't let her fool you," Jeremy said. "She carries a .357 Magnum on duty, and she knows how to use it."

"Trained by you, no doubt," another man said.

"If she knows how to use explosives, we could use her," another said. "Can't afford another disaster."

"It wasn't my fault," Beard said.

"Nobody's blaming you," Jeremy said. "Come on, Lydia. Let's step outside before these show-offs start bragging."

Once they were outside, Jeremy asked, "Are you all right?"

"I'm fine."

"Rough night?"

"Yes. I just needed to talk to someone."

"We can go up to the cabin and talk, if you want."

"Who are those guys in your barn?"

"Friends," Jeremy said. And then added, "Actually business acquaintances—of a sort."

"Business acquaintances?" Lydia said, incredulously. "They look like a Seal team celebrating a successful operation."

"They're something like that. Only they're a hell of a lot better." Jeremy reached out and placed his hand lightly on her shoulder. "Listen. I'm really concerned about you. Is there anything I can do to help?"

Lydia looked at his hand on her shoulder. He began to withdraw it, thinking he had offended her, but Lydia grasped it and held it in place.

She smiled. "I'm okay. Just being here helps. Can we go back inside? I'd like to sit and watch for a while."

"Of course. Can I get you a drink? We don't have wine, but we have a cooler loaded with beer. And Tommy has a bottle of whiskey."

"A beer would be fine, thank you. Let's go back inside with your friends."

"Okay, but we'll be up most of the night. You can head up to the cabin anytime you want."

The man who had been watching the game while standing, pulled up a chair for Lydia while Jeremy got her a beer. Except it wasn't a chair. It was a sawed-off log.

Once Lydia was seated with a bottle of Scrimshaw beer in her hand, the man pulled up another log and sat next to her.

"I suppose you forgot my name."

Lydia smiled. "I did."

"It's Alex." He was a tall muscular man with whitish blonde hair.

"Hi Alex. I'm Lydia in case you forgot in the confusion."

"I know. We heard a lot about you."

"I imagine you did."

"All good, of course. You're a police officer?"

Lydia nodded. She was staring at the embroidered image on Alex's ball cap. What looked like two falling bombs from a distance were the barrels of two Revolutionary War cannons with the muzzles pointed down.

Alex noticed her looking at the ball cap.

"Loose Cannons," Alex said eagerly. "That's what we call ourselves."

"I see." Lydia tried to recall if Jeremy had mentioned anything about his friends when they went out to dinner last Sunday night. They had talked a lot, getting to know each other, but nothing was mentioned about his buddies.

"So, what have you heard about us?"

Lydia shrugged. "Nothing actually. Are you in the military?"

"Was."

"What did you do?"

"They call it direct action. It involved flying drones, blowing things up, infiltration, rescue, exfiltration, that sort of thing."

"Drones?"

"Yep. Also, surveillance and assault."

"So, what do you do now?"

"I'm not sure I should be telling you this."

"I can keep a secret."

"Of course, you can. I do the same thing I did before in the military. Only this time, I do it for fun. And a lot more money."

"How much money?"

"More than a police officer makes. You couldn't afford us."

That's what you think, Lydia thought.

Lydia finished a second beer and stood up. She caught Jeremy's eye and he nodded. She looked down at Alex. "It's been nice talking to you. I hope we can meet again."

"So do I."

"Are you ready to hit the sack?" Jeremy asked.

"I am. I can find my way up the cabin."

"I'll take you," Jeremy said. "It's dark outside, and the road is a little uneven." He grabbed a high beam spotlight that was hanging from a hook on the barn wall.

Once they were outside, Lydia said, "I thought I saw something moving by your cabin."

A coyote howled in the hills above them, and it was joined almost immediately by another on the other side of the canyon. Within seconds, the call was taken up by at least a dozen coyotes.

Lydia felt goosebumps on her arms. She had never heard anything so chilling in her life.

"They're talking to each other," Jeremy said. "Leo must be in the canyon tonight. They don't like him, and he doesn't like them."

"Leo?"

"The mountain lion that comes down and visits."

Lydia remembered that last Sunday night Jeremy had told her that a mountain lion occasionally visited his ranch.

"Is he harmless?"

"I wouldn't bet on it. He doesn't seem to mind me or my horses being in the canyon, but you can never tell what a wild animal will do."

They continued walking up the slope toward the ranch house. The porch lights were on, making the rustic cabin look as inviting as a Thomas Kinkade painting.

"I'm almost afraid to ask," Jeremy said. "What do you think of my buddies?"

"I like them. It's interesting to see the male species in a single gender environment."

"A single gender environment?"

"That's what I call a poker party. My stepfather used to have one every Friday night. The company he kept weren't anywhere near as pleasant as yours."

They walked silently for a few moments. Lydia drew in a breath of the scented air and sighed.

They had arrived at the front door to the cabin and stopped on the porch. Laughing erupted from the barn.

Lydia turned to look down the canyon toward the barn.

"When are you going to ask?" Jeremy said.

"Ask what?"

"About my friends."

"Okay. What exactly is it you guys do when you're not playing cards?"

Jeremy smiled. "We all have a Special Forces background. Mostly direct action."

"What do you guys do, now that you're no longer in the Army?"

"We're private contractors. We get paid to do jobs for the government when it doesn't want anybody to know about its involvement. And we make a lot more money than soldiers who do the same thing."

"How much more?"

"Chickenfeed by your standards."

"How much more?" Lydia repeated.

"Five million for a job less than a month, plus expenses. Sometimes, expenses can be twice as much."

Lydia couldn't help but glance at Jeremy's left leg. He was wearing jeans, but no one would ever know by the way he walked that he had a prosthetic leg below the left knee.

"You should know that I'm a part of it if we're going to continue seeing each other, Lydia. I'm telling you this in case I'm off the board for a week or two."

"So, what do you do? I mean, you as in yourself."

"I can't run as fast as the rest, but I play a role in our operations."

"If you can't tell me, that's okay."

"I fly drones," Jeremy said.

"So, you're a spy of sorts?"

Jeremy shook his head. "The drones I use have cameras, but they're primarily used to locate targets that need to be destroyed."

The cabin was just as Lydia remembered it when she had spent the night here last Sunday. Jeremy told her that it had been built by an actor from the silent movie days who wanted a place where he could get away from the city. The cabin was small and consisted of three rooms; the front room that was a combination parlor and kitchen, and two small bedrooms in the rear.

The rustic furniture and the mounted heads of deer and antelope looked as if they might have come with the place, but Jeremy told her that the original furnishings were so decrepit and vermin-ridden that he burned them on a wood pile.

Even though the interior of the cabin looked old fashioned, everything in it, including the furniture and the mounted heads of deer and antelope, was purchased from a catalogue specializing in furnishings for hunting cabins or lodges. The presence of a replica of an upright radio cabinet and the absence of a television gave the cabin the appearance that it belonged in another century.

"What time do you have to be up tomorrow?" Jeremy asked.

"I have an appointment in Santa Monica at nine," Lydia said.

"Then you're not going to get much sleep."

"Which bedroom should I use?"

"Use mine. You know the way."

Lydia smiled mischievously. "Afraid to show me the way?"

"I suppose I'd better get going."

"I suppose you should."

He leaned over and kissed her on the cheek.

Lydia stared at the closed door for a few moments after he left. Jeremy was really a good guy and totally unlike her former fiancé, Jake Nilsson, who had an air of sophistication that she later discovered was as thin as a layer of varnish over a piece of plywood.

She could not help but think of Jake without thinking of her stepfather, Jonathan Benedict, who Lydia suspected was conspiring with Jake to seize control of her deceased mother's estate. Jake was in jail now—Lydia had helped put him there. So, she put him out of her mind and went to bed, thinking only of Jeremy.

CHAPTER SEVEN

IT WAS 8:13 when Lydia woke the next morning. She was going to be late for her appointment with her attorney, Eric Milburn. It would take over an hour to get to his office on Ocean Avenue in Santa Monica. She took a quick shower, dressed, headed for the door, and found an unexpected roadblock. A mountain lion was stretched out on the porch, chewing on a freshly killed jackrabbit that lay between its paws. Its attention was momentarily diverted from the jackrabbit when she opened the door.

It looked up at her and growled softly.

"Sorry, Leo," Lydia said as she slowly closed the door. She paused for a few minutes, thinking how in hell she was going to get out of the cabin without attracting the attention of the lion.

She decided to go out the back door. But there was another problem. To get to her car, she still had to pass the lion and walk at least a hundred yards of open ground. The best way to do that was to go around the side of the cabin that the lion was not facing and hope that it was so occupied with its breakfast it wouldn't see her. She quietly left the cabin by the back door, walked around to the front, and peeked around the corner.

All that she could see of the lion was its rear haunches. The only sounds she could hear were the muted sounds of the lion munching on bones and the morning songs of the birds that inhabited the little canyon.

At this time of year in California, grass was still green from the winter rains, so she thought her best bet to remain unheard by the lion was to walk slowly down the hill in the grass alongside the dirt road so that it would mask any noise she would make. She walked slowly down the hill, not looking back. She felt a soft wind on the back of her neck that made her feel as if she were being watched.

About halfway to her car, she stopped and looked back.

The lion had looked up from its breakfast and was watching her, its face frozen in an expression of curiosity. She thought about warning Jeremy and his friends about the lion, but when she managed to make it all the way down to the barn without the lion leaping up and chasing her, she found that the barn door was shut. She decided not to disturb the men. They were big boys. Surely, they could handle a little old mountain lion.

Lydia got into her BMW and backed out of its parking spot. She let the car coast down the dirt road to the paved road. Once she got out onto the open road, she called Eric Milburn and let him know she would be late for her appointment

Most people would have no problems facing the challenges posed by Lydia Harte's inheritances, but for her, it was a distraction from doing what she really liked. She had two sources of wealth coming to her through the deaths of Vivienne Benedict, her mother, and Sophia Benedetto, the woman who Lydia called grandma but who really wasn't.

Lydia knew that her mother had put nearly all her assets in a trust with Lydia as the sole beneficiary, with the proviso she would receive $10,000 a month from the estate until her mother died. Lydia would not be eligible to receive the corpus of the estate until she reached twenty-six years of age.

Eric Milburn had been Vivienne Benedict's attorney for years, but a few weeks ago, Milburn told Lydia that her mother had gone to another attorney, namely William Landry, to change the trust at Jonathan's insistence. Vivienne had named her husband, Jonathan Benedict, as alternate beneficiary, thus giving him the incentive to kill Lydia's mother and Lydia.

When Lydia discovered that Jonathan had ordered the death of her mother and was actively plotting to kill her, Lydia solved the problem very neatly. She put a bullet to Jonathan's head using a stolen .357 Magnum revolver that was given to her by Sergeant Billy Vernor who happened to be a burglary detective at Century Division.

Thus, Lydia became the sole beneficiary of her mother's estate that was worth six hundred million dollars or more. The reason this estate was not a headache for Lydia was that her attorney, Eric Milburn, was overseeing the bank that managed the trust assets.

The second inheritance that Lydia received was from Sophia Benedetto. Lydia was surprised when she learned that Sophia had placed her assets in trust with Lydia as sole beneficiary. Lydia was already the owner of Oceania Manor, thanks to Sophia naming her as a joint tenant of the property, but there were other assets as well.

Eric Milburn was in the process of transferring the trust assets to Lydia, which included two acres of commercial real estate located on Santa Monica Boulevard that housed a restaurant called Schroeder's Deutsche Hofbraumarkt and a small fortune in several stock brokerage accounts. There was only one problem with Sophia's estate. The restaurant business was not included in the trust. Milburn was in the process of filing a probate action on behalf of Lydia to transfer the ownership of the restaurant to her as Sophia Benedetto's sole heir.

Lydia had no idea of what to do with the restaurant when she got it. The real problem, and it was a major problem, was Jonathan Benedict's estate. The sole beneficiary listed in his trust was his son, Milo. Since Jonathan's trust mentioned no other beneficiaries, his property would pass to his nearest relative by the laws of intestate succession in California. Jonathan's only living relative was Lydia whom he had adopted at her mother insistence. His estate, according to what Milburn discovered, included a seventy-five percent partnership interest in a warehouse and trucking company in Culver City, an automotive conversion facility called Pacific Coast Car Conversions in Culver City, a weapons manufacturing plant called Benedict Armory on the East Coast, assorted strip joints and adult book stores throughout California, and a small casino located just across the border in Nevada.

According to Sergeant Hector Maldonado of the Organized Crime Unit of LAPD's Intelligence Division, the property in Jonathan's estate didn't belong to him even though he held legal title to it. It was being held by him for someone else, namely whoever was in charge of organized crime in Southern California. Maldonado wanted Lydia to assist him by taking control of the property and waiting to see who approached her to get it back.

LYDIA HARTE'S REVENGE · 45

Lydia's first impulse was not to get involved, but it occurred to her that while Jonathan had arranged the death of her mother, he was acting on someone else's behalf. The idea that someone else was ultimately responsible for Vivienne's death was percolating in the back of her mind.

Lydia was sitting on a sofa in Eric Milburn's office on Ocean Avenue in Santa Monica. Directly in front of her was a coffee table and on it was a colorful figurine about ten inches tall of a decrepit knight on horseback, his horse being led by an overweight squire. Lydia had seen the figurine on her prior visits to Milburn's law offices. But today when she shifted her gaze from the rider to Milburn who was sitting in an easy chair on the other side of the coffee table, she realized that the intensity of the expression on the knight's face seem to resemble that of Milburn's.

"Before we begin, Miss Harte, I want to show you something," Eric Milburn said. He handed her an envelope.

The envelope was addressed to Eric Milburn. The return address was a post office box in Malibu, and the postmark showed it was mailed last Wednesday.

Lydia opened the envelope. She pulled out a single piece of yellow legal paper with a note stapled to it that contained Sophia Benedetto's signature. The note read, "For Lydia's estate."

But the handwriting on the yellow sheet of paper wasn't Sophia Benedetto's. It was her mother's.

"What is this?" Lydia asked, looking up at Milburn.

"It's a codicil. If that's your mother's handwriting and signature, it changes the terms of her trust."

"It is her handwriting. But is this legal?"

"It is."

Lydia began reading.

"It makes two changes to the trust," Milburn continued. "One that is important, one that is not. It changes the trust so that you no longer have to wait until you're twenty-six before you receive the trust assets. Your mother's property is now yours. That codicil also removes Jonathan as an alternate beneficiary, but it is moot since he is deceased."

Lydia looked at the date next to her mother's signature. "My God," Lydia muttered.

"Is there anything wrong?" Milburn asked.

"My mother signed this one day before she was murdered." Lydia looked up at Milburn. "She left Jonathan the day after she signed this. She found out he was cheating on her."

"I understand. Perhaps, we can discuss the reason why you wanted to see me after you have time to digest this information."

"No, no, Mr. Milburn, this doesn't really change anything. I need to talk to you about Jonathan's estate."

"I can guess why you wanted to see me, Miss Harte," Eric Milburn said, "but I'm afraid the answer is going to be no. I don't want to get involved in an estate that is contaminated with organized crime."

"I know that, Mr. Milburn, but I need some advice. I've already been approached by someone who wants me to assign my rights to Jonathan's estate."

Milburn held up a hand. "Who was this?"

"He said his name was Moretti."

"And this conversation occurred in Landry's office?"

"Yes."

"Was he an attorney?"

"I don't know."

"What did he offer you for the assignment?"

"Five million dollars."

Milburn smiled. He didn't look like the statue of the decrepit man on horseback when he smiled. As a matter of fact, he bore no resemblance to the figure at all except when his face had an expression of seriousness. Unlike the decrepit knight who was skinny as a barn pole, Milburn inspired confidence. He dressed well, had an earnest face, and spoke with a pleasing baritone voice.

"Of course, they wouldn't pay a lot for something they think they already owned," Milburn continued. "I assume Landry wanted to represent you in filing a claim on your behalf in probate court. They would need to do that for the assignment to be valid."

"I think that's exactly what he wanted. Both he and Moretti seemed taken aback when I told them I wanted my own attorney to handle it for me."

"What did Landry say when you said you wanted to hire your own attorney?"

"That's what I wanted to talk to you about. He recommended that I hire a big firm that has offices in Century City."

"Do you remember the name of the firm?"

"I believe it was called Mayes and McMurray."

"Perhaps he meant Mayes, Murphy and McBride."

"Yes, that's it."

Milburn stood up. "Pardon me, Miss Harte." He went to his desk and picked up a manila folder. He took a slip of paper out of it and handed it to Lydia. "These are the three firms I recommend using. They all have the resources to do what you need to have done."

Lydia took the paper and looked at it. Mayes, Murphy and McBride was the second name on the list.

"You can do no better than hiring the Mayes firm, Miss Harte. They are the best in this town for the work you need to do. Their senior partner is running for mayor and is likely to win the primary. They are also the most expensive when it comes to litigating a probate claim, but you can afford it."

Lydia thought about it for a moment. She trusted Milburn. If he recommended Mayes, Murphy and McBride, she would not question any of his motives for doing so. Plus, the law firm had offices in Century City. It was the closest of the three firms to her condo. As a matter of fact, if she walked out to the balcony of her condo, she could see Century City looming to the northwest.

She looked up at Milburn. "Can you make an appointment for me with them tomorrow morning?"

"I'll do that, Miss Harte." Milburn paused for a moment. "I don't know if this occurred to you. Jonathan Benedict died last Saturday morning. Not more than three days go by, and you already have Jonathan's attorney contacting you about assigning your right to his estate when you haven't even established your right to it. It seems to me that these people are getting ahead of themselves."

"I think they're running scared, Mr. Milburn."

"How so?"

"They don't completely understand what I'm capable of."

When Lydia got back to her apartment, she found that Milburn had already left a message for her saying that she had an appointment to meet an attorney named Reece Tanner at the law offices of Mayes, Murphy and McBride the next morning at 9:00 a.m.

The first thing Lydia did after she had put on her uniform at the station was to walk back to the detective squad room to pay a visit to Sergeant Billy Vernor who worked the Burglary Unit. She found Vernor at the four-man desk-table, writing out a report in long hand. Vernor's partner was off on long term leave for an injury he received on duty. Sergeants Finlayson and Gordon, the other two men on the Burglary Unit, were out of the station.

Vernor, like most senior detectives, was overweight, but unlike the other detectives, he wore clothes that fit him, and he didn't let his weight slow him down. He always dressed well and looked as if he had just shaved even though it was late in the afternoon. Lydia had worked temporarily with him when she was taken out of the field because of the difficulties she had with a group of officers who made it clear she wasn't welcomed on P.M. Watch. During the first week she worked with Vernor, they made five arrests, more than the entire detective division combined. She was amazed by his energy and aggressiveness.

Lydia would have liked to continue working with Vernor, but she was still a rookie and on probation. She was sent back to the uniform side when the Women's Coordinator in the Chief's Office made a stink about her being taken out of the field and not receiving proper training.

Vernor looked up at her when she took a seat opposite him.

"Miss me already?" Vernor asked.

"I dream about you," Lydia said, as she looked over at Lieutenant Hardemann's office.

Hardemann's office was tucked in a corner of the squad room. It had a large plate glass window that allowed him a view of the entire room. The small office was crowded with several detectives who were mostly standing. Hardemann was seated behind his desk listening to what was being said. Lydia recognized one of the men as the officer-in-charge of the Homicide Unit.

Vernor either smiled or grimaced in response to Lydia's comment. Lydia couldn't tell which.

"I hope they're good dreams," Vernor said.

"Mostly nightmares," Lydia said, as she continued looking at Hardemann's office. "What's going on?" She nodded her head in the direction of the office.

"Well, you know about the double homicide on Lyon last night. I heard you and Hagerty were there. But something else must have happened, and they're keeping it a secret. The Captain has been in to see Hardemann several times today, and Hardemann didn't even take a break for lunch."

Lydia frowned.

"What was it like out there?" Vernor asked.

"Pretty bad," Lydia said. She remembered the little girl huddled in the cooler. "What's even worse about it was that a little girl was there and may have seen what happened."

"There's nothing you and I can do about the little girl. But there's a lot we can do about the assholes who killed her grandparents."

"That's hardly reassuring."

"Look, Lydia, you have your own problems. You never came back to see me since what happened over the weekend." He smiled. "So, why now? What do you really want?"

Lydia looked around to make sure no one else was nearby. Two teenage boys were adding and removing green marker pins from the wall map showing the area of responsibility of Century Division. The boys were police student workers, volunteers, who wanted to be police officers and who did menial tasks around the station.

When Lydia had been assigned to work with Vernor, he had her plot the locations of the latest burglaries on the wall map. She was upset when she later found out that the task was normally done by teenagers. Vernor told her there was a good reason why he had her do it. It was the quickest way to familiarize herself with the burglary problems in Century Division.

One of the boys, a good-looking teenager of Indian descent, was looking at them with a frown on his face.

Vernor also noticed the boy. "What's the problem, Akim?"

"Is 12403 Santa Monica in your team area?"

Lydia knew the answer was important. Santa Monica Boulevard was the dividing line between the area that Vernor was responsible for and the area Finlayson and Gordon had.

"What did I tell you boys about how addresses worked in Los Angeles?"

The boy looked up at the ceiling.

"The answer is not written on the ceiling, Akim. Tell me what you remember about street addresses in L. A."

The boy looked at him. "Odd numbers are north, even are south."

"So, does that burglary belong to me or to the other team?"

"Oh," Akim said. He walked back to the map.

Vernor said. "I expected an answer to my question."

The boy turned and looked back at Vernor with a sheepish look on his face. "It means that the burglary belongs to the other team, doesn't it?"

"Of course." Vernor stood up. "Let's go outside for a minute," he said to Lydia as he tossed his head toward the boy.

Lydia understood.

Vernor didn't want the boy to hear what they were saying.

"What did you want to see me about?" Vernor asked, once they were in the parking lot behind the station.

"Will you run some license plates for me?"

"Why can't you run them?"

"Because I don't want Hagerty to know what I'm doing."

"Mr. Straight Arrow, isn't he? Give me the numbers."

"I don't have the numbers yet. Maybe in a day or two."

"Another clandestine operation?"

"Something like that."

"Need any help?"

"Nope."

"Give me a call. The usual method."

Vernor was letting Lydia know she should call his throwaway phone.

Lydia looked at her watch. "I've got to hurry to roll call."

They began walking toward the back door of the station.

"You know I shouldn't tell you this, but you look really sharp in uniform."

Lydia smiled. "I know I do. That's what happens when you stay in shape."

"An intended slur on my physique?"

"Maybe."

"Have you heard the latest on Jimmie Spahn?"

Vernor and Lydia had arrested seventeen-year-old Jimmie Spahn two weeks ago after they chased him for nearly a mile in a stolen car. Vernor had suspected that Spahn was responsible for residential burglaries in which two guns were stolen and would be trying to sell them as soon as he had the opportunity.

Jimmie Spahn attended Jefferson High School. So, on the weekday after the burglaries had occurred, they had staked out the high school from a vacant house across the street and waited for him to come out. Lydia followed Spahn on foot to a nearby shopping center where he stole a Mercedes sports car. They finally captured him after a wild pursuit. In the aftermath of the chase, they also arrested the boy's mother who was a professional shoplifter.

Lydia stopped walking, the smile fading quickly. "I haven't heard anything about him since we put him in Juvenile Hall."

"Well, they decided to try him as an adult. That's the good news."

"What's the bad news?"

"The bad news is that the little shit escaped."

Lieutenant Morton, the P.M. Watch Commander, had a serious look on his face when he took his seat on the raised platform in front of the roll call room. Lydia remembered that he had the same look when Captain Kemper came into the room and announced the murder of Les Cooley, the Assistant Watch Commander two weeks ago.

Morton stared at the clipboard that lay on the desk for at least a minute before he was nudged by Sergeant Joanna Watson. He looked up and scanned the faces of the thirty-three officers in the roll call room.

After a moment or two, he began reading from the clipboard. "Last night at approximately 8:20 p.m., two male Caucasians robbed the store located at 3600 Lyon and killed the owners. Suspect number one is described as a dark-featured male Caucasian, six foot, in his early twenties, wearing a Raider baseball cap, dark blue shirt and black pants. Suspect number two was a male Caucasian about five six to five eight, also in his early twenties, wearing a baseball cap under a black hoodie and light-colored pants. Suspect number one fired a shot at a witness across the street as they fled southbound on Lyon where they drove off in a blue car. Another witness said that after the police had arrived, the tall suspect had come back to the scene and watched what was going on for a few minutes before leaving."

"I heard they were Mexicans," a voice said from the back of the room.

"One witness initially described them as Mexican, but when he was interviewed, he couldn't say for sure," Morton said. "The other witness said that the suspect who came back to the scene could have possibly been black."

Morton paused for a moment, looking first at Hagerty and then Harte before continuing. "The granddaughter of the owners was in the store when the shooting occurred. Hagerty and Harte found her hiding in the cooler. She was taken to the station and interviewed by the Juvenile Unit. At approximately, 12:15 a.m., Sergeant Brenda Lamy from the Juvenile Unit left the station with the girl on the way to a DPSS home. A suspect, presumed male, no further description, appeared out of the bushes at the rear gate and fired three shots at the little girl who was seated in the passenger side of the car. The suspect fled the scene. The girl received a cut to the side of her face and was treated at a hospital before being released to DPSS."

Morton looked up again. "Now, I know most of you were already on your way home when that happened. But, if any of you saw anything suspicious on the street behind the station last night, you need to report to Sergeants Fentress and Doyle in the Homicide Unit and tell them what you saw."

"Morton didn't mention it," Hagerty said to Lydia after they had gotten into their police car, "But we had a similar robbery of a liquor store a few weeks ago in Pacific Division. There were two suspects, description about the same as ours, one of them was wearing a black hoodie. They shot the cashier, but he survived."

Lydia said nothing, thinking of the little girl and how terrified she must have been.

Hagerty stopped at the exit of the parking lot where the shooting had taken place last evening. A chain link fence ran across the back of the parking lot. Between the fence and the sidewalk was a thick row of bushes about six feet high.

"They need to cut that back," Hagerty said. "Makes it awfully easy to ambush anyone in the lot."

"Did you hear that Jimmy Spahn escaped the detention center?" Lydia asked.

"You're thinking about the one with the black hoodie?"

"Yes."

Hagerty shook his head vigorously. "I know the little bastard. He doesn't have the guts to pull off something like this. He's a mama's boy." Hagerty pulled his car to a stop for a red light. "We need to catch these bastards. Most liquor store bandits usually take the money and run. These two assholes shoot first, and then take the money. When we run across them, they will not surrender peaceably."

CHAPTER EIGHT

March 23, 2006. Thursday

THE LAW Offices of Mayes, Murphy and McBride were on the second, third, and fourth floors of the Mulholland Building on Century Park East in Century City. By the time Lydia had gotten on an elevator in the underground parking lot deep in the bowels of the building, she was wishing she had walked from her apartment, since it seemed like she had walked two miles just to find an elevator to the second floor.

The main floor of the law offices was no surprise to Lydia. It was an open space with a glassed-in conference room behind the receptionist's desk. The receptionist was a pretty woman in her mid-twenties with short blonde hair. She smiled when she saw Lydia come out of the elevator.

"May I help you?"

Lydia was distracted for a moment by a large poster board showing a grinning man in his early fifties sitting behind his desk with a caption that read, COMING SOON, MAYOR EAMON MURPHY. In large letters beneath the picture was an invitation to attend a fundraiser at the home of the candidate in Holmby Hills with a suggested donation of $5,000.

"Mayor Murphy," the receptionist said, seeing that Lydia's attention was focused on the poster. "It has a nice ring to it, doesn't it?"

"Yes." Lydia nodded, thinking that the name sounded like the name of a moronic sitcom that passed for entertainment on television these days. "I have an appointment with Reece Tanner."

"Oh yes, of course. You're Miss Harte, aren't you?"

"I am."

"Before I ring Mr. Tanner, would you like something to drink? I can arrange for tea or coffee service to be set up for you."

"Just water, please," Lydia replied.

Moments later, a well-dressed woman in her forties with neatly sculptured blonde hair came through a doorway to the right side of the receptionist's desk. She wore a green dress that was cut two inches above her knees. Her makeup didn't look like what one would expect to see in a business office; it looked like what a woman would wear if she was planning on attending the Academy Awards or some other formal event.

The woman had a beaming smile on her face. "Miss Harte, I'm Jane Halloran, Mr. Tanner's assistant. Will you please come with me?"

Lydia followed Jane Halloran down a hall to a small conference room that was empty except for a small circular mahogany table and chairs. A picture of three men, arms around each other, was hung on one wall. A photoshopped picture of City Hall sitting on a small barren island was on the opposite wall.

Jane Halloran again offered Lydia a choice of tea or coffee. Lydia asked for coffee just to avoid being pestered again.

Halloran looked around the room to make sure everything was all right, and then said, "Mr. Tanner will be along presently. Please have a seat."

Lydia went to the window, which looked out to the east. In the distance, she saw the golf course that was behind her condo. Once she had a frame of reference, she easily spotted her building. She was mentally counting the floors and balconies, trying to determine which apartment was hers when Reece Tanner entered the room.

"Hello Miss Harte," he said in a pleasant voice while offering to shake her hand. "Will you have a seat?"

Tanner was a tall man with short blonde hair that was combed upwards in a spiky style. He was wearing a tan suit with a yellow tie, and everything about him including the light blue eyes and the blonde hair gave one the impression that here was a man who rarely ventured outdoors. The cologne he wore was faint and slightly effeminate.

The first thing Tanner said when they took their seats at the table was to tell Lydia that coffee was on the way. The second thing was to express sorrow for her loss, which took Lydia aback for a second before she realized he was referring to the deaths of Jonathan Benedict and his family.

Once the formalities were over, a young woman in a black dress, looking very much like Hollywood's version of a maid, entered the room, and poured coffee for Lydia. Once she had left, Tanner began his pitch.

"We are very pleased that you have chosen Mayes, Murphy and McBride as your law firm, but I have to tell you that our services are very expensive."

Lydia couldn't resist. "So, I noticed by the clothes your staff wears." She immediately regretted saying that. It was catty, and Lydia didn't like cats.

Tanner had a dumbstruck look on his pale face for just a moment before it turned into a faint smile. "A little joke, perhaps?"

He leaned closer to Lydia bringing his cologne with him. It smelled like peppermint. Lydia fought off an involuntary shudder. What kind of man wears peppermint cologne?

"We've worked with Mr. Milburn before, and he assured us you have the financial resources to employ us, so there should be no problem," Tanner continued.

"How much do you charge for your services?"

"Five hundred an hour. We also require a retainer of $50,000."

Lydia was not all that surprised. She couldn't help thinking of the contrast between the fees charged by Mayes, Murphy and McBride and that of the law offices of Eric Milburn who charged $200 an hour and never requested a retainer.

"How much will your services cost to handle this?" Lydia asked.

"We will need to file a probate action and it may be contested. I have no way of predicting what that will cost, but it could be expensive. It's always expensive to litigate. We try to keep the costs down by using paralegals as much as possible. We bill them out at $150 an hour. But once we have established your right to the Benedict estate, attorney's fees are set by statute."

Lydia thought about what Charles Dickens wrote in his novel, Bleak House. The author took the English Chancery Court and the legal profession to task by including as a central element in his novel the fictional case of Jardyce v. Jardyce, in which a massive estate was laid waste by attorney's fees charged by a multitude of attorneys litigating claims against the estate.

She really didn't need Jonathan's assets, so her interest in Jonathan's estate wasn't about money. There were questions about her mother's death that needed answering. Lydia had already established that Jonathan was responsible for the death of her mother, but there was a nagging feeling that Jonathan wasn't working alone. There was also the question of who exactly he was entertaining during his nightly poker games at Oceania Manor. When she had penetrated the estate grounds last Friday night, she saw five black sedans and four bodyguard/chauffeurs parked in the circular drive in front of the mansion.

"Okay, let's go to work and file a probate action," Lydia said. "How soon can this be done?"

"I can file the petition on Monday. It will take several weeks to get a hearing scheduled."

"How quickly can this be resolved?"

"Are you in a hurry?"

"No, I'm not," Lydia said, thinking about the case mentioned by Dickens, a case that benefitted none of the contesting heirs but lined the pockets of a host of attorneys. "I just don't want this to drag on."

"It won't," Tanner said.

"How long will it take to resolve it?"

"Less than a year."

"Not good enough."

"If you hire me, I'll do my best to expedite this case. I know how to do it. My firm has influence with some of the judges downtown." He paused for a moment. "Do you have any idea of what's in his estate?"

There was something about the tone of Reece's voice that caused Lydia to think he already knew the answer to that question.

"Not completely," Lydia answered. "I know the name of several businesses Jonathan owned, but I have no idea of the true extent of his holdings. I have been informed that his estate is worth over five hundred million dollars."

"Eric Milburn told me that an attorney by the name of Bill Landry drafted his trust."

"Yes. Do you know him?"

"No, I don't."

"I asked Landry what was included in the estate, and he wouldn't tell me. Can you find out?"

"I'll call him. I'm sure I can get the information you want."

"Why would he tell you but not me?"

"Well, you're not a beneficiary. But usually, attorney to attorney, there's no problem finding out information like that."

"I see."

"Do you have any idea of what you will be doing with the estate? Will you be selling it?"

Lydia stiffened slightly. Why did he want to know?

Tanner noticed. "What's wrong?"

"There was a man with Landry who wanted me to assign it to him."

"When you got the estate?"

"What?"

"Did he say he wanted you to assign it after you established your claim to the estate?"

Lydia decided not to answer the question. "Mr. Tanner, you asked me if I wanted to sell the estate. I don't even have it yet, so I don't know what I'll do with it. But what I need to know is what's in it before I decide to do anything, and I want the information as soon as possible."

"Okay. I understand."

"I would like it by tomorrow."

"Then, you'll get it tomorrow." Tanner stood up, trying hard to keep the smile on his face from fading. "Can you wait a half hour while I see about getting a retainer agreement drafted for you to sign? We expect the retainer to be paid within twenty-four hours of your signing."

Lydia nodded. "If you don't mind, I'll write out a check right now."

"That would be fine. And please help yourself to coffee."

"I will," Lydia said, as she opened her purse to take out a checkbook from her brokerage account. She had more than enough money to pay the retainer in her account. Her mother's trust had been giving her $10,000 a month ever since she started her freshman year at U.C.L.A. Lydia spent little of it, since she had an athletic scholarship and immediately went to work with LAPD a few weeks after she had graduated from college.

Fifteen minutes later, Tanner came back into the room with Jane Halloran who passed a five-page retainer agreement to Lydia. After carefully reading every word, Lydia signed the agreement. Tanner signed on behalf of the firm. Jane Halloran notarized the signature and Lydia slid the check across the table to Tanner.

Tanner looked at the check briefly and then gave it to Halloran.

"Can I come by tomorrow to pick up a list of the property in the estate?" Lydia asked.

Halloran answered. "I'll have it for you tomorrow morning, by noon at the latest. I can either fax it or send it to you by email."

"Email would be all right."

Tanner produced a four-by-six card from his coat pocket and said, "If Mr. Murphy were present, he would have personally wanted to give this to you."

He slid the card across the table and Lydia looked at it. It was a beautifully engraved invitation for two to attend a fundraiser at Eamon Murphy's residence on Sunday afternoon.

Lydia looked up at Tanner. "I don't donate to politicians, Mr. Tanner. I'm afraid I can't attend."

"You don't have to donate, Miss Harte. This is a complimentary ticket that will allow you and a guest to attend the event free of charge. These are given out sparingly and only to our major clients. The firm would like you to attend as its guest."

At roll call that evening, Lieutenant Morton reported that the Tactical Operations Division would be staking out most of the liquor and convenience stores in Century Division for a week starting on Friday night. Lydia had never heard of Tactical Operations before. She waited until she was in the police car before asking Hagerty what it was.

"Whoever tries to rob one of those stores is going to get the surprise of their life," Hagerty said. "Tactical Operations sets up two officers in concealed positions in each of twenty stores. They'll put a video camera on the cashier, so that they can see what's going on. As soon as a bandit pulls out a gun, the officers will step out from their cover, identify themselves, and order the suspect to drop his gun. When the suspect turns with the gun in his hand, he signed his death warrant."

"That's awful," Lydia said. She was thinking about the photographs that she had seen during a class by an instructor from Robbery Homicide when she was at the Police Academy. The photos showed several bodies of men on the coroner's table who had been hit with double aught buckshot at close range.

"Think about what you saw two nights ago," Hagerty said. "Robberies are usually committed by a suspect who carries a gun and is prepared to use it. Do you think the two bastards who shot the Hamadas gave them a chance before they killed them?"

Lydia nodded, thinking of the old couple who had been murdered merely because they owned a store. It was a brutal world she had chosen to be part of.

Twice during the night, they parked their car a half block down the street from the home owned by Willie and Emily Spahn. Billy Vernor had asked them to check out the place to see if Jimmie Spahn had returned home after he escaped from custody. Jimmie had no relatives in the area; in fact, he had no relatives in California, and Vernor suspected he might have gone back to the house.

The house was vacant.

The father, Willie, was serving time in prison. The mother, Emily, had been arrested by Vernor and Lydia several weeks ago when she had pointed a gun at Lydia while she was in the process of handcuffing Jimmie, after a pursuit in which he was driving a stolen car. When Vernor and Lydia searched the house after the arrest, they found a treasure trove of merchandise stolen by Mrs. Spahn from department stores and items stolen by Jimmie from houses he had burglarized.

The Spahn home was freshly painted. It was a pre-World War I, Cape Cod, with an immaculate lawn. On one of the occasions that Hagerty and Lydia checked the house out that night, they snuck into the back yard from the alley and listened for five minutes at a back window. The house was dark and was quiet. It was apparent that no one was inside.

"Do you think," Lydia asked Hagerty once they were back in the police car, "there is any chance of Spahn being involved as an active participant in the Hamada robbery?"

"Not actively," Hagerty said cautiously. "Spahn is a little shit with a pale face. He doesn't match the description of the suspects."

"He may have supplied them with guns," Lydia said.

"Or he might have been driving the getaway car."

"That too."

Fifteen minutes later, Hagerty stopped a driver who was so drunk he had problems trying to keep his car from drifting into an oncoming lane.

When Hagerty got out of the car, Lydia heard him say, "Oh, shit!"

He was pointing at the license plate of the car they had just stopped. It had a City license plate.

"We're not going to like this one," Hagerty said to Lydia as he walked up to the driver's side of the car.

Lydia walked at an angle behind Hagerty so that she could keep an eye on the driver. Her hand was resting on the butt of her revolver.

Hagerty politely asked the man to step out of the car. The man was so drunk that he had to hold onto the car door to keep from falling. Hagerty asked him for his driver's license. He kept his flashlight on the man's hands as he fumbled through his wallet.

The man pulled out an i.d. card and held it up to Hagerty's face. "Do you see what this is?" the man said. "Can I go now?"

Hagerty took the i.d., looked at it, and said, "Please stay right there, sir."

"What have you got?" Lydia asked as she met Hagerty at the rear of the car.

Hagerty handed her the i.d. card.

She looked at it. The name on it was Danny Black. The i.d. card showed he was a Lieutenant with the Los Angeles Police Department.

"So, what do we do now?"

"He's drunk and he's in a City car. We call for a supervisor."

Lydia was surprised at what happened next. She expected that Lieutenant Morton would order them to release Black, but he told them to stay where they were, and he would meet them.

The first thing that Morton did when he got to the scene was to look in the back seat of the police car where Danny Black had fallen asleep. He then walked around the City car that Black had been driving, inspecting it for damage.

Lydia thought the contrast between Lieutenant Morton and Lieutenant Black could not have been more different. Morton was a tall man with ginger hair and was strikingly handsome. He wore a police uniform to perfection. Danny Black had black hair and was dark featured with an aquiline nose that made him look menacing. He dressed impeccably in a charcoal pin-striped suit and would have looked like a corporate attorney if it wasn't for the fact that he was slouched in the back seat of a police car with his head lolling off to one side and saliva drooling from his mouth.

Once Morton had completed his inspection of the car, he met Hagerty and Lydia on the sidewalk.

"Do you really want to do this?" Morton asked Hagerty.

"Lieutenant, I wouldn't have expected you to ask a question like that," Hagerty said.

Morton looked away in disgust.

"Sorry," Hagerty said. "I didn't mean to imply . . ."

Morton whipped around. "Listen Hagerty. Of all the people who are on the Department, that bastard in your police car deserves to be in jail. But he's also buddy buddy with the Chief. They play golf together once a week, for God's sake."

"Are you saying we should let him go?"

"Fuck no!" Morton said, his face reddening. He turned away again and looked at the ground.

Lydia and Hagerty exchanged glances.

After a moment, Morton turned back toward them. "I should call the Captain before we decide to book him," Morton said, his voice much softer now. "But I'm not going to do that." He paused once more, deep in thought, not looking at either of them.

"I'm going to release him, Lieutenant," Hagerty said firmly.

Morton looked up at him. "No, you're not, Dick. I've got a hunch that if we book that asshole we'll never hear another word about it."

An hour later, Hagerty and Lydia, accompanied by Lieutenant Morton as an observer, booked Lieutenant Danny Black into the Wilshire jail. As they drove back to the station, Lydia glanced at Hagerty.

"I've got a question," Lydia said. "It sounded like Lieutenant Morton has a history with that man. Where does he work?"

"You've never heard of Danny Black? It was in all the papers."

"What was in the papers?"

"Well, I guess not all of it was in the papers. Some of it was hushed up. A couple years ago, Danny Black's wife was murdered after she had called Internal Affairs and told them she had information that he was taking money from a prostitution ring and tipping them off when vice was working in their area. Black was the P.M. Watch Commander at Metro Central at that time. The wife didn't want to come to Police Headquarters, so they arranged to meet her at the Police Academy. That part of the story was not in the papers. For all I know, it might just be police gossip. There's an exit called Stadium Way off the Pasadena Freeway that will take you to the Police Academy. Do you know where that is?"

Lydia nodded.

"Someone in the bushes above Stadium Way opened fire on her with a semi-automatic rifle and killed her. That part was in the papers. The story was that it was a contract hit, that someone was out to get Danny Black."

"Did they ever find out who shot her?"

"Of course not."

"Do you know if they investigated the claim that Black was taking bribes?"

Hagerty snorted. "They did. They couldn't find any evidence that he had been taking bribes. They put him in charge of the vice unit. He got into trouble there, too."

"What happened to him?"

"They transferred him out to one of the Valley detective divisions."

Lydia blew a soft whistle. "Sounds like he's got friends on the Department."

Lydia didn't get home until 1:30 a.m., but when she did, her telephone began ringing immediately. She picked it up and heard the same gravelly voice.

"You will be asked one more time to sign over your rights to Mr. Benedict's property. You will be well paid when you do so. If you don't sign, you will suffer consequences."

Before Lydia could say anything, the caller hung up. She was halfway down the hall when it occurred to her.

How did the bastard know she was home?

She grabbed her Springfield XDS from the end table in the living room and headed out the door. The elevator was already on her floor, so she took it, and arrived in the lobby not more than a minute after the caller had hung up.

The security guard who worked the night shift was smoking a cigarette under the porte cochère just outside the lobby door. Lydia ran past him and onto the sidewalk. She looked up and down Pico Boulevard. There were no cars parked in either direction. There was a large building across the street with a driveway alongside it. There were no cars there either.

Lydia walked back toward the building entrance.

The security guard carefully watched Lydia as she entered the lobby. A cigarette dangled out of the corner of his mouth. He stared at the gun in her hand.

"You know we have a policy . . ."

Lydia cut him off. "I'm a police officer. What is your name?"

"Sandling. You must be Miss Harte from the third floor."

"I am, Mr. Sandling. Did you happen to see any cars parked on the street just a moment ago?"

"That's why I came out of the office," the security guard said. "I saw a car pull up across the street about five minutes ago. No one is supposed to park over there, so I went out to take a look."

"What kind of car was it?"

"It was a black sedan, a Mercedes, I think."

"Did you get a license number?"

"I'm not allowed to leave the property, Miss Harte. Not while I'm working."

"If you see it again, can you get a license number for me?"

"Like I said, Miss Harte, I'm not allowed to leave the property. You have to ask the manager to let me do that."

"I will," Lydia said. She started to go back inside the condo but stopped and turned to face the security guard. "You're not French by any chance, are you, Mr. Sandling?"

"No. Why?"

"Because the only people I've seen who talk with a cigarette in their mouths are in the movies and are usually French."

CHAPTER NINE

March 24, 2006. Friday.

EARLY THE next morning, Lydia called Billy Vernor. She could always count on him being the first to arrive in the detective squad room, and he didn't disappoint.

"Billy, I need some advice."

"Okay, what is it?"

"I'm being followed."

There was a long pause on the phone before Vernor said anything. "Does this by any chance have to deal with the fabulous riches you are about to receive?"

"The tainted ones, yes."

"You should call Maldonado. He'll know what to do."

Lydia didn't answer.

"Stubbornness has a way of keeping you from what you should be doing, Lydia."

"Billy, knock off the bullshit. I called you for advice."

"What kind of car was following you?"

"I didn't see it. I got a call on my phone last night when I got home, so I knew I was being followed. I went down to the lobby to see if there was anyone out in the street, and the security guard told me that a black Mercedes had been parked across the street but left just before I got to the lobby. I know that some of Jonathan's friends use to drive that kind of car."

"What did the caller want, if you don't mind me asking?"

"He wanted me to assign my rights to the Benedict estate."

"You should do it. Get rid of the headache."

"I'm thinking about it."

"Let me talk to Hardemann about it. Maybe he can have you covered by the Gang Unit for a few days."

"What the hell are you talking about, Billy?" Lydia knew exactly what he meant. Hardemann would have the Gang Unit put a tail on her. She wasn't sure that was a good idea. She had plans she didn't want the Department to know about.

"Let me talk to Hardemann and I'll get back with you. He's good at this kind of shit. He might be able to help you."

"Okay."

"Did you guys check out Spahn's place last night?"

"We went by twice and spent a little time round back. Nobody was there."

"Keep looking. He's got to be around somewhere. I'll talk to you later."

Just before noon, Lydia received an email from Jane Halloran from the law offices of Mayes, Murphy and McBride that contained a list of property in Jonathan Benedict's estate. Lydia printed out the list. She then went out to the balcony of her condo, sat down, and looked out on the golf course.

It was a pleasant day with a slight breeze coming in from the west. There were golfers out on the course beyond the small park that was directly below her condo.

She began reading.

Miss Harte,

The following is a list of property in the Jonathan Benedict Trust that we received from the law offices of Johnson and Landry. Please note that neither I nor Mr. Tanner have seen the trust document. The following is a list of property that Mr. Landry said was in the trust:

Pacific Coast Car Conversions in Culver City.

The Benedict Armory near Greenville, N.C.

Red Dog Trucking and Shipping in Culver City.

Bar and business called Juicy Lucy in Hollywood.

Bar and business called Lucy's in Van Nuys.

Bar and business called Lucy Too in Reseda.

Bar and business called Lucy's Tutu in Bakersfield.

Bar called Lucky Lucy in Modesto.

Adult video and paraphernalia stores in Hollywood, Reseda, Van Nuys, Modesto, and Bakersfield, all are attached to the above bars.

Please note that Mr. Benedict had a seventy-five percent interest in the trucking company. The other twenty-five percent is held by Jacob Nilsson who is the managing partner of Red Dog Trucking.

Mr. Tanner will file an action in probate court this coming Monday, March 27, 2006.

Please call me if you have any questions.

Sincerely and at Your Service, Jane Halloran, personal assistant to Mr. Tanner.

Lydia read the document twice before setting it down. There was a lot of property in the trust she had never heard of before, but there was also something missing. She got up from her chair and went back inside the apartment. She sat down on the sofa, leaned back, and closed her eyes.

What was missing?

Then it came to her.

A casino!

Someone told her a week ago that Jonathan owned a casino just across the state line in Nevada.

Who was it? Was it Sergeant Maldonado or Milburn?

She couldn't call Maldonado. He'd asked questions without giving any answers. So, she got up from the sofa and called her attorney, Eric Milburn. He confirmed that he had been told by Bill Landry that the trust included a roadside casino.

"Is there a problem?" Milburn asked.

"Yes. Jane Halloran at the Mayes law firm gave me a list of property, and the casino wasn't listed."

"So, you have hired Mayes, Murphy and McBride?"

"I have. Reece Tanner will be my attorney."

"Do you feel comfortable with him?"

"Why do you ask?"

"I've worked with him before. I just wanted to know what you thought of him."

"He's a little too rich for my blood. I don't know how to describe him. When I was with him, it felt like I was taking a bath in maple syrup."

"I know the feeling. Do you think you can work with him?"

"I do."

"Well, that's good. Have you thought that maybe the casino was omitted from the list by accident? That it wasn't purposeful?"

"Mr. Milburn, I'm paying these people $500 an hour. I expect them to earn that money."

"I'm not defending that law firm, Miss Harte, but they have a reputation for quality service. Maybe, it wasn't their fault that the property was not on the list. Maybe, Bill Landry didn't tell them about it."

Lydia remained silent for a moment.

"Are you still there, Miss Harte?"

"I am, Mr. Milburn. Thank you for your time."

Jenny Hamilton had once been Lydia's best friend when she was at U.C.L.A. She was still Lydia's friend but not so "best" anymore. Jenny was bisexual. Lydia was not. The bond between the two of them weakened, particularly one night after the track season ended when Jenny got Lydia drunk and managed to get her into bed without her consent.

Lydia had maintained her friendship with Jenny, but she kept her distance. Jenny did have something that Lydia needed and that was her skill as a computer programmer in a large investment firm in Century City where she helped analysts by designing programs that would allow them to look at financial data in new and different ways.

Jenny was also a proficient hacker. She had helped Lydia on previous occasions with hacking into secure databases.

"Are your phones monitored?" Lydia asked when Jenny came on the line.

"I think they are. What do you want, sweetie?"

"Call me from a secure phone when you get a chance. Do it before 2:30 if you can."

Jenny called her five minutes later. "What do you need?"

"I always seem to be calling you nowadays when I need something," Lydia said.

"I got no problem with that, Lydia. I love the kind of things you want me to do. Work can be so fucking boring."

"Do you remember when I asked you to get information on Jonathan's assets?"

"I do."

"Did you uncover any information about a casino he owned?"

"Have you looked at the report I gave you?"

"It's not mentioned in the report."

"I don't remember seeing anything about a casino. Do you want me to check?"

"Did you check property records in Nevada?"

"I didn't check any property records outside of California. Even if I did, I might not have turned up anything on the casino. He might be leasing the property."

"Are you saying you might not be able to find out?"

"No. There're other sources I have access to. When do you need the information?"

"As soon as possible."

"I may be able to get what you want by seven. Do you want to meet for dinner?"

"I'm working tonight."

"Why don't we meet at Donovan's at midnight?"

Lydia remembered the last time they met at Donovan's. U.C.L.A. basketball fans were celebrating a victory, and the restaurant was so crowded that she and Jenny were crammed into a corner of the bar and could hardly move without invading each other's space. But U.C.L.A. wasn't playing tonight, so Lydia agreed to meet Jenny at Donovan's after she got off work.

Shortly after the noon hour, Lydia received a call from Lieutenant Hardemann's secretary, asking her to come to the station immediately and meet him in his office. This was not the first time she had received a request like this. Just last Sunday, she was called into the station to be interviewed by that obnoxious lieutenant from Sheriff's Homicide.

Lydia was a little worried as she drove into the station. When she walked across the detective squad room toward Hardemann's office, Billy Vernor saw her and mouthed, "What's happening?" Lydia shrugged her answer.

Hardemann saw Lydia coming and waved her inside. Hardemann was a big man. He was black, bald, and extremely intelligent. He had just returned after a month at the FBI Academy in Quantico and was scheduled to be promoted to Captain in a few weeks.

"What did you do now?" Hardemann asked.

"Is something wrong?"

"What have you been doing in the last twenty-four hours? At work, I mean?"

"I worked with Hagerty last night. We didn't do much . . ." She stopped suddenly, putting a hand to cover her mouth. She paused for a few seconds before speaking again. "We arrested a police lieutenant last night for D.U.I."

"Oh, who was that?" Hardemann was frowning.

"Danny Black."

Hardemann looked away, muttering something under his breath. After a moment or two, he turned to Lydia. "Who approved the booking?"

"Lieutenant Morton."

"I suppose you didn't know that Black and the Chief are golfing buddies."

"Does that make a difference? I mean he was really drunk. He blew a .13 on the breathalyzer."

"I don't know how to tell you this, but just one hour ago, Captain Kemper called me from a community event he was attending. He told me to take you down to the Chief's office."

On the way to Police Headquarters, Lydia turned to Hardemann who was driving. "How come Hagerty hasn't been asked to go to the Chief's office? He was driving the police car last night and made the decision to pull Danny Black over."

"Maybe, he wants to see you about something else."

Lydia considered this for a moment before saying anything. "Lieutenant, do you think I need to have a representative with me at this meeting?"

"I don't think so," Hardemann said. "If this was a disciplinary matter, I'd be taking you to Internal Affairs."

"So, it's got to be about Lieutenant Black."

"I honestly don't know."

"Hagerty told me he ran into trouble a couple of years ago when he worked vice."

"It was two years ago. Internal Affairs had an informant who said that the entire vice crew at Metro Central was taking bribes from a bookmaker. When Internal Affairs tried to set them up, one of the vice officers got a call saying they were under surveillance and that the bookmaker they were meeting was wearing a wire." Hardemann started laughing. "So, Danny Black and his crew managed to escape getting arrested. But a sergeant working Internal Affairs named Charlie Wolf got arrested because they discovered it was his phone that was used to tip off the vice unit. Anyway, Wolf hired a good attorney and beat the criminal charges against him, but the Chief fired him anyway."

It was silent for a moment in the car until Hardemann became aware that Lydia was staring at him.

"Something else on your mind, Officer Harte?"

"How did they get away with something like that? An entire vice unit is corrupt, and nobody takes the fall. And then you got this sergeant who tips off the vice unit and doesn't get convicted."

"Well, there is some issue whether the sergeant was even the one who made the call to vice. He filed a multi-million-dollar lawsuit against the

City for wrongful termination. From what I hear, his attorney is blasting holes in the case against him."

Chief Thomas Fletcher's office was on the sixth floor of Police Head-quarters. Joyce Fleming, the Chief's secretary, rose from her desk when Lydia and Hardemann entered the room. Fleming's face beamed with pleasure when her eyes fell on Hardemann.

"Lieutenant Hardemann, how nice to see you again. The Chief is ex-pecting you and Officer Harte in the conference room."

Lydia looked around the office. It was large for a reception area. Next to the door to the Chief's office was another desk occupied by a young man with a large head who was wearing a white shirt and tie. He looked up from his computer when he heard Hardemann's name. The name plate on his desk simply read, LIEUTENANT KIRBY, ADJUTANT.

"I saw your name on a letter to the Personnel Department approving you for promotion to Captain," Kirby said to Hardemann. "I don't know how the hell you made it before me."

"I work in the trenches," Hardemann said. "I have actually done real police work."

Kirby glared at Hardemann.

"If we're through insulting each other, gentlemen," Joyce Fleming said, "the Chief of Police is waiting." She opened the door to the Chief's office and led the way in.

The first thing that Lydia noticed about the Chief's office was that it looked grander than the President's Oval Office but lacked its simplicity. Even though the mahogany desk and plush carpet were high quality, the office was marred by a clutter of memorabilia that included a variety of trophies and plaques and a multitude of photographs showing the Chief posing with celebrities.

Joyce Fleming led them through the office to a door on the left side of the Chief's desk. It opened into a long conference room with a shiny par-quet table that was nearly fifteen feet long.

Chief Fletcher in uniform sat at the head of the table at the far end of the room. Two men sat to the left of the Chief; a third one sat some dis-tance away.

Fleming led Lydia and Hardemann to the side of the table where no one was sitting.

Lydia muttered, "Oh shit," under her breath when she saw Sergeant Hector Maldonado seated on the opposite side of the table.

Maldonado was a short, dark-featured man who Lydia had first met when she was applying to become a police officer. Just last week, Maldonado showed Lydia evidence that tended to prove how she managed to sneak back into her apartment after she had killed Jonathan and Milo Benedict without being discovered by the Robbery-Homicide surveillance team. Maldonado then displayed good faith by showing Lydia that he had subsequently destroyed that evidence. But still, she found herself unable to trust the man, even though he seemed pleased at what Lydia had done. She felt as if she was being manipulated by Maldonado, and she didn't like it one bit.

To Maldonado's right was a man dressed in a well-tailored suit that Lydia had never met before. He was a burly man with a florid face.

Seated three empty chairs to the left of Maldonado was Captain Kemper, who seemed as if he were distancing himself from the other two men.

Didn't Hardemann say Kemper was attending a community relations function? Lydia thought.

The Chief rose as Lydia approached. "Officer Harte, I would like you to be seated next to me."

He didn't offer to shake hands.

Lydia sat down. There was a bottle of water in front of her. She took it and cradled it with both hands.

The Chief sat down.

Lydia had met Chief Fletcher before, but so did everyone else in her Academy class. He had presented her with a certificate at their graduation ceremony. Not much of a conversation accompanied the certificate. Just "Congratulations Officer Harte. Proud to have you as a member of our Department."

Two weeks later, Lydia had been shot while on duty and her partner was killed. During her stay in the hospital, Lydia had a vague recollection that the Chief had come to visit her, but she was in a fog and didn't remember much about it.

Chief Fletcher was a tall man, ascetic in appearance, lively blue eyes, baldheaded, except for a one-inch band of gray hair that circled the back of his head. He started off the meeting by pointing to the three men on the other side of the table.

"You know, of course, Sergeant Maldonado and your boss, Captain Kemper. The big guy to the Sergeant's right is Captain Smith, the Commanding Officer of the Intelligence Division."

Lydia nodded her head but didn't say anything.

"I suppose you're wondering why we brought you here," the Chief continued.

"What I am wondering," Lydia said, choosing her words carefully, "is whether I need a union representative at this meeting."

Chief Fletcher looked at Captain Kemper for a moment who shrugged. He turned back to Lydia. "I can't imagine why you would need a union representative. This is not a disciplinary meeting."

Lydia heard Hardemann shifting in his chair.

"The reason we're here, Officer Harte, is because of an on-going investigation into the criminal activities of your stepfather, Jonathan Benedict. I have been informed that the trust he set up has no living alternate beneficiaries, and that by California law, you may be entitled to his estate. Is that true?"

"I think so," Lydia said cautiously.

"I understand that you have retained Eric Milburn as your attorney?"

"Mr. Milburn is my attorney, but he is not involved with the Benedict estate."

"Then you don't intend to seek your share of the estate?"

"I've hired separate legal counsel to do that."

The Chief's eyebrows went up. "I didn't know that. Are you at liberty to tell us who you hired?"

"Yes. Mayes, Murphy and McBride."

The Chief sat back in his chair and looked at Captain Smith, who, in turn, looked at Maldonado.

"I didn't know that either," Maldonado said, uncomfortably.

"I only met with them, yesterday," Lydia said.

"Can you afford a firm like that on a police officer's salary, Officer Harte?" the Chief asked.

"I have independent means, sir."

"I see," the Chief said, eyebrows raised. "Have you met Mr. Murphy?"

"I have not. But I suppose I might have an opportunity in the next couple of days. I was invited to his fundraiser."

"You were?"

"Yes, sir."

The Chief, a twinkle in his eye, turned to Captain Kemper. "Eamon Murphy lives in your Division, Thomas. Have you heard anything about this fundraiser?"

"No, sir. I have not."

"You received no requests for security?"

"The people who live in Holmby Hills usually hire private security."

The Chief stared at Lydia for a moment or two.

Lydia stared back.

The Chief suddenly turned to Captain Smith. "Tell her what we know about the Benedict estate, Malcolm."

"Yes, sir." Smith leaned forward, placing his arms on the table as he directed his attention to Lydia. "On paper, Jonathan Benedict legally owns the properties in his estate. But he really doesn't own them. He holds them for a criminal syndicate we call the Swamp for want of a better name. We don't know who is at the top of that organization, and we don't know what kind of hold he has on Benedict. But whatever the arrangement he had with Benedict, it made him enormously wealthy. We believe that Benedict and his son, Milo, were skimming money off the top of the businesses and that was why he was murdered."

Lydia blinked her eyes, trying to keep them from looking at Maldonado who looked up at the ceiling to avoid eye contact with anyone in the room. She looked at Captain Kemper whose dark face grew darker. He had once told Lydia that Milo Benedict, her stepbrother, was one of the best reserve officers in the division. He had obviously not been informed that Milo was mixed up with Jonathan's businesses.

"We expect that you will be contacted in the next few weeks by these people who want their property back," Captain Smith continued. "They will offer to buy the property from you, but the offer will not be anywhere near the value of the property in the estate. They do not want to pay a lot for property they think they already own. We want you to work with us on this. We want you to engage these people, talk to them, deal with them, and find out who they are. You will continue to work your regular assignment at Century Division, but you will also be working for Intelligence."

Lydia held up a hand to stop him, but it didn't keep him from continuing.

"Please hear me out, Officer Harte," Smith said. "You will not be doing this alone. You will be covered by detectives from Intelligence, so you will be completely safe. Also, the Chief has authorized overtime for this work." Smith paused for a moment and then said, "Do you have any questions, Officer Harte?"

Lydia shook her head. "I don't have any questions, Captain, but you must already know that Sergeant Maldonado and I already have had a conversation like this. I told him that my cooperation is contingent on him giving me the names of the men who visited the Benedict mansion during the Friday night poker games. He refused to do it."

"Why do you want their names?" Chief Fletcher asked Lydia.

Lydia didn't know how to answer the question, so she decided to be a little evasive. "They might have been involved in Jonathan's murder. They might come after me. I want to be able to identify them if they are coming for me."

"Why would they come after you?" Fletcher asked.

"Because they might be part of the Swamp you're talking about." Lydia realized she was talking in circles.

"May I say something?" It was Hardemann.

"Of course," the Chief said.

"I was told that Officer Harte is being followed by unknown persons. I plan on having my Gang Unit covering her going to and coming from work."

"I don't want anybody covering me at all," Lydia said vehemently. "I can handle myself."

"Very well. We'll talk about this later," the Chief said. "Tell us what happened when you were followed."

Lydia did so, starting with the phone call she received when she got home after work, and what Sandling, the security officer, told her about the Mercedes illegally parked across the street. She didn't tell them about the meeting with the man who called himself Vincent Moretti. If they were not going to help her, she sure as hell was not going to help them.

"Doesn't it bother you that you have unknown people calling you on the phone about the estate, Officer Harte?" the Chief said.

"Telephone calls don't bother me."

"But you think you're being followed?"

"Yes."

"So, will you work with Intelligence on this?"

"No!"

The Chief smiled. "What if I give you a direct order to do so?"

"Then I would probably have to apply for a job with another police agency. I hear that San Diego is looking for lateral police officers."

"I wouldn't want you to do that, Officer Harte." The Chief looked at Maldonado. "Is there any reason why we can't give Officer Harte the information she needs."

"Yes, sir. It's confidential."

"Do you agree, Malcom?"

"I do, sir. As you are aware, we have a protocol that no one in the Department is allowed access to information we have uncovered until we have enough to send to the D.A.'s office. You already know the reasons for this policy. There are no exceptions."

"Okay, then." The Chief suddenly turned to Lydia. "We'll not badger you any further, Officer Harte." He stood up. "If the rest of you don't mind, I'd like a few minutes with Officer Harte, alone."

After the others had left the room, Chief Fletcher signaled Lydia to take a seat. "Are you going to attend the fundraiser at Eamon Murphy's house?"

"I don't think so, sir. I don't like big parties. Besides, I'm scheduled to work on Sunday."

"I want you to go to that fundraiser. I'll make sure you'll have the day off. I need to know who shows up and who spends time talking to Eamon Murphy."

"You want me to spy on someone running for political office? Is that legal?"

"You were invited to be there, Officer Harte, so I see no problem with you merely reporting what you see."

"Let me think about it," Lydia said. She was also thinking it would be a great way to start the week. After Sunday, she was scheduled for two days off.

"I want you to understand that I'm not interested in partisan politics. I have other reasons for finding out who Eamon Murphy associates with. He may very well become mayor of this City, and I want to know everything I can about him. It will give me some idea who I'm dealing with if he becomes mayor."

"He might fire you."

"He might."

The discussion piqued Lydia's interest about one of the heavy players in the law firm she had hired. Maybe, it might be in her interest as well to see what this Eamon Murphy was like.

"Okay," Lydia finally said. "I'll do it."

The Chief took a business card out of his pocket and handed it to her. "This card has my cell phone number on it. Call me Sunday night and tell me what happened at the fundraiser."

"Okay."

Chief Fletcher leaned forward. "Officer Harte, I didn't want to say this before you made your decision. But when your first year is up at Century and you're due to be wheeled out to another division, I want you to tell me where you would like to be assigned and I'll see to it."

Lydia immediately thought of Billy Vernor. She had worked with him for a few weeks and liked the way he aggressively pursued the miscreants who dared commit burglaries in his assigned area. But would the Chief let her work with him? The policy of the Department was that a new officer had to work three different patrol divisions before moving into a specialized assignment.

"Thank you, sir." Lydia stood up to leave but hesitated a moment. "Chief, are you aware that my partner and I arrested one of your friends last night for D.U I.?"

"Are you talking about Danny Black?"

"Yes."

"What makes you think he's my friend?"

"I was told you were golf buddies with him."

"I wouldn't use the word 'buddy' with respect to Lieutenant Black, Officer Harte. But there, I've already said too much. You're dismissed."

The change in Chief Fletcher at the mention of Danny Black was sudden. He was no longer smiling.

"You are certainly one of the most stubborn females I have ever met," Lieutenant Hardemann said as he drove back to Century Division.

"And what do you call the attitude of the people in that conference room?" Lydia responded.

"What do you mean?"

"All I wanted is the names of the men who played cards with Jonathan. That's not too much to ask for, is it? I may be stubborn, but I'm not the only one."

"They have had leaks before. That's why they have the policy."

Lydia turned to look at Hardemann. "Can I ask a favor of you?"

"Of course."

"Don't have the Gang Unit follow me. They have more important things to do. I can take care of myself."

"All right, I'll do what you ask. But you need to know that Intelligence may still put a tail on you. Be careful you don't do anything that you don't want them to know about."

Hardemann's statement bothered Lydia and she couldn't let it go. "Lieutenant, what exactly is it you think I do when I'm off-duty?"

"You misunderstood what I said. I don't want you to get into a situation where you think you may have to take some action against whoever is following you. I don't want one of those incidents where we have police officers shooting at each other."

As they drove back to the station, Lydia thought about what the Chief had asked her. He never used the word 'spy' when he asked her to attend the fundraiser. But that was exactly what he was asking her to do. Did he suspect that Eamon Murphy was crooked, or was it just Department politics, the Chief wanting information that he could use in the future for the benefit of the Department?

It occurred to her that she had wasted a good bargaining position. She wanted the names of the men who attended the poker game at Oceania Manor, and she should only have agreed to attend the fundraiser in exchange for those names.

She realized there was another way she might be able to get what she wanted and that involved a trip to Oceania Manor under darkness. She had the means to do that at her disposal. In planning for the final confrontation with Jonathan, she had rented a Jeep Wrangler and had accessed Oceania Manor from the fire road in the hills behind the property. After she accomplished what she had set out to do, she stored the Jeep in a garage she had rented about two miles away from where she lived. She still hung onto the Jeep because she had ordered a new set of wheels and tires for it just in case the lieutenant from the Sheriff's Department discovered the tire tracks behind Oceania Manor. Even though Lydia considered that unlikely because of the limited brain power possessed by Shepherd, her partner was smart enough to go poking around and find the tire tracks.

Everything she needed to get back into Oceania Manor was in that rented Jeep, a large backpack: bolt cutters, mag light, and the dark clothing and trainers she wore early last Saturday morning.

Numerous plainclothes cars flooded the streets in and around Century Division as Hardemann drove his car into the station parking lot. "Tactical Operations will begin their stakeouts tonight," Hardemann said to Lydia. "I'll never understand why they show up for roll call at the division they're assigned. Apparently, they don't think the crooks are smart enough to check out the police station before they pull off a 211."

Lydia followed Hardemann into the detective squad room and caught Vernor's eye. She nodded her head to indicate she wanted to talk to him without anyone around. The hallways of the station were too crowded with plainclothes officers from Tactical Operations, so they met outside in the parking lot.

"What's going on?" Vernor asked. "Are you in trouble?"

"I need a favor. Hardemann wants to cover me with the Gang Unit. I asked him not to do that. Can you let me know if he goes through with it?"

"I will. How did the meeting with the Chief go?"

"Okay, I suppose. I didn't get what I wanted."

"What do you want?"

"The names of the people who played poker with Jonathan the night he was killed." She looked around the parking lot to make sure no one was listening. "I asked you the other day if you could run some license numbers for me. Now, I'm not so sure you should do that. They can be traced back to you, can't they?"

Vernor smiled. "Not the way I do it. You get the numbers. I'll get the names of the owners."

Roll call was quick. Lieutenant Morton explained that Tactical Operations would need the roll call room in ten minutes. He didn't read from the rotator, a clipboard that contained the latest crime information over the past twenty-four hours. Hagerty was on a night off, and Lydia found she was working with the third person assigned to the car, Kenny Ferris, a lean man in his late twenties who had the odd habit of looking out of the corner of his eyes at the person he was speaking to.

Morton ended roll call by explaining that a two-man team from Tactical Operations would be on stakeout in nearly every liquor and convenience store in the Division. Before leaving the roll call room, he looked down at Lydia and motioned her to meet him upstairs.

When Lydia entered the Watch Commander's office, Morton was already busy with paperwork. Sergeant Joanna Watson, who sat behind a desk opposite Morton, motioned her to come forward.

"I show you working on Sunday," Watson said unexpectedly.

"But the Chief . . ."

Watson looked up at her, smiling. "I know what the Chief wants. You will be scheduled to work on Sunday, but you don't have to report to work. You'll be on special assignment for the Chief."

"Yes, sir . . . I mean, yes ma'am. Is it possible to get a day off tomorrow?"

"Fraid not. Hagerty's not here. It's just you and Kenny Ferris on the car."

"Okay, thank you."

Just as Lydia was about to leave the room, she heard Lieutenant Morton call out her name. She turned to look at him. He was smiling.

"Good luck on Sunday."

It was like any other Friday night in Century Division. She and Kenny Ferris got five calls all at once when they began their shift. They handled ten more calls that night including six family disputes. It was the kind of call that Lydia disliked the most because she never left one of them feeling she had accomplished anything other than tossing a glass of water on a raging fire that would not go out.

Kenny Ferris did not have the instincts that Hagerty had, but he was an excellent policeman. Lydia was impressed with how he handled one family dispute. The husband was an obnoxious drunk who would not let the wife have her say. Ferris asked her to step out onto the sidewalk where he could talk to her. The husband came roaring out of the house demanding to know what they were doing with his fucking wife. The moment he stepped onto the sidewalk Ferris arrested him for disturbing the peace.

They did have time to do a check of the Spahn house that night. Again, the lights were out, and there was no sound coming from inside. When they left the house and were driving away, Lydia spotted some movement in a parked Ford Taurus that was facing the wrong way. Somebody was seated so low in the seat that only half of their head could be seen.

Lydia told Ferris what she had seen. He made a U-turn and lit up the Ford with the police car's emergency lights. Lydia and Ferris got out of the police car with guns drawn. A man emerged from the driver's side of the car with his hands up.

It was Billy Vernor.

"You guys really know how to fuck up a stakeout," he hissed. "Turn off those damn lights and get the hell out of here!"

Although it was busy that night, nothing was happening in the liquor and convenience stores. It seemed as if the criminals knew that officers from the Tactical Operations Division were sitting in the backrooms of the stores, waiting with their shotguns for someone stupid enough to pull off an armed robbery.

Just before end of watch, Lydia got a call on her cell phone from Jenny Hamilton who had to cancel their meeting at Donovan's. Jenny had not finished doing what Lydia had asked her to do, because she had unexpectedly caught an assignment at work that required her to work overtime. They agreed to meet tomorrow for lunch in Westwood.

That was okay with Lydia, because there was somewhere she had to be early the next morning. Because of that, she realized she would have to put off going to Oceania Manor for another day.

CHAPTER TEN

March 25, 2006. Saturday.

IT TOOK Lydia nearly an hour to get to Santa Clarita the next morning. Once she had driven past the small community where four CHP officers had been killed in a gunfight in 1970 that lasted no more than two minutes, she turned west on a small country road that ran alongside a wide but shallow creek. After a half mile, she turned left onto a dirt road next to a sign containing the words, RIVERCREEK RANGE. She drove over a cobbled concrete strip through the creek bed and entered the gun range owned by Jeremy Morgan that was once an off-road motorcycle park.

She was surprised to see so many cars parked in front of the white double-wide trailer with a sign over the entrance reading, HOME OF THE GUNFIGHTER'S COMBAT COURSE. Underneath it was another sign in smaller print that read, ONE SHOT, ONE KILL.

Nearly half of the parked vehicles were four-wheel-drive Jeep Wranglers. She recognized a blue Toyota SUV belonging to Dick Hagerty. Strangely enough, there was a late-model Porsche painted in olive green parked next to it.

When she got out of the car, she heard three quick shots coming from one of the ranges. She knew it had to be Hagerty. He came here to practice shooting every Saturday morning.

Three men of Hispanic descent who were Jeremy's employees were sitting at a picnic table under a scrub oak tree and drinking coffee.

Jeremy for some reason was hesitant to call his employees by their real name, so he called each of them Jose.

Lydia opened the trunk of her BMW and took out her polished service belt containing her .357 Magnum revolver in its holster. She was about to enter the double-wide trailer when she heard a voice that called out from her right.

"They told me not to come in."

She saw a man who was standing behind the Porsche. Lydia had met the man about two weeks ago when she began the gunfighter's combat course. Morgan's strange habit of not identifying anybody by their real name extended to his customers. Jeremy had called the man Jim. Two weeks ago, he had been at the range with another man named Jules, but today, Jules was nowhere to be seen. When Lydia arrived to attend the first session of the combat course, Jeremy had introduced her to the two men as Jane.

Lydia, thinking she had a better relationship with Jeremy than Jim, disregarded what he had said and entered the double-wide trailer.

Jeremy Morgan was sitting behind his gunmetal gray desk. Seated in a loose circle in fold-up chairs were four of the men she had seen playing poker in Jeremy's barn. The man who was named Beard was pointing at a drawing of a rough map on butcher paper that had been tacked to the wall. He rapidly pulled the map off the wall when he saw Lydia enter the trailer.

Jeremy stood up. "Jane!" he said, alarm in his voice.

"Sorry," Lydia said as she backed out of the trailer.

"I told you not to go in there," Jim said when he saw Lydia come out.

Seconds later, Jeremy opened the door and looked around until he spotted Lydia by her BMW.

"Jane, get yer butt in here!"

"I'm sorry, Jeremy, I didn't . . ."

"Nothing to be sorry about. We took a vote. It was unanimous. The guys wanted to see what you look like when they were sober."

"I told you," one of the Loose Cannons said when Lydia entered the trailer. "I told you."

"Be polite," Jeremy said.

"All I said was that she's wearing black jeans and a black pullover. That's gonna be a big mistake."

"What kind of mistake?" Lydia asked.

"Wait until you see what Morgan has planned for you."

"I'd bet you don't even remember the names of these reprobates," Jeremy said to Lydia.

"Wait a minute," Tommy said. "You just called her Jane a minute ago. I thought her name was Lydia."

"It's Jane here," Jeremy said. "Remember that when we go outside."

"I remember two of the names," Lydia said, getting back to Jeremy's original question. "The guy with the beard is named Marcum, and the guy who tore the map off the wall is named Beard."

"Good," Jeremy said. "Let me re-introduce the others."

As Jeremy did so, Lydia tried to associate the names of the men with their physical features. Alex was tall, muscular, good-looking and had hair so white that it looked like sand. The guy with the flaming red hair was named Tommy, and the musclebound guy who looked like a younger Arnold Schwarzenegger was named Rocky. Except for Jeremy who wore khaki shorts, they wore olive-green T-shirts and desert camouflage pants. They wore their trademark ballcaps with the falling cannons.

"So, where are you guys off to?" Lydia asked.

"Breakfast," Marcum said. He had a raspy voice that sounded a little bit like the man who had been calling her on the telephone. "But only after we try out Morgan's combat course."

"Actually, I was referring to the map that was on the wall when I came in," Lydia said. "Where are you guys going?"

"Top secret," Marcum said. "Do you want to come along with us?"

"You're carrying a .357 Magnum," Rocky said. "Do you use Magnum rounds on the course?"

"Yes and no," Lydia replied, recognizing that her attention was being deliberately drawn away from the map. "Just for a few scenarios, and then I switch to a .38+P."

"Did you ever shoot someone with a Magnum round?"

"Never," Lydia lied.

"It is truly a sight to behold."

I bet, thought Lydia. When she had shot Jonathan Benedict with a .357 Magnum, Jonathan's entire nose had disintegrated.

"I have a question," Lydia said. "Jeremy told me you charge five million dollars a month."

The men all looked at Jeremy.

"How much," Lydia asked, "would you want if you did a job for a civilian?"

Nobody said anything.

"I asked," Lydia repeated patiently. "how much would you charge a civilian for a month's worth of work."

"What civilian would you be talking about?" Marcum asked.

"Me."

"You can't afford us," Tommy said.

"Yes, I can."

"What are you thinking, Lydia?" Jeremy asked.

"I'm just asking a hypothetical question."

"We would charge you the same rates we charge our regular customers," Tommy said. "Plus expenses. And expenses can get pretty high. I don't know what you have in mind, but we don't work in the homeland. And we don't do revenge work. We are hired to solve problems. Big problems."

And I, Lydia thought, have a major fucking problem. But not the kind these guys can take care of.

The mood lightened up when they went outside. "You have quite a set-up here," Beard told Jeremy."

"You haven't seen anything yet," Jeremy said. "Wait until you see what's in some of those ranges."

There were eight ranges on the property, all of them backing up against a hill scoured with motorcycle trails.

Hagerty was firing his .357 Magnum revolver from behind a barricade at the first range. It was neatly maintained with covered wooden cubicles and concrete paths leading to human-shaped targets at the twenty-five-yard line. Next to it was a combat range with mechanically operated targets on swivels.

But the six other ranges shared none of the orderliness of the first two. They were separated from each other by tall concrete walls covered with rough lumber. They contained a variety of targets. Shooting positions consisted of ordinary wooden posts, window frames, fences, wooden walls, barrels, concrete culverts, fireplugs, telephone poles, a mailbox, and even an abandoned car shot full of holes.

"Where's Jules?" Jeremy asked.

Lydia turned and saw Jim approaching them.

"I think he quit."

"Did he say why?"

"Too much running and not enough shooting."

There was a lot of running in Jeremy's Gunfighter's Combat Course. Jeremy believed that officers should be prepared for any contingency, and one of the most difficult situations was chasing a suspect for a quarter of a mile and then turning a corner only to find the suspect had stopped and was firing at them. Consequently, Jeremy insisted that his students should practice shooting on the run or shooting from cover after running at least two hundred yards at full speed.

In addition, Jeremy had built in the unexpected. He used all six of the combat courses in his training. He would station his three employees at various intervals along the ranges. The trainees would be driven down to the far end of the property. From there, the trainee would be required to run toward the ranges. When one of Jeremy's employees pointed at a range, the trainee had to enter and be prepared for anything.

The drive down to the far end of the range was nearly a quarter of a mile. Jeremy took Lydia, Jim, and Tommy down there in his open Jeep. The other four men followed in one of the Wranglers.

They stopped at the chain link fence separating Jeremy's property from a training facility used by LAPD and LASO SWAT. Jeremy took a handheld radio out of the Jeep and began positioning his employees for the first drill.

"Okay," Jeremy said when he put down the radio. "Jane and Jim, load up with Magnum rounds for this first scenario only. The rest of you pansies use whatever weapon you brought with you. The first drill is an easy one. You will run hard, and you will stop and fire two rounds at a bullseye target in each of the first three ranges. You will need to reload before continuing to the next three ranges. But we will do something different on the last three. You will fire two shots into the last three ranges while on the run. Remember, keep your finger off the trigger until you are ready to shoot. Jane, you're first. Put on your safety glasses.

Show these dudes what it looks like when they're competing with a world class athlete."

Lydia had no problem with the targets in the first three ranges. She was certain that she had scored direct hits on each of the targets. But she was not at all certain that she had hit any of the remaining targets while she was running. Her gun, loaded with Magnum ammo, had a powerful recoil, and it was not easy to bring it back down on the target after firing it. The first time she had shot at Jeremey's range, she had fired a hundred rounds through her Magnum revolver, and her shoulders ached so much afterwards that it felt as if she had been doing bench presses.

When Lydia got back to the starting point, Jeremy sent Jim off on his run.

Tommy sidled up next to Lydia. "Were you serious about hiring us?"

"I was just curious," Lydia said.

"What did Jeremy mean when he called you a world class athlete?"

"I have no idea."

Jeremy placed the radio on the hood of his Jeep and turned to Lydia. "You hit all targets on the first three. A miss on number four, two hits on five, one hit on six."

Lydia nodded.

"What did you mean when you said she is a world class athlete?" Tommy asked Jeremy.

"Ask her."

"I already have. She didn't answer."

Jeremy smiled. "She ran track and field at U.C.L.A. and holds two PAC 12 records. She could outrun all five of you assholes into the ground."

Two and a half hours and two breaks later, it got so hot under the blazing sun that Jeremy had the group huddle up. "This will be the last drill. I don't see the need to put anybody in the hospital."

"What, you can't take it?" Beard said.

Jeremy ignored him. "We will work as a team on this one. Two at a time. Be ready for anything, but make sure when you're shooting that your partner is not in front of you. Keep your finger off the trigger until you are ready to shoot. Jane and Rocky, you will go first."

There was a thin film of sweat on Lydia's face as she reloaded her re-volver. When she had finished, she looked up at Jeremy and nodded. Her partner, Rocky, chambered a round in his Springfield 1911.

"I'm ready," Rocky said, adjusting his safety glasses with his free hand.

"Okay, go!"

They ran at least a hundred yards when Jose pointed to a range they were to enter. Lydia noticed two things about Jose that were different; one, that he stood well back from them, and two, he had a sly smile on his face.

Rocky took up a position three yards to the left of Lydia as they turned to face the range.

The range looked like any of the others. It had at least a half dozen ar-tifacts to use for cover.

It was eerily quiet. Nothing was moving.

Rocky signaled Lydia to move forward. They began walking slowly into the range, their guns pointing downward at a 45-degree angle. Six targets popped up from the ground at the back of the range. Rocky and Lydia brought up their weapons to fire, but before they could, a hail of neon-colored pellets about the size of peas, came flying at them from sev-eral directions accompanied by the sound of multiple gunshots.

Lydia felt one of the pellets sting her right cheek.

"Hit the deck!" Rocky yelled to Lydia.

Lydia flopped down in the dirt.

They were at least twenty feet away from the nearest cover, a broken piece of concrete culvert and a large engine block.

"You're exposed!" Rocky yelled.

The first thing Lydia thought was that her jeans might have slid off her butt, but she quickly realized what Rocky meant when she saw him crawling toward the concrete culvert. Lydia began crawling toward the engine block.

"What are they shooting at us?" Lydia yelled.

"I believe they're airsoft bullets."

"I got hit by one."

"Are you okay?"

They had now reached cover. An explosive was set off down range. Dirt began raining down on Lydia.

"I'm okay," Lydia yelled back.

"When I say now, we knock down the targets," Rocky yelled to her. "I'll take the three on the left. Keep a low profile when you fire."

Lydia nodded. She looked up. A steady stream of pellets was flying over her head. Lydia adjusted her safety glasses and peered around the engine block, showing only the right side of her face.

"Now!" Rocky yelled.

Just as she was about to fire, there was another explosion behind the targets. Lydia flinched, recovered quickly, and began firing, two bullets in each of the targets.

The pellets suddenly stopped flying.

Lydia looked at Rocky. His face was red with anger.

"I guess we're done," she said. Lydia looked down at her clothes. They were covered with grit, and she began brushing herself off.

"You think that's goddamn funny!" Rocky said in a threatening tone of voice.

Lydia looked up.

Rocky was glaring at Jose who had a grin on his face.

"I wish you had told me to bring a change of clothes," Lydia said to Jeremy as she emerged from the restroom in the double-wide trailer where she had tried to wash up and dust off her clothes as best as she could.

"Sorry about that," Jeremy said. "I didn't know you were going to meet someone for lunch."

The Loose Cannons had gone back to Jeremy's ranch, and they were alone in the office. Jeremy's employees were out on the range, supervising a group of women from a quilt guild who came in every other Saturday for target practice and had to be watched very carefully to prevent them from inadvertently shooting one another.

"I know you guys are planning something," Lydia said. "I saw a little bit of that map. It looked like a compound of some sort with several buildings. Will you be going with them?"

Jeremy was slow in answering. "We'll be gone for about a week. Maybe less."

"You're going with them?"

"Of course."

"When are you leaving?"

"Early Monday morning."

Lydia shook her head. "That's too bad, I have two days off starting Monday."

"That is too bad."

"Wait a minute. Are you free on Sunday? Mid-afternoon?"

"Yes. Why?"

"I've been invited to a fundraiser at Eamon Murphy's estate. I need an escort."

"I thought you had to work."

"I do. But I have been told I need to make an appearance at the fundraiser."

Jeremy looked away. "I don't like politicians, Lydia, and I especially don't like Murphy."

"Sorry, I bothered you, Jeremy. I didn't mean to put you on the spot like that."

"How did you ever get invited to one of his fundraisers?"

"I hired his firm to work on Jonathan's estate. The invitation came as soon as I wrote out a check."

"You'll need an escort to keep you from the freaks, won't you?"

"An escort would be nice. What can I do to change your mind? I would really like you to go with me."

"I take it that this is a formal affair?"

"Afternoon formal, I guess."

"I should wear a suit, maybe? What will you be wearing?"

"The navy-blue dress I bought for my graduation at U.C.L.A."

"I'll try to match you. Not the dress, but the navy blue. Where do we meet?"

"How about at my condo at 2:30 tomorrow. You've never seen it. I'd like to show it to you."

"Okay."

"Can I ask you something?"

Jeremy nodded.

"What are you guys going to be doing?" Lydia saw the pained look on Jeremy's face and quickly added, "Sorry, I shouldn't have asked."

"It's all right. I can't tell you what we're doing. But if you pick up a paper that carries international news, you might find it out on your own."

"Five million for a week's work."

"Plus expenses, of course."

CHAPTER ELEVEN

THE HOSTESS, most likely a U.C.L.A. student, looked at Lydia in disbelief when she entered the Japanese restaurant called Minako's in Westwood.

"I'm sorry, but we . . ."

Lydia knew she should have gone home to clean up before she met with Jenny Hamilton, but she didn't have time. She tried her best to brush out the dirt from her clothes, but she couldn't get it all.

"I'm supposed to meet someone here."

"Really!"

"Really!" Lydia mimicked the teenager's nasal voice. "My friend is waiting for me. Jenny Hamilton. I see her now. She's sitting at the table in the back. The young lady in the green dress who's looking at her cell phone."

The hostess stared at Lydia for a moment.

"Listen, kiddo, Lydia said, "I don't have time for this. Now either seat me or get the manager."

Lydia was quickly led to Jenny's table.

Jenny looked her up and down. "You look like you've been dragged across the desert."

"You might say that," Lydia said as she sat down. "You, on the other hand, look quite lovely."

Jenny studied Lydia for a moment. "I'm sorry I said that Lydia. I sit on my ass all day in an office, trying to keep my legs crossed to keep my work buddies from salivating. I know what you do for a living. It can't be much fun."

Lydia could understand why the nerds in the office where Jenny worked spent so much time sneaking peeks at her. Jenny Hamilton was a beautiful woman. Her black hair was the same color as Lydia's but was kept short. Whereas Lydia's skin had a healthy glow to it, Jenny's skin was so pale she had to stay out of the sun. The contrast between Jenny's black hair and pale skin required the skillfulness of a makeup artist to prevent her from looking like a stand-in for a television personality who went by the stage name of Elvira, Mistress of the Dark. When Jenny went out in the evening and needed to dress up, she had to work hard to avoid looking like she was part of the Goth subculture.

"Have you ordered yet?"

"I've ordered sushi and a double order of shrimp and vegetable tempura for two. I've ordered tea. Would you prefer sake instead?"

"I would, but I have to work tonight."

"How did you get your clothes so dirty?"

"I was practicing on the range. A lot of dirt gets kicked around."

Jenny cocked her head, a puzzled expression on her face. "That's so unlike the young lady I knew in college. You were so fastidious back then."

Lydia shrugged. "So, tell me, what's going on with Rod?"

Jenny giggled uncomfortably.

"I guess I shouldn't have asked you that," Lydia said.

"No, it's all right. We're back together again." Jenny paused.

Lydia waited for her to continue.

"He called me a few days ago. We talked about what he called my problem. My problem! That's what he called it. My problem! He was so intrigued that we met for drinks. I think my so-called problem turned him on."

"So, are you going to marry this guy?"

"Well, yes. Why not?"

"Congratulations. I wish the best for the two of you," Lydia said, wondering how long the marriage would last.

"Thank you," Jenny said, flashing a big smile on her face. "I believe you really mean it."

"I do," Lydia said. She tried to sound sincere.

"Now, down to business," Jenny said, still smiling as she reached below the table and picked up a bound document with a red cover that looked about the size of a script for a motion picture. She handed it across the table to Lydia.

"What's this?" Lydia said, staring at the document.

"It represents everything I could find that was owned by Jonathan Benedict."

"Jenny, you shouldn't have gone through the trouble of binding it like this."

Jenny shrugged. "No problem at all."

Lydia opened the binder to a page with a title that read CALIFORNIA PROPERTIES. The next page contained a list of properties with references to page numbers. It included the properties owned by Jonathan Benedict that Lydia already knew about with four exceptions. These included four bars located in the San Francisco Bay area that Lydia was sure weren't on the list that Jane Halloran emailed her.

Lydia flipped through the pages and saw the source material for each of the properties. Jenny had found the title transfer documents for all of them. Some of the material included the original real estate listing. Lydia looked up in amazement at Jenny.

"You must have spent most of the night putting this together."

Jenny shrugged. "You haven't looked at the next section yet, sweetie."

Lydia turned to the section entitled OUT OF STATE. There were four properties listed; the casino in Nevada, the Benedict Armory in North Carolina, and a big surprise, a large ranch and a smaller parcel of property with a house on it in Arizona. Lydia knew about the casino and the armory, but this was the first time she had seen any information about property owned by Jonathan in Arizona.

"What do you know about this ranch?" Lydia asked.

"Jonathan bought it about eight years ago."

"Where is it located?"

"In Arizona on the border with our friends from the South. It's big, Lydia, over a thousand acres."

Lydia turned to the page where the ranch was featured. It was in Cochise County, Arizona, off Highway 92 near Miracle Valley. There were satellite pictures showing a large rectangular building on flat land about a mile north of the Mexican border. The records indicated that it was sold to Jonathan Benedict in 1999 for $1,200,000.

The records for the house showed that it was located on Highway 82, northeast of Sierra Vista, Arizona, and that Jonathan had purchased the property in 1999 for $125,000. The plat map showed that the house was on fifty acres and was set back nearly a half mile from the highway.

Lydia looked at a map of the area thoughtfully provided by Jenney and noticed that even though the house was located about twenty miles due north of the ranch, there was no direct route between the two properties. Getting from one to the other on paved roads required a rather circuitous route.

She closed the binder when the server brought food to the table. She waited until the server left before speaking. "Jenny, you did a lot of work on this. I owe you."

Jenny speared a piece of raw tuna with a chopstick. She looked at Lydia and smiled.

Lydia knew what she was thinking and said, "How about I pick up the check and we call it even?"

Lydia was assigned to work with Kenny Ferris that evening. During roll call, Sergeant Joanna Watson reported that no one had robbed any of the stores that Tactical Operations covered the previous evening. She then read a list of eighteen liquor and convenience stores that were being staked out by Tactical Operations that evening and reminded the officers to stay away from them unless they were called. Eleven of the stores were in the district assigned to Lydia and her partner. Roll call was quickly finished, and the officers filed out to begin their shift while officers from Tactical Operations began filing in to begin their briefing.

Officers Benny Workman and Roger Neff from Tactical Operations were assigned to Nate's Liquor in a small strip mall on Sepulveda just south of Pico. They met the owner, whose last name was Patel, at a little after 4:30 p.m. They installed a small camera in a space between petite liquor bottles located on a shelf just behind the cash register. Workman set up the monitor in the office at the back of the store while Neff adjusted the camera until it had a clear view of anyone who entered the store.

Neff had a little problem trying to make it clear to Patel what he was supposed to do if someone entered the store and pulled a gun on him. Patel thought the word 'duck' meant a two-legged bird that liked water, and Neff had to explain to him that 'duck' with an exclamation point also meant that he was to drop to the floor.

Once Neff was able to get the idea across to Patel that he needed to take cover in case of a robbery, he asked Patel if he kept a gun under the counter.

He did.

Neff asked for it, explaining that if a bandit came into the store his job was to hit the ground and not engage in a gunfight. Patel reluctantly handed the pistol over to Neff. It was a two-shot .22 caliber derringer spotted with rust. Neff marveled at what he believed to be a totally use-less weapon.

He headed to the office at the rear of the store where Workman was setting up the monitor. Neff would be the point man that night, charged with confronting the suspects should they be foolish enough to try and rob the store. He carefully studied the layout of the store from the van-tage point of the hallway door which was located a few steps from the office. From there, he would have a clear view of the area in front of the cash register.

There was no question as to what would happen if someone tried to rob the store. Neff would take cover behind the door frame, aim the shotgun at the suspect, and yell, "Police! Freeze! Drop that gun!" The startled suspect would turn to see what was going on. When he did that, the gun would turn with him toward the officer, and he would get blasted by nine pellets of double-aught buckshot before he realized he had made the biggest mistake of his life.

Neff had experienced this scenario on three separate occasions. On each occasion, the shooting had been videotaped. When played back, it looked as if the suspect was turning the gun on the officer instead of complying with the command to freeze and drop the gun. The result was always the same; the death of the bandit and a Coroner's ruling that the death was justifiable homicide.

Neff joined Workman in the office and loaded his twelve-gauge Ithaca shotgun with double-aught buckshot. He and Workman settled in for the night, watching the monitor, and listening to the muted sounds of Indian music coming from Patel's portable radio.

While the officers in the back room of Nate's Liquor fought off boredom on what they thought was a quiet night, officers assigned to Century Division were faced with a deluge of calls for services that kept them running from one end of the Division to the other the entire evening. Strangely enough, there was not a single robbery call until later that evening. It was as if word had gotten out on the street that Tactical Operations was in the Division.

Lydia and Kenny Ferris had handled eleven radio calls and were ready to call it a night when things really broke loose. At 11:15 p.m., right before they began thinking it was time to head to the station to finish their tour of duty, a small man wearing a black ski mask entered Nate's Liquor Store, pointed a semi-automatic pistol in Patel's face, and said in a loud voice, "Hello, motherfuckers!"

Neff and Workman immediately sprang in action. Neff stood up and clicked off the safety of his shotgun. He moved quickly toward the hallway door and braced his shotgun on the door frame, his finger on the trigger, ready to fire.

Nobody was in the store!

Neff rushed to the cash register and Workman ran past him out onto the sidewalk. Neff looked over the counter. Patel was face down on the floor, his hands held over his ears, waiting for gunfire.

"Are you all right!" Neff yelled.

Patel didn't move.

Neff reached over the counter and hit the silent alarm.

Workman stuck his head back inside the door. "I'm going after him. He's running south on Sepulveda. Set up a perimeter."

Neff paused before doing so. Something strange about the whole encounter bothered him. Patel was the only person in the store, yet the would-be bandit clearly yelled, "Hello motherfuckers!" Neff realized that the bandit had no intention of robbing the store. He knew there was a stake-out in place and was taunting them.

Lydia and Kenny Ferris heard the call come out.

"Any unit in the vicinity, a 211 silent at 2058 Sepulveda."

"Shall we take it?" Lydia asked.

"Why not? I've got nothing else to do tonight," Ferris said.

Lydia picked up the mike and rogered the call.

The female dispatcher came back on the line in a monotone voice. "Five-Adam-99, handle the 211 silent at 2058 Sepulveda, Code Three."

Ferris turned on the siren and the emergency lights and made a quick U-turn. A minute later, the dispatcher came back on the line and said something that Lydia couldn't hear over the siren. She leaned forward and asked the dispatcher to repeat what she had said.

Lydia listened as the dispatcher cancelled the call. She reached over and turned off the siren.

Ferris looked at her.

"They cancelled the call. Tactical Operations is handling."

"Another bandit hit the dust," Ferris said. "Shall we head to the barn?"

Lydia turned the radio to the frequency used by Tactical Operations. They were setting up a six-block perimeter around 2058 Sepulveda.

"They must have lost the suspect," Ferris said, as he pulled the car over to the curb. They listened as Tactical units began responding to the scene of the call.

"Shall we go over and take a look?" Lydia asked, forgetting that she had plans for later that night.

"Let them handle it," Ferris said. "If we went over there, we'd get stuck at directing traffic for half the night while the heroes would be conducting a search for the suspect."

Lydia switched the radio back to their channel as Ferris drove to the station. The dispatcher came back on the air.

"All units. Suspect of attempted robbery at the liquor store at 2058 Sepulveda is described as a Male Caucasian, 18 to 21 years, five foot seven, dark hair, wearing a black hoodie, dark pants, last seen running east from Sepulveda through an alley toward Bentley. Suspect is armed with a small revolver."

Ferris pulled the car to the curb and looked at Lydia. "How about we make one quick check before we call it a night?"

"Jimmie Spahn?"

"Sounds like him, doesn't it?"

Lydia couldn't help but comparing her partner for the night, Kenny Ferris, with her other partner, Dick Hagerty. Ferris was a hard worker, like Hagerty, but Hagerty seemed to have a greater imagination and eye for detail that Ferris lacked. But tonight, Ferris once again surprised her. He turned onto Maple Street where Jimmie Spahn had lived with his parents and immediately pulled the car to the curb.

"You check the right side of the street," he told Lydia. "I'll check the left. Feel the hood of every car. If you find one that is warm, let me know and we'll check it out to see if it belongs here."

"Okay," Lydia said.

When they reached the Spahn residence without finding any cars that had recently been driven, Ferris crossed the street and joined Lydia on the sidewalk.

The house was dark and appeared to be empty.

They walked up onto the porch. Ferris took a position next to the right of the front door, while Lydia covered the other side. They listened for five minutes without hearing anything coming from inside the house. After checking the sides and the rear of the house, they headed back out onto the street. They saw a man on the porch across the street waving at them to come over.

The man was in his late fifties and was wearing shorty pajamas that exposed a pair of spindly legs. "If you're looking for the little bastard, he's not there. He left nearly two hours ago."

"How long has he been staying here?" Ferris asked.

"A couple of days. Comes and goes. He sneaks in at night and never turns on the light. Never seen him during the daytime."

"Does he have a car?" Lydia asked.

"I don't know. He usually comes in on foot from that direction," the man said, pointing to the east.

"Thank you," Ferris said.

"Who should I call if I see him?"

"Call the station and ask for the watch commander. If you see him during the day, ask for Sergeant Billy Vernor."

Five minutes after the police car left the area, a car thirty yards east of the Spahn house started up, made a U-turn, and drove off. The man who had reported what he had seen to Kenny and Lydia sat on the porch smoking a cigarette in the darkness. He got up and watched the car as it made a right turn at the next intersection.

"Damn," he said to himself when he realized that he had never seen anybody get into the car. He wondered if he should call the police station and tell them about it.

He didn't.

"Do you think Lieutenant Sloan would assign a car to watch the house," Lydia asked Ferris while they were on their way to the station.

Lieutenant Sloan was the A.M. Watch Commander.

"I doubt if he would pull a car out of the lineup on a Saturday night."

Lydia thought about it for a second. She pulled out her cell phone and called Vernor. He answered immediately. She told him what had happened that night and what the neighbor had said.

Vernor paused for a moment and then said, "I'm coming down as soon as I can. Let the Watch Commander know I'll be inside the house tonight."

"You have a key to the place?" Lydia asked.

Vernor hung up without answering.

Just before they arrived at the station, Kenny looked at Lydia out of the corner of his eye. "I've been expecting another 211 call to come out."

Lydia realized what Ferris was talking about. It was highly likely that the apparent robbery attempt of Nate's liquor store was a ruse to draw Tactical Operations off their stakeout locations, leaving other stores without cover.

"You know, Kenny," Lydia said. "none of this makes any sense to me. Tonight, they pull a gun on the owner of a store and then leave without trying to take the money. Earlier this week, they killed a Japanese couple in a convenience store and get away with less than a hundred dollars. What kind of people are we dealing with?"

"They could be doing this as an initiation rite to get into a street gang, or they could be thrill seekers who get their kicks by hurting people. Either way, these guys are dangerous. I seriously doubt we'll be able to take them down without some copper getting hurt."

CHAPTER TWELVE

March 26, 2006. Sunday

LYDIA CHECKED to make sure she wasn't being followed after she left the station. She wasn't worried about the man with the gravelly voice who had been calling her about assigning over her rights to Jonathan's estate. She was concerned that Lieutenant Hardemann didn't do what she had asked and had assigned the Gang Unit to cover her despite her wishes. She had a long night ahead of her and didn't want anybody from LAPD following her.

The first thing Lydia did when she entered her apartment was to check for telephone messages. There were none. The anonymous caller must be taking the night off.

She went to her bedroom and changed into dark-blue workout clothes and pulled on a matching hoodie over her T-shirt. She walked past a full-length mirror in her bedroom and stopped. She looked tired. She felt tired. But there was something important she needed to do.

The front lobby was not manned by a security guard after midnight, but the front door was locked. Lydia pulled the hood over her head to prevent her face being seen by the video camera as she left the building. A minute later, she had slipped around the building and was jogging across the golf course on her way to the storage facility where she kept a rented Jeep in the garage.

The Jeep contained everything she needed to get inside the fenced property at Oceania Manor without being seen. A trash bag held the black clothes she had worn the night she had killed Jonathan, and a large backpack contained a mag light and a heavy-duty bolt cutter.

After retrieving the Jeep, she drove west on Interstate 10 toward Santa Monica and then north on Pacific Coast Highway towards Malibu. It was a beautiful night. The ocean sparkled with reflected lights of the oil rigs ten miles offshore. Traffic was heavy going on PCH in both directions, but it was a weekend night and was to be expected.

As she approached Oceania Manor, the traffic had gotten considerably lighter. She drove past Vermillion Canyon Road and continued north. She slowed down as she approached what was left of the estate. The entrance to the estate had a line of sawhorses acting as a feeble barrier. The wrought iron gate was set too far back in the driveway to be able to see it. She continued driving north until she found a street where she could make a U-turn.

On her way back, she pulled over to the shoulder of the highway. From her vantage point, she could see that the wrought iron gate had been damaged so badly it looked ready to fall off its hinges. The only thing holding the two sections together was a chain with a padlock. Just beyond the gate was the two-story gatehouse where Carlos Aldana and four other bodyguards took turns controlling access to the estate.

The mansion itself was a couple hundred yards up the drive. The stone front gleamed ghostly white in the moonlight. In the past, it was the finest house on this part of the highway, but now it looked threatening with black gaping holes for windows and a massive front door that had been reduced to rubble by the fire.

Lydia drove on and turned east on Vermillion Canyon Road. She stopped her Jeep across the road from the gate to a fire road. The iron bar that stood for a gate had a padlock on it.

Waiting a minute to make sure no cars were coming, Lydia turned onto the fire road, stopped the Jeep in front of the gate, and turned off the lights. She got out of the Jeep and waited for a few seconds, listening for cars. Satisfied that no one was on the road, she cut the lock with her bolt cutter and swung the iron bar to one side. She drove past the gate, parked the Jeep, got out, and pulled the gate shut.

The fire road was scoured with ruts and the ride was bumpy. After driving a few hundred yards, Lydia crossed a shallow creek lined by scrub oak trees. She stopped and backed the Jeep into a rough parking spot under a clump of trees. She was certain it would be hidden from any ranger who happened to be checking the area.

She got out of the Jeep, opened the back hatch, and began taking off her clothing, belatedly realizing she should have changed into the dark clothes while she was still in the storage space. She removed the .45 Springfield XDS she carried off-duty from her belly band holster and placed it in the rear of the Jeep. It was extremely unlikely that she would be needing the gun tonight.

Once dressed in night combat black, she put on black leather gloves, slung the backpack over her shoulder, and set off in a light jog up the fire road.

Getting to the twenty or so acres occupied by Jonathan's estate required a serious amount of effort even though Lydia was highly familiar with the fire road. When she was in her early teens, she and her friends would race up, down, and across the hills in ATVs. Jonathan had even installed a gate that she could use to access the roads. But since then, he had blocked off the gate and had a contractor drop heavy boulders onto a trail that led up to the fire road, so there was no easy way to get onto the property.

Lydia climbed halfway up the steep fire road until she reached the area directly behind the mansion. She then slid down a hill studded with loose dirt, rocks, and chaparral, and crossed a deep creek bed with little water in it. She entered the property without having to go over the boundary fence by scooting underneath a concrete culvert. It held a half foot of stagnant water over a layer of slime. Several rats scurried out of her way.

Two weeks ago, when Lydia visited Carlos Aldana in the gatehouse, she discovered that the estate was now covered by fourteen CCTV cameras. Not one of them covered the area around the culvert. She didn't know if the CCTV system still worked, but she didn't care. Tonight, she would make sure it wasn't working.

The first thing Lydia did once she was on the property was to head for a large garden shed that was nearly a hundred yards behind the house.

Once inside, she turned on her mag light and looked around. It was just as she remembered it. There was a trapdoor in the floor. Lydia pulled the trapdoor open and climbed down the ladder to a tunnel.

Lydia had discovered the tunnel quite by accident several weeks ago. She had driven up to Oceania Manor to borrow one of the many guns Jonathan kept in a large vault in the basement. She had known about the vault and its extensive collection of revolvers and semi-automatics, but neither she nor anyone else knew about the tunnel that Jonathan had built as an escape route.

Jonathan had been getting ready to leave for dinner with his girl-friend, Victoria, and his son Milo. He invited Lydia to go with them, but she declined. She didn't want to spend any more time than necessary with her stepfather.

Lydia needed to borrow a .357 Magnum revolver from Jonathan to use on duty, because the one she had purchased was on back order and would not be available for several weeks. Since he was in a hurry to leave for the dinner reservation, Jonathan gave Lydia the combination to the vault and told her to take what she needed.

It was while Lydia was exploring the vault that she noticed a steel door in the rear. It was painted the same color as the walls and was virtu-ally undetectable from a distance. When she opened the door, she discovered the tunnel. It occurred to her that she might have a need to sneak into the mansion in the near future. She took the time to make sure the keypad on the tunnel side of the door had the same combina-tion as the main door.

She found a .357 Magnum in the model that Hagerty had suggested and put it in a duffel bag. When she was ready to leave, she took one last look around the room. It occurred to her that she might need a gun in the future that couldn't be traced back to her.

But she didn't take just one gun. That night, she stuffed nearly a dozen guns into a duffel bag. On the night she killed Jonathan Benedict, she put them back.

Lydia slowly made her way through the tunnel toward the house. The tunnel was dark and full of cobwebs. Lydia hated spiders, and there had to be a thousand of them living down here in the dark. Even though she kept the mag light on, she could not avoid having cobwebs glide over her face as she made her way through the moldy darkness. About halfway to the vault, Lydia became aware that the floor was wet.

When she arrived at the entrance to the vault, she shone the light on the keypad. She paused for a moment, hoping it was battery operated. If it wasn't, she would have to go back to the shed and find something she could use to pry open the door. She punched in the first number into the keypad and it lit up.

When she opened the door, a stream of water about two inches deep came gushing out. She played the light around the vault and was astonished at its condition.

Even though most of the main floor had not collapsed, there was considerable water damage to the display cases. Instead of looking like the bright and shiny display room it had once been, it now looked like it was a setting in a haunted house attraction.

The room was dank, the air heavy, smelling of burnt refuse. At the far end of the room, the floor had partially collapsed. A beam or rafter with part of the underfloor attached to it had fallen into the vault, blocking the entrance into the room from the basement. In the gloom, Lydia could see a ladder coming down from a hole that had been chopped in the ceiling.

All the weapons in the vault were modern weapons manufactured in the past 100 years. Jonathan had bragged that he had every single model of handgun that had ever been made, including guns manufactured by Smith and Wesson, Kimber, Colt, Taurus, and Ruger. If a model had an optional barrel length, he had one of each. If a model came in different kinds of finishes, he had one of each.

From her previous visit to the vault, Lydia knew that revolvers were stored in the cabinets on the south side of room and semi-automatics on the north. Each gun was displayed in a felt-backed niche with a brass plate that showed its make, model, serial number, and date of manufacture.

Over a third of the guns had been removed, mostly from the front of the room. Apparently, LASO Homicide had taken them out to be tested.

Lydia was relieved when she found the Springfield semi-automatics had not been removed. She favored that gun in the XD series using the .45 ACP cartridge. She grabbed a couple of those models and placed them in her backpack.

At the bottom of the display case was an XDS that was not in its correct position. She had used that gun to kill Carlos Aldana and Milo Benedict and had placed it there on her way out of the house. She decided she didn't want that gun found by Lieutenant Shepherd. Even though Lydia had worn gloves when she fired it, there might be something on the gun that could be traced back to her.

Lydia put the gun in her backpack, intending to dispose of it as soon as possible. She sloshed her way through the water across the room to the door and left the vault, forcefully closing the door behind her.

When Lydia had been on the grounds of Oceania Manor last Sunday morning, she had to move cautiously to avoid detection by one of the many CCTV cameras. The power was now out, so she didn't have to worry about her image being recorded as she walked along the south side of the now derelict mansion toward the gatehouse. She could hear the waves breaking on the beach and an occasional car passing by on Pacific Coast Highway.

She climbed the stairs at the back of the gatehouse and entered the large room at the top where Carlos Aldana and his buddies kept watch over the estate. There were four windows on each side of the room, giving it a magnificent view of the estate and the ocean. There was also enough light coming through the windows from PCH that would allow her to move around the room without using the mag light. The room looked just the same as Lydia had seen it when she visited Carlos Aldana three weeks ago. It also looked as if it had not been searched.

She went to the bank of CCTV monitors. They were not on. She looked around for the recorder, hoping that Shepherd had not found it. She breathed a sigh of relief when she saw it on a shelf under the monitors. It was about the size of a satellite DVR and could easily fit in her backpack. When she turned the recorder sideways, she found an array of wires protruding from the back. It took less than a minute for her to detach the wires from the recorder.

Just as she slid the recorder into her backpack, she heard a door slam shut. She went to one of the windows overlooking the entrance to the estate. A sheriff's car was parked in the driveway on the other side of the line of sawhorses. A deputy was out of the car and walking toward the gate with a flashlight in his hand. A second deputy was getting out of the car.

Shit!

She had not heard the car drive up to the gate. She scooted down and waited, her heart pounding so furiously that it felt as if her eardrums were throbbing.

Why do I do shit like this? Lydia thought.

If they caught her, even someone as dumb as Shepherd could make a case against her for murder. It would be hard to explain why she had the gun that killed Carlos Aldana and Milo Benedict in her backpack.

There was a sound of a rattling chain and then voices. She waited, trying to calm her breathing. It was a good two minutes before she got up and looked out the window.

Two deputies, one of them a woman, were standing by the gate. The male deputy was talking over a handheld radio.

Lydia decided she had to get out of there fast. She slung the backpack onto her back. Keeping low, she headed for the door and made sure it was closed before heading down the stairs. Once on the lawn, she ran diagonally toward the creek on the south side of the property, keeping the gatehouse between her and the deputies.

The creek had a trickle of water running through it. She stepped into the creek and began working her way slowly toward the culvert. When she drew near the culvert, she heard a helicopter coming up the coast. She stumbled through the water as fast as she could.

Behind her, a brilliant light turned on. The helicopter had arrived and was beginning a slow circle over the estate.

Lydia ducked into the culvert and knelt in the murky water. All she could see of the mansion was the top floor with its missing roof. The helicopter was lazily circling around it, its spotlight searching the grounds.

After fifteen minutes, it went away.

Lydia waited for another fifteen minutes before she crawled out of the culvert and climbed up the hill toward the fire road. It occurred to her that the estate belonged to her as a result of the joint tenancy established by Sophia Benedetto, and she had a right to be there. But the fact that she owned Oceania Manor would not help her if it were discovered the gun that killed Carlos and Milo was found in her possession.

While heading south on Pacific Coast Highway, Lydia passed a storage area for a roadside construction site with a portable toilet. She made a U-turn and parked next to it. After making sure no one was around, she entered the portable john and held her breath. After checking to make sure the pit was nearly full, she tossed the gun she had used to kill Carlos and Milo into the stinking mess.

Back on the road, Lydia drove carefully, making sure she drove only a mile or two above the speed limit. The last thing she needed was to get stopped by the police.

The night was not over yet. There was still work to be done. She needed to get the CCTV unit into her apartment without being seen.

Then, there was the problem of trying to figure out how the unit worked and retrieving the information she needed. If she was lucky, she might be able to find instructions on the internet. And if she was really lucky, she might be able to get the license numbers of all the cars that entered the estate for Jonathan's Friday night poker party.

When Lydia pulled the Jeep into the garage at the storage facility, she looked at her watch. It was 3:40 a.m. She had planned to return to her condo at 5:45 a.m. to make it look like she had been out for an early morning jog. After setting the alarm on her watch, she lay back on her seat and dozed off.

The alarm didn't work. Lydia woke suddenly and looked at her watch. It was ten minutes after six. She got out of the Jeep, opened the rear hatch, and changed into her work-out clothes.

When she entered the lobby at 6:30, she found the security guard named Pedersen on duty. He was a pleasant man who was starting a second career after he retired with twenty-five years as a corrections officer in the state prison system. He greeted her with a warm smile as she approached him.

"Mr. Pedersen, I'm expecting a visitor around 2:30 this afternoon. Could you let him have one of the parking spots out front and send him up to my apartment?"

"I will."

Once she was in her apartment, Lydia took a long shower and then slipped into bed.

CHAPTER THIRTEEN

LYDIA WOKE just before noon, put on a T-shirt and jeans, and went down to the garage to get her car. It took her less than an hour to retrieve the CCTV recorder from the storage unit and bring it back to her apartment. She placed it on the counter in the kitchen. After jotting down the model and serial number, she went back to her den where she kept her computer. She spent nearly an hour searching for a user manual for the CCTV system called Pro-Surveillance before giving up.

The first person she thought that could help her was Jenny, but she didn't want to call her. She didn't want to risk losing Jenny as a friend by making it look like the only reason she called her was to ask for a favor.

Thinking about Jenny sparked a memory of what had been in the bound document binder she had given her. There was some information in the document that needed further investigation. She was thinking about the ranch property that Jonathan owned in Arizona. Was it really a ranch, or was it being used for something else?

Jonathan had never mentioned anything about owning a ranch. He was not an outdoorsman, and he was not the type of person who would be interested in raising cattle. There was not much money in it. The ranch was right on the border. Therefore, the ranch likely had something to do with Jonathan's illegal business activities.

Lydia had the next two days off, so it shouldn't be a problem flying to Arizona and taking a look at the ranch. She got on the Internet and made a reservation on a direct flight to Tucson early tomorrow morning.

At 2:00 P.M., Lydia began getting dressed for the fundraiser. She put on the navy-blue dress and pearls that she wore at her graduation from U.C.L.A. last year. After she finished dressing, she went back to the kitchen and pulled a bottle of chardonnay out of the refrigerator and set it with two wine glasses on the counter. She then began examining the controls on the front of the CCTV recorder in the hopes of finding out how to retrieve what was stored on the device. The doorbell rang just as she found a USB slot that she could use to attach to her computer.

She was surprised when she opened the door and found Jeremy standing there in Army dress blues.

They both said, "Wow" when they saw what each other was wearing.

Lydia tuned out the compliments by Jeremy as she looked at the twin silver bars on his shoulders and the ribbons on the breast of his jacket. When Lydia was at U.C.L.A., she had befriended an Army veteran who had been a member of the Special Forces. He had once attended a formal event with her in his dress uniform. When they were seated at a table with some mutual friends who were athletes, the conversation turned to the ribbons and badges he wore on his jacket. He didn't want to discuss them. After some prodding and several drinks, he explained what they meant. Lydia was impressed by what he had accomplished in four years of military service.

Lydia knew from the badges and medals on Jeremy's uniform that he had been an infantry Captain, that he had been in the Special Forces, and had earned the Combat Infantry and Parachutist badges. He also wore three rows of ribbons including a Silver Star and two Purple Hearts.

Lydia raised a hand to her mouth as she stared at the ribbons.

"It's the only suit I have that isn't a K-Mart special," Jeremy said when he saw her reaction. "Do you think those people in Beverly Hills would approve?"

Lydia shook her head. "It's Holmby Hills, and I really don't care what anyone up there thinks. You look great." She paused for a moment, her head cocked sideways. "You're not on active duty, are you?"

"Negative on that. Did I say you look gorgeous?"

"I think you said that already."

"Sorry."

"Don't be sorry. I love flattery. Do you want a glass of wine before we go?"

Jeremy looked at his watch. "Do we have time?"

"We have plenty of time. It doesn't matter if we're late."

Lydia headed to the kitchen while Jeremy walked across the living room toward the balcony. There were golfers out on the course. He turned to Lydia who was behind the kitchen counter opening a bottle of wine.

"Do you own this place or rent?"

"I own it. It's a long story. My mother bought it for me when I was at U.C.L.A."

"It's very nice."

"Beats the hell out of living in one of the cells in a dorm." She watched him for a moment. "So, where did you go to college?"

"Arizona. In Tucson."

It occurred to Lydia that Jeremy might know the area she planned to visit tomorrow and might be a good source of information. But it was not a good idea right now to let him know what she was planning.

Jeremy walked over to the counter and looked at the CCTV recorder. "What are you doing with this recorder?"

Lydia, surprised, looked up. "You know what this is?"

"Of course. It's a Pro-Surveillance 1810. One of their top line models. If you have the right camera, it has the capability of seeing anything in high definition fifty yards out."

"Do you know how it works?"

"I do. I helped set up a CCTV system like this in some armpit in the Middle East. What are you doing with it?"

"I'm trying to figure out how to get some pictures off it."

"But what are you doing with it?"

"It came into my possession rather suddenly. No more questions on its provenance, okay?"

Jeremy stared at her as she poured a glass of wine.

"I know you have a computer, but do you have a data transfer cable?"

Lydia looked up. "I do."

"Take me to your computer."

Lydia passed a glass of wine to Jeremy.

"Did I tell you how good you smell?" he asked.

"It's the wine," Lydia said. "They claim it has accents of raspberry and peach."

Jeremy passed the wine back to Lydia. "You carry the fruit. I'll carry the recorder. Where's your computer?"

Lydia watched as Jeremy hooked up the recorder to the computer. It didn't take long before he had a menu on the monitor. He turned and looked up at Lydia who was standing behind him.

"This thing was connected to fourteen cameras. What are you looking for?"

"The front gate. I want the license numbers of cars who were at Jonathan's poker party last Friday night. I don't know what time they got there, but they left just after midnight."

Jeremy, looking thoughtful, stared at her for a good long while.

"What's wrong?" Lydia asked.

"This recorder is from your stepfather's estate, isn't it? Are you trying to find out who murdered him?"

Lydia was stunned by the question. "I don't care who murdered him. I want to find out who attended his poker game last Friday night."

"How did you get this?"

Lydia didn't answer.

"All right, I'll get what you want. But we need to turn this over to the police after we're done."

"Jeremy, I can't turn this over to the police. You don't have to do this. I'm sorry I asked you."

"Tell me why you want this information."

Lydia stared at her mother's picture that was in a little niche above her desk. She wasn't sure how much to tell Jeremy about why she wanted the license plate numbers but decided on an abbreviated version. She told him about how people wanted her to assign her rights away to Jonathan's estate and the phone calls she had been getting.

"So, you think that the person or persons who are giving you a bad time might be the same people who were playing cards that night?"

"They might. As a matter of fact, I'm sure of it."

"Okay, let's see what we can find," Jeremy said. "We need to find out which camera covered the front entrance."

He went to work on the computer and quickly found what Lydia wanted. The camera that covered the front gate was set low on the gatehouse, so there was a clear view of any vehicle entering and leaving the grounds of the estate. The last image recorded on the system for the camera that focused on the front gate was at 2:23 a.m., March 18, 2006, when power had been cut off to the estate. Jeremy scanned backward through the video file until he came to a place where there was movement at the front gate. He stopped the recorder at that point and played it back. The monitor showed firefighters forcing the front gate open and entering the estate.

"Do you want to watch this?" Jeremy asked. "We could find other cameras that showed what was happening at the mansion."

"No," Lydia said. "Keep rewinding it."

Jeremy began winding the recording back until there was movement again. He stopped it, and it showed a black sedan passing through the open gate toward PCH.

"There," Lydia said. "That's one of the cars. I need the license number."

Within five minutes, Lydia had five license numbers. She knew who one of the cars belonged to by sight. It belonged to her former fiancé, Jake Nilsson, who was now in jail for participating in a burglary where the owner of the property had been killed. She needed to get the other plate numbers to Billy Vernor, so that she could find out who the cars were registered to, but she didn't want to do that in front of Jeremy. She would do it later that night.

"What are you going to do with the recorder now that you found out what's on it?" Jeremy asked.

"I don't know," Lydia finally said when she became aware that Jeremy was staring at her with a quizzical expression on his face. "Maybe keep it. After all, I own the damn place where I got it from."

"Shall we take my Jeep, or do we want to go classy and take your BMW?" Jeremy asked Lydia as they left her apartment.

"Let's take your Jeep," Lydia replied. "Maybe shake things up a little when those rich people see what a real soldier looks like."

They took the elevator down to the lobby and walked past Pedersen who had a broad smile on his face when he saw how Lydia was dressed.

Holmby Hills was a fifteen-minute drive from Lydia's condo. It was less expensive than its neighbor Bel Air to the north and was first developed in the 1920's. Most of the estates currently on sale in the community were worth over ten million dollars, although a one bedroom, one bath, condo could be had for a mere half million dollars. Its most famous property was the Playboy Mansion. Its most famous residents included people in the entertainment industry, professional athletes, and a sheik on the lam from a Middle East vendetta over his choice of a wife.

Caroline Drive was partially blocked off by a barricade manned by security officers. One of the officers tossed Jeremy a lazy salute when he saw the twin bars on his epaulettes.

The front of Eamon Murphy's estate was shielded from the street by a tall hedge that stood directly behind a wrought iron fence with a scroll-work design. On the opposite side of the street were several television crews who turned their cameras on the Jeep as Jeremy pulled into the driveway of the estate. Two burly men in black suits stopped them at the gate entrance. Lydia showed the invitation to the man who came to her side of the car. He seemed more interested in her thighs than the invitation. They were waved through without a word being said.

Eamon Murphy's home was a three-story mansion painted a blinding white. Although the homes in Holmby Hills were expensive and extravagant, Murphy's mansion didn't fit any known style in Los Angeles. The central structure with its columns and colonnades looked as if it had been magically transplanted from a southern plantation. The addition of two wings on either side of the main building, an afterthought by the look of it, caused it to sprawl over the length of three quarters of a football field.

When Lydia saw the size of the place, she thought someone could live in one end of the mansion, go about their daily business, and not see anyone from the other end for days.

The driveway was an ellipsis that circled around an immaculate lawn. A pond in the center of the lawn had a fountain that was shooting a stream of water thirty feet in the air.

Lydia knew that California was experiencing a drought. She wondered how Eamon Murphy, being an aspiring politician in a City where water-saving measures were being enforced, would deal with that in his campaign.

A valet greeted them at the massive front entrance and took the keys to the Jeep. Jeremy watched the valet carefully as he drove the Jeep off the property. He looked at Lydia who shrugged.

Jeremy led Lydia by the arm up the marble stairs to the front door. The foyer was almost as large as the lobby in Lydia's condo. It was two stories high and featured two curving staircases finished with brass railings that circled either side of the entrance hall. A narrow hallway led to an open door at the rear of the house.

Just inside the door were two matrons wearing fluffy pink dresses sitting at a small mahogany table. They were trying their best to look like Southern belles.

"What is your name, dear?" one of the ladies asked as Lydia approached the table.

Lydia gave her name.

"And this soldier is your guest?"

"Captain Jeremy Morgan is my guest."

"How nice. Would you like to donate to Mr. Murphy's campaign?" the woman asked Lydia. "A minimum of five thousand dollars is suggested."

"I've already donated fifty thousand," Lydia said. She became aware that Jeremy whipped his head toward her. Lydia presented the invitation to the lady. "My invitation includes a guest."

"Very well," the lady replied. "The fete is just outside the door to the back. Mrs. Murphy requests that you do not walk on the lawn. There is a large patio and lots of walkways that will allow you to enjoy the gardens. Mr. Murphy is in a receiving line on the patio out back. If you hurry, you might be able to see him before it shuts down."

As they walked through the hall towards the open door at the far end, Jeremy walked so close to Lydia that their shoulders touched. He leaned over and whispered in her ear, "You donated fifty thousand dollars to his campaign? I'm surprised you would do something like that."

"It was the retainer his law firm charged me." Lydia stopped and turned toward Jeremy. "And do you know what? I don't like this place. It reminds me too much of Jonathan's mansion."

"Which you own."

Lydia smiled. "What's left of it."

There was a massive lawn out back that led down a gentle slope to a brick fire pit and beyond that a swimming pool. The patio and the walkways were lined with brilliant red and yellow rose bushes. The area around the pool was crowded with guests.

A large bar had been set up on the patio to the right, but there was no line waiting at it because there was least a half dozen waiters taking drink orders from the guests. Another half dozen servers were carrying trays of canapes.

"Hello there."

Lydia turned to find Reece Tanner standing behind her.

"The receiving line is now closed, but I'm sure that Mr. Murphy will want to talk to you. Will you introduce me to your guest?"

Tanner was wearing what Lydia thought was a strange get up. A white sport coat and knee length pink shorts that exposed clean shaven legs. Trailing behind him was a pretty girl about twelve-years old. She was wearing a light blue taffeta dress with frills along the neckline and waist that looked as if it was designed for someone much younger.

Lydia introduced Tanner to Jeremy.

"We don't see a lot of that in Holmby Hills," Tanner said, looking at the ribbons on Jeremy's uniform.

"You should get out more often," Jeremy said, pleasantly.

Tanner half-smiled, his mouth partially open. After a moment, he said, "I'm sorry if I offended you in some way, Mr. Morgan."

"You didn't, Mr. Tanner. I was just making an observation about where the people in our military come from."

"I see."

Lydia decided to interrupt before hostilities broke out. "Who is the young lady with you, Mr. Tanner?" Lydia asked.

Tanner turned. "I'm sorry. I should have introduced you. This is my daughter, Charlene. Charlene, say hello to Miss Harte and Captain Morgan."

Charlene smiled, said hello shyly, and then hid herself behind her father.

"I've told Mr. Murphy all about you," Tanner continued. "When I mentioned you're a police officer, he said he wanted to meet you. He wants to hear all about your work."

"I would be glad to talk to him," Lydia said. "I've heard a lot about him." She didn't mention the fact that what she knew about Eamon Murphy came solely from the Chief of Police.

"Make yourself comfortable. There's a bar and food on the promenade above you and plenty of comfy chairs with a great view of the Hills."

Lydia and Jeremy turned and looked up. The second floor of the rear of the house had a long balcony with white railings. It stretched across the central portion of the mansion.

"You can get up there by taking the stairs in the main hall," Tanner said. "When I see Mr. Murphy, I'll tell him you're here." Tanner took his daughter by the hand. "If you'll excuse me, I have to find my wife."

"Mr. Tanner," Lydia said, stopping him, "are you ready to file in the probate court tomorrow morning?"

"Yes. The petition has already been drafted. It'll be messengered to the court first thing tomorrow morning."

"Thank you."

Tanner turned and led Charlene down the walk toward the pool.

After a moment, Jeremy asked in a low whisper, "He has a wife and not a husband?"

"Be nice."

"I am being nice. His having a wife raises my opinion of him."

"Are you talking about the way he dresses?"

"Yes."

"Many people on the Westside try to be clever with clothes."

"You don't," Jeremy said.

"I don't usually dress to show off," Lydia said.

Jeremy scratched his head. "What kind of wife would let her husband dress like that?"

"The same kind of wife who dresses her teenage daughter like a six-year old."

"Point taken. What do you know about this guy Tanner?"

"I don't know much about him personally. But I do know he charges $500 an hour. Did you notice what he said about the petition being drawn up? He didn't say he drafted the petition. He had someone do it for him. Probably a paralegal at $150 an hour. I can't wait to see how they bill for it."

"Shall we go up to the promenade and get comfy?" Jeremy asked, mimicking Reece Tanner.

"Of course."

Lydia thought she would never see Jonathan Benedict's girlfriend Victoria again, but there she was, walking out of the house as Lydia and Jeremy were walking inside.

"Lydia, what a surprise to see you here," Victoria said. She was holding a champagne flute. "I thought you stayed away from politics."

Lydia recovered quickly. "I'm not involved in his campaign. I hired his firm to handle a legal matter."

"Let me guess. The matter involves Jonathan's estate, doesn't it?"

"It does."

"Good. I'm glad you're doing that. I wouldn't want the State of California to get their hands on it."

Lydia nodded. "Yes. What are you doing here if I may ask?"

"My firm is doing some publicity for Eamon," Victoria said. She smiled coyly at Jeremy. "And who is your friend? Is he substituting for Jake?"

Lydia tried her best to repress a cringe. "This is Captain Jeremy Morgan. He's my shooting instructor and my friend."

"How nice," Victoria said.

"Are you two related?" Jeremy asked.

Lydia and Victoria did look alike. Victoria wore almost the same style of dress with pearls that Lydia was wearing, except that Victoria's dress was black. They both wore their dark hair in a ponytail, but there were differences between the two of them that anybody who was close enough could easily see. Victoria was a good fifteen years older than Lydia, and her face showed it. Her face was thinner and more angular than Lydia's, her hips slightly broader, her calves slightly weaker, but she still was a beautiful and elegant woman.

"We're not related," Victoria said in response to Jeremy's question. "But we do have something in common. I was a friend of Lydia's father."

Lydia resented Jonathan being called her father. It rankled her so much that she nearly always corrected anyone who had the misfortune of referring to Jonathan as her father by hastily replying that Jonathan was her stepfather, not her father. She didn't think now was the right time to do this in Jeremy's presence.

"So," Victoria continued, "I imagine you know all about what happened at Oceania Manor last weekend. I suppose you've been interviewed by that dreadful policewoman. She is easily the most annoying woman I have ever met."

"I have been interviewed by her," Lydia said.

"What do you think happen up there?" Victoria said, her eyes locking on Lydia's. "Do you have any idea who might have done it?"

"I have no idea," Lydia replied. "What about you? What do you think happened?"

"I suppose it had something to do with that card game he threw every Friday night."

Lydia shrugged.

"You know I attended some of those parties," Victoria continued. "I even played a hand or two."

"I didn't know that," Lydia said, wondering why Jonathan would ask Victoria to attend one of his poker parties. The Friday evening events were for Jonathan's business associates only, and they were all men. But she knew Jonathan always liked being seen with beautiful women.

"So," Victoria said, "will you be attending the funeral tomorrow?"

Lydia was not aware of any funeral plans for what was once her family. "No one told me about any funeral. Who's being buried tomorrow?"

"All of them except for Carlos. He'll be cremated and his ashes tossed in the ocean. The police released their bodies on Friday. I hope to see you there. It'll be at Meadow Lawn in Malibu at eleven."

"I can't come. I'll be out of town."

"Something important, I hope?"

"Yes. It's a seminar the Department already paid for. I've already made reservations for the flight."

"That's too bad. Listen, I won't keep you. I assume you two were heading out."

"Actually, we're going up to the promenade. Nice to see you again, Victoria."

Once inside the house, Jeremy tapped Lydia on the shoulder. "Let's talk for a second." He led Lydia to the side to let people through.

"What's going on?" Lydia asked.

"Several things. Who is that woman?"

"She was Jonathan's girlfriend, but I don't know her all that well. She handled public relations for Benedict Armory. I don't even know her last name, and I don't know who she works for."

"Did you get the impression she wasn't all that broken up about what happened in Malibu?"

"I had the same impression. But it's been over a week since Jonathan was killed."

"She was pumping you for information."

"I know that. I said as little as possible."

"I don't like her."

"Neither do I."

"And you really didn't know about the funeral?"

"I didn't. I would have liked to have been there for Sophia, but I can't. I have something important to do tomorrow."

"Why do you suppose nobody told you about it?"

"I don't know, Jeremy. Maybe, they thought I already knew about it."

Jeremy looked up at the ceiling.

"Do you want to go up to the promenade," Lydia asked, "or does that look on your face mean you have something else on your mind?"

Jeremy turned his attention back to Lydia. "What's this about you having a reservation for a flight tomorrow? I didn't know you had a seminar."

"I don't."

"Where are you going, or is it a secret?"

"My God, Jeremy, you'd think we were married. It's no secret. I'm flying to Tucson."

"And what will you be doing there?"

"What will you and your buddies be doing tomorrow?"

"I can't tell you. You know that."

"Do you know what ditto means?"

"I do. Do you want to leave, or shall we go up to the promenade?"

"Let's go up to the promenade." Lydia didn't want to tell Jeremy she was spying for the Chief of Police, and that she needed to stay a little while longer.

The promenade was not as busy as it was on the patio. Lydia ordered a lemonade from a passing waiter and Jeremy a scotch whiskey. She filled a plate with finger food from the buffet, and the two of them found a table in the shade overlooking the back lawn.

"It's the first time I've been in Holmby Hills," Jeremy said. "Actually, it's quite pleasant and peaceful, but all things considered, I like my place better."

"I'm with you on that," Lydia said, looking out over the lawn.

She spotted an actress, walking up from the firepit, a woman whose cinematic skills didn't come anywhere near matching the size of her breasts. A man walked down to meet her. They talked for a few seconds, and then the man took the actress by the arm and led her toward the house.

The man looked familiar. Then Lydia recognized him. He was Robert MacFarland III, the Democratic mayor of Los Angeles who was serving his last term after seven years in office. Lydia had often heard of him referred to by some of the officers at Century Division as Bobby the Turd.

"It must be wonderful having more money than you can spend," Jeremy said suddenly.

"What did you say?" Lydia asked, realizing that she had been distracted by seeing the Mayor with an actress.

Jeremy waved his hand horizontally as if bestowing a blessing over the crowd below them. "It must be wonderful having more money than you can spend," he repeated.

"It is," Lydia said, deadpan.

Jeremy paused for a second, then caught the subtlety in Lydia's remark and laughed. After a moment, he looked back down at the lawn below them.

Lydia saw him suddenly squint his eyes as if he were looking in the direction of the setting sun. There was no sun over the backyard. She tried to follow his eyes. At first, she didn't see what he was looking at.

Then she saw it.

Victoria was talking to Reece Tanner by the firepit, and her arms were gesticulating wildly. Several people were watching them.

Lydia leaned forward to get a better look.

"If I didn't know better, I'd swear they were a married couple arguing about some family matter," Jeremy said.

Lydia didn't respond. She was wondering what in the hell was going on. If Victoria was doing publicity for Murphy's campaign, why was she arguing with one of the partners?

"Can I ask you a personal question?" Jeremy asked.

"Depends on the question."

"Are you Republican or Democrat?"

"Neither. I never registered to vote. I have only two expectations of government. My personal safety and less taxes. The government has failed miserably in both."

"So, you're an Independent?"

"In a personal sense, yes. I have no idea what Independent means in a political sense. I won't ask whether you're Republican or Democrat. I already know."

"What am I then?"

"Republican."

"Good guess. I am registered as a Republican, not that the party makes one hell of an impact in California politics."

"Do I hear politics being discussed?" a baritone voice asked.

Lydia looked up.

Eamon Murphy was standing directly behind her.

How in hell did he sneak up without either of us hearing him? And how long had he been there?

Jeremy started to rise to his feet, but Murphy stopped him with a casual wave of the hand. "Please, sit down, Captain." He looked at Lydia. "Am I intruding, Miss Harte?"

"Not at all, Mr. Murphy."

"May I join you?"

"Of course."

Jeremy got up, retrieved a chair, and offered it to Murphy.

Murphy nodded his thanks and positioned the chair so he could see both of them.

Eamon Murphy was a burly man, built not like a football player, but more like one of the wrestlers who had once performed in the Olympic Auditorium every Saturday night. He wore a dark-gray tailored suit, but his white shirt was open at the collar. He had wavy rust-colored hair that sat atop a massive head

When Lydia first visited Mayes, Murphy and McBride, Lydia had seen his picture on the posterboard advertising his fundraiser. His face in that photo looked smooth and pleasant and not at all like the rugged face of an Irishman who drank a lot and was now sitting across the table from her

Murphy looked at the bars on Jeremy's shoulders. "Are you on active duty, Captain?"

"No sir. Discharged on a medical."

Murphy frowned. "But you still keep physically fit?"

"I do."

"What unit did you serve with?"

"Special Forces, Fifth Special Forces Group."

Murphy's eyes focused on the bars on Jeremy's shoulder.

"So, you were the commander of an O.D.A.?"

"I was."

"I wanted to join the military as an officer. But my father convinced me to go to law school. There are times when I wonder if I should have ignored his advice."

Jeremy didn't say anything in response, so Murphy turned his attention to Lydia. "When I walked up, I overheard that you said you were an Independent."

"I'm not a registered voter, Mr. Murphy. I'm not a member of any political party."

Murphy leaned forward. "You'd be surprised how many people there are in this City who are just like you, Miss Harte."

"Maybe so."

"I am truly independent with the small letter. I am beholden to no party, neither Democrat like my friend Bobby McFarland, nor Republican, nor Green Party. I have spent nearly thirty years as an attorney, and I feel it is time to retire from the practice of law and serve this community. My only interest in running for office is to make Los Angeles a better place . . . for everyone."

Lydia was trying desperately to listen attentively to what Murphy was saying. Listening to self-aggrandizement from a candidate for public office on the campaign trail bored the hell out of her.

"The only way I can do that," Murphy continued, "is by listening to everyone, and that is one of the reasons why you have been invited to my home."

That comment got Lydia's attention. She exchanged glances with Jeremy.

"As a police officer on the front lines, so to speak, I'd like to hear what you believe the Department needs in the way of resources to do its job more efficiently."

Lydia paused for a moment before saying anything. She wondered whether Murphy really wanted a serious answer or was just making conversation.

"I'd like to think about it for a few days, Mr. Murphy, but I suppose you want feedback that is a little more spontaneous."

"I do."

"My Division does an analysis of overall crime trends, but the field police officer gets shortchanged on information. Is this the kind of thing you want to hear about?"

"Yes. Please continue."

"The first way that the officer in the street gets crime information is at roll call. The watch commander reads a list of serious crimes that have occurred Division-wide. But if the officer wants to know what's going on in his district, he has to go back to the detective squad room and look at a pin map that shows the locations of major crimes. There is a different color pin for each type of crime. For example, a green pin denotes the occurrence of a burglary. The problem for the field officers is that they can't tell from that green pin if that burglary occurred on their watch. The second problem with the pin map is that they have teenagers putting up and taking down the pins. Based on what I've seen, I don't trust a teenager to do the job right. Just a few days ago, I heard one of them ask a detective on which side of a street a pin should go."

"So, do you have a solution?"

"I have one, but it probably isn't the only one. The City needs to hire a computer programmer to come up with a system that allows every officer at roll call to get a print-out of all the crimes and the times they were committed in his or her patrol area during the past twenty-four hours."

Murphy sat back in his chair. "I see. Anything else?"

"Do you have the entire afternoon?"

Murphy heard his name being called from the far side of the promenade. He looked back and frowned. He stood up and turned his attention back to Lydia. "I'm being summoned, and I must go. Thank you for your time, Miss Harte." He looked at Jeremy. "Safe journeys, sir.

You have my admiration." He looked back at Lydia. "The next time you visit our office, ask to see me. I would like to speak with you again."

"Sir, I have a question to ask of you," Lydia said.

Murphy looked away for a second to the other side of the promenade. When he turned back to Lydia, he looked annoyed. Lydia thought he might be irritated with her, but he wasn't.

"Pardon me, Miss Harte. I don't like people yelling at me. What did you want to ask me?"

"What does Victoria do for your campaign?"

Murphy's brows furrowed. It looked like a plowed field on his massive forehead. "Victoria?"

"I don't know her last name," Lydia said.

"I'm afraid I don't know anyone named Victoria working on my campaign. Pardon me. I must leave the two of you for now."

Lydia watched him walk away.

Jeremy shifted uncomfortably in his seat. "Someone lied to us, and I'm not sure who it is."

Lydia continued watching Murphy. He joined a distinguished looking man in his forties who had been talking to a tall woman wearing a shimmering black sheath that was much too short for her age. The man smiled and shook hands with Murphy when he joined them.

Jeremy leaned toward Lydia and said, "That's the Governor."

"Which one, the man or the woman with the knobby knees."

Jeremy shook his head. "You really don't know who the Governor is?"

"Just messing with you." Lydia set her lemonade on the table. "Let's go."

Jeremy declined Lydia's offer to come up to her apartment, saying he had to get up early the next morning, and there were things he needed to get done. Despite that, they talked for another fifteen minutes in Jeremy's Jeep.

As she was getting out of the car, Jeremy stopped her. "Listen Lydia, I don't know what you're up to, but be careful. And remember, if you need any help or back-up, you got six men with a lot of experience who would do anything for you."

Lydia thanked him and went inside.

Once inside her condo, Lydia changed into a blue T-shirt and white shorts. She then walked barefooted into the living room and called the Chief of Police on her cell phone.

He answered immediately.

Lydia told him about the conversation she had with Eamon Murphy. The Chief said nothing for such a long time that she thought she had lost the connection.

"Sir, are you still there?"

"Yes, yes. I'm sorry. I was just thinking. Do you think he really wanted to know what you thought about how we can improve the Department?"

"I do."

"Then, I may have misjudged the man. Who else did you see there?"

"The Governor and the Mayor."

Another pause before he spoke again. "And Murphy told you he would like to talk with you again?"

"He did."

"If that happens, I would like you to call me."

"I will."

Lydia's next call was to Billy Vernor using her throwaway cell phone. She needed to find out who owned four of the five cars that the CCTV system had picked up leaving Oceania Manor two Fridays ago.

"Can you run these plates for me without setting off any tripwires?" Lydia asked.

"Since when did you start using military jargon?" Vernor said.

"Maybe watching too many war movies," Lydia said, thinking of Jeremy Morgan and how wonderful he looked in his uniform.

"I can get the names of the people who own these cars, and nobody will ever know it was me who did it." He paused for a moment. "Who are these people?"

"Jonathan's friends."

"What are you going to do when you find out who they are?"

"I don't know. I'll be out of town for a few days. Thank you for your help. You're a real friend."

Before Vernor could ask where she was going, she hung up.

Originally, Lydia thought she wanted those numbers because she wanted to find out who might be making those threatening calls. After

Vernor hung up, she wondered what exactly in hell she was going to do with that information once she had it.

Lydia spent the rest of the evening getting ready for her trip to Arizona. Part of that time was on the computer trying to locate the two properties owned by Jonathan Benedict on a satellite map. She found the properties and zoomed in as close as she could. When she had a clear image, she printed the maps. She then moved the cursor along the road on either side of the properties trying to find landmarks that she could use as reference points that would help her locate the properties once she was on the ground.

When she was satisfied that she had what she needed, she recorded the geographic coordinates of the entrance to both properties in a notebook. Finally, she checked her cell phone to see if her mapping application used GPS coordinates. It didn't. She would have to buy a GPS tracker at the airport tomorrow.

There was one more thing she needed for the trip.

A gun!

She did an Internet search and located a gun shop in Vail not far from the Tucson airport.

She opened a concealed wall safe in her den and took out five thousand dollars in hundred-dollar bills. Except for her airfare, she wouldn't be charging anything on this trip.

It didn't take long for her to pack the few things she needed for the trip in a gym bag before heading off to bed on the early side.

CHAPTER FOURTEEN

March 27, 2006. Monday

EARLY MONDAY morning, Lydia left for the airport wearing a dark blue ball cap, a blue jacket over a loose-fitting T-shirt, desert-tan cargo pants with an elastic waistband, and hiking boots. She found a GPS on sale at the airport and paid for it in cash.

She arrived at the Tucson airport an hour and half after she boarded her flight in Los Angeles and went to the car rental counter with the largest national presence. Even though she wanted to pay cash, the rental agent insisted that Lydia provide a credit card for a hold on damages. Lydia wanted a four-wheel drive Jeep. They didn't have any available. She settled for a Ford F-150 pickup with four-wheel drive.

Fifteen minutes later, she was on Interstate 10 heading southwest. She didn't stop until she reached Vail, Arizona, a desert town with a population of around 10,000 people near Saguaro National Park. The houses that she passed on Colossal Cave Road were mostly adobes and ranches and were landscaped with assorted desert plants.

What interested Lydia the most was not the scenic attractions of the area but a rundown store that sold firearms in a small shopping center next to a gasoline station just north of the Interstate.

The owner was a small man in his fifties with long gray hair and a gray beard that nearly reached his waistline. He was sitting on a stool behind a counter and looked up from a newspaper when Lydia entered the shop.

"Do you rent guns?" Lydia asked.

The man stared at her, uncomprehending at first, and then smile lines appeared around his light blue eyes. "I don't rent guns," he said. "What do you plan on doing with the gun."

"Self-defense against rattlesnakes."

"Going hiking, are you?"

"Yes."

"What kind of gun are you looking for."

"A compact Springfield in .45 ACP."

"Don't have one of those. Got a small Smith & Wesson semi-automatic in that caliber."

"That might work. You wouldn't want to rent it to me for a few days, would you? I can't take it home with me on a plane."

The man put both arms on the counter and stared at her for a moment. "Okay, young lady, here's what I can do. I can sell you that gun. If you return it without having to use it by the end of the week, I'll buy it back from you at eighty percent of the selling price. If you shoot it, I'll give you sixty percent of the selling price."

Lydia paused for a few moments. If she had to use that gun, she would not be returning it. "All right," she said. "It's a deal."

"I need to see some I.D. for a background check."

Lydia produced her California driver's license.

Twenty minutes later, she walked out of the gun shop carrying a S&W four-inch semi-automatic and a box of .45 ACP bullets to go with it. She put the gun under the seat of the truck and began looking for a restaurant to have breakfast.

After eating and stopping at a convenience store to buy a case of half liter bottles of water, Lydia located Arizona Highway 83 and began driving south. Lydia had visited both Phoenix and Tucson while participating in the 440 and 440 hurdles when she was on the U.C.L.A. track team, but she had never been out in the real desert. As she headed south, she was amazed at how barren the landscape was. Occasionally, she saw small patches of grass among grayish-green bushes that she assumed were some type of sagebrush. If there were ranches in southern Arizona, she was not sure how animals were able to live on them.

As she proceeded south, the landscape slowly changed from sparse vegetation to sagebrush surrounded by clumps of grass and then to a broad grassland with an occasional stunted tree. She saw a sign indicating that she was passing through a Federally protected area called Las Cienegas National Park.

She turned east on Arizona Highway 82 at a small town called Sonoita that was set in a wide valley of rolling grasslands with mountains off in the distance. As she drove east, the grasslands faded out and more and more sagebrush began to show up. She drove past Highway 90 which led south to Sierra Vista where she would be spending the night.

It took another fifteen minutes before she reached the area where she thought the smaller of the two properties owned by Jonathan Benedict was located. She pulled over to the side of the road and began looking at the satellite maps. They were of no help. She couldn't correlate what she was seeing in front of her with what was on the maps. The scrub brush that Lydia thought might be greasewood was at least six feet high and dominated the landscape, blocking the view from either side of the road.

She found the GPS in her purse, connected it to the cigarette lighter, and turned it on. Once it was up and running, she entered the GPS coordinates of Jonathan Benedict's property. From the map on the screen, it looked like she needed to drive another mile and a half. She set the GPS on the dash and was prepared to get back on the road. When she looked in the side view mirror, she became aware that a car was parked on the road next to her. It was a police car with the markings of the Cochise County Sheriff.

The officer, a young man of American Indian descent, rolled down his window.

Lydia rolled down hers.

"Are you lost?" he asked, smiling.

"I'm okay. Just trying to get my bearings."

"Tombstone is on this highway if you keep going east. What are you looking for?"

"A place to go on a short hike."

The deputy's smile broadened. "Go to Tombstone. Lots of places to hike around there." He looked down the road for a few seconds before turning back to her. "Tell you what. My uncle's ranch is about two miles down the road on the right. You can't miss it. The first hundred feet is paved. Park at the gate. A dirt road runs due south. It leads to some hills that have a nice view over the valley. Don't go off into the brush. You'll get lost."

"Would your uncle mind?"

"He doesn't live there. Take care. I've got a call to handle near Tombstone." He waved at her and drove off.

Lydia waited until his car was out of sight before she got back on the road.

The entrance to Jonathan Benedict's property was a dirt road that cut through a berm. There was no mailbox or marker of any kind alongside the road.

Lydia resisted the temptation to get out of the car to find out if she could see the house from the top of the berm. Instead, she drove farther down the road until she found the entrance to the ranch the deputy talked about. She parked on the shoulder next to the gate.

She put on gloves and loaded the Smith & Wesson and two magazines. The gun and magazines fit snugly in her belly band holster. She adjusted the gun so that it rested on the back of her right hip. After she loaded the backpack with four half liter bottles of water and several granola bars, she slung it over her back. She picked up her binoculars and began walking down the road toward Benedict's property. If a car came along, she could duck into the tall bushes before she was seen.

Jonathan Benedict's property was not that far along the road. She walked up the slight incline over the berm to find that the dirt road was blocked by a locked gate. It was not attached to a fence. She walked around it.

A quarter mile to the south, the dirt road crossed over a saddle between two barren knobs. Lydia began walking south, carefully checking each side of the road for a warning device that would let anyone on the property know that a visitor was coming.

The dirt road was deeply rutted and studded with large rocks. The truck Lydia rented would have a difficult time driving over it, even if it were in four- wheel drive.

Ten minutes later, Lydia was at the top of the saddle looking south. The house was about a quarter mile off. Lydia picked up her binoculars. The house was dirty white with a rust-colored roof. No one was around. A dilapidated water tower about to fall over was on the left side of the house.

Lydia sat down on the rocky hillside after making sure she was not intruding on the space of any rattlesnakes. She looked at her watch. It was half past one. She decided to watch the house for at least an hour to make sure no one was there before going down to look at it.

The sun was as high as it was going to get, but it was not hot. A cool wind flirted with the face of the slope, bringing with it the scent of the desert.

A soft whirring sound began rising from the southwest. A minute later, Lydia saw a flight of six helicopters flying east. They eventually passed about a mile south of her, not more than a thousand feet above the ground. She confirmed through her binoculars that they were military, most likely coming from Fort Huachuca near Sierra Vista.

After an hour had gone by, Lydia got up, brushed the dust off her butt, and headed down the slope toward the house. It took her just a few minutes before she noticed something unusual about the condition of the road on this side of the hills. It was smooth and had been recently graded. She looked back at the slope leading up to the saddle. It was rocky and scoured with deep ruts.

Why grade this part of the road and not the front part?

Puzzled, she looked back toward the house.

Was this a runway?

The graded part of the road could not have been more than two hundred yards long. It was too short for even a Cessna to land or take off.

So, why was it graded?

She moved on toward the house.

The area around the house had been cleared of vegetation for at least fifty feet. The house itself was old and small, the roof of the front porch sagged, the boards on its floor were uneven. Lydia stepped onto the porch and looked in through a dirty window. There was no furniture inside. The house looked abandoned.

She opened the front door but did not go inside. There was one large room in front with wooden floors. It was old and musty with faded yellow paint on the walls. A hallway led to the back

A layer of dust covered the wooden floor. She noticed that when she had opened the door, it left a faint sweeping arc in the dust, but there were no other tracks on the floor.

Lydia paused for a moment.

What in the hell was Jonathan doing owning a place like this? This wasn't his style, so it must have been purchased as an investment.

She decided to go outside and look around. She stepped off the porch and walked around the side of the house.

Usually, places like this had abandoned farm equipment laying around, but there were none here. The water tower had one of its stilts broken and was leaning to the right.

When she reached the backyard, Lydia discovered that a yellow grader was parked alongside the back of the house. She took a closer look. It was small, but it was large enough to grade the dirt road. And it was not abandoned. It was a recent model, and it had been recently used because there were tracks leading through the tall grass that led around the other side of the house.

Lydia took one more swing around the house before she decided it was time to leave.

She paused at the front of the house and looked up the graded road.

What in hell was Jonathan doing with this property? she asked herself one more time.

By the time Lydia got to the city of Sierra Vista on Highway 90, it was past four o'clock and getting too late to take a look at Benedict's ranch near the U.S./Mexican border. She checked into the Windermere Hotel, took a shower and then flopped onto the bed for a quick nap before heading out for dinner.

Sierra Vista was a rather large city for Arizona, and it was located next to Fort Huachuca, once the base for the Army's hunt for Geronimo. It had also been the home of the Buffalo soldiers, a distinguished cavalry troop composed of black soldiers. Lydia didn't know what the Army did nowadays at the fort, but she quickly discovered what a pain in the ass its soldiers were when she entered a Western-themed bar and grill and sat down for a steak dinner.

It seemed as if everybody in the place wanted to buy her a beer and talk to her.

Finally, the owner, a burly man in his fifties with military tattoos on his large biceps shooed the men away. When she left the place an hour later, there were seven untouched bottles of beer on her table.

CHAPTER FIFTEEN

March 28, 2006. Tuesday.

THE ENTRANCE to Jonathan Benedict's ranch was in an isolated area of Arizona Highway 92. The part of the road heading east paralleled the border for about sixteen miles and then changed directions northeast toward Bisbee, an old mining town that was now a tourist attraction. The border with Mexico was about five miles to the south.

There were cattle ranches on either side of the highway. The terrain was mostly grassy but was sparsely dotted with the same kind of sagebrush that Lydia had seen on Benedict's property to the north.

It was early spring, the grass was green, and the weather was pleasant, but Lydia was not out for a pleasure drive.

She didn't bother trying to locate Jonathan Benedict's ranch by using the satellite maps. She fired up the GPS, entered the coordinates, and found the entrance to the ranch a half dozen miles east of the small town of Miracle Valley, where in 1982, members of a nondenominational church engaged in a fierce gun battle with law enforcement officers who were trying to serve a bench warrant on three of its members.

Benedict's ranch was fenced like all the others that Lydia had seen along Highway 92. A freshly graded dirt road provided access to the property. Thirty yards in from the highway was an opening in the fence with a cattle grate.

Lydia pulled up to the grate and got out of the pickup. The terrain in front of her consisted of gently rolling hills covered with knee-high grass and patches of sagebrush. There were recent tire tracks on the dirt road.

Using her binoculars, she tried to locate the building she had seen on the satellite map. She couldn't see it, nor did she see any sign of cattle. In the distance was a mountain range that had to be in Mexico.

Lydia decided to explore the property and determine what it was being used for. If she got caught trespassing, she already had a story made up to explain why she was there. She got back into the truck and headed south on the dirt road toward the border with Mexico.

After driving a mile and a half on the dirt road, Lydia spotted the building she had seen on the satellite map. It was at least two miles in front of her. So far, so good. The dirt road was smooth with graded ditches on both sides.

Lydia had no worries about being discovered on the property until she drove past a small ranch house that was set halfway down a small slope a hundred yards off to her right. She didn't recall seeing that building on the satellite map.

A Humvee and an ATV were parked on the shady side of the house, but no one was in sight.

She drove on, kicking up a trail of dust, hoping nobody had seen her go by. About a mile farther on, she looked in her rearview mirror and saw an ATV coming up fast behind her. The man riding it was waving a hand and pointing to the side of the road.

Lydia pulled over and got out of the truck.

The man parked his ATV twenty feet behind Lydia's pickup and got off the bike slowly like he was an L. A. motorcycle cop getting ready to write a ticket. He was tall and wearing an old-fashioned pair of aviator goggles. He was wearing a black baseball cap, a multi-colored Western style shirt, and jeans.

Lydia waited for him to approach.

"What are you doing here?" he asked in an authoritative voice after he took off the goggles. "This is private property."

"I'm sorry," Lydia said. "I didn't see a sign."

The man glared at her. He was suntanned and his eyes were dark, almost black. He took a couple steps forward. "I asked, what are you doing here?"

"I heard they were installing a fence along the border. I wanted to see it."

"Are you one of those damn reporters?"

Lydia shook her head.

"Turn around," the man said brusquely.

"What?" Lydia asked, mistakenly thinking that the man was asking her to get into her truck and leave.

"I said turn around, goddammit! I'm going to search you."

"Like hell you are!"

The man took another step toward her.

Lydia felt like she had no choice. She swiftly moved her right hand around her back, pulled out the Smith & Wesson out of the belly band holster, and pointed it at the man.

The man hastily backed away, holding out his hands, palms up. "Take it easy, lady. Do you know how to use that goddamn thing? It might go off!"

"I know how to use it, buster, and I can't guarantee it won't go off."

"How do I know it's loaded?"

"I don't want any trouble, mister! Back off and I'll leave!"

The man looked back up the road.

Lydia followed his eyes. He was expecting backup. There were probably more people in the house. She had to get out of there.

"I'm not going to say it again," Lydia said, using the command voice she was taught in the Police Academy. "Back off! Now!"

The man didn't move.

Lydia lowered the gun at a forty-five-degree angle and fired one shot between his legs. The bullet creased the inside of his jeans and missed his balls by less than two inches.

The man jumped back a few feet and yelled, "Jesus!"

"I'm not going to fuck around with you! Get back!"

The man stared at her for a moment and then begin backing slowly until he was alongside of his ATV. "Who are you?"

"Turn around."

The man did as he was told, keeping his eyes on Lydia until his back was turned toward her.

Lydia jumped into her truck and started it. She looked in her rearview mirror. The man was opening a storage area in the back of the ATV.

She spun the truck around in a U-turn, throwing up dirt.

The man had his head down, looking for something in the ATV.

Lydia pulled alongside the ATV and stopped. She rolled down the window and pointed the gun at his head. "Get your hands up where I can see them!"

The man looked up, saw the gun, and raised his hands. "You're going to regret this, lady."

"I already have. Now back off the road!"

The man did so, his hands still over his head.

Lydia guessed that the man had a gun in the ATV's storage area, but she didn't have time to remove it. Reinforcements might be arriving at any minute. She did the next best thing she could think of without having to shoot the man.

She fired a bullet into one of the front tires of the ATV and got the hell out of there.

About a half mile down the road, Lydia saw a Humvee coming toward her at a high speed. When it got within a hundred yards, it turned sideways blocking at least three quarters of the road, the passenger side of the heavy utility vehicle facing her.

There were two men in the Humvee, and the one on the passenger side was getting out. Lydia decided she didn't want to stop and have another chat with men who were intent on dominating her. She didn't slow the truck down. Instead, she drove off the side of the road around the back of the Humvee and across the slope of the ditch, hoping her truck would not roll over.

The truck performed as well as any off-road vehicle should, and she was back on the dirt road within seconds. She stabbed the pedal to the floor and looked back in the rearview mirror. There was a cloud of dust behind her, and she couldn't see anything.

Within minutes, she turned west on Highway 90. She checked her rearview mirror. The pickup had left a dirt trail on the paved road. The men in the Humvee would not have any problem seeing what direction she took.

She picked up speed until she was doing well over eighty miles an hour. After traveling a few miles, she slowed down and began thinking. She didn't need to get stopped by the Cochise County Sheriff, but she sure as hell didn't want the men in the Humvee to catch up with her either.

The town of Miracle Valley was dead ahead. She pulled into the first gas station she saw and parked on a dirt lot behind the store.

She got out and walked around the building toward the front of the store. Once inside, she bought an ice cream bar and ate it while looking out onto the highway. Two minutes later, the Humvee drove by doing about thirty miles an hour. The passenger didn't even look in her direction.

Lydia waited a few minutes, then got into her truck, and headed east toward Bisbee intending to circle her way back to Sierra Vista. It was a longer way to get back to the motel, but she didn't want to run the risk of encountering the Humvee again.

As she drove east, she looked for places near Benedict's property where she could hide her truck when she came back later that night. She found a turnout about a mile and a half east of the entrance to the ranch. She drove in to check it out and discovered a dirt road that ended at a small parking area about fifty yards off the highway.

It would do for what she had in mind. She headed back onto the highway.

Lydia had time on her hands, so she stopped in Bisbee for lunch, played the role of tourist for an hour, and then drove on. She stopped in Tombstone, found a military surplus store, and bought a knapsack, bolt cutter, a pair of cloth gloves, a mag light, and a small crowbar.

She didn't stop to take in the re-enactment of the gun battle at the O.K. Corral. If the Earps were still around, she could teach them a thing or two about taking down bad guys.

It was 6:00 p.m. when Lydia got back to her hotel. She set the alarm on her cell phone for 9:00 p.m. and then flopped into bed with her clothes on.

CHAPTER SIXTEEN

LYDIA LEFT the hotel in Sierra Vista at 9:15 p.m. and stopped at a fast-food restaurant to pick up a burrito. After she ate in the truck, she carefully drove south on Highway 92 not wanting to attract any attention. The grasslands along the isolated highway were stunning under the light of the moon. She was tempted to make a stop and take in the beauty of the night

When Lydia arrived at the entrance to Benedict's ranch a half hour later, she stopped and checked out the dirt road. There was no sign of any lights to the south, so she drove on and parked in the turnout she had spotted earlier that day.

It took her less than five minutes to get ready. She stuffed the bolt cutter and crowbar she had purchased in Tombstone in the knapsack, cinched it tight, and slung it over her back. After putting on her new gloves and adjusting her black ball cap to keep moonlight from reflecting off her face, she grabbed the mag light and headed off to the southwest. She expected that she would have to walk at least four miles before she located the building she had seen on the satellite map.

A minute later, she stopped. How in hell was she going to find the truck if she had to come back in a hurry? She went back to the truck, picked up the GPS, and set the coordinates for her position. She put the GPS in her pocket and started off once more toward the Benedict ranch.

Even though the area was mostly rolling hills, Lydia found it difficult trudging through the knee-high grass. Occasionally, she would come across a bald and rocky patch of earth on top of a knoll and crossed over it, hoping she would not disturb a rattlesnake in its nighttime foraging. It was quiet out here. There was no traffic out on the road. There was no wind and no movement under the moonlight. It was surprisingly peaceful, but all of that changed when a nearby coyote began howling.

Lydia stopped and listened. The animal could not have been no more than a hundred yards behind her. She doubted very much whether a single coyote would attack a person, so she trudged on. Seconds later, another coyote began howling. This one sounded like it was a good distance to her left. Then another started howling, then another, and another, all around her, some close, some distant.

She stopped, shifted the mag light to her left hand, and felt around to the belly band holster until her hand rested on the Smith & Wesson. A lone coyote would not bother her, but a pack of them might. She pulled the Smith and Wesson out of the holster and kept walking. A minute later, the howling stopped as suddenly as it had begun.

Lydia trudged on until she found a fence that ran south and north. It was a simple fence, three strands of barbed wire attached to metal stakes. Lydia had no problem crawling under it.

An hour later, Lydia walked onto the dirt road on Jonathan's property. She could see the building not more than a half mile to the south, gleaming in the moonlight. Lydia began walking toward the building, staying on the grassy side of the ditch alongside the road. A hundred yards farther on, Lydia spotted a hulking object about thirty yards to her left. She went to check it out.

It was a large backhoe, painted the same color yellow as the grader on the property to the north. And then she smelled something she had smelled on several occasions while on patrol in Century Division. The smell of death.

She walked around the backhoe and saw a partially dug hole. Beyond it, she saw three dark forms in the grass. She went to take a closer look.

There were three bodies lying side by side. Holding her breath, she turned the mag light on, shielding it with her left hand, so that the light reflected downward. She played the light over the bodies. They were all men, all had black hair with swarthy faces, all wearing rough clothing. She settled the light on the face of one of them. He had a bullet hole in the forehead just above the nose. She checked another one. He had two bullet holes in his right temple.

Lydia walked away from the bodies and began breathing again.

What in the hell was going on here?

She decided to continue walking toward the building, but this time she stayed fifty feet off the dirt road. Within a few minutes, she came to a bare patch of earth. Using the mag light, she saw a fresh mound of dirt and tracks left by the backhoe

The earth was soft. Could it possibly be a grave?

Before she reached the clearing where the building was located, she had come across three more mounds. It became evident that whoever controlled the property was killing trespassers.

The building was large, and its exterior was covered with sheets of bare metal. It was at least twenty-yards wide and fifty-yards long and sat on a leveled clearing that was about the size of an acre. There was a tall set of double doors in the front that was held together by a chain and padlock.

Lydia pulled the doors open as wide as the chain would allow and shone her light through the three-inch space. All that she could see inside was bare ground. She didn't want to cut the lock just yet, so she walked around the building to see if it had any windows. It did, but they were all painted black from the inside, and they were all locked.

She didn't want to leave any evidence she had been there, but she had no choice but to cut the chain with the bolt cutter. The first thing she saw when she entered the building was a large object directly in front of her that in the dim light looked like a large insect. She flashed her mag light on it, and the light was reflected back by a large glass bubble. When she walked around to the side, she saw what it was.

It was an ultralight aircraft.

Lydia played her light over it. It was a one-seater, with a glass canopy in front and no doors on the sides. The small aircraft was painted desert tan and had no markings on it.

She remembered the road leading up to the building was level and freshly graded. The road on the Benedict property to the north was also level and graded. Both could easily function as an airstrip for a small aircraft. She looked into the interior of the aircraft. Behind the pilot's seat was a space that could store a large amount of cargo. She realized what was going on. Someone was using the light aircraft for smuggling.

After a moment or two, she flashed her light around the building. There was a large stack of rough timber off to the left that nearly reached the ceiling. She saw tools of all kinds; shovels, picks, and crowbars, lying in the dirt. There was also a stack of thick metal bars about six feet long that had flat metal plates welded to each end. When she looked closer, she saw that the bars could be telescoped to make their length adjustable.

She shone her light to the right side of the building where she saw a medium-sized grader painted yellow and behind it two smaller devices, one an excavator on tires, the other a skid steer on tracks with a bucket attached to the front. Behind the equipment was a late model Ferrari covered in dust. She began walking toward the Ferrari and nearly stepped into a hole.

After she recovered her balance, she saw that it wasn't a hole at all, but a long concrete ramp. She turned her light on it. It was narrow, about eight feet wide, and led downward about fifty feet before it curved to the right. It was also steep. She began walking down to see what was below.

She thought she would find an underground storage area. But it wasn't a storage area. It was a manmade tunnel about seven feet high and seven feet wide with dirt walls buttressed by rough boards. She saw that the roof was supported by timbers held in place by the round metal bars with the flat ends she had seen earlier.

It was cool down here, and there was the unhealthy smell of moldy earth. Lydia didn't like the smell, so she went back up the ramp where she paused to take several deep breaths and to think things over. The tunnel led directly south toward Mexico. She had a rough idea of the kind of businesses that Jonathan was involved in, but she had no idea that he was involved in smuggling.

But what was he smuggling? It had to be narcotics, but the tunnel was also large enough to move people, a lot of people.

An idea occurred to her. She flashed her light again on the equipment parked along the south wall. The skid steer and the small excavator were too large to be used inside the tunnel. But how did they dig that hole? They had to use people. Slave labor, perhaps? She remembered the burial sites along the road. They had to be using illegal border crossers to dig the tunnel. She wondered how many burial mounds were covered by grass alongside the dirt road.

It was then she heard the sound of a fast-moving vehicle that was approaching the building. She rushed to the door and looked out.

She saw headlights coming down the dirt road. There was no time to shut the door. She ran across the open area and reached the grass just as the vehicle drove onto the space in front of the building. She heard doors slamming and muted voices. And then a loud voice.

"Damn! Somebody's inside!"

Lydia flopped to the ground, thinking someone might have seen her. Then it was quiet for a few seconds before she heard a different voice.

"I'm going inside. Joe, you come with me. And you, you stay out here."

Then it was silent.

Lydia waited a moment before shifting her body and looking back at the building.

The Humvee she had seen earlier was parked in front of the building. A man was standing by the door. He was aiming his flashlight at the ground. She was certain he had spotted her tracks because the light was now following the direction she had just taken. He raised the flashlight in her direction. Lydia ducked her head.

She looked up again when she heard muted voices. The lights inside the building were on. The man with the flashlight had moved toward the door and was looking inside the building. Lydia got to her knees and began crawling farther into the grass. She dropped flat onto the ground when she heard voices again.

The first words she heard were, "Look here."

Then muted voices. After a moment, she turned and looked up over the grass. There were three men standing in front of the door. They were quietly talking. She could not hear their voices.

Then one of the men walked toward the Humvee and said quite loudly, "It's the fucking wetbacks!"

Another one said, "It might be the girl."

The man who was walking toward the Humvee stopped and said, "No, goddammit. We get wetbacks here all the time, looking for a place to stay once they made the crossing."

"Whatever you say, boss."

Lydia lowered herself in the grass and waited until the Humvee drove off. Before she set off for her pickup truck, she looked back to make sure they had left no one behind. The lights in the building were out, and the doors pulled closed. A few minutes later, she got up and began the long trek back to her truck.

During the walk back to her truck, Lydia had time to think about what she had seen and heard. She knew that the man with the flashlight had discovered her footprints, but it appeared as if the discovery had been disregarded. From the conversation she heard, it seemed as if a conclusion had been reached that a border crosser had broken into the building.

She realized that a border crosser would not have been carrying a tool that could cut the lock to the building. The three men had to know that too. What she heard while lying out there in the grass was a rehearsed speech. They wanted her to think they would not be looking for her.

They would be waiting for her out on Highway 92.

Lydia's GPS didn't take her directly to her vehicle. She emerged from the tall grass onto Highway 92 about thirty yards west of the turnout where her truck was parked.

She paused before moving on. No vehicles were parked on the highway. She walked on the shoulder along the highway until she came to the turnoff where her truck was parked. She paused again and listened. It was quiet except for the rustle of the grass as a cool breeze blew in from the west.

It didn't surprise her when she saw the Humvee parked twenty yards behind the pick-up she had rented. In the faint light of the setting moon, she could see the driver and passenger in the front seats.

She knelt in the dirt and pulled out the Smith and Wesson from her holster.

Damn. What do I do now?

Her unspoken question was answered when the interior lights in the Humvee came on and the driver's door opened. The driver slid out of the vehicle and turned to face her.

"We see you back there! Get your ass over here!"

Lydia remembered the bodies and the graves she had seen. If she didn't do something, she would end up in one of those graves.

She raised her Smith & Wesson. Although she could barely see the sights on the gun, she could see the man quite clearly in the moonlight. She became aware the passenger was also getting out of the Humvee.

The man called out again. "I have a gun trained on you. Stand up so I can see you!"

Lydia didn't hesitate. She fired three shots at him, the blasts shaking the night air.

The man staggered and turned, trying to grab hold of the door for support. He made whoofing sounds like a bear ripping apart a rotten log and then fell to the ground.

Lydia turned her attention to the other man, but she couldn't see him. The flash of fire from her gun had dampened her eyesight. She waited, still on one knee, listening. The interior lights were still on in the truck, and she could not see any sign of the passenger.

A few minutes later, she heard rustling in the grass to her right. The passenger was trying to outflank her.

She stood up and tracked her gun in the direction of the noise. A moment later, she saw a figure rising out of the grass.

She didn't hesitate.

Three more quick shots and the figure was down.

Lydia waited a few minutes. There was no sound or movement coming from the grass where she had last seen the man. She got to her feet, reloaded her weapon with a fresh magazine, and cautiously moved toward the Humvee.

The driver of the Humvee was dead. Blood was seeping out of a bullet hole in the center of his chest.

Lydia turned on the mag light and looked at his face. It was the same man who had stopped her earlier that day, the one who had been driving the ATV. She paused for a minute, trying to decide what she needed to do.

The first thing she did was to pull the body off the road and into the grass far enough so that it could not be easily discovered. Once that was done, she went looking for the man who had been crawling in the grass.

She found him, lying on his back. He was also dead. A bullet had hit him just below the right eye.

Lydia cursed softly. It was a lucky shot. She had been pointing her gun at the center of his body and had missed two of the shots. This man didn't need to be moved. He was far enough off the road that it would be difficult to find him.

Next, she searched the ground, looking for the six shell casings that had been ejected from her gun. When she found them, she put them in her pocket.

Her next step was to move the Humvee off the dirt road. There was no way of avoiding traces of her in the truck once she had driven it, but she made it more difficult by pushing her hair up into her cap. If there were any hairs belonging to her left in the Humvee, it would be because they had been shed from the back of her clothing.

Lydia backed the Humvee out onto the highway and drove it a few hundred yards to the west where she found another dirt road that led to the north. She parked it off the road in a shallow depression so that it could not be easily seen from the highway.

Fifteen minutes later, she was in her truck heading west toward Miracle Valley and swearing at herself for what had just happened. She realized she was killing far too many people than she wanted to.

CHAPTER SEVENTEEN

March 29, 2006. Wednesday.

IT WAS just before the noon hour when Lydia returned to her apartment on Pico Boulevard. The only sleep she had was a nap on the first plane she could catch back to Los Angeles, and she was too tired to do much of anything but flop into bed for a quick nap.

She had had a long night. The first thing she did when she left the dirt road where she had killed the two men was to get rid of the gun. She wiped it clean to make sure she didn't leave any fingerprints. On her way north, she stopped and took the gun apart. She tossed all of the parts except for the barrel into the grasslands of the Las Cienegas National Park. Farther up the road where the grasslands gave way to the desert, she pulled alongside the road, rolled the oily barrel into the dirt so that it lost its sheen, and then dropped it in the center of a sagebrush. She dumped the rest of the bullets she had purchased in a trash container next to a convenience store that was closed after making sure there was no CCTV on the premises.

Once in her motel room, she took off the clothes she had been wearing and stuffed them in a trash bag she had removed from a waste basket in her room. After taking a shower, she checked out of the motel and was on the road again.

The only thing she needed to do before going to the airport was to get rid of the trash bag and run the truck through a car wash. When she arrived at Tucson International Airport, she believed she had done everything she could to remove any trace of her being involved in the killing of the two men in Southern Arizona. The only problem was that there was another man on Benedict's ranch who knew she had been there and knew the other two men were missing after going to look for her.

When Lydia woke up from her nap, it was approaching 1:30 p.m. She checked for phone messages. There were a few hang-ups and a call from Jenny saying, "Let's meet for lunch."

There were also two calls that caused some worries. One was from Jane Halloran stating that Mr. Tanner had filed the probate action on Monday and that everything was going well. Lydia decided that she needed to talk to her other attorney, Eric Milburn, about her concerns that the law firm of Mayes, Murphy and McBride had failed to tell her about the properties in Arizona.

But it was a call from someone named Jamie that caused Lydia the most concern. The only Jamie that Lydia knew was a waiter at Schroeder's Deutsche Hofbraumarkt, a German restaurant that had been owned by Sophia Benedetto, Lydia's pretend grandma. About a week before Sophia's death, Lydia had met her for lunch at the restaurant and Jamie had waited on them.

After Sophia Benedetto traded insults with Jamie and he left them to peruse the menu, Sophia waggishly told Lydia that Jamie was in the witness protection program. But it was a different kind of witness protection program that Sophia was talking about. The Feds were not protecting Jamie. He was hiding from them.

Jamie had never called Lydia before, and she was surprised he even had her number. She thought about this for a moment or two before she remembered that she was the heir apparent to Sophia's estate that was not included in the trust. The manager of the restaurant probably had Lydia's contact information, at least that was what Lydia hoped. The thought that Jamie might have gotten her phone number from another source was disturbing.

The call raised another question. Lydia wondered if Jamie's call had anything to do with the two men she had shot in Arizona. Jamie's connections with the underworld brought back memories of her experience in the desert. She wondered if she should tip off someone about the tunnel she had found in the building on Benedict's ranch. The building and tunnel were being used for smuggling and something needed to be done about it.

And those bodies! The ranch was also being used as a graveyard.

She decided that she would anonymously tell someone about what she had discovered, but not now. She would wait a few days before she did anything about it.

Later, as she sat on her balcony feeling refreshed from a shower and feeling like she was ready for anything the world could throw at her, Lydia called Eric Milburn. Once he was on the line, she said, "I need some advice Mr. Milburn."

"How can I help, Miss Harte?"

"A few days ago, I received a list of properties owned by Jonathan Benedict from Reece Tanner at Mayes, Murphy and McBride. I have since discovered that Jonathan owned two pieces of property in Arizona that they didn't tell me about. Should I be concerned about this? I guess my real question is do I need to find another attorney to handle my case?"

Milburn paused for a moment before answering. "What kind of property?"

"A house on fifty acres of mostly desert in Southern Arizona. A large ranch on the Mexican border with a house and a warehouse."

There was another long pause on the phone before Milburn answered. "Mayes, Murphy and McBride is a reputable law firm. I doubt they would intentionally conceal this property from you."

"Are you suggesting they might not know about it?"

"I am. It's likely the property you discovered might be held in an Arizona trust."

"How do I find out if there's another trust?"

"It's difficult. There's no requirement that a trust be filed with a court. But there's the possibility that the property might be the subject of a probate action. I can find that out for you if you tell me where the property is located."

"Cochise County, Arizona. Should I tell Reece Tanner what I found?"

"By all means."

After thinking about it, Lydia decided not to call Tanner. She remembered when she was at the fundraiser at the home of Eamon Murphy that she saw Tanner talking to Jonathan Benedict's former girlfriend, Victoria, and that they seemed to be arguing about something. She was not sure he was to be trusted despite what Milburn had said.

Before Lydia reported for work, she received a call from Billy Vernor. He asked if she could come in a half hour before her shift and meet with him.

She agreed.

Billy Vernor was sitting at his desk when Lydia stepped into the detective squad room. The other burglary team, Finlayson and Gordon, were not in their usual place alongside Vernor at the table the detectives called a desk.

Vernor with a casual flick of a hand motioned for her to sit down.

The serious look on his face caused Lydia to cock her head.

"What have you got yourself into?" Vernor asked.

Lydia paused for a moment. "I'm fine, Billy, thank you. And how are you doing on this wonderful day in paradise?"

Vernor leaned back and pointed to a manila envelope on her side of the desk. "There is some serious shit in there, Lydia. I ask again, what have you gotten yourself into?"

"What's in the envelope?"

Vernor looked around before answering. "I did more than run those license plates for you, Lydia. I ran a criminal records search on the men who owned those cars. All of them have been arrested at one time or another on some rather serious charges. One or two have been arrested for murder but were acquitted when the witnesses had a sudden loss of memory."

"I know these men are bad guys, Billy. They played poker with Jonathan the night before he got killed."

Vernor sighed. "What do you plan on doing with the information?"

"I don't know."

"Jesus Christ, Lydia! These men are rattlesnakes."

"I already know that."

Vernor paused before speaking again, his fingers drumming on the desk. "Listen, if you need help, you know where to come."

Lydia picked up the manila envelope and stood up. "Thank you, Billy. I really appreciate that."

"Can I offer you some advice?"

"Why not?"

"Be careful."

Lydia found the locker room occupied by a half dozen women officers who were preparing for roll call. She had hoped for some privacy so she could look at the material Vernor had given her, but she could not do that without arousing the curiosity of her fellow officers. Ignoring the lively chatter, Lydia put on her uniform and equipment and took the envelope with her to the roll call room.

The second that Lieutenant Morton entered the roll call room, followed by Sergeant Watson, Lydia knew something was up by the gloomy expressions on their faces.

Morton rapidly read roll call and the assignments and then looked up at the assembled group. "Did any of you happen to see or stop a small late model blue car with three men in it last night?"

"There are a lot of late model blue cars out there, Lieutenant," a voice said from the back of the room.

"This one had three men in it. At least one of them was Hispanic."

No one answered.

"Anyone?"

Again, silence.

Morton nodded at Watson, who picked up the phone and began dialing. Morton looked down at the rotator and began reading. "Sometime between 1:00 and 1:15 a.m. this morning, two men entered the gas station at Overland and Venice and shot and killed the cashier and a customer who was inside the store using an ATM. They took an unknown amount of money from the cash register and $50 the customer had just withdrawn from the ATM." He looked down at the officers. "They were last seen getting into a small late-model blue car that was driven by a male Hispanic with a chalky white face. Does that ring any bells? Did any of you see a car like that last night?"

"We work the P.M. Watch, Lieutenant. That robbery occurred on Mornings," someone said from the back of the room.

"I know we work P.M. Watch, Carter! But the bastards might have been driving around the Division looking for a place to hit earlier in the evening."

"Do we have a better description of the suspects?" another voice asked.

Lydia recognized the voice as belonging to Hagerty.

"We do." Morton got up and turned on the television monitor on the wall behind his table. He turned and nodded to Watson who was holding the phone in her hands.

Watson said something into the phone, and a few seconds later, a grainy image popped up on the television monitor and showed the interior of a convenience store. A young man behind the checkout counter was reading a newspaper spread out before him. A tall man dressed in dark clothing and a hoodie that covered his face entered the store. He was followed by a shorter man, also wearing dark clothing and a hoodie. The cashier looked up. The pleasant smile on his face became frozen when he saw a gun pointing at him. The tall man shot him in the face at point blank range. The smaller man looked to the right, raised his gun, and fired at someone off camera.

"You asked for a description," Morton said bitterly. "This is the best we can do. Both men were armed with nine-millimeter semi-automatics."

Lydia watched as the screen showed the tall man lean over the counter and fire a shot into the area where the cashier had fallen. The other man dashed off to the right and disappeared from view. The tall man reached over the counter, opened the cash register, and grabbed a fistful of bills. Seconds later, the other man reappeared and headed for the door, followed by his partner. Both were wearing ski masks.

"Thirty-two seconds," Morton said. "That's all they needed to kill two people and steal less than a hundred bucks. We need your help, people. If you see a small blue car with three young men in it, call for backup before you red light them. These men are dangerous, and we need to stop them."

"Did you work last night?" Lydia asked Hagerty as he drove the police car out of the station parking lot.

"I did."

"What happened to Tactical Operations? Were they gone by the time these guys robbed the store?"

"They pulled Tactical Operations off stakeout two nights ago."

After a moment thinking about it, Lydia said. "Could they have been watching the station to see what was going on?"

"They've been watching us all right. But they aren't very smart. If they were, they wouldn't be doing all this killing and driving the same kind of blue car, wearing the same clothing. Even the dumbest crooks are not that stupid."

"Thrill seekers?"

"Either that, or they just want to show us how superior they are." Hagerty hitched a finger over his right shoulder toward the back seat. "What's in the envelope you tossed in the back?"

"Something Billy gave me to look at."

"Vernor?"

"Yes."

"I damn well know it has nothing to do with his informants. He keeps those names in a black notebook and guards it with his life. Have you seen what's inside?"

"The black book?"

"No. The envelope."

"I haven't, but I need to look at it before the night is over."

"Okay."

Ten minutes later, Hagerty turned into the parking lot of a donut shop. He parked the car. "Do you want any coffee? Say no."

Lydia stared at him for a moment.

"I'm going inside," Hagerty continued. "Be back in ten. Wait for me. I'll leave the car running so you can keep the air on. Honk the horn if we get a hotshot."

Lydia watched him get out of the car and enter the donut shop.

The envelope contained four separate sections that consisted of papers stapled together. Lydia pulled out one of the sections and set the others on the seat next to her. The first page was a copy of a driver's license of someone she knew.

It was Robert Moreno, the man she had met in Landry's office who was introduced to her as Vince Moretti and who had tried to get her to sign a document turning over her rights to the trust. He had an address on Stone Canyon Boulevard in Bel Air. Attached was his criminal record. He had been arrested eight times. The arrests were for multiple burglaries, assault with a deadly weapon, battery, and rape. He was never convicted. Moreno was now forty-two, and Lydia noticed that all of his arrests had occurred in his late teens and early twenties.

The next page contained a property evaluation of his home in Bel Air. It was worth 2.4 million dollars. The last page was a copy of property records listing the current and past owners of Moreno's home. Lydia wasn't interested in that, so she placed it back in the envelope and took out another section. Putting it away was a mistake. If she looked at the last page more closely, she might have seen there was a joint tenant on the property.

The second section contained the driver's license of a man named Eduardo Santini who had an address on Channel Road in Pacific Palisades. Lydia had never seen Santini before. She skimmed through his criminal history. He had a record that included an arrest for murder but no conviction, multiple arrests for battery and disturbing the peace, one for robbery, and one conviction for disturbing the peace that resulted in a fine but no jail time.

The picture on the driver's license of the man in the third section caused Lydia to take a second look. She had seen this man before. But where and under what circumstances?

His name was Jimmie Woodson, and he had a house on Bouquet Canyon Road near Santa Clarita, not far from where Jeremy Morgan lived.

Lydia sat back in her seat, thinking. She saw movement out of the corner of her eye. Hagerty, carrying a cup of coffee, came out of the donut shop. He glanced at Lydia and then turned quickly away. He took a seat at a wooden picnic bench and pretended to look off in the distance, cradling the cup of coffee in both hands.

Suddenly, a sparkle of memory caused Lydia to look at the picture again. An image came to her mind, a man getting off an ATV with the practiced movement of an L. A. motorcycle cop getting ready to write a ticket. Two days ago, he was wearing an old-fashioned pair of aviator goggles, a black baseball cap, a Western style shirt, and jeans. The last time she saw him was when she pulled his dead body into the grass in the turn-out where she had parked the rented pickup truck.

Woodson's criminal record was extensive, many arrests, few convictions. One arrest and one conviction stood out like a beacon from the others. He had been convicted of murder when he was nineteen and spent seven years in prison.

Lydia looked at his property records. The house on Bouquet Canyon Road sat on three acres, ranch property she guessed, many horse trails winding around the hills in that area.

Well, he was dead now. Lydia didn't have to worry about him anymore.

The last section included information about a man named Henry Mariani who lived in one of the many condos in Marina Del Rey. Lydia looked closer at the picture. She had never seen him before. He also had an extensive record, two of them for carrying a concealed gun, one for assault with a deadly weapon, which was pleaded down to disturbing the peace with no time served, and three burglary arrests with no convictions.

How in hell do you get arrested for burglary and not get convicted? Lydia thought.

It occurred to her that these men had far too many arrests where there were no convictions. Was the criminal justice system that fucked up, or was there something ominous going on?

Lydia was staring off into the distance when Hagerty opened the car and looked in.

"Are you finished?"

"Yes."

Just as Hagerty slid behind the wheel, a hotshot came out over the radio.

"Five-Adam-99, and all units in the vicinity, a shooting in progress at 1134 Maple. Five-Adam-99, handle the call, Code Three."

"Seatbelts on!" Hagerty said in an even voice as he started the engine. He reached over and turned on the emergency lights and siren.

Lydia put on her seat belt and Hagerty took off, rear wheels spinning as he pulled out of the parking lot.

A Code Three run was an exhilarating experience, Lydia had found. It seemed as if the siren charged the body with a double shot of insulin. The effect was probably caused by the combination of the sound of the screaming siren and the prospect that at the end of the call you could be facing a life or death situation. Lydia had been on several Code Three runs before and two pursuits involving stolen cars at high speeds, and each time she felt her nerve endings were on fire.

"Do you recognize the location of the call?" Hagerty yelled over the sound of the siren.

"What?" Lydia, yelled back, already knowing where they were going.

"It's . . . goddammit!" Hagerty said as he swerved the car to the left to avoid hitting a car that drove through an intersection in front of them.

"It's the same street where the Spahns live," Lydia said.

"And right across the street."

"Oh shit!" Lydia yelled over the siren. "Kenny and I talked to the man who lived across the street last week. He saw Jimmie Spahn sneaking in and out of the house at night."

The Code Three run to Maple Street took only three minutes. Lydia and Hagerty were the first to arrive. They found a man lay sprawled on the porch steps of a house across the street from the Spahn residence. A man in his thirties wearing athletic shorts and a T-shirt was bent over the stricken man's face administering CPR. A baseball bat lay in the grass next to the porch. Several bystanders on the sidewalk were watching what was going on.

Lydia was the first one out of the car, and she ran toward the porch. She looked down at the stricken face. It was the same man who told her and Ferris about seeing Jimmie Spahn surreptitiously entering his parent's house at night. Under the porch light, Lydia could see blood seeping from the man's chest. She bent over and looked closer. There were two bullet holes in his chest and one in the throat. She gently pushed the man administering CPR aside.

"He's gone," Lydia said. "You can't help him."

"I know that," the man replied. "He was a good neighbor. I had to try."

"Did you see who shot him?"

"I don't know. I heard the shots. I came out and saw him lying there." The man looked up at the sky. Tears were rolling down his face. "It had to be that little asshole, Jimmie Spahn. He's been hanging around here."

"Did you see him tonight?"

The man shook his head.

"Lydia!"

She looked up.

Haggerty was standing behind her. "This is a crime scene. I want you to secure it. I'll put out a broadcast and try to locate witnesses."

Lydia nodded and looked down at the man who had been doing CPR. "Sir, what is your name?"

"Wilcox."

"Mr. Wilcox, I need you to go back to your house and wait there. The detectives will want to talk to you."

"I understand."

The man stood up and walked over to pick up the baseball bat.

"Wait a minute," Lydia said. "Put that down."

The man looked at her bewildered. "It's mine."

"Okay, could you leave it there for a moment?"

"Well, I guess so."

Other police units began rolling in as Lydia did her best to secure the area with a roll of crime scene tape that she obtained from the trunk of the police car. She heard a woman talking to Hagerty and overheard the name, "Jimmie Spahn."

Lieutenant Hardeman and two detectives from his Homicide Unit appeared at the scene of the shooting thirty minutes after the call came out. It wasn't until after 2:13 a.m. that Lydia and Hagerty were relieved from the crime scene by a Morning Watch unit.

On the way back to the station, Lydia said, "I heard Jimmie Spahn's name mentioned by the lady you were talking to. Did she see him?"

"She saw him shoot the man. The little bastard drove off in a blue Hyundai. She got the license plate. It was a stolen plate. He's hit big time now. He'll be tried as an adult and put away for a long time." Hagerty sighed. "What was with that baseball bat? Did you ever find out?"

"It belonged to the neighbor. He was going to confront the shooter with it."

Lydia was thinking about the neighbor as she drove home. Taking a baseball bat out to confront an active shooter took a lot of courage. Most people would turn and run away from a person with a gun. She wondered what she would do if she were unarmed and confronted an active shooter. She hoped she wouldn't run away.

The Police Academy didn't teach much in self-defense. She was small, but she was also very strong. But was she strong enough to take on a man twice her size? Probably not.

Lydia was so engrossed in her thoughts that she didn't notice the black Mercedes following her. When she finally looked up and spotted it in the rearview mirror, she didn't see the black Humvee with an iron grill guard on the other side of the road that crossed the double-yellow lines and slammed into her BMW.

CHAPTER EIGHTEEN

March 30, 2006. Thursday.

OFFICERS ANNA Browning and Mike Witman, assigned to Five-Adam-95 on A.M. Watch, discovered Lydia's wrecked car at 3:12 a.m. The force of the collision was so hard that the front end of the BMW had been pushed up onto the sidewalk.

Browning got out of the police car while Witman typed in the BMW's license number into the computer. Browning looked around. There was some traffic on Pico Boulevard at night, and she was amazed that no one had bothered to report the accident. She inspected the car. There was a smear of blood on the driver's side window, but no one was inside. She checked the front of the car. The left front fender and the suspension had been pushed all the way up against the engine block. Whatever hit the car had hit it hard.

"Anna!"

Browning stopped and turned to look at Witman who had gotten out of the police car and was standing by the door.

"The registration is flagged," Witman said.

Browning paused for a moment thinking about what that meant. No one could find out the name of the owner of a car if its registration was flagged. It meant that someone in government owned the car, a politician, perhaps, or maybe even a police officer.

She had a bad feeling as she opened the passenger-side door of the BMW, a growing apprehension of what she was about to find inside. The first thing she found in the car was an empty pint bottle of whiskey on the floorboard. Its cap was off. The interior of the car smelled of alcohol.

Browning pulled a pair of black leather gloves from her rear pocket and put them on. She reached inside the car, opened the glovebox, and retrieved the car registration from the document folder.

She shone her flashlight on the registration. When she saw the name on it, she muttered, "Oh shit!"

"What is it?" Witman was now alongside her.

Browning showed him the registration.

Witman looked at it and frowned. "I don't get it. Who is she?"

"It's Lydia Harte. She's a probationer on P.M. Watch."

"I don't know her. She wasn't in my class at the Academy."

"She was in the class before yours."

"What do we do?"

"We call the Watch Commander."

When Lydia woke, she was lying with her head turned, her right cheek was flattened against a cold floor. She lifted her head. A sharp pain surged from the middle of her forehead to the back of her head. She shut her eyes to make the pain go away. When she opened her eyes again, it was almost as dark as when they were closed.

Lydia slowly got to her knees and tried to look around. When she looked up, she saw a small, red light that seemed floating about ten feet off the ground.

She began trembling. It was cold in this place, whatever it was. She wrapped her arms around herself to stop the trembling. It didn't work.

Then she felt something on her head. It was in her hair just above the left ear. She gently touched it. It felt crusty, like dirt. She ran a hand over it to wipe it off and felt a sharp pain. She had a laceration on the side of her head.

How in hell did that happen? She didn't remember getting hit on the head. She tried to picture where she had last been. She remembered leaving the locker room at the station. She had no idea what happened to her after she left the station.

Fluorescent lights came on. Lydia got to her feet, feeling a little wobbly. Blinking her eyes against the harsh light, she looked around. She was in a large room with gray walls. There were no windows. She saw a door.

It was large and painted the same color gray as the walls. It had a large handle shaped like a banana. She reached for the handle and tried it. It was frozen in place and it wouldn't move.

A metallic clicking sound came from the other side of the door. Lydia bent close to the door and listened. Suddenly, the door was thrust open, its blunt edge slamming viciously into the laceration on the side of her head.

She dropped to the ground. The pain was excruciating, and she felt herself on the verge of blacking out. She heard a male voice that seemed to come out of nowhere.

"That's what you get, you nosy little bitch."

She opened her eyes. A man was standing above her. He was wearing a baseball cap over a ski mask and a yellow rain slicker that fell below the knees.

The man grabbed her by the hair and pulled her to a sitting position. "Look over there." He twisted her head. "Do you see it?"

All that Lydia could see was the wall.

"That pot, do you see it?"

What pot? Lydia thought.

"Damn you! Answer me!"

"She's dazed," a voice said behind her. "Let her sleep it off."

The voice was smooth and elegant, and Lydia realized that the person behind her was a woman. She belatedly realized that the man who was treating her so roughly had a gravelly voice.

"We ain't got the time," the man said.

"Let her sleep it off. We can come back in a couple of hours."

The man roughly shoved Lydia back to the floor. For a few seconds, Lydia looked up at the ceiling. There were four rows of metal bars that ran across its length. They had slots in them, and she saw a hook or a hanger of some sort on one of them.

And then she saw the man in the slicker raise a foot.

"Goddammit, Hank! Don't do that!"

Lydia screamed in pain as the man kicked her in the ribs.

"Now look at what you did!" the woman's voice said as Lydia blacked out.

At first, Lydia didn't feel any discomfort when she woke. But when she moved, the pain struck savagely in her left side. She brought her hand up to her mouth to keep from crying out. After a moment when the pain subsided, she turned on her right side and gingerly rose to her knees, holding the left side of her ribs with her hand, trying to slow her breathing.

Where in hell am I?

She remembered what she saw just before she lost consciousness; metal bars running across the ceiling with slots in them, gray walls that seemed to be made of composite material.

The lights came back on. It was blinding after the darkness. She rose a hand to shield the glare.

The door opened. She didn't look up, but she was aware that someone was watching her. After a few moments, she heard a scraping sound, and she slowly raised her head.

The man in the slicker had dragged a card table into the room and was setting it up. Another person wearing the same kind of ski mask and yellow rainslicker placed a metal folding chair in front of the table. It was obvious from her size that this was a woman. A third person entered the room, wearing identical clothing. For a wild moment, Lydia thought the three of them looked like aliens from a science fiction film from the 30's.

The man with the gravelly voice walked up to her. "Get up and sit down in the chair."

Lydia didn't move.

"Pick her up, Hank." This voice belonged to the woman.

Lydia held one hand up. "I can get up. I need time."

"We ain't got time," the man called Hank said.

Lydia began slowly rising to her feet, trying to keep from groaning. A sharp pain arced suddenly across the left side of her ribs like a jolt of electricity. She screamed and fell flat on the concrete floor. She shut her eyes and passed out.

When Lydia woke up, she found herself on her back. The lights were on, and the woman was standing over her.

"Relax," the woman said. "It's Oxycodone. It will make the pain go away. Sit up and drink this."

Lydia felt something on her tongue. She opened her mouth to spit it out. The woman poured a glass of cold water into her mouth, the excess water splashed across her face and down her neck. Lydia began choking and tried to spit the pill out, but it was too late. She had swallowed whatever it was.

The lights went out.

Twenty minutes later, the lights were turned back on. Lydia was lying on her right side, the side away from where she had been kicked. She felt groggy. Someone wearing a pair of trainers came alongside her. The trainers were tan with diamond-patterned brown spots, meant to look like camouflage, but looking more like the back of a desert rattlesnake.

"Come on, get up." It was the man called Hank who spoke. The tone of his voice was softer now.

Lydia found herself fighting to keep her mind clear. She had to remember certain things about these people in case she got out of this alive.

Need to remember Hank's voice. Associate it with rattlesnake trainers. He wears black trousers with cuffs under the slicker.

Lydia used her right arm to push herself off the concrete floor to a sitting position. The pain was still there in her left ribs, not as sharp as it had been before, but dull enough that she could tolerate it.

The woman was standing ten feet away. Lydia looked at her shoes. She wore black flats and gray slacks that was cut just above bare ankles.

The third man was wearing black trainers. His legs were bare. He was either naked under the rainslicker or wearing shorts.

"Get to your feet," the woman said.

Lydia complied, moving slowly. She felt unsteady on her feet, as if she had too much to drink. "I need to go to the bathroom."

"There's no bathroom, here. You can use that when we're done." The woman was pointing to one side of the room where there was a blue enamel pot, the kind used for cooking stews.

"I need to use the bathroom," Lydia repeated.

"You need to do what I tell you," the woman said. She stepped aside. "Sit down." She pointed to the card table and a metal chair that had been placed in the room.

Lydia took notice of the woman's hands, long and graceful, clear nail polish, no wedding ring. She walked unsteadily toward the card table.

A document was lying on the table, its upper half concealed by a sheet of heavy paper. A ballpoint pen lay next to it.

"Sit down," the woman repeated.

Lydia sat down on the metal chair.

"Now sign it."

"Sign what?" Lydia mumbled. Her voice was hoarse.

"Sign on the line above your typed name."

Lydia picked up a ballpoint pen and studied the document. There was no date alongside the signature line. Although heavy paper concealed the top half of the document, she knew what it was. An assignment of her rights to Jonathan's trust.

"What am I signing?" Lydia asked.

"It doesn't matter," the man called Hank said as he came alongside her. "Sign it and we'll let you go."

Lydia looked up at the ski-masked face under the black baseball cap. This man had dark eyes just like the woman. She then noticed something unusual about the man's slicker. It sagged slightly off the right shoulder. Something was weighing it down. The slicker had a pocket, and there was a bulge in it. He was carrying a gun.

"You'll let me go if I sign it?" Lydia said.

The man nodded.

Lydia picked up the pen and looked at the signature line on the document. She paused for a moment, thinking. Would they really let her go if she signed the document? Somehow, she doubted that. But would they kill her after she signed it? She doubted that too. They were wearing masks. If they were going to kill her, they wouldn't be wearing masks, would they?

Lydia began writing, not her signature, but "Fuck you" with an exclamation point.

"Goddamn you!" the man cried in rage. He stepped forward and hit her as hard as he could with his fist.

Lydia blacked out and fell to the floor.

CHAPTER NINETEEN

Four Days in Hell.

"**DOESN'T LOOK** like there's a lot of blood," Hardemann said as he opened the passenger door of Lydia's BMW and looked inside.

Billy Vernor looked up from his kneeling position at the damage in front of the BMW. Hardemann and Vernor were in the police impound lot, having decided to look at Lydia's car in an effort to uncover anything that the traffic accident reconstructionist had missed.

The report completed by the accident expert had said that there was no debris left at the scene of the crash from the hit and run vehicle, which was unusual. The only marks left behind on the BMW by the hit and run vehicle were traces of black paint embedded in the silver paint. The report further stated that samples of the black paint had been sent to the FBI lab for identification.

Vernor stood up. "They're not going to find the car that did this."

Hardemann looked at him. "Robbery-Homicide has some top-flight detectives working on this case. I trust them to do everything they can to find out what happened to Harte."

"I'm not talking about the competence of Robbery-Homicide. What I'm talking about is the location of those black marks. That black paint didn't come from a car. The marks are too high, higher than a standard bumper. I think this car was hit with a heavy-duty bumper guard. One that was aftermarket."

When Hardemann didn't respond, Vernor continued. "The kind you sometimes see on a heavy-duty pickup."

"Rumors are going around she's an alcoholic," Hardemann said, looking at Vernor and expecting a reaction.

Vernor shook his head. "I only saw her once when she came to work with a hangover. I never smelled any booze on her during any other time we worked together."

"Do you know what she drinks?"

"Wine," Vernor said as he walked to the back of the car. "Can you pop the trunk release? I want to look inside."

Once Vernor had the trunk open, he stood back and examined the contents. Nothing was there except for a squeegee and jumper cables. He pulled up the cover to the spare tire and looked inside. Nothing there either. Just the spare tire.

"Billy!"

Hardemann's voice sounded urgent.

Vernor went to see what he wanted.

Hardemann was holding a manila envelope in one hand and a sheaf of papers in the other.

Vernor frowned when he saw what was in his hand. It was the unauthorized research he had done for Lydia.

"Where did you find it?" Vernor asked.

Hardemann frowned when he saw the look on Vernor's face. "Under the rear seat."

"Pardon me, Lieutenant," Vernor said, "but you don't need to be looking through that material."

"You know what's here?"

"I do."

"Dammit Billy, did you do this for her?"

Vernor looked away.

"Who are these men, Vernor?"

"Lieutenant, please trust me on this. You really don't want to know anything about this. Give it to me and forget you ever saw it."

Hardemann stared at Vernor for a long hard minute. He put the papers back into the envelope. "Do you suspect these men might have something to do with Harte being missing?"

"I don't know."

"We need to turn this over to Robbery-Homicide."

"You go ahead and do that, Lieutenant, and watch what happens. This information will spin this investigation into a direction you never dreamed of."

"But what if this material has something to do with her disappearance?"

"I already said I don't know if it does, Lieutenant. If you give it to me, I'll do what I can to find out if there is a connection. If there is a connection, I'll share it with Robbery-Homicide."

Hardemann thought about this for a moment. Then he said, "I hope you know what you're doing, Billy." He handed the envelope to Vernor and turned away.

Lydia regained consciousness to a throbbing pain on the right side of her face. She put a hand to her cheekbone and instantly regretted it. There was a lump the size of a baseball there, and the pain was sharp, sharper than the pain in her ribs. She pushed herself to a sitting position and looked around.

The red light in the ceiling was still on. Earlier, when she came awake for the first time and started moving, the fluorescent lights turned on, and someone entered the room. This time nothing happened.

She waited a few minutes and then began crawling on all fours in the darkness toward the place where she thought the enamel pot was located. It took her five minutes before she located it next to a wall. It was difficult getting her sweatpants off because the movement set her ribs on fire. It was a lot more difficult having to pee in a soup pot, but she did it.

Lydia found a place where she could sit against a wall. She shut her eyes and waited. No one came into the room. She began wondering what kind of place this was. It had to be a factory of some sort. It smelled funny, like something dead and moldy. The long rails on the ceiling rack might have been used to install a row of hangers, but they seemed too high to hang clothing. She wondered what they had been used for.

It didn't take long before she fell back asleep.

When Lydia woke up, the room was dark. She had no idea what time it was, nor how long she had been out. She rose from a sitting position very slowly, not wanting to stir up the pain in her ribs and was relieved to find that it had subsided to nothing more than a dull throbbing. Even so, she was careful not to move fast.

The first thing she did was to locate the door and see, if by some miracle, it was unlocked. Using the wall to guide her around the room, she found it. She tried the banana-shaped handle. It moved slightly but it wouldn't open.

She began thinking about her predicament, and how she could get out of here alive. The big question on her mind was what these people would do to her if she signed the document. She doubted they would kill her.

But there was one point that bothered her. The document was undated. That meant they wouldn't take any action on it until she had established her right to Jonathan's trust. But what could they do to prevent her from claiming she signed the document under duress? They must have a plan in mind that would keep her from doing that. But what?

Well, damn it, Lydia thought. They weren't the only people who had a brain. She could come up with a plan to beat these people if she thought long and hard enough.

Lydia began walking around the room, letting her hand trail on the wall as a reference point, only to find that on the first circuit she nearly kicked over the cooking pot full of urine.

She had to pass the time somehow. When she ran out of ideas of how to counter what these people were doing to her, she imagined she was back at U.C.L.A. at Drake Stadium, in the blocks, getting ready for a 440 sprint. She began walking more quickly as she imagined dashing around the track. Using the door as the reference point, she began counting laps around the room.

No one . . . and that meant no one . . . in the PAC 12 beat me in any race during my last two years of college, she thought. The same goes for these assholes in the ski masks. They are not going to beat me!

Lydia had counted 763 circuits around the room when the lights came on. She stopped, turned, and looked defiantly at the door.

A minute later, the tall man, the one that the woman called Hank, entered the room wearing the silly ski mask and the rainslicker. This time he was holding a semi-automatic pistol. It was a 1911 .45 ACP.

He pointed the gun at her. "No more funny business, sister. This time you're going to sign that fucking document!"

The woman and the smaller man came into the room. The man carried the card table and metal chair and set them up in the middle of the room. The woman then placed the document and a ballpoint pen on the table.

The man with the 1911 waved the gun at the table. "Are you going to sign, or do we have to rumble?"

Lydia didn't respond. There is no way she would be able to handle a fight with this man. She was beginning to understand that if she wanted to continue being a police officer, she should start taking lessons in some form of martial art.

The woman nodded at the man with the gun.

He stepped forward and pressed the semi-automatic against Lydia's forehead. "So, what do you think?"

Lydia could see that the hammer was in the cocked position and the man had his finger on the trigger. Every 1911 that Lydia had ever seen had a safety, but she couldn't see if the safety was off on the gun the man was holding.

"I don't think you're going to kill me," Lydia said calmly.

The man's eyes blinked several times rapidly before he spoke. "Why not?"

Lydia wasn't thinking of an answer. She was remembering how they were taught at the Police Academy that the biggest mistake a gunman could make was getting too close to the person they were threatening. The recruits were taught two maneuvers on how to disarm a suspect during their self-defense classes. One technique was how to take away a weapon from someone who was standing directly in front of you. The other technique was how to do the same thing if the gun was held to your back.

Lydia hadn't practiced the maneuver since she graduated from the Academy, and she was uncertain whether she was still able to execute it. Once you were committed, there was no room for error. The maneuver had to be executed smoothly and quickly or else you were dead.

The man with the gun interpreted Lydia's silence as defiance, so he tapped the gun on her forehead. "Why not, bitch?"

Lydia didn't flinch. "Because you need me."

The man grunted and turned to the other two. "See, I told you she was a wiseass."

For just a second, Lydia was tempted to try and take the gun away, but the man suddenly turned back to face her. He waved the pistol at the table.

"Sit."

Lydia didn't move.

"Sit down. Goddammit it!"

Lydia remain still.

"Okay," the woman said. "Let's motivate her."

The other man, the smaller one who hardly ever said anything, came forward. He was holding a billy club in his hand.

Lydia stepped back as he approached.

Both men came alongside her. They grabbed her by the arms and pulled her toward the door. The maneuver caused a streak of pain across the side of her bruised ribs, a pain so intense that she would have fallen to her knees if she wasn't being held up by the two thugs.

The men dragged her out of the room into a long dusty hall that was lit by a string of fluorescent lights. Despite the intensity of the pain, Lydia realized she needed to learn as much as possible about the place where she was being held if she ever had a chance to escape, so she began paying attention to the layout. There were a series of doors on the left side of the hallway that had the same kind of lever-like latch that had been on the door to her room.

It finally dawned on her what this place was.

It was an abandoned meat packing plant. The room where she was being held had been a meat locker.

The men dragged Lydia down the hallway toward an open door. When they got there, they stopped and turned Lydia to face the interior of the room.

There was a woman in the room bound to a chair with strips of duct tape wound around her chest. Her head was leaning forward, her chin resting on the upper part of her chest so that her black hair fell across her face. Even though she was wrapped with duct tape, Lydia could see under the harsh lights in the room that the woman was nearly naked, wearing only a black bra and panties.

The two men pulled Lydia into the room, so that she was standing a few feet away from the stricken woman.

Lydia stared at the woman and drew in a deep breath. She smelled a perfume she recognized.

God, no! Is that . . .?

The woman wearing the ski mask walked up to the injured woman in the chair and rapped her on the head with her knuckles. "Okay now. You need to look up. We didn't hurt you that bad."

The woman slowly raised her head. Even though the disfigured face was purpled with bruises and one of the eyes was swollen shut, Lydia had no problem recognizing her friend, Jenny Hamilton.

"Lydia," Jenny murmured through bruised lips, "did they fuck you too?"

Lydia stared at her for a moment, her mouth moving, not being able to form any of the words she wanted to say. She screamed, spun around, and threw her right elbow as hard as she could into the face of the smaller man. The pain in her ribs flared up for an instant, but just as quickly dissolved when she felt a sharp blow to her head and lost consciousness.

Lydia woke to find that the lights were on in the room where she was being held. She rolled over and pushed herself up on her hands and looked around. The card table and the metal folding chair were still there, but no one was in the room. She felt something crawling on the right side of her face. She rubbed it. Something sticky clung to her fingers. She looked at her hand and saw blood, drying into a crust. Reaching up into her hair, she felt another crusty laceration, this one on the left side of her head.

Great, she thought, another one to match the one on the right. How symmetrical!

She thought of Jenny and what they had done to her and the grim humor left her. As she stood up, a rage began roaring inside her. She was going to kill these bastards if it was the last thing she could do. She looked around. The cooking pot full of piss was not heavy enough to kill anyone. The metal folding chair would make a nice weapon. If she was lucky, she could pick it up and hit the bastard with the gun before he could shoot her.

But she knew they were watching her. They seemed to know when she began moving around.

Before she could formulate any plan, the man called Hank opened the door and entered the room. He was carrying the gun and was followed by the woman. There was no sign of the smaller man. The blow to his face with her elbow had been a hard one. If he didn't have a broken tooth or two, he surely would have a broken nose.

The man pointed the gun at her. "Sit down!"

Lydia didn't move.

"Jenny Hamilton is your friend, right?" the man continued. "If you want to see her alive again, you will do what I tell you."

Lydia wanted to say something in response but didn't. So, this is how it was. They were using Jenny to get her to sign that document.

"I said, sit down!" the man screamed.

Lydia walked slowly to the table. When she got there, she gripped the back of the chair as if she was going to pick it up.

The man, his eyes gleaming, raised the gun, and pointed it at her face.

"You won't kill me," Lydia said.

The woman stepped forward and put a hand on the man's gun and gently lowered his arm. "You're right," she said. "We won't kill you, but we will make life very difficult for your girlfriend if you don't do what we want. Sit down!"

Lydia pulled out the chair and sat down.

The woman stepped forward and laid a document and a ballpoint pen in front of Lydia. She had been careful to lay a sheet of heavy paper over the document that covered most of it except for an undated signature line at the bottom.

Lydia looked up at the woman. There was nothing in her hands. There were no pockets in the slicker that Lydia could see. The woman might have a gun somewhere under her rainslicker, but there was no visible outline of one.

The man moved behind Lydia. He held the gun loosely in his right hand.

Lydia picked up the pen and looked at the document.

"Sign it!"

The man was hovering over her left shoulder, his breath smelling of whiskey.

Lydia could feel his right hip against her shoulder. She turned and looked up at him.

"You raped Jenny," Lydia said. Her voice was flat and listless, but her mind was not. She held the pen in her lap, below the table, so that the man and the woman couldn't see her changing her grip.

The man said nothing in response.

Lydia stared up at him for a moment, gauging the thickness of the ski mask. It was made of a thin material and was tight against his face and neck. She fumbled the ballpoint and adjusted it so that she held it in her fist with the nib pointed up. She dared not look down at it but was confident that at least four inches of it protruded above her fist.

If Lydia sprang into action, she had two people to contend with, and she didn't know for sure if the woman was carrying a gun. Lydia looked at the woman. She was waiting expectantly, staring at Lydia.

"Are you going to sign it or not?" the woman asked.

Lydia gripped the pen tightly. She turned back to the man. "Can you step back a little. Your dick is rubbing my shoulder."

The man looked startled for just a moment and backed away a few inches. Lydia quickly stood up and slammed her left elbow into the man's solar plexus. He stumbled backwards.

When Lydia thought about it later, she wondered why she felt no pain when she made her move. The pain would not return come until much later.

Grabbing the metal chair with her left hand, Lydia awkwardly threw it at the woman, without looking to see if it connected. She spun around with the pen in her right hand and plunged the ballpoint pen as deep as she could into the man's neck, hoping to hit the carotid artery.

The man called Hank dropped the gun and stumbled backwards, clutching his throat with both hands. Lydia stooped down and grabbed his gun. She stood up and looked back at where the woman had been standing. There was only a fleeting glimpse of her as she dashed out of the room into the hallway.

Lydia ran to the door and looked to the right. The woman was running down the hall as fast as she could. Before Lydia could raise the gun to fire, the woman darted into a room and disappeared. After firing a single shot down the hallway to make sure the woman didn't plan on coming back, Lydia stepped back into the room where she had been held captive.

The man called Hank was on his knees. He had pulled the ballpoint out of his neck and taken off the ski mask. He was holding his neck with two hands, trying to stop the bleeding.

The man looked familiar, but Lydia couldn't remember where she had seen him before.

"Hey!" Lydia said.

He looked up at her and tried to speak. Lydia thought she heard his thickened voice mumble, "Hospital."

"Hospitals don't admit dead people," Lydia said.

She shot him in the face.

Lydia cautiously looked down the hallway where she had last seen the woman. There was no sign of her, so Lydia stepped out into the hallway and began looking for the room where they were keeping Jenny.

When she found the room, she was surprised at what she saw. The chair that Jenny had been sitting in was overturned. Pieces of duct tape were scattered across the floor. There was no sign of Jenny.

Lydia stepped back into the hallway and was greeted by a burst of gunfire from down the hall. She ducked back inside the room and waited.

"Drop the gun and come out!" the woman called out.

Lydia realized that the shots the woman had fired had bounced off the cement floor. She was not shooting to kill. The woman needed her alive. Lydia was under no such restriction. She would kill the woman if she got a chance.

After a moment, Lydia knelt and cautiously looked around the edge of the door jamb. The hallway was empty. Lydia rose to her feet, using the door jamb as a brace for the gun. She waited for at least another minute before she saw the woman's head peeking around a door sixty feet down the hall. Lydia didn't hesitate. She fired three quick shots at the woman and ran in the opposite direction.

Behind her, she heard gunfire. The shots went over her head. She found a darkened hallway to the right and skidded into it.

Lydia ran until she found an open room with long wooden tables and conveyor belts. Moonlight filtered through high windows. There was just enough light to allow her to cross the floor without running into anything.

She saw a doorway leading toward a glassed-in office at the back. It was twenty yards away. Lydia ran toward it.

There was a loud click, and suddenly the entire room was lit up.

When Lydia got into the office, she looked back. The woman was at the far end of the room, looking around. It was a matter of time before she found where Lydia was hiding.

Lydia looked at her gun. The slide was open. There were no bullets left in the gun. She looked around. The office was small with a desk and several wooden chairs. Behind the desk was a row of windows. She grabbed one of the office chairs and used it to break out a window. After clearing out the glass, Lydia boosted herself up on the windowsill and dropped onto a patch of knee-high weeds.

The moon was out, shining down on a huge expanse of a parking lot with weeds coming up through the cracks in the paving. Beyond the pavement was a six-foot chain link fence. Lydia ran toward it.

Two shots rang out!

Lydia lofted herself over the top of the fence and landed onto the dirt. In front of her was a hill strewn with rocks. She ran up it. When she was halfway up, she stopped and looked back.

The abandoned meat-packing plant was isolated in a small valley-like depression. The only light she saw in the area below her was from the building.

The woman who had been chasing her was standing in the middle of the parking lot, looking up the hill.

Lydia kept climbing until she reached the top. She began breathing heavily, gasping for air.

What the hell is wrong with me?

One year ago, she was running sprints at U.C.L.A. She kept in shape by working out on a regular basis and shouldn't be breathing that hard.

She finally realized that a lack of physical fitness wasn't the problem. The cumulative effects of the beatings she taken from the man called Hank were catching up with her. And that was when the pain came roaring back with such an intensity that she fell to her knees. She stared at the ground, fighting with her mind and body to keep from passing out.

CHAPTER TWENTY

April 3, 2006. Monday

LYDIA DIDN'T know how long she was out, but when she regained consciousness, it was still dark. She looked around and discovered she was on top of a knoll.

Below her was what looked like an arroyo, barely visible in the darkness. She shakily got to her feet and started down the hill, having no idea of where she was going or what direction she was taking. She began to slide through the grass and loose rocks. Still on her feet, Lydia desperately tried to stop her momentum, but couldn't. She tumbled into a wide ditch and struck the back of her head on a rock.

Lydia lay still for a while. When she felt as if the world had steadied itself, she turned over and struggled to get back on her feet. She climbed out of the ditch onto the side of another hill.

It took her nearly twenty minutes to get to the top. Once there, she fell to her knees and looked over the knoll, half expecting to see the abandoned meat packing plant. She sighed with relief when she saw what was spread out in front of her. It was a large residential area that stretched for miles. In the distance, maybe two or three miles away, was a cluster of tall buildings.

She got to her feet and began carefully making her way down the rock studded hill to the houses below her. The pain in her ribs was still there, not as bad as before, but she now had pain attacking her head from three separate directions.

The tract directly below Lydia consisted of large ranch homes. A five-foot wall of ornamental concrete blocks ran along the backyards of the homes. Lydia easily climbed over the wall into the backyard of the nearest house.

When she dropped into the backyard, she was greeted by a little dog who began yapping at her. As she walked to the gate next to the house, the dog followed her, setting up a racket that made Lydia's bruised head throb. She shut the gate behind her and walked out to the front.

When she got to the sidewalk, she stopped and considered what she should do. The easiest thing would be to go up to a house and knock on the door. But who, at this time of night, would open the door to their house without a gun in their hand?

The little dog was still yapping furiously like an alarm that couldn't be turned off. The lights came on in the house.

Lydia needed to get to a main street where she could either find a police car or an open gas station who could call the police for her. She began walking down the sidewalk, hoping to find a way out of the subdivision when she heard someone calling from behind her.

When she turned, she saw an elderly man who was wearing a robe and pajamas standing on the sidewalk about fifty paces away. He held a large gun loosely in his hand.

"What were you doing in my backyard?" he yelled.

Lights began turning on in other houses.

"Call the police!" Lydia yelled back.

"I already have. What were you doing in my back yard?"

Lydia didn't answer. She turned and continued walking down the street. She was tired and felt sick. Her head was spinning, but she kept walking.

The street ahead of her curved away sharply to the right. She heard a rapidly accelerating car in the distance that was getting closer. A minute later, a police car, its emergency lights on, rounded the curve ahead of her.

Lydia stopped and raised a hand, but the car sped past her. Just when she began to think the officers didn't see her, the brake lights of the car came on and it slid to a stop. The car began backing up. Lydia began walking toward the car. The car stopped and an officer got out, holding a gun in one hand and a flashlight in the other.

"Don't move!" the officer yelled in a commanding voice. "Get your hands on top of your head now!"

Lydia stopped, confused.

The officer began moving toward her, the light from the flashlight playing over Lydia's body. The other officer had gotten out of the car and was walking toward Lydia, staying in the middle of the street.

"Put your hands on top of your head and turn round. Do it now!"

Lydia realized that the officer talking to her was a young woman.

"I'm a police officer," Lydia said. "I've been beaten. I can't put my hands up. I need to go to a hospital."

Lydia was concentrating so hard on the female officer that she didn't see the other officer rushing her from the side. He tackled her, throwing his shoulder into her ribs, and knocked her to the ground. He turned her over, pushing her face down into the sidewalk.

Lydia screamed in pain as he pulled her arms up behind her and hand-cuffed her.

He turned her over. "Come on, now," he said. "I didn't hurt you."

Tears streamed from Lydia's eyes. "Ribs broken," she muttered in a high-pitched voice.

"Quit being a baby. I didn't hit you that hard."

"Did you hear what she said?" the female officer said.

"I didn't break her ribs."

"She said she's a police officer."

The male officer looked down at Lydia's face. "Bullshit."

"What's your name?" the female officer asked.

"Lydia Harte."

The male officer looked up at his partner. "Give me that fucking light."

The female officer handed the light to him.

He shone it on Lydia's face. "She's on drugs," he said, "We better call a supervisor. I think this is the officer from Century everyone is looking for."

The ride to Valley Station took nearly a half hour. The male officer was driving, and the female officer was in the passenger seat. A burly sergeant by the name of Matthews who smelled of cigar smoke and whiskey rode in the back seat of the police car with Lydia. She was handcuffed and seatbelted. The pain in her ribs struck her viciously every time the car hit a bump.

Matthews asked her several times about what she had been drinking and what drugs she had been taking. He refused to listen when Lydia tried to explain what had happened to her, and how important it was that they find Jenny Hamilton. By the time they arrived at Valley Station, Lydia was so pissed off that she stopped trying to talk to Matthews.

When she got to the station, she hoped that things would get better. She was placed in an interview room used by Valley Division Detectives and left alone. A few minutes later, the Watch Commander entered the room with Matthews. His name tag showed his last name was King. Like Matthews, he was a sergeant, but the rocker under the stripes indicated that he was a senior sergeant.

King sat down. At first, he was very pleasant, asking Lydia how she was feeling.

Lydia looked at him in stunned belief. "Do you really want to know?"

King smiled and nodded.

"I feel like you people don't give a damn. I already told Matthews they're holding my friend, Jenny Hamilton. She needs medical attention, but no one here seems to care."

King leaned forward and looked into her eyes. Under normal circumstances, Lydia would have considered him attractive, but there was something sinister about that handsome face. Maybe, it was something she saw in his dark eyes. Lydia felt for the second or third time in her life that she had encountered a man who had no soul.

King sat back and looked up at Matthews who was standing beside him. "Are you seeing what I'm seeing?"

Matthews nodded.

King looked back to Lydia. "What kind of drugs have you been taking?"

"I haven't been taking any drugs. They gave me something that made me compliant."

"Compliant?"

"Yes."

"What kind of drug was this?"

"I don't know."

"Where was this? Was it with your friends?"

"Goddammit, they weren't my fucking friends!"

"So, you have no idea who you share drugs with?"

Lydia stared at his name tag. "I don't do drugs, Sergeant King. If this is what this questioning is all about, I want to talk to my attorney. As a matter of fact, I feel sick. I want to go to the hospital right now."

"Why do you want an attorney?"

"I'm not saying anything else until I see my attorney."

"Who were you doing drugs with?"

Lydia looked at King's badge to make sure he was LAPD.

He was wearing an LAPD badge. She couldn't believe that this man had never heard of the Miranda decision.

"I want to call my attorney," Lydia repeated.

"You know you are required to answer my questions? You can get fired if you don't."

Lydia looked away for a moment. She was tired. She felt sick. And she was hungry. And she wasn't going to answer any more of this asshole's questions.

King got up and signaled to Matthews with a roll of his shoulder that indicated they should leave the room.

Lydia leaned over, laid her head on the table, and shut her eyes.

An hour later, Lydia was awakened when the door opened. She looked up. A tall man with coal black hair and wearing a tailored suit entered the room. He was followed by King.

The man didn't take a seat. After he looked at Lydia's face, he turned back to King. "You didn't tell me she was injured."

"I was planning on having her looked at by the jail nurse."

The man stared at King for a moment before turning back to Lydia. He leaned over the table and looked into her eyes.

He had dark eyes, like King, but they weren't menacing. Lydia smelled coffee on his breath.

He frowned, straightened up, and spoke to King. "Why do you think she's on drugs?"

"Look at her eyes, sir."

"I have, Sergeant King. She's not on drugs, goddammit. She's got a concussion. Where's Matthews?"

"Outside. In the detective squad room."

"Tell him we need an ambulance here, Code Three."

"Yes, sir."

King left the room and the man sat down opposite her.

Lydia looked at him through tired eyes.

He leaned forward and lay his arms across the table. "I'm Captain Mitchell, Officer Harte. Did my people do this to you?"

Lydia shook her head. "No."

"You have several lacerations on your head. Who did this to you?"

Lydia saw that the man was genuinely interested in hearing what she had to say. "I don't know. I was kidnapped. They got my friend, Jenny. You've got to find her. She's badly hurt."

Mitchell's eyes widened. "Is she a police officer?"

"No. She's a friend."

"Where is she?"

"She was in a meat packing plant with me. She was in one of the coolers."

"You were in a meat packing plant?"

"Yes."

"Where was this?"

"Near where the officers picked me up."

"There's no meat packing plant here in our Division. They say they picked you up in a residential area."

"It was abandoned. Back in the hills."

Mitchell, looking skeptical, sat back in his chair. "Okay, we'll try to find her." He stood up. "We've got an ambulance on the way. I've taken the liberty of calling your Commanding Officer. Do you need anything?"

"My ribs are broken. I need to get these cuffs off me."

Mitchell nodded and stood up.

"And coffee," Lydia added.

"Done," Mitchell said. He started to leave the room but thought better of it. "How many people were holding you prisoner?"

"Three of them. They were wearing masks."

"How did you escape?"

"I stabbed one of them with a ballpoint pen. Then I took his gun and shot him."

"You shot someone?"

"Yes. Listen, sir, you've got to find that place and get Jenny out of there. They beat her badly. She needs help."

Mitchell nodded. "We'll do our best. I can't promise you anything because I don't know where it is. If it's here in Division, we'll find it and your friend."

Lydia was taken to Valley General in an ambulance accompanied by a female police officer. The officer stayed with her throughout her treatment in the emergency room. It was confirmed by a doctor that Lydia had a concussion. The x-ray showed she also had three broken ribs. The good news was they would heal without medical intervention. After the lacerations on her head were cleaned and stitched, Lydia was admitted to the hospital for observation.

It was beginning to get light outside when Lydia was placed in a hospital bed and attached to a web of tubes. She didn't know what they were pumping into her blood stream, but she fell asleep the moment she lay down.

It was five-thirty in the afternoon when she woke up. A woman entered the room with a dinner tray and asked if she was hungry.

Lydia said that she was. She asked the woman if there was a police officer sitting outside.

There was.

She asked the woman to get her. She did.

The police officer who entered the room was a tall blonde who was as slender as a runway model. She was wearing a name plate that said her name was Rainey.

The officer walked over to the bed. "Are you all right?"

"Yes. Did they find Jenny Hamilton?"

"They found the place where you were being held, but no one was there. Were you raped?"

Lydia shook her head. She had been fucked over but good, but not raped. "Why are you here? Am I in any danger?"

"Not that I know of. They wanted me to call Lieutenant Grayson when you woke up." Rainey stepped closer, bent over her, and whispered, "Did you shoot someone?"

Lydia knew why she had asked that question. Lieutenant Peter Grayson from Robbery-Homicide was in charge of the Officer-Involved-Shooting Team. He was not someone Lydia trusted. A few weeks back, he had her followed by a surveillance unit because he believed that Lydia had killed two police officers.

"I did," Lydia said, in response to Rainey's question.

"Good for you."

"Can you wait until after I eat dinner before you call Lieutenant Grayson?"

"I will."

"Can you do me another favor?"

"If I can."

"Can you get me a phone number for my attorney? His name is Michael Honshino."

"I can do better than that. I know Mike. I'll call him. What do you want me to tell him?"

"Tell him I need to see him as soon as possible."

An hour later, there was a knock at the door of her room, and Lieutenant Peter Grayson entered. He was accompanied by a severe-looking young woman wearing a black suit with the skirt cut above her fat knees.

"What did they do to you?" Grayson asked, peering at the bruises on Lydia's face. He was a big man, over six feet tall with a military bearing that suggested a stint in the Marine Corps. He wore a tailored light gray suit with business-like pin stripes.

Lydia misinterpreted what he asked. "They patched me up. That's pretty much it, except I have to stay here another day."

"I mean at the place where you were held."

"Oh that. They starved me and beat the shit out of me, Lieutenant."

"They told me you shot one of your captors."

"I did." Lydia looked at the woman standing at the foot of the bed. "You haven't introduced your partner."

Grayson smiled and looked at the woman. She wasn't smiling.

"This is Grace Wicker. She's from the Civil Rights Division of the D.A.'s office."

Lydia knew what that meant. It was a euphemism for let's try and put a cop in jail who shot someone in the line of duty.

When Lydia didn't respond, Grayson continued. "I'd like to hear what happened out there."

"So would I," said a voice behind Grayson. "Except she's not going to do that until I get a chance to talk to her."

Lydia recognized the voice. It was her attorney, Michael Honshino.

Grayson turned toward him. "Mike, what are you doing here?"

"I see you got Grace Witcher with you, Pete. What the hell's wrong with you people?"

"It's Wicker," said the woman angrily. "Have the courtesy to pronounce my name correctly."

"I'll pronounce your name right when you have the courtesy to treat police officers who are doing their job with the respect they are due." Honshino turned his attention back to Grayson. "Okay, Pete. I want her out of here now!"

"Come on, Mike. You know the procedure after an officer is involved in a shooting."

"I follow procedure too, Pete. It's called the Police Officer's Bill of Rights. Neither you nor that woman in the black suit are going to talk to my client under these conditions. Any interview of her will be at a reasonable time and place after she has been released from the hospital and with me present."

Lydia could see the fury building up in Grayson's face, but he said nothing. He nodded to Wicker and they left the room.

Michael Honshino was well known among police officers who had gotten into trouble with their employers. He specialized in helping police officers counter the false narrative favored by some politicians bent on making a name for themselves by nailing police officers to a cross when all they had been doing was their job under very stressful circumstances.

Honshino was a small, stocky man who had offices in Little Tokyo not more than two blocks from Police Headquarters. He had once represented Lydia in an incident where it looked like she might have accidentally shot her partner, and he had done a fantastic job of making sure she was treated right.

He pulled up a chair and sat down. "Okay. Tell me what happened."

Lydia did so

After he listened to what Lydia had to say, he got up. "From what I can see, I don't think you're going to have any problems. There will be a number of people who want to talk to you about what happened, but I'll make sure they don't harass you."

"Do you have any pull with any of the brass in the Department?"

"I might. It depends on what you mean by pull."

My friend, Jenny. I want to make sure someone is looking for her."

"I'll see what I can do."

Later in the evening, there was a knock on the door and Dick Hagerty and Kenny Ferris walked into the room. Both were in uniform.

Lydia drew the covers up to her neck and smiled when she saw them. "My, but you two are way out of your assigned district."

"We have been given special dispensation by Lieutenant Morton," Hagerty said. "Everyone wants to know if you really had been drinking while you were driving."

"Why would they think that?" Lydia asked. "I was on my way home from work."

Hagerty exchanged glances with Ferris. "They found an empty bottle of whiskey in the car."

Lydia stared at him for a moment. "I don't drink whiskey. I don't like it."

"Okay."

"I drink wine. A little beer now and then, but not whiskey."

"I believe you."

"Do you know if they fingerprinted the bottle?"

"I'm sure they have."

There was silence in the room for a moment.

"Are you all right?" Hagerty asked.

"Broken ribs. A concussion. But I feel pretty good right now. The doctor says I will be able to go home tomorrow."

"Are you sure?" Ferris asked.

"Well, the doctor says so."

"You look like hell."

"Thanks," Lydia said. She suddenly remembered she had kept the research Billy Vernor had given her under the back seat of her BMW. "Do you know what they did to my car?"

"It's in the impound lot," Hagerty said. "And it's totaled. The entire front quarter panel was pushed all the way into the engine. You're going to need a new car." He paused for a moment studying Lydia's face. "Is there anything we can do for you? You do know there are some guys in patrol who really like you."

That revelation surprised Lydia. She thought the only person she got along with at the station were these two men standing before her and Billy Vernor.

"Do you know if Jeremy Morgan is back?"

Hagerty smiled. "He is."

"Do you have his phone number?"

"Don't you have it?"

"I've lost everything. My off-duty gun. My purse with my credit cards. Everything."

"Did someone take a report?"

"No. All they were concerned with was if I was on drugs." The instant Lydia said this she knew that it wasn't strictly true. Captain Mitchell seemed genuinely interested in her.

Hagerty nodded. "We'll take a lost report."

"I don't have the serial number of my gun."

"No problem. We can follow-up tomorrow."

"Have you actually talked to Jeremy," Lydia asked Hagerty.

"I have. I saw him at the range."

"Is he okay?

"Why shouldn't he be? He had a smile on his face like he had just hit the lottery."

CHAPTER TWENTY-ONE

April 4, 2006. Tuesday.

LYDIA WAS released from the hospital at 11:30 the next morning. She had contacted Jeremy Morgan the night before, and he volunteered to pick her up at the hospital and take her home. The only problem was that the press had gotten wind of Lydia's release and were waiting to interview her when she came out the front door. So, she was wheelchaired by a nursing assistant out the back door where Jeremy Morgan was waiting for her in his Jeep.

Jeremy groaned when he saw her bruised face. "I'd kiss you, but it looks like it would hurt."

"Who? Me or you?" Lydia smiled.

Jeremy helped her into the Jeep. He leaned in and looked closely at her face.

"I look a mess, don't I?" Lydia asked.

"Do you mind if I tell you something that might make you mad?"

"At you?"

"Probably."

"Go ahead."

"You got three bald spots on your head, and your hair isn't long enough to cover them."

"I already know that," Lydia said as she put a hand to the laceration on the right side of her head and felt a short row of stitches. She smiled, and said, "Do you know where I can find a good wig shop nearby?"

"No, I don't," Jeremy said. "Never had the occasion to use one."

"I know one in Beverly Hills. Can you take me there?"

"It'll be our first stop."

When they drove around to the front of the hospital, Lydia saw dozens of reporters, some with television cameras, under the porte cochère. None of them saw the Jeep as it swept down the drive and onto the main road.

"So, you hit the news big time?" Jeremy said.

"I did. What about you?"

"Nada."

"Are you disappointed?"

"Negative."

"You're being remarkably laconic today."

"Just thinking of what happened to you. It disturbs me. Is there anything I can do to help? I'd like to find the people who kidnapped you and give them a good dose of what they did to you."

"I'm not sure who they are. I saw one of their faces, and I thought maybe I had seen him before." Lydia paused for a moment, thinking about Jenny and what they did to her. "I'm not worried about them right now. I'm more concerned about my friend, Jenny Hamilton. They beat her pretty badly, and I don't know if the Department gives a damn about her."

"Well Lydia, they do. They've put out a bulletin with her picture on it and an announcement that her company has offered a hundred-thousand-dollar reward for anyone who can provide information on her whereabouts. The papers also said the police found the location where you were being held, but they said nothing about finding your friend."

They drove in silence for a while.

"I'd like to kill the bastards who did this to her," Lydia said.

Jeremy looked at her and saw that she was serious. "You wouldn't want to do that, Lydia. If you got caught, you'd go to jail."

Lydia looked at him, a question mark on her face. "Loose Cannons, maybe? A job for them?"

"What are you talking about?"

"Maybe, your guys could help with my problem."

"There's one hitch. We have a rule. We usually don't take jobs like that in the U.S. Plus you don't know who these people are."

"I don't know who they are, right now." Lydia paused, trying to decide how to frame her next question without getting a negative answer. "Was your mission overseas successful?"

"Yep."

They were now passing under Mulholland Drive overpass, and Lydia looked up. Just a few miles east of here, Jonathan's bodyguard, Carlos Aldana, had pushed her mother's dead body in a car over a cliff and made it look like she was driving drunk. Lydia had taken care of that problem, but it created a whole new set of problems, and she needed to do something about that too.

Jeremy was talking to her. "Lydia!"

Lydia broke out of her reverie. "What?"

"Are you all right? I thought I'd lost you there for a while."

"Just thinking." She was thinking that maybe Jeremy and the Loose Cannons might have a solution to her problems even though she was not certain who was causing those problems. She turned to Jeremy and tapped him on the shoulder. "Jeremy."

"What?"

"Can you tell me what you did and where?"

"No." Jeremy looked at her and shrugged. "I guess there's no harm in telling you. We blew up a manufacturing plant and made it look like someone else was responsible for it."

"What kind of plant?"

"Weapons grade nuclear."

"It didn't make the news?"

"No. The people who run that country wouldn't want to admit their security forces failed them."

"There must be some other way."

"Huh?"

"If I got rid of these people, more of them will step in and take their place."

"Excuse me, Lydia. I don't understand what you're driving at."

"I'm talking about the people who beat the hell out of an innocent woman just to get me to sign some papers. There has to be a way to destroy these people without more of them coming after me."

Lydia made coffee while Jeremy stood at the balcony window watching several overweight golfers make their way across the course. There was a ton of mail on the counter that Jeremy had brought up from the lobby.

She decided the mail could wait. There were also at least a dozen messages on her answering machine. One of them was a message from Jamie at Schroeder's Deutsche Hofbraumarkt who said it was important that she get in touch with him. There were two others that had just been recorded that morning, one from Jane Halloran at Mayes, Murphy and McBride who stated that Mr. Tanner had an urgent matter that needed to be discussed and to call him as soon as she got in. The second call was another one from Jamie who sounded on edge and said that it was urgent she return his call. He left a number that looked like it was from a cell phone.

"Who in hell is that?" Jeremy asked.

"Nobody important," Lydia said as she dialed the number for the law offices of Mayes, Murphy and McBride.

After inquiring about her health and Lydia giving the same answer she had given to many others, Reece Tanner got right to the point.

"I've got an offer for you that I'm obligated, as your attorney, to pass along."

When Lydia didn't reply, he continued, "The offer is for 10 million dollars for your signature on an assignment of rights to the Benedict property. We've got a hearing on your petition two weeks from now, and we could get rid of this problem within days after the judge makes his ruling."

"What problem are you talking about?"

"Well." He paused for a few seconds. "I assume your kidnapping is related to this issue."

"Mr. Tanner, who made the offer?"

"It came through Bill Landry's office."

"From Vince Moretti?"

"Yes."

Lydia sat the phone down on the counter and looked at Jeremy.

"Is anything wrong?" he whispered.

She shook her head and picked up the phone. "You tell that bastard that we can talk about assigning my rights away once they release Jenny Hamilton." She slammed the phone down hard on the counter.

Jeremy stared at her with a look of concern.

The phone rang again.

Lydia picked it up and shouted, "What do you want?"

"Is everything all right?"

It was Michael Honshino.

Lydia took a few seconds to settle down. "I'm all right, Mike. What's going on?"

"Grayson set up a meeting in your Captain's office. Can you be there in one hour?"

"Damn."

"We can postpone if you want. I'll tell them you aren't feeling well."

"Let's get it done, Mike. I need some time. Can you reschedule later this afternoon, say after four o'clock?"

Honshino said he would see what he could do and hung up.

"So, what's next?" Jeremy asked. "What can I do to help?"

"Can you hang around while I cancel my credit cards and checking account?"

"My day is yours."

It took Lydia less than an hour to cancel her credit cards and checking account and open new ones. Honshino telephoned and said the meeting was changed to four o'clock in the Captain's office at Century Division.

Jeremy drove Lydia to the impound lot where her BMW was stored. She was astonished at the amount of damage sustained to the car and amazed that she hadn't been seriously injured. But she didn't come to see how bad the car was damaged. She opened the rear door and looked under the seat. The envelope containing the research Billy Vernor had done for her wasn't there.

Jeremy saw the look of pain on her face. "What's wrong?"

"Something important is missing."

"What about your car? It's totaled."

"Cars can be replaced." She looked away, wondering who had the folder. She turned toward Jeremy. "I need a new car. Drive me?"

Jeremy drove her to a BMW dealership in Beverly Hills where she bought a blue BMW coupe without taking it for a test drive and paid for it by a check drawn on one of her brokerage accounts.

Before she got into her new car to go to the station, Jeremy took her aside and said he wanted to talk to her.

"You're going to work?" There was concern on his face.

"It's just for an interview. Probably won't last more than an hour."

"The doctor said you should take a week off. You should follow his advice."

"Okay."

"You're not going to listened to me, are you?"

"I won't get into a police car until I'm released by a doctor."

"Am I missing something here?"

Lydia frowned. "What are you talking about, Jeremy?"

"I'm talking about what you just said. About not getting back in a police car until you're cleared by a doctor. That leaves a lot of wiggle room."

"Wiggle room for what?"

"You know what I mean. You're going to do something I don't even want to think about."

"Jeremy, thank you for your concern. But if we keep talking like this, I'll be late for my meeting."

Jeremy took her by the shoulders and pulled her gently toward him. "I don't want to lose you, Lydia."

"Thank you, Jeremy. I really appreciate that." She turned to get into her new car.

After she settled in, Jeremy leaned in on the windowsill. "Listen," he said. "I know you. I know you aren't going to leave this alone. I know you will go after these people. Before you do anything, think twice. Call me. Maybe my crew can help."

Lydia thanked him and left him standing at the curb next to his Jeep.

Lydia met Michael Honshino in front of the station. He was on the sidewalk, looking at the plainclothes cars that lined the street.

"What's going on," Honshino asked Lydia. "Don't they have enough space in the lot for all of their cars?"

"They belong to Tactical Operations," Lydia said. "They have a robbery problem in this area."

"The one where the bandits kill the owners?"

"Yes. You know about that?"

"It was in the papers two days ago."

"They hit again?"

"Yes. At a small liquor store in Venice."

Lydia paused for a moment. Venice was an eclectic community in Pacific Division next door to Century Division. The thugs who were on a murder spree were expanding their area of operations. But why was Tactical Operations here? Did they know something about where the bandits were going to hit again?

Lydia and Honshino went in the station together. She had expected some reaction or comment from the officers she met in the hallway about her bruised face and her injuries, but nearly everyone she ran across smiled or said hello without making any reference to the ordeal she experienced.

The long table in the Captain's conference room was full. The seat at the head of the table was reserved for her with a space open to her right for Michael Honshino. Seated to her left was Lieutenant Hardemann. Next to him in line was Captain Kemper, Lieutenant Morton, and Lieutenant Linda Jeffreys, the Day Watch Commander. At the far end of the table was Sergeant Hector Maldonado from the Organized Crime Unit who always had a ready smile when he saw Lydia. On his left was his boss, Captain Malcom Smith. Also, on that side of the table was Lieutenant Peter Grayson and a very young but tough-looking lady detective that Lydia didn't know by name.

Lydia thought the placement of Grayson was strange, because as leader of the Officer-Involved-Shooting Team, this was his show.

Hardemann warmly greeted Lydia and invited her to sit down. She did so. Before he could say anything, Honshino spoke up.

"Before we begin, I'd like to reiterate the rules we have established for this meeting. First of all, I have been assured by Captain Kemper and Lieutenant Grayson that what is said in this room will not be recorded."

Lydia looked down at the table and tried to repress a smile. She knew Honshino had a small tape recorder in his jacket pocket that was probably already running.

Honshino continued. "This interview is being conducted for administrative purposes only. Anything that Officer Harte has to say in this room will not be used to discipline her or as a basis for filing criminal charges against her. Is that the understanding of everyone in this room?"

Honshino paused, making sure he got a confirmation from everyone. "And it is also understood that Lieutenant Hardemann is the only person in this room who will be asking questions. I've been told that Lieutenant Grayson has agreed to this."

"I have," Grayson said. "Captain Hardemann has had experience working for me, and he understands what we do when we investigate an O.I.S."

"Then, we may begin."

"I have a question," Lydia said, looking at Hardemann and wondering why Grayson had addressed him as Captain. She then remembered that Billy Vernor had once told her that Hardemann was next in line to be promoted to Captain.

"Yes."

"I understand they have located the place where I was being held as a prisoner."

"They have."

"What about Jenny Hamilton? Did they find her?"

"They didn't. We will be taking you there after we get done here, so you can point out the room where you last saw her."

"What is being done to find her?"

Hardemann looked at Grayson and nodded for him to respond.

"To answer your question, Officer Harte," Grayson said, "we searched the area around the factory and found no trace of her. We checked all of the hospitals in Los Angeles County and the Coroner's office, and there was no trace of her."

Lydia put the fingers of both hands to her forehead and lowered her head. The mention of the Coroner had gotten to her. She didn't want to think of Jenny Hamilton being dead.

"Are you all right?" Hardemann asked.

Lydia looked up. "I am. Let's get this damn thing over."

But Grayson wasn't finished. "We also saw no evidence that you had been there either."

Lydia looked up. "What?"

"One of the officers who picked you up told me that you appeared delusional. He thought you were coming down off drugs. He doubted if you knew what you had been doing for the past few days."

Honshino made no attempt to conceal the anger in his voice. "God-dammit Grayson, are you accusing her of being under the influence of drugs?"

"There was trace evidence of barbiturates in her blood."

"And how do you know that, Lieutenant? Did you look at her medical records without authorization?"

"We had a subpoena, counsel."

"Based on what grounds?"

"I already told you. One of the officers said she looked like she was on drugs."

Honshino was furious. "What are you trying to do, Grayson? Set her up on a murder charge?"

Hardemann interjected, "Now, hold on here. No one is trying to set up Officer Harte on any kind of charges."

Grayson ignored him. "State of mind is relevant to an investigation of an officer-involved-shooting, Counsel. You should know that by now. You've been representing police officers for nearly twenty years."

Honshino turned to Hardemann. "Can we stop this bullshit and begin?"

Before Hardemann could answer, Lydia spoke up. "A couple of days ago . . ." She stopped for a moment. Everyone was looking at her. "Anyway, I think it was a couple of days ago. They gave me some kind of drug. I don't know what it was. It made me feel lethargic."

"Do you remember how long ago that was?" Hardemann asked.

"It had to be either the same day I was kidnapped or the day after. I lost track of time. They kept me in the dark and I slept a lot."

"Did you feel lethargic when you shot that guy?" Hardemann asked.

"I wasn't lethargic. I was pissed."

Someone in back of the room started laughing but stopped when Lydia looked down the table, her face turning angry red. "I was pissed because I saw what they did to my friend."

Hardemann paused for a moment, watching Lydia closely.

"I know what you're thinking, Lieutenant," Lydia said. "I was angry, I admit that. But I wanted to get out of there and do something for Jenny.

They beat her so badly that her face was lopsided. One of her eyes bubbled out and was swollen shut. I would have killed all three of those people to get her out of there."

Lydia felt Honshino's hand touching her forearm, signaling her to stop.

After a moment, Hardemann put down his pen and looked at her. "Okay, Lydia, let's start from the beginning. What time did you leave the station after work on the morning of Thursday, March 30?"

Hardemann walked Lydia through the events that led up to the shooting step by step. The only time when he deviated from the order of events was to ask a few questions about the meaning of the document that the kidnappers wanted her to sign.

When Lydia explained what it was and the fact that she had hired an attorney to establish her rights to Jonathan Benedict's estate, there was silence for a moment. And then Hardemann asked the question that seemed to be on everyone's minds.

Did she know how much the estate was worth?

When Lydia answered that she had been told that the estate was valued over five million dollars and could be worth as much as a billion dollars, the silence in the room lasted for nearly a minute before Hardemann resumed questioning.

The interview lasted for an hour and a half. A few notes were passed down the table to Hardemann. He looked at each of them and then looked up at Lydia.

"Do you know who the people were that held you captive?"

"I don't. The man I shot was called Hank. I saw his face when I shot him. I think maybe I've seen him before, but I couldn't put a name to him." Her attention was drawn to Hector Maldonado who was hastily scribbling a note.

"Has anyone approached you before about assigning away your rights to the Benedict estate?"

"Yes. I was contacted by an attorney named Bill Landry. He was representing a guy who called himself Vince Moretti. I was offered five million dollars to assign my rights away to the estate."

"And you rejected it?"

"I countered with five-hundred million dollars."

Lydia saw Grayson shaking his head.

Hardemann was now looking at the note passed to him by Maldonado. He laid it down and looked up at Lydia. "You mentioned that you heard that the guy you shot was named Hank."

Lydia nodded.

"Do you know a man named Henry Mariani?"

"I don't know him personally, but the man I shot looked like him."

"You've met him before? I mean, before the incident?"

"I believe I have. At Oceania Manor. I believe he was an associate of Jonathan's." She was thinking that if she had the material Billy Vernor had given her, she could check his picture and see if it was him.

Hardemann looked at another note and then grimaced as if he tasted something bitter. "Officer Harte," he began slowly, looking up at her, "a whiskey bottle was found on the floorboard of your car. Was that yours?"

The question surprised Lydia. "No sir. It wasn't mine. I don't drink whiskey." She frowned and then continued. "Did they find my purse or my gun?"

Hardemann smiled. "We didn't find your purse. And we didn't find your gun."

"What about my personal papers?"

"All we found in the car was your registration and insurance information."

Hardemann looked around the room. "Any more questions before we go out to the plant?"

Captain Kemper raised his hand. "I don't have a question, but I do have a comment. Based on what I've heard, I think we need to put round-the-clock protection on Officer Harte."

"I don't need any protection," Lydia said, hurriedly. "I can take care of myself."

The last thing Lydia needed was having a surveillance team watching her every move. There were things that needed to be done that she didn't want the Department to know about.

When Lydia and Michael Honshino stepped out into the cool night air in front of the station, they found Billy Vernor standing on the sidewalk smoking a cigarette. A manila envelope was tucked under his arm.

"How bad was it?" Vernor asked Lydia.

"Do you mean my lost weekend or what happened in the Captain's office?"

"The weekend."

Lydia shook her head. "I killed a guy."

"That's usually not a good thing."

"That was the only good thing about it."

"You were beaten badly?" Vernor was staring at the fading bruises on her face.

"I was." Lydia paused for a moment as she watched Honshino walk to his car. "Billy, do you know if they are seriously looking for my friend, Jenny Hamilton? I got the feeling that some people in there don't think I'm telling the truth."

"They were looking for her yesterday. I think they called the search off this morning."

"Shit."

"I have something for you."

Vernor pulled the manila envelope out from under his arm.

Lydia recognized it immediately. "Where did you get that?"

"Hardemann found it in your car."

"Did he look at it?"

"Yes."

"What did he say?"

"Nothing. He told me to take care of it."

He handed the envelope to Lydia.

"What's wrong?" Vernor asked.

"Hardemann never mentioned it when he was asking questions about what happened to me."

"I think he's giving you a lot of slack, Lydia. If Grayson found out what was in there, he would be asking you a lot of embarrassing questions about it."

Lydia nodded her head, in deep thought. "Billy, why would he do that?"

"Do what?"

"Not ask me about what was in the folder."

"He knows where you got the information. He doesn't want to know what you're doing with it."

"He made Captain, didn't he?"

"He did. He'll be transferring to some cushy job downtown in a couple of weeks."

"Thanks, Billy. I'll see you when I get back to work."

"Maybe, sooner."

"Okay by me. Maybe we can go to lunch."

Lydia started walking toward Honshino's car but stopped when she realized the plainclothes cars that were parked earlier on the street were no longer there. She turned back toward Vernor. "I saw Tactical Operations parked out here a little earlier. Have you heard anything on the street about those killers?"

Vernor nodded. "I heard nothing useful, but I expect they'll take down another place when Tactical Operations leaves. These guys are not in it for the money. They're in it for the thrill."

When Lydia got into Honshino's car, Lydia opened the manila envelope Vernor had given her.

"What's that?" Hoshino asked.

"I need to look up something, Mike. It'll take a few seconds."

Leafing through the documents, she found what she was looking for. The picture of the man she shot. It was Henry Mariani. The same man whose name Maldonado had written in a note and passed to Hardemann to ask if she knew him.

Lydia closed the envelope and nodded at Honshino. She began thinking as Honshino pulled away from the curb. Two of the men whose names were in the envelope were dead. Hardemann had seen what was in the folder. If another one of these four ended up dead, there might be a problem if Hardemann spotted the pattern. Billy Vernor could be trusted. She wasn't entirely sure about Hardemann.

"God," she mumbled to herself. "How bad can it get?"

Honshino looked at her, thinking she was talking about the investigation into her shooting. "Take it easy, Lydia. This is a piece of cake."

Lydia realized that the meat packing plant was still being treated as a crime scene when she saw two police officers standing guard next to the gate. Honshino drove his car onto the massive lot and parked it next to two police cars where the investigating team was waiting for them.

When Lydia got out of Honshino's car, she looked around. It was dark, and the plant was lit up and no longer looked abandoned. Even the air felt fresher and cooler than when she had been here last.

"Are you ready?" Honshino asked.

"I am," Lydia said, suddenly aware that everybody was looking at her.

It took Lydia five minutes to locate the hallway where the freezers were located. She walked down the long hall with Hardemann on her left, Honshino on her right, and the others following.

"I guess I didn't realize how big this place was," Lydia said.

"Are you sure this is the area where you were held?" Hardemann asked.

"Yes," Lydia said, looking around. "I exchanged shots in this hallway with the woman. I ran down the hallway in that direction."

"Forensics went through this area," Grayson said, who was behind them. "They couldn't find any shell casings."

Hardemann glanced back at Grayson with a look that told him to shut up. He turned to Lydia, "Let's see if we can find the room where you were held."

Lydia looked at three meat locker rooms before she was sure she found the one where she had been held prisoner. It was empty. There was nothing in the room that had been there when she left, no sign of the piss pot, no sign of the table and chair, and most importantly, no sign of blood on the floor.

"How do you know this is the room?" Hardemann asked.

"Up there," Lydia said, pointing to the ceiling near the door.

They looked up.

"Do you see that hole? That's where I saw a red light. I think they had a camera up there."

Grayson shook his head. "There's nothing up there right now."

"Wait a goddam minute!" Honshino angrily said, turning toward Grayson. "Is this how you run a shooting investigation. Treating Officer Harte at every step as if she is lying?"

"I'm only doing my job, counsel."

Honshino was about to explode, but Hardemann intervened.

"He's right, Pete. Let's hold off on the skepticism. The purpose of this walkthrough is to hear the officer tell us what happened."

"But there's no goddamn blood in this room. She says she shot the guy in the face. There should be blood splattered all around."

"Maybe, they cleaned it up," Lydia said, trying desperately to keep calm.

"How sure are you that this is the room?" Hardemann asked.

"I'm positive," Lydia said.

Hardemann turned his attention back to Grayson. "We need to get Forensics back out here, Pete. If there was blood on the floor, they can find traces of it even if it has been swabbed up."

Grayson grunted.

"Okay, Lydia," Hardemann said, "let's find the room where they held your friend."

The room where Jenny had been held was easier to find. Lydia knew it was the second room down from hers. When they entered, they found it empty. The chair that Jenny had been strapped to was no longer there. There were pieces of duct tape on the floor the last time Lydia had been in this room, but there wasn't evidence of any of it on the floor now.

"How badly had she been hurt?" Hardemann asked.

"Really bad."

"Was she bleeding?"

"Yes."

Hardemann turned to Grayson. "We need Forensics in this room also."

Grayson nodded.

This was Lydia's second shooting since she had been on the job. The first one had been in a warehouse where she had fired a single shot that everyone, except the Department brass, thought had killed her partner. She knew the drill conducted by detectives in the aftermath of a police shooting and was not surprised when Hardemann had walked her through every step she had taken in her flight from the plant and located every spot where she had exchanged gunshots with the woman who held her captive.

A search of the areas where shots had been fired revealed no sign of empty cartridge casings, and Lydia was beginning to understand the reasons for Grayson's skepticism. The only evidence that Lydia was able to identify that confirmed her story was a hole in the ceiling where she believed there had been a camera.

Finally, they entered the office where Lydia had made her escape.

Lydia turned to Hardemann. "Do you remember what I told you in the office about how I had to break a window to get out of here?"

Hardemann nodded.

She pointed to the window she had broken to get out of the building. "That's the window I broke with a chair," she said.

After Grayson inspected the window, he turned to Hardemann. "It's definitely broken from the inside."

"I see that," Hardemann said. He turned toward Lydia, "Did you cut yourself when you went out the window?"

"No."

"Do you know where the woman was when you jumped out the window?"

"I don't know exactly where she was. All I know is she fired two shots at me while I was climbing a fence across the lot."

Grayson shone his flashlight around the area below the window. He looked up at Hardemann. "No empty cartridge casings here."

"They must have swept this place clean," Hardemann replied.

"Maybe," Grayson said.

"There has to be bullet holes somewhere in the plant."

"We haven't found any."

"Were you looking for them?"

"Hell, yes!"

'Then you need to look harder."

Lydia ignored them and looked out the window. The lights in the parking lot were on, and she could see the chain link fence that she had jumped over. The hill beyond it was a vague shadow.

"Lieutenant," Lydia said, forgetting that Hardemann had been promoted to Captain. "If you lend me your flashlight, I might be able to give you proof I've been here."

"How?"

"Give me the light."

Lydia took a running leap at the fence and vaulted herself over. Hardemann looked at Grayson. "Can you do that?"

"Maybe when I was in high school," Grayson said.

"She is an athlete, you know," Honshino said.

"Doctors say she has broken ribs," Hardemann said. "I sure as hell couldn't do that even when I was in high school."

They watched the flashlight bobbing as Lydia climbed the hill. When she reached the crest, she began moving along the ridge, playing the flashlight on the ground.

"What is she looking for?" Hardemann asked Honshino.

"Hell, if I know."

A minute later, Lydia called down to them. "I found it. Come on up."

"Found what?" Hardemann called back.

Lydia didn't answer.

"I suppose we need to find a way over the fence and take a look at what she found," Hardemann said, looking down at his tailored suit.

It took them five minutes to climb the hill after they found a hole in the fence. When Hardemann got to the top of the hill, he looked off in a direction he believed to be south. He saw the shadowy outline of another hill about a quarter mile across a small arroyo, its outline framed by dim city lights in the distance.

"Is that the direction you took to get out of here?" Hardemann asked Lydia, pointing to the hill.

"It is," Lydia replied. "Do you want to see what I found?"

Hardemann nodded.

Lydia shone the flashlight on the ground. A 1911 semi-automatic pistol was lying in the dirt.

"This is the gun I shot the bastard with," Lydia said.

As they were leaving the meat packing plant, Hardemann told Lydia she had nothing to worry about. It was clear that she had been held hostage for four days, and there was no evidence that she had been under the influence of drugs when she was picked up by the police on Monday morning.

The discovery of the 1911 on the hill behind the abandoned plant blunted any skepticism on the part of Grayson that Lydia was not telling the truth. He ordered Forensics out to the warehouse to go through the plant again, this time more thoroughly.

At Hardemann's insistence, Grayson took steps to have his investigators begin searching the area around the meat packing plant for any possible traces of Jenny Hamilton.

CHAPTER TWENTY-TWO

April 5, 2006. Wednesday.

ON WEDNESDAY morning, Lydia noticed that the pain in her ribs seemed sharper than it did yesterday evening. She attributed that to her foolish decision to loft herself over the chain link fence to go looking for the semi-automatic pistol. At the time, she was so excited at the prospect that the gun could still be on the hill that she forgot about her damaged ribs. Now she was paying for her mistake.

She showered and then went to the kitchen to make coffee. It was then she noticed that she had a message on her house phone.

It was another message from Jamie. Due to the urgency in his voice, Lydia listened carefully, playing the message twice. He told her in a dramatic tone of voice that he tried to warn her last week that she was going to be kidnapped, but she never returned his call. Now, it was going to happen again, and she needed to call him right away.

She didn't call Jamie right away. Instead, she called her attorney, Eric Milburn. The first thing he did was to ask Lydia how she was feeling after her ordeal. Lydia gave him the stock reply that she was fine and on the road to recovery.

Milburn then said, "I've been meaning to call you. I've got some good news."

Good news, Lydia thought. It was about time.

"I found a retired banker who did a lot of trust management," Milburn continued. "His name is Brian Thornberry. He agreed to manage your trust assets if you and he are compatible. When would you like to meet him?"

"Maybe in a few days, Mr. Milburn. Did you say he was retired?"

"He's retired, and he's bored. I get the idea that he needs to get out of the house. Even so, he won't decide to take on the job until he talks to you first."

"In other words, he wants to make sure he can work with me."

"You might say that."

"How much is his fee?"

"One hundred fifty thousand dollars plus traveling expenses, if necessary. It might sound like a lot, but it's not, considering the size of your estate. And he even knows that you have an interest in Jonathan's estate and will handle that for another fifty thousand dollars if you get title to it."

"Can you set up a meeting with him?"

"I'll do that. But you called me. What did you want?"

"I need the name and cell phone number of the manager of Schroeder's Deutsche Hofbraumarkt."

Lydia arrived early at the restaurant and gave her name to the young lady at the hostess station. She looked in the direction of the dining room and saw Jamie laying out silverware and glasses on a table. It was early and no customers had arrived yet.

Lydia asked the hostess where the ladies' room was, knowing full well that it was at the back of the restaurant. Jamie looked up at her on her way to the restroom and smiled. Lydia returned the smile.

She waited in the restroom for a full five minutes before going back out to the dining room. On her way out, she grabbed a cloth serviette from the makeup counter.

Jamie was now busy seating two customers and didn't see Lydia emerge from the restroom.

Lydia saw her chance. Using the serviette, she grabbed one of the wine glasses that had been set on the table by Jamie and stuffed it into her purse. She walked to the front of the restaurant where she was escorted to the private room by the hostess.

It was a pleasant room, small but classically decorated. Its walls were paneled in mellow oak and contained niches displaying tiny marble statutes. On the wall between the niches were miniature paintings of medieval town squares.

The hostess asked Lydia what she would like to drink, and Lydia ordered iced tea. The young lady then left the room and closed the door behind her.

A minute later, Jamie entered the room and set a glass of tea in front of Lydia. He sat down opposite her and leaned on the table with both forearms.

When Lydia met Jamie for the first time a few weeks ago, he and Sophia exchanged smart-ass comments in a light-hearted manner. But today, Jamie seemed very tense.

"They really fucked you over, didn't they?" Jamie said.

Lydia realized that Jamie was staring at the fading purple and yellow bruises on her face. "Why did you ask to meet me?" Lydia said, ignoring his question. "You said something about me being kidnapped again."

"Yes, yes," Jamie said. "But I need information from you in exchange."

Lydia scooted her chair back and stood up. "You lured me here under false pretenses? So you can get information?"

"Wait, wait," Jamie said, holding up his hands. "I have information you need. All I'm asking for is a guarantee."

Lydia slowly sat back down. "What kind of guarantee?"

"Did Sophia tell you who I am?"

Lydia shrugged. "Actually, I don't know who you are. I don't even know your last name."

"But she told you the F.B.I. is looking for me, right?"

"She said something like that."

Lydia began wondering why on earth she didn't tell Maldonado about what Sophia told her about Jamie. The Organized Crime Unit would surely like to know who this guy was, and what he did that made him go underground.

"Actually, it's not the Feds I'm worried about," Jamie explained. "It's LAPD. There's some asshole in the headquarters building that's got a hard on for me." Jamie glanced nervously over his shoulder and then back at Lydia. "Look, I know you're LAPD. I know you could have reported me but didn't. What I want is a guarantee that you won't tell anyone about me. That's the quid pro quo. You guarantee my anonymity, and I'll keep you clued into what they're planning. If you don't give me a guarantee, I'll have to move and find a new place to work. I don't want to do that. I like working here."

Lydia folded her arms. "Who are the people you're talking about?"

"The people who kidnapped you. They're going to do it again. If I get the guarantee, I'll give you the names and tell you what they're planning to do."

Lydia thought about the proposition. Was this guy naïve? Did he really believe her guarantee would be honored?

"How do you know I would keep my promise?" Lydia said. "What if I said I won't tell anyone about you and then went ahead and did it?"

"Because Sophia said you could be trusted. I trusted her. You haven't told anyone about me yet, so I trust you. Besides, I know a few things about you that you wouldn't like your cop buddies to know."

"Like what?"

"Like there's a rumor going around that you killed Jonathan."

Lydia smiled. It was more than a rumor that she had killed Jonathan.

"Okay," Lydia said. "You got a deal. But there's something I need to find out. What happened to Jenny Hamilton?"

Jamie frowned. "Who's Jenny Hamilton?"

"You don't know who she is?"

"No."

"She is my friend. Whoever kidnapped me kidnapped her. They tried to use her to get me to sign a document."

Jamie nodded. "I know who you're talking about. They dropped her off in the desert up in Palmdale."

Lydia felt her heart fluttering. It was a feeling she had never experienced before. "Did they kill her?" she asked, holding her breath.

"I don't know for sure. I just know they dumped her in the desert."

"Where exactly did they dump her?"

"I don't know. Look, if she was dead, they would have buried her. But they didn't."

"Can you find out from someone where they dumped her?"

"Only if somebody brings it up. I can't just ask them."

"Who are these people you're talking about?"

"Roberto Moreno and his wife, Angela. They're the ones who kidnapped you, along with Henry Mariani."

Lydia was silent for a moment. She felt an urgent need to get out of this room and begin looking for Jenny even though she knew that was not possible without knowing the exact location where they left her.

"You said they were going to kidnap me again."

"Yes."

"When?"

"I don't know. They're bringing two guys in from Las Vegas to handle it."

"Why do they need someone from Las Vegas?"

"They specialize in this kind of thing. They have a way of making people do things they don't want to do."

"Okay," Lydia said. "Thank you for the information."

"So, do we have a deal?"

"What? . . . oh, yes . . . we have a deal, Jamie."

"Do you want to order something? After all, you own the place."

"No thanks. I have something to do."

Lydia picked up her purse and stood up. She cringed when she heard the wine glass in her purse clink against her car keys, but Jamie seemed not to notice.

Fifteen minutes later, Lydia entered the detective squad room at Century Division. Vernor was sitting at his desk alone, still without a partner. The other burglary team consisting of Finlayson and Gordon was not at the desk-table they shared with Vernor.

Vernor saw her coming and stood up, his face turning red. "What in hell are you doing here, Lydia? You're off-duty! You're supposed to be at home resting!"

"I need to use the phone for a minute, Billy. I think I know where they dumped Jenny. She might be in Palmdale."

"How do you know that?"

"I'm not the only one in this building that has informants."

"Bullshit," Vernor said as he sat down. "Do you need help finding her?"

"I do. Are you going to help?"

"Where do we check first? The morgue or the hospital?"

Lydia grimaced. "The morgue."

Vernor opened a desk drawer and pulled out a County Directory. He handed it to Lydia. "The County morgue is in Lancaster, a few miles north of Palmdale. What is Jenny's last name?"

"Hamilton," Lydia said.

"You check the morgue. I'll get a list of hospitals in the area and start calling."

Lydia was relieved when she learned that the Coroner's office in Lancaster didn't have an unidentified body in storage. When she hung up the phone, she saw Vernor talking on the other phone. He pushed a hand-written note across the table. There were two major hospitals in Palmdale, the Palmdale Regional Medical Center and Antelope Valley Hospital. The Regional Medical Center was checked off. Lydia reached for the phone on her side of the table and started to dial the number for the Antelope Valley Hospital when she became aware that someone was standing next to the desk.

She looked up and saw Hardemann.

"What's up?" Hardemann asked.

"We're trying to see if one of the hospitals in Palmdale has someone fitting the description of Jenny Hamilton," Lydia said.

Vernor held up a hand, asking them to be quiet. They watched him as he listened on the telephone for a good minute. Finally, he said, "Thank you," and set the phone down, and looked across the table at Lydia.

"They have an unidentified woman in her twenties who was found lying across some railroad tracks by a farm worker," Vernor said. He looked at Hardemann. "Shall I let Grayson know?"

"No. Let's make sure it's the person we're looking for." Hardemann turned to Lydia. "Are you in good enough condition to travel?"

"To Palmdale? Absolutely!"

Palmdale was only sixty-two miles away from West Los Angeles, but it took them nearly an hour to navigate the traffic on the freeways before they even reached the Antelope Valley Freeway. Once there, they drove through desert-tan hills and jagged rock formations before they reached the desert plain that led into Palmdale. Ahead of them was a flat, listless city that was surrounded by square plots of barren land and farms that relied on irrigation to grow crops and fruit trees.

Palmdale Regional Medical Center was a modern hospital located southeast of the city's center. They were met in the lobby by a detective named Obregon from the Palmdale Sheriff's station. He took them aside to a small room off the lobby and asked why they were interested in the woman. Lydia ignored him and asked Obregon how badly she was hurt.

Obregon looked at her, a curious expression on his face. "Are you a member of the family?"

Lydia took offense. "She's my friend," Lydia said, barely holding back her temper.

Hardemann butted in before Lydia could explode. "Officer Harte is a police officer. She was kidnapped and so was her friend who is still missing. I explained this on the phone to your lieutenant. We have information she was dumped in the desert near Palmdale. We think the woman you have in this hospital might be her."

"What's the friend's name?"

"Jenny Hamilton," Lydia said. "The last time I saw her was either last Saturday or Sunday."

"Well, this might be the person you're looking for. She was discovered Monday morning lying on the railroad tracks near 116th. Street."

According to Obregon, the woman was discovered in the early morning hours by an employee of a citrus orchard who saw a truck or large SUV drive onto a dirt road located on the western border of the orchard. The employee thought it might be railroad maintenance personnel, but when he saw the vehicle leave a few minutes later, he saw no markings on its sides. He became suspicious and decided to investigate. He got into a utility vehicle and drove along the railroad tracks to see if any damage had been done to the orchard's property. It was on his way back when he saw a naked woman lying across the tracks. When he saw she was alive, he picked her up, placed her in the cargo bed of the utility vehicle, and drove back to the warehouse to call 911.

Lydia sucked in air when she saw the battered woman. A tube was inserted in her mouth and oxygen was being fed through tubes in her nose. Her face was a shapeless mass of abrasions and contusions.

"Is it her?" a voice said behind Lydia.

"It looks like her," Lydia replied. "But her face . . ."

"Are you sure?"

She turned to look to see who had spoken. Vernor was standing behind her. Hardemann and Obregon were standing near the door.

"She had a tattoo," Lydia mumbled.

"Where?" Vernor said.

Lydia moved to the head of the bed.

"Wait!" Obregon said. "I'll get a nurse."

Obregon left the room.

"Where is the tattoo?" Vernor asked.

"On the back of her leg, just above the ankle. A red rose."

A minute later, Obregon came back with a nurse.

The nurse pulled the blanket away from the feet and lifted the left foot. Lydia leaned down to see the back of the leg.

Nothing was there.

The nurse lifted the right foot. Lydia moved around the bed. There wasn't a single rose tattoo on the woman's leg. There was a cluster of a half dozen red roses just above the ankle.

The rest of the night and the early morning was a fog in Lydia's mind. When she saw the red roses, the life seemed to flow out of her. The nurse caught her as she nearly fell to the floor. She was led to an easy chair by the nurse who carefully examined her. She heard voices, talking about her, talking about leaving her there while they went out to the railroad tracks.

There was an argument. Vernor and Hardemann were trying to convince someone in charge that Lydia should stay there for a few hours and they would come back for her. They left. The room was darkened, and Lydia fell into a deep sleep.

Lydia was awakened hours later when the lights in the room came on.

Vernor entered the room. "Come on, Lydia. We're done here. We need to get back to L. A."

Lydia got up from her chair and looked at Jenny. Her breathing was slow but steady.

"I need to see her doctor," Lydia said.

"I already have," Vernor said. "She's going to be okay."

"But why is she unconscious?" Lydia looked down at Jenny's face and felt tears forming in her eyes. "It's been how many days since she's been here?"

"She's in an induced coma."

Lydia looked up at Vernor. "That means she has brain damage, doesn't it?"

"Not so," Vernor replied. "The doctor expects a full recovery." He looked impatiently at the door. "It's late. We need to get going."

Lydia was sitting in the back seat of the car as Vernor drove to L. A. She was thinking about what had happened to Jenny. She was also thinking about what she needed to do. She needed a plan to deal with the people who did this to Jenny, a proper plan, a plan that would take care of these people once and for all.

Her reverie was broken when she heard Vernor say something to Hardemann about tire tracks.

She leaned forward to listen. They were talking about the railroad tracks where Jenny had been found. Lydia broke into the conversation and asked what they had seen there.

Vernor said they found recent tire tracks in the area. They called Lieutenant Grayson who came out to the scene with a woman from Forensics. After the woman measured and photographed the tire prints, she concluded that the tire marks probably came from a large pickup truck or Humvee.

Lydia sat back in her seat, thinking. Why did they do this to Jenny? Why lay her on the railroad tracks? Why not just kill and bury her?

She didn't realize that she had been thinking aloud until Vernor turned and answered her question.

"It's a message."

"What?" Lydia said.

"Whoever did that to your friend. It was a message."

A message to me, Lydia thought.

By the time, they got back to West Los Angeles, Lydia had an idea of what she needed to do to answer that message. How she was going to accomplish that was another matter altogether.

CHAPTER TWENTY-THREE

April 6, 2006. Thursday

LYDIA WAS making coffee in her kitchen when she noticed that the light on the answering machine was blinking. It was two o'clock in the afternoon. When she picked up the phone to listen to the message, she saw it had come in earlier that morning. The call was from Jamie. He told her he had just learned that the two men from Vegas were in town and were asking about her address.

She called him at the restaurant. When he answered, she got right to the point.

"Who are these guys?"

"I told you. They're from Las Vegas."

"What do they look like?"

"I don't know. I've never met or seen them before."

Lydia paused for a moment.

Jamie continued. "I don't know them by sight or name. All I know is they are in town, and you need to be careful."

"How do you know this?"

"I stay in touch."

"With whom?"

"Robert Moreno." Jamie paused. "Actually, his wife. They want another crack at you."

Lydia slammed the phone down in anger. She hastily made coffee and threw the spoon in the sink. She went out to the balcony and sat down, barely noticing the nice weather and a foursome of inept golfers plodding across the course.

She began thinking about her options. Should she call the station and ask for help? If she did that, they would assign someone to follow her. That was not an option. She knew Hardemann would help, but there would be questions, like who gave her that information? She didn't want to tell anyone at LAPD about Jamie. Not yet anyway. If she did, they would pick him up, and she didn't want that. Jamie was a useful source of information.

Five minutes later, she dumped the coffee in the sink and went down to the lobby. A few weeks back, she had been followed by a surveillance team from Robbery-Homicide. They had parked their car in a driveway alongside the building across the street. There was no car parked there today.

She stepped outside under the porte cochère.

Pedersen, the security guard, joined her. "Nice day, isn't it?" Pedersen said.

"Yes, it is." Lydia turned to him and said, "Mr. Pedersen, do you remember a few weeks back when you thought you saw an undercover police car parked across the street?"

"I do. Are you expecting any trouble?"

Pedersen was looking at her warily, and Lydia knew she had to come up with some bullshit to ease his mind. "I've had a problem with a stalker, and I'm afraid he may have followed me home."

"Are you in any danger? I mean . . ."

"I don't know, but I would appreciate it if you would let me know if you see anyone hanging around that doesn't belong here."

Lydia made a few phone calls when she returned to her apartment. The first was to Jeremy who asked how she was feeling. Lydia brushed aside the question and asked if he could come down to dinner tonight.

Jeremy's response was guarded. "Is there anything the matter? You sound different."

Lydia told him about what Jamie had said. After she was finished, Jeremy was quiet for so long that Lydia thought the call had been dropped.

"Are you still there?" she asked.

"Yes, I am. Just thinking."

"Okay, so what do I do?"

"Nothing. Let me take care of it."

"What about dinner?"

"That's part of what I have in mind."

"What do you have in mind?"

"Lydia, I know how independent and stubborn you are. But you have to listen to me."

"Okay."

"Are you listening to me? Really listening?"

Lydia sighed. "Yes."

"Okay then. First of all, do not go out. Do not open your door for anyone but me. I'll pick you up at seven."

"I need to do some shopping."

"What kind of shopping?"

"Food."

"Don't."

"What should I do about those guys from Las Vegas?"

"No worries. Let me take care of them. I've got to go now. A problem on the range. Pick you up at seven. Don't go anywhere."

He hung up, leaving Lydia looking at the phone.

Fifteen minutes later, Lydia got a call from Eric Milburn. He told her that Brian Thornberry would like to meet her in Milburn's office tomorrow afternoon at 3:00 p.m.

That was fine with Lydia. She already had an idea of what she was going to do about Jonathan's estate, but she needed information from both Milburn and Thornberry to determine if her plan was feasible.

"Mr. Milburn," Lydia asked, "how much do you know about my mother's shipping business?"

Milburn's reply was guarded. "A fair amount. I did a lot of work for your mother, so I got to know a little bit about the business."

"Does the company ship to areas where maritime piracy is prevalent?"

"They do. They occasionally travel to the Middle East through the Indian Ocean."

"Do you know how often they do that?"

"A lot. Several times a month."

"Are we insured for this type of thing?"

"For piracy?"

"Yes."

"Your company has insurance against piracy."

"Is it expensive?"

"Yes."

"What can we do to decrease the risk?"

"I imagine the surest guarantee would be to stop shipping through any area where piracy is a problem."

"How much business would we lose?"

"I'm not sure, dollar wise. Maybe twenty percent. Maybe thirty. I would have to inquire to be more specific."

"Are there any alternatives to decrease the risk?"

"Just the one I mentioned above. Avoid shipping in that area. You might discuss this with Mr. Thornberry when you meet him. Tell him what you have in mind. If he agrees to work for you, he could research this issue and give you a better answer."

Lydia thanked him and hung up.

Lydia was waiting at the lobby door at 7:00 p.m. when Sandling, the night security guard, came out the door and stood alongside her. She looked up at him expecting a comment from him about the way she was dressed, but the man was not at all interested in the form-fitting, sheath she was wearing. He was looking across the street.

"Pedersen told me to tell you that he spotted a man in the shrubs alongside the driveway over there," the security guard said. "He called the police, but the man was gone when they arrived."

Lydia nodded and stared across the street at the bushes lining the driveway. They were thick and could easily hide someone.

"Do you think he might have come back?"

"Don't think so. I went over there to check just a few minutes ago."

"Thank you."

Sandling turned to go back inside but stopped. "You look very nice this evening."

"Thank you, again, Mr. Sandling." Lydia had checked a mirror before leaving her apartment to make sure her makeup covered the bruises on her face and that her wig was on straight.

A few minutes later, Jeremy drove into the circular drive. He was out of his Jeep to open the door for Lydia but stopped when he saw she had already gotten into the vehicle.

Lydia was not smiling when Jeremy got back into the Jeep. "The guard told me that they saw a man hiding in the bushes across the street this afternoon."

"They're not there now."

"I know that, but how do you know?"

"They're a block down the street. One is sitting on a bus bench. The other one has been standing by an ATM for the past thirty minutes. He's been looking up and down the street as if he is waiting for someone."

"Maybe, we shouldn't go out."

"Why not?"

"Because they might follow us. They want me, but they don't need you. The first thing they would do is to shoot you."

"I don't think so, "Jeremy said. "The biggest mistake these guys will make in their miserable life is if they follow us."

"You got plans for them?"

"I got plans for you. Dinner and a nice bottle of wine. Those guys won't be bothering us."

Jeremy didn't drive straight to the restaurant. He took a route that Lydia had never taken before. He went south through a residential neighborhood and then turned west into a dark industrial district.

About ten minutes after they left Lydia's condo building, Jeremy got a call on his cell phone. He answered, listened, said, "Okay," and then hung up. He turned to Lydia. "The boys from Vegas will be taking an unexpected tour of the mountains."

Lydia smiled.

Once they were seated at a trendy Italian restaurant called Ferrentino's in Santa Monica and ordered a bottle of wine, Jeremy leaned over the table to take a closer look at Lydia's face. A lit candle cast a soft yellow glow on her face. He pushed the candle off to one side.

Lydia frowned.

"You shouldn't do that," Jeremy said. "It makes you look mean."

"Do what?"

"Frown."

"I know I shouldn't do that," Lydia said. "It still hurts."

"What hurts?"

"The bruises on my face."

"I don't see any bruises," Jeremy said as he leaned in for a closer look.

"They're under my makeup."

Jeremy smiled. Lydia held out her hand. Jeremy took it, held it gently, and looked at it.

"What are you thinking?" Jeremy asked as he looked back up at Lydia.

"About those two guys. There will be more."

"All you need to do is to let me know, and I will take care of them."

"I've been thinking about a more permanent solution."

Jeremy sat back in his chair. "Oh, oh."

"Do you mind if I ask you for some professional advice?"

Jeremy shrugged. "Ask away."

"I'm wondering why I even bothered with Jonathan's estate." Lydia looked away for a moment. "I had real doubts about going after it, but I went ahead and did it anyway. I guess I was just curious about who wanted it so badly."

"It's not too late to back out of it then, is it?" Jeremy said. "You can cancel that thing you got going in court."

"But that won't make the problem go away. These people will keep coming after me until they get what they want. They'll try and kidnap me again. Or worse yet, go after someone close to me to force me to give them what they want. This won't go away as long as the property they want exists."

"You could hire a bodyguard. You can afford it."

"That won't make the problem go away."

"Is there anything I can do to help?"

Lydia gave a slight shrug. She took a sip of wine and set the glass down forcefully. "Does your group ever operate in the United States?"

"We haven't in the past. Two of my guys are against it."

"Would you consider it?"

"I imagine we would take on a job in the U.S. if it looked like something we could do in keeping with our standards."

Lydia saw that a man and woman at the table next to them was listening to their conversation. She leaned forward and whispered. "What are your standards?"

Jeremy also lowered the tone of his voice. "We don't accept collateral damage. And we wouldn't ever do something in the U.S. where there was the remotest chance of that ever happening. There are too many people in Washington who would recognize our style."

Lydia gripped his hand and lightly squeezed it. "Have you ever worked for a private person?"

"All the time, but only if we get paid up front."

"And your standard fee is five million dollars?"

"Yes. No exceptions. No discounts." Jeremy squeezed her hand. "What's on your mind?"

"Just thinking."

"You said that before. What are you thinking of?"

"The possibilities."

The two men who had been watching the condo building were sent down from Las Vegas to deal with Lydia. Their names were Junior Tizano and Mikey Balter.

Tizano was a short man, dark featured, and nearly bald except for a ring of coal black hair that circled the back of his head and covered his ears. Tizano was the handsomer of the two men, but that wasn't saying much because his taller partner, Balter, had a face that was so pitted it looked like the surface of the moon. Both men wore expensive suits and carried recently stolen Colt 1911 pistols that had been provided to them by a guy named Moreno who met them in a coffee shop not far from the airport. They were also given keys to a dark blue Mustang that had been stolen off a long-term pay parking lot just that morning.

The two men were good at what they do, but the first time they had ever been taken by surprise while on a job was that night.

"That was too easy," Tizano told Balter as he began following the Jeep that contained the woman they were told to grab.

The driver of the Jeep began driving swiftly as if he knew exactly where he was going. Tizano had no problems keeping up with him. He followed the Jeep into Culver City where it drove a few blocks through a residential neighborhood and then turned sharply into an industrial area.

Tizano stepped on the gas and followed. When he turned into the industrial area, a trash truck, its lights on, was parked at an oblique angle, blocking most of the road. The Jeep was no longer in sight. Tizano stopped the Mustang and swore under his breath. He was going to lose their best chance to grab the girl if he didn't get around this truck in a hurry.

Balter reached over and hit the horn.

"What the fuck are you doing here?" Tizano yelled. "Keep your paws off the fucking horn! I'm driving here!"

Tizano realized something his partner hadn't. There was no need to blow the horn to get the attention of the man behind the wheel of the truck. There might be enough room between the rear of the truck and the dock behind it to get past. Tizano turned the steering wheel and began driving toward the rear of the truck.

There was enough room to pass all right, but it was going to be close. He began inching the car forward. Just when the nose of the Mustang nudged into the space behind the dump truck, the truck lurched backward, hit the front end of the Mustang, and pushed it into the dock wall.

"What the fuck is he doing!" Balter screamed.

Tizano put the car in reverse and jammed his foot on the accelerator. The Mustang's rear wheels spun uselessly. The front end of the car was wedged between the dump truck and the dock and wouldn't move.

"I'm going to kill the motherfucker who did this," Tizano screamed. He opened the door and got out of the car.

In the dim light, Tizano saw two men standing a few feet behind the Mustang. Pissed, he walked toward them, thinking that one of them might be the driver of the trash truck and intending to give him a piece of his mind. He froze when he saw they were wearing black ski masks and black utilities. Worse yet, the men were pointing AR-15s at Tizano, and it looked like they knew how to use them.

Tizano didn't have time to even think about reacting because someone hit him on the head with a blunt object.

When Tizano woke up, he had the sensation that the world was rocking. He looked up and saw nothing. It was dark. He heard the deep-throated rumble of an engine and the thrumming sound of tires rolling over the highway. He tried to move but couldn't. His hands were tied behind his back and his feet were tied together. He tried to roll onto his side but couldn't.

"Are you awake?" a voice said out of the blackness.

"That you, Mikey?" The sound of his own voice started a vibration in his head. "Where the fuck are we?"

"In the back of a fucking pickup."

"I can't see anything. I'm going blind."

"You're not blind, stupid. There's a cover over us."

Tizano considered this for a moment, thinking of all the enemies he had made in his long miserable life.

"Who are these guys, Mikey?"

"I don't know. When the boss finds out what they did to us, they're dead meat."

It was quiet for a while. Just the sound of the engine and the rough humming of the tires.

"My feet are cold, Mikey."

"They took our shoes and socks off."

"Why the fuck did they do that?"

"I don't know."

"They're going to kill us, Mikey."

"I don't think so. They're wearing masks. If they were going to kill us, they would have taken them off. They said they were going to drop us off on a mountain."

"Shit!"

"What?"

"Maybe you heard wrong. Maybe they said they were going to drop us off a mountain."

The truck slowed down and made a turn. Seconds later, the bed of the truck began bouncing. They were now travelling on a dirt road. The heads of the two men bounced on the metal floorboard like basketballs.

Fifteen minutes later, the truck stopped. And then it backed up and turned in one direction, then stopped, and turned again. Tizano heard doors opening. A minute later, the tailgate opened, and someone pulled Tizano out of the cargo space. He fell to the ground. Someone grabbed him by the shirt and roughly pulled him to his feet.

Tizano's attention was on a man who now held him by his shirt. He was not wearing a ski mask, but it was so dark that Tizano could barely make out his face. The man shoved him, and Tizano found himself standing beside Balter. In the dim light, he could see four men, two of them pointing rifles at him and Balter. None of them were wearing ski masks.

"Now listen up assholes," one of the men said. "Look off to your right."

Tizano did. Far below them, miles off, was the glow of lights of a small town.

"That's where you need to go. It's a truck stop called Gorman. When you get off this mountain . . . if you get off this mountain, you will hitch a ride to Bakersfield. You will not ever come back to L. A. again. Do you understand me?"

"We sometimes got business in L. A.," Balter said.

One of the men carrying a rifle stepped forward and slammed the butt into his gut, knocking him flat on his back.

"You," the man said in a menacing voice, "will never go back to L. A. again. You got that? Instead, you will go to Bakersfield. You will catch a plane or a bus out of California and not come back. Do you understand me?"

Balter nodded his head up and down.

The man pulled Balter up to his feet. He cut the plastic cuffs off his wrists with a box knife and looked Balter directly in the face. His breath smelled of cigars.

"Don't try and take a shortcut off this mountain. There are mountain lions up here. You wouldn't want to wake up one of those beauties. They get pissed off when they don't get their sleep. Go down the dirt road. It looks like it's going in the opposite direction, but it will take you down to the highway. If you're lucky, you might even catch a ride to Gorman."

He handed the box knife to Balter. "Cut your idiot friend loose after we leave."

The man with the cigar breath snapped his fingers, and one of the other men stepped forward, holding something up in his hand.

"We're going to give you back your wallets. We took money to pay for our gas, but we left your credit cards. We also took your driver's licenses.

Remember what I said. L. A. is fucking off limits. We know who you are. We knew when you got into town, and we'll know if you come back."

Tizano and Balter watched the men get into the pickup truck and drive off. They looked at each other, shrugged, and began gingerly walking down the rock-studded road in their bare feet.

Minutes before Jeremy dropped Lydia off at the front door of her condo building, he received a call on his cell phone. He answered, said nothing, and listened. When he put the phone back in his jacket pocket, he looked at Lydia. "You're not going to have to worry about those two men following you again."

Lydia smiled. "Where are they?"

Jeremy shrugged. "Somewhere up in the mountains, about a dozen miles from Gorman."

"Dead?"

Jeremy shook his head. "The last I heard was that they were walking off the mountain barefooted."

"What if they come back to L. A.?"

"They won't be coming back to L. A. Not after my boys had a chat with them. Take my word for it."

The first thing Lydia did when she got back to her apartment was to change into her jogging clothes. She grabbed a knit cap and headed out the front door.

It was well after midnight when Lydia turned her BMW onto Stone Canyon Drive. The area was upper-class residential. Most had landscape lighting, but very few of the houses had their interior lights on. She found the address she was looking for, the house that Roberto Moreno shared with his wife, Angela Rossi, and drove past it. Two blocks up the street, she made a U-turn and came back down Stone Canyon, this time driving slowly so she could get a good look at the house.

The front room was on the right side of the house. The porch light was on, and the interior of the house was dimly lit. To the left of the front door was a three-car garage and a driveway that was illuminated by two lights mounted on ornate lamp posts on either side of the driveway. There were no cars in the driveway.

A sidewalk ran along the left side of the garage, leading up to a wrought iron gate with a light above it. The sidewalk behind the gate continued up an incline until it disappeared into the darkness.

Lydia concluded that the house had multiple levels and was partially set into a gently sloping hillside. She decided she would come back tomorrow night and enter the property through the wrought iron gate on the side of the garage. If there was a lock securing the gate, a small crowbar could take care of it.

She would also bring along a .45 Springfield XD semi-automatic with two spare magazines which she kept in the Jeep she stored in the rented garage. It was one of the guns she had taken out of the display vault in the ruins of Oceania Manor. If she had to use the gun, it would be untraceable to her.

CHAPTER TWENTY-FOUR

April 7, 2006. Friday

ON FRIDAY morning, Lydia called the Palmdale Regional Medical Center to see how Jenny was doing. Even after Lydia tried explaining she was a police officer and a friend, they refused to give out any information regarding Jenny's condition. She then called the Palmdale Sheriff's Station and left a message for Obregon to call her.

Michael Thornberry was a short stocky man who wore a pristine charcoal gray suit and a scarlet bow tie. Lydia always had a negative feeling about men who wore bow ties because nearly everyone she had met who wore one turned out to be a little odd.

Lydia was introduced to Thornberry by her attorney, Eric Milburn, in his office. Milburn seated them in easy chairs around the coffee table that had a small statue of a rickety old man on horseback holding a forward-pointing lance.

While Milburn went to arrange for coffee, Thornberry immediately begin talking about the assets controlled by Lydia and how he intended to manage them if he was hired by her. He was still talking five minutes later when Milburn brought in a coffee service and sat down.

By the time Thornberry finished with his spiel, Lydia had changed her opinion about men who wore bow ties. He was obviously competent and knew what he was doing.

When Thornberry finished his presentation, he sat back in his chair. "I hope I haven't bored you."

"You haven't." Lydia must have seemed bored, or he wouldn't have asked that question. She had other things on her mind.

"Do you have any questions?" Thornberry asked.

Lydia didn't respond. Instead, she stared at the statute of the man who thought windmills were dangerous. Was she like him? Was she just as screwed up as the man on horseback?

"Do you have any reservations about what Mr. Thornberry said?" Milburn asked.

Lydia had been so busy thinking about Thornberry's bow tie, she had not even noticed how oddly Milburn was dressed. He was wearing a white short-sleeve shirt with white riding pants. The bottom half of the pants seemed cleaner than the rest, looking as if he had been wearing tall boots. Lydia looked at the statute of the old man on horseback again. If you took away the helmet and the lance, the old man's physique resembled Milburn's. The whole effect of what she was seeing reminded her of how quixotic her plans were for dealing with the problem that confronted her.

"Actually," Lydia said, "I would like to hire Mr. Thornberry. But I have some questions, and I'm afraid that if I ask them, he might not want to work for me."

It was silent in the room for a good full minute, the two men staring at Lydia. Thornberry leaned forward and put two teaspoons of sugar in the cup of coffee Milburn had poured for him. He took a sip, frowned, and set the cup back down, spilling some of the coffee into the saucer. He looked up at Lydia.

"I will do anything you ask, provided it's not illegal. I might go so far as to say, my actions might bump into the side of law, but I never break it. What did you want to ask?"

"How would I go about drawing a million dollars a year out of my estate for five years without raising questions?" Lydia calmly said.

Thornberry cocked his head. "Are you talking about using income generated from your properties?"

"Yes."

"Would you be doing something illegal with the money?"

"No," she said, "I will be paying someone for doing a service."

"You could be talking about money laundering."

Lydia thought about this, realizing what Thornberry was saying, realizing what she had in mind had to at least look legit, although it might raise some questions if someone was interested enough to find out why she was doing it.

"It would be for a legitimate service, for security to protect my assets," Lydia replied.

"Okay," Thornberry said slowly. "I'm not sure I would want to get involved with this without knowing more."

"You can trust her, Brian," Milburn said. "I have known her and her mother for a good number of years. I can vouch for her honesty."

Lydia had to fight off a smile. She was honest all right. Being a murderous vigilante had nothing to do with being honest.

"Well, you do have some liquid assets," Milburn said. "About eight hundred thousand dollars."

"When can it be withdrawn?" Lydia asked.

"The quickest way would be to wire the money."

"I need it in cash."

Milburn glanced at Thornberry and then looked at Lydia. "I imagine we could get it by end of business on Monday."

"And the rest?" Lydia was hoping that Thornberry would bring up the shipping company without her having to lead him into it.

Milburn intervened. "Brian, this is what Lydia asked me about the other day. I believe she's thinking about hiring a security firm to protect her shipping company from piracy."

"But you do know your company is insured for this kind of risk," Thornberry said to Lydia. "And it's cheaper than what you're thinking of doing."

"I just don't want to be insured for risk," Lydia said. "I want absolute security against piracy. If we had that, there would be no need for insurance at all."

Thornberry stared at the statue of the old man on horseback. After what seemed an eternity, he looked up.

"Okay, if I found a way for you to do this, I would want a letter of authorization from you telling me what you intend to do with the money. I would want the money to be characterized as a legitimate business expense. Even then, it may provoke the interest of the IRS."

"You'll get my letter, and it will be characterized as a legitimate business expense."

"Then I think I can do this," Thornberry said, getting up. "I'll get back to you by tomorrow."

On the way home, Lydia stopped and bought a small crowbar from a hardware store. Her cell phone began ringing when she got back into the BMW. She pulled over to the curb to take the call.

It was Obregon from the Palmdale Sheriff's Station.

"I called the hospital. Your friend is still in a coma, but she is otherwise stable. I also talked to the head nurse. You can call the nurse's station at any time for an update. Just ask for the nurse supervisor on duty. They'll even let you visit. Make sure, you don't run across her parents when you do. They're really pissed at you and her boyfriend."

Lydia was stunned at hearing this. Jenny had never talked about her parents. The only thing that Lydia recalled Jenny saying about her family was that she was glad they lived somewhere on the coast above San Francisco.

"You told her parents everything about what happened?" Lydia said.

"I did. They weren't too happy."

"Why are they mad at Rod?"

"Rod?"

"The boyfriend."

"You haven't heard this story?"

"What story?"

"Jenny's father was a judge. In L.A. County. He was disbarred. The boyfriend had something to do with it."

"What happened?"

"I don't know the details. I remember reading about it in the newspapers. The judge didn't go quietly. He turned on everybody in the courthouse. Kept the gossip columnists busy for weeks."

Lydia thought about what Obregon had said on her way home. No wonder Jenny didn't want to talk about her family. Then, a thought occurred to her. What if Jenny didn't come out of the coma? What if Jenny died?

She shut her eyes far too long before she realized what she was doing. Her car was drifting over the double yellow line. She corrected it.

By the time she entered West Los Angeles, she cleared her mind of all thoughts of Jenny and began thinking about what she had to do later that night. She couldn't take her BMW to Stone Canyon. She needed to rent a vehicle that was so new it had temporary plates. She stopped at a car rental agency and asked for the newest car they had. It turned out to be a small Toyota SUV that had the features Lydia wanted the most . . . a temporary license made of flimsy paper pasted to the rear window. The lady at the service counter asked Lydia about the Jeep that she had previously rented. She told them to extend the rental for another week.

When Lydia got home, she parked the SUV on the street. Before going inside, she took a picture of the temporary license plate on the rear window with her cell phone. Once in her apartment, she got onto her computer and began searching for a numerical font that matched the numbers used on the temporary plate. When she found what she wanted, she printed out seven numbers on white paper, intending to paste the numbers over the temporary plate. They weren't a perfect match, but they were close enough to pass inspection if a picture of the plate was taken by a traffic camera.

Lydia spent the rest of the afternoon thinking about the things that could go wrong when she broke into the Moreno residence. Was there a private security patrol in the area? If so, how often did they come around? When she had last visited the area, she remembered seeing several alarm company signs posted in the front yards along Stone Canyon. She didn't bother to look to see if any of them had mentioned private patrol. On her last visit, she didn't recall seeing any sidewalks in the area. She wondered if it would be unusual to see a jogger running in the road later at night.

By six o'clock, Lydia thought she had looked at everything that could possibly go wrong.

She was mistaken.

Lydia had no problem finding a parking place on Stone Canyon Drive. Most of the residential lots were so small that cars had to be parked on the street. She found a spot that was only three blocks away from the Moreno residence. The Springfield XD in her belly band holster was larger than what she was used to, and the bulk of it felt uncomfortable riding on her right hip.

She put on a black watch cap that matched the sweats she was wearing, put on a pair of gloves, and began jogging up the road. One minute later, she noticed a tiny pinpoint of red light about eight feet up on a light standard. She barely had gotten pass it when she saw another one on the opposite side of the road.

Damn! Infrared cameras were taking her picture.

When she jogged past another one, she stopped to check it out. It looked like it was a trail camera, the kind used by hunters. There were no wires attached to it, so it was unlikely it was being monitored. And it was high enough off the ground so that she couldn't dismantle it. She continued up the road.

By the time she got to the house, she had seen four flashes of red light and had concluded that her foolproof plan was not so foolproof. If she had to shoot someone, she was going to be in deep shit. But she had come this far and was not going back home empty handed. She was going to get inside that house and find out everything she could about the people who lived there.

There were no cars in the driveway in front of the garage. When she had driven by the house on the previous evening, the driveway in front of the garage as well as the sidewalk alongside it were fully illuminated. Not so, tonight. Even the dim landscape lighting was turned off. The only light showing evidence that someone was inside the house was a flickering light in the windows. Someone inside was watching television.

Lydia looked up and down the street to make sure no one was around before entering the narrow walkway that ran alongside the garage. She had plenty of experience doing this. How many places had she broken into during the last month? At least three she could recall, maybe more.

Even so, she felt a tingle of nervous excitement when she arrived at the gate. She took out a pencil flashlight and found that the latch was not secured by a padlock. Being careful not to make any noise, she opened the gate and made her way up the sidewalk.

The backyard was amazing. The house had been built into the side of a hill that was landscaped with flowering tropical plants. A waterfall flowed through an artificial rocky outcrop into a large spa that was illuminated by a pale-yellow light. Hidden lights cast a rosy glow over the lush garden and the patio.

After making sure no one was relaxing on one of the several lounge chairs spread around the spa, she entered the backyard.

The entrance to the house was an open double-wide glass door with a screen. She slid open the screen door and entered. There was a short hallway in front of her with stairs dropping down to another level. To the left was an office with a massive desk facing the door. A computer sat on one corner of the desk and a small lamp, dim light on, sat on the other corner. The open door to the right led to the master bedroom.

She stopped and listened. The sound of a monotonous voice broadcasting a basketball game came from the front of the house. Lydia moved toward the stairs leading down to the next level and stopped.

The house was a lot bigger than it appeared from the outside. The sound from the television was distant. It was not coming from the level below her. There had to be another level below that one. She made her way slowly down the stairs.

The middle level was twice as large as the first. On her right was an open dining area, and next to it was a kitchen with a swinging door that was open. On the opposite side were two rooms with closed doors. No sounds came from either.

Satisfied that no one was on this level, Lydia proceeded to the top of the stairs leading to the next level and listened. The voice coming from the television was louder now. She could hear the announcer talking in an annoying tone of voice at how much better U.C.L.A. basketball was when he played on the team.

At the base of the stairs was a glistening marble walkway that led to the front door. The sound from the television was coming from a room to the right that Lydia assumed was the living room. She slowly stepped down the flight of six stairs and peeked around the corner. A man, his back turned toward her, was sitting on a sofa and watching television. No one else was in the room and Lydia wondered where the wife was.

There was another room to her left. She checked it out. It was a formal living room, lit by dim lighting. No one was in it.

She looked back at the man watching television and fingered the Springfield in its holster. Even though she could not see his face, she was sure this was the man who had held her captive in the abandoned meat processing facility. She wanted to put a bullet into the back of his head, but she couldn't because of the cameras that caught her image as she was jogging up the street.

Someday she would get the chance to shoot this sonovabitch, but not now.

She moved slowly back up the stairs, hoping that the wife was not in one of the rooms on the second level that she had not checked. She listened at both doors, and hearing no noise in either one, she went up the stairs to the office on the top level.

The office was large, furnished with a sofa and two easy chairs on the right facing a television mounted on the wall. On the wall to the left was a small bookcase, a metal filing cabinet, and then a large window that overlooked the back yard.

The filing cabinet interested Lydia the most. The top drawer contained financial information, including banking statements and insurance policies for the couple who live there. It suddenly occurred to Lydia that she might be in the wrong house. She had a thought that maybe she had fucked up big time, like the time she went out to jog at Drake Stadium and had forgot to put on jogging shorts. She checked the names on the accounts to make sure she was in the right house and then breathed a sigh of relief. The records were for Roberto L. Moreno and Angela V. Rossi.

The second drawer proved more interesting. Bookkeeping files, summarization of accounts, audits, all contained in marked manila folders. The third held banking records and the fourth held property records. Most of them had the name of Jonathan Benedict on them. Some of them referenced the names of businesses owned by Jonathan, companies like Pacific Coast Car Conversions and Benedict Armory.

The first question that came to Lydia's mind when she saw the records was how in hell did Moreno get hold of them. She studied one of the files more closely. The papers inside weren't originals. They were copies.

Lydia looked around the room once more and saw something she had not noticed when she first entered. There was a business grade copier next to the desk.

But how did Moreno manage to get copies of Jonathan's records? Did Jonathan give them to him? Or did Moreno sneak them out to be copied?

All of these records concerned companies that she would eventually own. There was no reason why Roberto Moreno and Angela Rossi should have them. Grabbing a handful of manila folders, she headed out the back door and dumped them into the spa. She looked down at the files floating in the bubbling water.

Why just these files? Why not all of them?

She worked fast, making as little noise as possible as she carried the files out to the spa. On her last trip out, she noticed that one of the files was markedly different. It was in an expandable redwell, whereas the others were in simple manila folders. Its label read, "Transfers." She opened it.

The documents inside contained a list of what appeared to be transfers of money into a single account number. Each item on the list had a number associated with it and the sums involved were considerable. Lydia didn't know what it meant, but she decided that this was one file she needed to keep.

Six minutes later, every document in the file cabinet with the exception of those in the redwell were in the spa. Lydia found the controls and turned the spa on full blast. Seconds later, the spa contained a churning mass of disintegrating paper.

Lydia decided she needed to look at what was inside the desk. She sat down in the chair and opened the top drawer. Maybe she should have been surprised at what she found in there, but then again, maybe not. There was a sheaf of papers held together by a clip. The title at the top read, "Assignment of Rights". At the bottom was a typed name above the signature line. It was dated approximately two weeks in the future. The name that had been typed in was, "Lydia Harte".

The document listed the property owned by Jonathan Benedict, including the property in Arizona. Lydia snorted when she saw what she was supposed to get in return for her signature on the assignment. It was a paltry sum, a lousy $10,000.

Lydia put the document into the redwell. She was getting ready to leave when she heard voices, and it wasn't the voices of the television announcer. Lydia picked up the redwell and moved quickly to the door. When she peered around the door frame, she saw two people coming up the stairs from the middle level.

She moved to the side of the room and tried to make herself invisible. Maybe they were going outside to the spa. If they did, she could make her escape out the front door without being noticed. She shifted the red-well to her left hand and drew the Springfield.

Seconds later, a man came through the doorway and switched on the lights. He began walking toward the desk but stopped when he saw the open file cabinet. "What the fuck!" he said in a high-pitched voice.

A woman, slim and graceful, walked into the room. "What's wrong?" Lydia knew she had heard that voice before.

The man rushed behind the desk and saw the open desk drawer.

The woman took a few steps forward, staring at the open doors in the file cabinet. "Somebody's been in here," she muttered.

The man looked up and froze when he saw Lydia inching her way toward the door. The woman caught his glance and turned to see what he was looking at.

Lydia was stunned. She had seen this woman just two Sundays ago at Eamon Murphy's home. It was Jonathan Benedict's girlfriend, Victoria.

The two of them stared at each other for a moment, not quite fathoming what each other was seeing.

It took Lydia a few seconds before she realized that this woman's real name was not Victoria, but Angela V. Rossi and that she was married to Moreno.

Victoria/Angela finally spoke. "How did you get in here?"

Lydia motioned with her gun toward the sofa. "Move!"

Victoria/Angela moved slightly to her right. Lydia now had a clear view of Roberto Moreno. He had shifted a little to the left, his right hand concealed by the computer. It was clear he was reaching down for something on the left side of the desk. There was a drawer there that Lydia had not searched.

Lydia pointed the gun at Moreno. "Get away from that desk, now!"

"What do you want?" Moreno asked, not moving.

Lydia brought the gun up and pointed it at Moreno's nose. "I said, get out from behind that goddamn desk! Do it now or you're a dead man!"

"How did you get in here?" Victoria/Angela repeated.

"Maybe you should lock your fucking doors," Lydia said, watching Moreno slide sideways from behind his desk. He was holding his hands up so that Lydia could see them.

"If you let us go, we will leave you alone," Moreno said. "We won't bother you again."

"Damn right, you won't! Sit on the couch, both of you!"

They did what Lydia commanded, both keeping their hands where Lydia could see them.

"How did you find us?" Moreno asked.

Lydia ignored him and stared at Victoria/Angela. She remembered seeing her nearly a month ago in Jonathan's library/den, wearing a tight cocktail dress and sitting demurely on a sofa. Lydia had envied her. She was a beautiful woman who carried herself with grace and elegance.

Today, Victoria/Angela was wearing a black pants suit made of what looked like silk with a white blouse that had a fluffy white bow at the neckline.

Today, Lydia wanted to kill her.

"It was that goddamn Jamie!" Victoria/Angela said bitterly to Moreno. "I told you that fool couldn't be trusted."

Lydia pointed the gun at her. She was thinking of what she had to do to get out of there without having to kill them.

They looked expectantly at Lydia. Victoria/Angela looking cool and calm, Roberto Moreno's eyes were terror stricken.

Lydia stared at them for a moment before she spoke. "Which one of you nearly beat Jenny Hamilton to death? And why did you lay her naked body on a railroad track to be cut in half by a train?"

Moreno and Victoria/Angela looked at each other. Lydia thought that Victoria/Angela looked surprised, but there was fear in Moreno's face.

Taking a step closer, Lydia looked at Moreno. "She's alive, and she's talking. I hope you wore a mask when you dumped her."

"I don't know what you're talking about," Moreno said, a crinkle of a smile on his mouth.

"You know she had gonorrhea, didn't you?" Lydia said, watching Victoria/Angela out of the corner of her eye.

It looked like a bubble, the size of a ping pong ball, that slid down Moreno's throat.

"What are you talking about?" Victoria/Angela said, looking at Lydia. Her voice was tense.

"You didn't know that, did you Victoria?" Lydia waved her gun at Moreno. "She was raped by this asshole and Henry Mariani."

The look on the woman's face told Lydia that whatever the current status of this couple's marriage, it was never going to be the same after tonight.

Victoria/Angela glared at Moreno. "You fucked her, didn't you?"

"I didn't. It was Henry."

"Don't lie to me! I know you, Bobby! You fucked her, didn't you?"

"Can we talk about this later? We have to deal with what we've got here right now. She's going to kill us if we don't make a deal."

"She's not going to kill us! She's not a fucking dummy! She had to have seen those cameras out on the street."

Victoria/Angela turned to Lydia. "What do you want?"

"I already have what I want."

Victoria/Angela's eyes darted around the room, to the open drawers in the file cabinet, the desk, and then at the redwell in Lydia's hand. "You can't take that with you."

Lydia ignored her, looking around the room one more time. She backed up to the desk and opened the drawer where Moreno had been standing. There was a Glock pistol in it. Lydia put it in the redwell.

"I'll be leaving now," Lydia said. "If you want to stay alive, you will not move until after I'm gone."

Moreno looked up at her. "You killed Hank!"

"Of course, I did. I would have killed you too if you had been there."

Victoria/Angela snorted. "You're lucky I didn't kill you."

"You're a piss poor shot," Lydia replied.

"So are you, for a cop."

Lydia shook her head. This was getting too catty.

"I have one more question before you go," Victoria/Angela said.

Lydia nodded.

"What did you do with those guys they sent down from Las Vegas?"

Lydia smiled. "I didn't do anything to them. The last I heard they were hiking off the top of a mountain in their bare feet."

"They'll send others," the woman said. "This is not going away."

"After those boys get done telling everybody what happened to them, I doubt if anyone will be dumb enough to try to kidnap me again."

Lydia backed her way out of the office into the hallway, keeping the gun trained on the husband and wife. Once she was in the backyard, she tossed the Glock into the roiling spa. She hurried down the sidewalk toward the front of her house. To her surprise, there was a black Humvee parked in the driveway in front of the garage. It had a massive bumper guard attached to the front, and it bore traces of silver paint, the same color as the paint on Lydia's wrecked BMW.

Lydia took out her cell phone and took several pictures of the bumper guard, making sure that she had at least one picture with the license number of the vehicle. When she finished taking pictures, she looked back at the house. The people inside that comfortable home were responsible for Jenny Hamilton's battered body lying in the hospital. She wanted to kill them but knew she could not get away with it. There were too many cameras on the street with her image in them.

As Lydia stepped out onto the street, she heard the high-pitched sounds of a woman shrieking coming from the back of the house.

Angela V. Rossi had found out that the records she and her husband had kept in the file cabinet were in the spa.

Lydia knew that the couple who lived in that house reported to someone higher, and he was going to be really pissed when he found out what happened.

She jogged down the street with a smile on her face.

CHAPTER TWENTY-FIVE

April 8, 2006. Saturday

LYDIA'S FIRST thought on Saturday morning was to drive out to U.C.L.A.'s Drake Stadium for a long run. She needed to clear her head from the surprise she received last night when she discovered that Angela V. Rossi had been Jonathan Benedict's girlfriend, Victoria. But when she reached down to tie her trainers, she felt a streak of pain across her ribs and knew she would have a difficult time breathing while running. She grabbed a cup of coffee and headed out to the balcony to think things over.

It was a pleasant day, the sun out, the distant sound of voices coming from the golf course across the park.

She again thought about what she had discovered last night. How in hell did Victoria/Angela get away with it? How could Jonathan not have known who she was? Jonathan was a very shrewd and intelligent man, not one who could be easily fooled.

Maybe Jonathan knew what Victoria/Angela was doing. Maybe he knew she was keeping watch over him for the organization and making sure he scrupulously reported the income from his businesses.

By noon, Lydia became so bored thinking about what she was going to do to fuck up the people responsible for kidnapping her and Jenny that she turned on the television in her living room. She dozed off after staring blankly at the screen for a few minutes. If she had been watching, she would have seen the news that two masked bandits had struck again in Century Division, this time at an Armenian market run by an elderly couple who were both murdered. The news ran a video clip showing the two masked murderers leaving the store. The taller of the two raised a hand and displayed his middle finger at the camera as he left the store.

The video was followed by a clip showing the Chief of Police at a press conference explaining what was being done to catch the killers. He was barraged by a host of questions about the failure of LAPD to catch the killers.

That was when Lydia woke up. She watched the rest of the news conference, sensing something big had happened. The report concluded with the television anchor reporting that the Mayor's Office had not responded to a request for a statement. The camera switched to a scene showing the Mayor playing golf at the Bel Air Country Club. Underneath the clip was a scrolling caption that said the Mayor's Office issued a statement that changes will be made.

What in the hell does that mean? Lydia thought. What kind of changes? Was the mayor going to fire the Chief of Police?

Lydia switched off the television and called Billy Vernor. He told her that the two bandits had struck in Century Division just after midnight and killed a man and a woman in their 60s. The Department was under fire for not doing enough to catch the killers. In response, the Chief of Police decided to flood Century Division and the eastern end of Pacific Division with every available unit from Tactical Operations.

"That won't do a damn thing," Vernor said. "So, they deploy over seventy officers into the area. They shake, rattle and roll every suspicious car they see. What good does it do? A goddamn week goes by. Nothing happens. They pull Tactical Operations out and the fucking suspects hit again."

"These guys are watching what we do, aren't they?"

"Hell yes. I told Hardemann that. He said Tactical Operations won't be holding roll call at our station like they usually do. They'll do that elsewhere. But any fool with half a brain will be able to figure out that we have extra cars on the street."

Lydia paused for a moment, thinking about Hagerty's and Ferris' reactions to what was happening. She didn't know about Ferris. He usually expressed no emotion, but Hagerty must be livid. He took it personally when some asshole had the audacity to commit a crime in his district.

"Are you still there?" Vernor asked.

"I am."

"How are you doing?"

"I'm fine."

"When are you coming back to work?"

"When the doctor releases me."

"How about that girlfriend of yours?"

Lydia winced when she heard the word girlfriend. There was already a rumor going around the station that Lydia was a lesbian, a rumor that infuriated Lydia.

"The last I heard she was still in a coma," Lydia replied, suddenly realizing that she had wasted nearly half the day and had not bothered to check on Jenny.

Fifteen minutes after Lydia said goodbye to Vernor, she was in her car on her way to the Palmdale Regional Medical Center.

Lydia stopped at the nurses' station before she went into Jenny's room.

"She's still in a coma," the nurse said, "but we had a specialist who came in and examined her. He was very optimistic about her chances of recovery."

Lydia thanked her for the good news.

When she turned to go to Jenny's room, the nurse called after her. "I think you should know that Miss Hamilton had visitors and things did not go well. Her parents have a conflict with her fiancé."

Lydia raised her eyebrows. "What happened?"

"I don't know what started it, but there was a shouting match, and it was in Jenny's room. We had to call security to put a stop to it."

"Have they left?"

"The parents are in the cafeteria. I think the fiancé went out for a smoke. I don't think you should be here when the parents come up. They sounded like they're holding you responsible for what happened to her."

Jenny Hamilton did look better. The bruises had faded, and she was no longer on a breathing tube. The wires leading to the heart monitor were still there as was the steady beat of the monitor.

Lydia touched Jenny's hand and stared at her face for a long minute. "Jenny, I'm so sorry. I will make this up to you."

Lydia hoped for some response, but there was none. Not a twitch of an eye lid, not the slightest movement of the hand. Just slow, steady breathing.

The nurse came into the room, and Lydia stepped away from the bed. "I think I ought to warn you. The fiancé is in the waiting room outside the nurse's station. I don't know if you want to be here when he comes in. We don't want another problem."

"Thank you," Lydia said. "I don't think I'll have a problem with him."

The nurse nodded and left.

Ten minutes later, Lydia decided there was nothing she could do that would help Jenny get better, so she decided to leave.

In the hallway, she encountered a man in his early thirties who reminded her of a suave actor she had once seen in a romantic film but whose name she couldn't remember. He was wearing a tailored navy-blue suit with a striped blue and yellow tie. As Lydia got closer, she suddenly realized that this guy was too good looking to be in the movies.

The man stopped when he saw her.

"You must be Lydia," the man said. "I'm Rod Mallory."

He offered his hand and Lydia took it, trying to ignore the electricity she felt racing up her arm. She had never met Rod before, but Jenny had always talked about him.

"I am," Lydia said. "What's going on with you and Jenny's parents?"

"They don't like me," Rod said. "The reason why they live on a stinking mushroom farm in Mendocino County is because of me."

Lydia paused for a moment, trying to remember what Obregon had told her about the incident in which Jenny's father was removed from the bench. "You were responsible for that?"

"I wasn't responsible for anything. I just happened to be in court waiting for a hearing when I saw an attorney walk into the court room and go straight back to the judge's chambers without even stopping to check in with the clerk. When I learned he was one of those attorneys who handled those class-action asbestos cases, I called up the lead defense counsel and told him what I saw. They did the rest."

Lydia had a hard time looking at this strikingly handsome man in the eye, so she looked away. She found it hard to believe that Jenny Hamilton was still engaged to Rod after he found out she was bisexual.

"Can you tell me what happened to Jenny?" Rod asked. "You were kidnapped. But why did they kidnap her?"

Lydia looked back at Rod. "They wanted me to sign a document. When I refused, they grabbed Jenny. They beat the hell out of her and threatened to kill her if I didn't sign."

"Who are the people who did this to her?"

Lydia stared at the man for a moment. A remarkable change came over his face. Rage transformed this man's face into something that was no longer pleasant to look at.

"I'll take care of them," Lydia said.

"Let me take care of them," Rod quickly answered. "I'll make them pay for what they did."

Lydia thought about the bodies and graves she saw in Arizona. "Rod, I don't know if you know this, but the people who did this to Jenny are ruthless. There are a lot more people involved, and I don't know who they are. Believe me when I tell you that you shouldn't tangle with them."

On her way back to Los Angeles, Lydia thought about the conversation she had with Rod Mallory. In the end, she had not only given him the names of Robert Moreno, Angela Rossi, and Eduardo Santini, but their addresses as well.

She didn't know what Rod intended to do with that information. Was he going to sue them on behalf of Jenny? Maybe. She didn't think it likely he would go after them personally, but she didn't know for sure. She had warned him about how dangerous these people were, but that didn't seem to bother him. Rod Mallory was going to do something to those people, but it didn't matter. Lydia was going to strike first.

She had plans.

When Lydia got home, she called Jeremy. He was glad to hear from her and wanted to talk. But she got right to the point. She wanted to meet with him and the Loose Cannons tomorrow to discuss a business proposition. The problem with that, according to Jeremy, was that his buddies had gone on a fishing trip and would not be back until late Sunday night. He agreed to have his team assembled at his ranch on Monday evening.

CHAPTER TWENTY-SIX

April 10, 2006. Monday

ON MONDAY morning, Lydia woke up earlier than usual and called the hospital to check on Jenny Hamilton. She was surprised to learn that Jenny Hamilton had come out of her coma and had been discharged from the hospital. The nurse on duty explained that Jenny's parents arranged for her to be moved to a private hospital against the advice of her doctor. When Lydia asked for the name of the hospital, the nurse replied that Jenny's parents wouldn't tell them.

Lydia then called the Sheriff's Office in Palmdale and asked the duty officer to leave a message for Obregon to call her. It took a while for Lydia to get hold of Jenny's fiancé, Rod Mallory, but when she did, he was just as surprised to hear that Jenny had been moved as she had. They talked for a while and concluded that it was likely that the Hamiltons had moved Jenny to a hospital near their home in Mendocino. They both agreed to do whatever they could to try and locate her.

Obregon returned her call. He had been informed by the hospital that Jenny had been moved, but he didn't seem all that concerned. He, also, didn't know where she had been transferred.

Lydia got on the computer and obtained the name and telephone number of every hospital in Northern California, but she didn't have time to call any of them. She talked to Rod again who asked for a copy of the list. She emailed it to him.

Before Rod hung up, he said he would call every hospital on the list and ask to be connected to Jenny Hamilton's room. Maybe, they would get lucky and find out where she was.

Lydia was in no mood to play games with the receptionist at Mayes, Murphy and McBride on Monday morning after the disappointing news about Jenny Hamilton. When she was told that Reece Tanner was unavailable, she said, "I don't give a damn if he is unavailable. I want to speak with him right now!"

"I'm sorry but . . ."

Lydia slammed the phone down. Fifteen minutes later, the phone in her apartment began ringing, but she was halfway out the door and was in no mood to go back and answer it.

When Lydia arrived on the second floor of the Mayes, Murphy and McBride offices, she approached the receptionist, told her who she was, and demanded to speak to Reece Tanner.

When the receptionist heard Lydia's name, the smile faded. "Could you have a seat while I call back to see if he is available?"

Lydia continued to stare at the receptionist. "Is there a problem with me standing here?"

"Not at all." The receptionist picked up a phone. Using her hand to cover the receiver, she spoke in a low tone of voice. After a moment, she put the phone down and looked up at Lydia. "Someone will be out in a moment. Perhaps you would be more comfortable if you sat down."

Lydia leaned over the desk. "Is Mr. Tanner actually in the office?"

"I'm sorry. I don't know. Someone will be out in a minute."

It was more like seven minutes before Jane Halloran came out. She spotted Lydia standing by the windows and went over to her.

"I'm sorry, Miss Harte, but Mr. Tanner is busy at the moment. If you'll come back with me, I'll brief you on the status of your case."

"I asked to see Mr. Tanner."

"He's busy at the moment."

"You already said that. This is important. I need to talk to him, right now."

Halloran nodded. "Please come with me. I'll see what I can do."

Lydia was led to a small conference room and was left alone while Halloran went out to fetch Reece Tanner.

The conference room windows faced west. Lydia stood at the windows for a moment or two before she realized she was looking down on the very area that she was assigned to patrol with Hagerty and Ferris. She tried to locate the market where they found the Japanese man and woman who had been murdered while their granddaughter was hiding in a beer cooler. She couldn't locate it. It was too far away to be seen.

The two murderers were also out there, probably planning another robbery. It was just a matter of time before they made a mistake. It would be their misfortune if Hagerty happened to be there when they did.

"Lydia, how are you doing today?"

Lydia turned to see Reece Tanner entering the conference room. He was followed by Jane Halloran who was carrying a manila file pocket with numbers on its side.

Tanner was smiling. "Would you have a seat?"

Lydia didn't sit down. "This won't be long, Mr. Tanner. I have a question or two that I'd like you to answer."

Tanner's smile turned into a look of puzzlement. "Well, if it's about the petition, I can assure you that all is going well. If you would care to have a seat, I can give you an update."

"I don't need an update, Mr. Tanner. I'd like to ask you a question. Do you know a woman by the name of Angela Rossi?"

The puzzled look didn't leave Tanner's face. He paused before answering. "I don't. Does she have anything to do with Jonathan's estate?"

"She might," Lydia said. "She also goes by the name Victoria."

There was a moment of silence in the room, and just for a second, Lydia thought she saw a flicker of recognition in Tanner's eyes.

"I don't know anybody by the name of Rossi. I did know a girl from college called Victoria, but I haven't seen her in ages."

"I saw you talking to her at Mr. Murphy's fundraiser."

"Victoria?"

"I'm talking about Angela Rossi who sometimes calls herself Victoria."

"Which fundraiser are you talking about?"

"The one a few weeks back on Mr. Murphy's estate."

Reece nodded. "I talked to a lot of people when I was there. I don't remember all their names, but I don't ever recall talking to an Angela or a Victoria. Can you tell me where I was when this happened?"

"Mr. Tanner, you're a liar! You're fired! Now get out of my way so I can get out of this goddamn place!"

Lydia was getting into her car when she saw Jane Halloran come dashing out of the building. Halloran looked around, saw Lydia, and began running toward her on wobbly heels.

Lydia was already backing her car up when Halloran came alongside and knocked on the window. Lydia stopped the car and rolled down the window.

"What in the hell do you want?"

Halloran paused for a moment, trying to catch her breath. "Mr. Murphy would like to talk to you. In his office."

"Why?"

"He wants to make things right."

"Tell him I don't want Reece Tanner as my attorney."

"Mr. Murphy wants to know why."

Lydia stared at the steering wheel for a moment. She put the car in gear and pulled back into the parking spot.

Halloran appeared again at the car window. "Shall I tell Mr. Murphy you're coming up?"

"Tell Mr. Murphy if he wants to talk to me, he can come down here."

Ten minutes later, Eamon Murphy appeared at Lydia's car window. He was dressed casually, wearing a blue polo shirt and tan slacks.

"Can we talk?" Murphy asked.

Lydia nodded.

"I mean, can I sit down . . . in your car?"

Lydia clicked open the door locks and Murphy got into the car. He wore a strong cologne with a bite to it that caused Lydia to feel nauseated. She regretted letting him in the car. The smell would linger for several days.

"What's this about Reece Tanner meeting someone at my fundraiser?"

"Do you know a woman named Angela Rossi?"

"I don't. Who is she?"

"She was at your fundraiser. I saw Tanner talking to her. She told me that she does publicity for you."

"When did she say that?"

"At the fundraiser."

"Well, I can assure you that I don't know this woman. If she worked for me, I would know it."

"Tanner was talking to her."

"I had a brief conversation with Reece before I came down. He told me what you said. He denied ever knowing a woman named Rossi."

"Well, I saw him having a lively conversation with her, and it was obvious they knew each other."

"Who is she?"

Lydia took a deep breath. "I assume you know all about my claim to the Jonathan Benedict estate?"

"I'm the managing partner of our law firm. I know about every case the firm is handling."

"Jonathan had a girlfriend who was named Victoria. I just learned the other day that her real name is Angela Rossi. She and her husband were the people who kidnapped me."

Murphy turned in his seat to look at Lydia. "I heard about that . . . the kidnapping, I mean. And you say that you saw Reece talking to her."

"I did say that," Lydia said.

"I'll talk to him about that. We can't have our attorneys dealing with criminals."

Lydia could hardly believe what he said. Lawyers deal with criminals all the time. Half of the attorneys in the United States wouldn't have a job if it weren't for criminals.

Murphy continued. "I know you're upset about this. I'll take care of whatever internal problem we have with Reece and this lady. But I'd like to keep you as our client. If you agree, I will personally handle your petition. Reece will no longer have anything to do with it. Is that a deal?"

Lydia stared ahead at the building where Mayes, Murphy and McBride had its offices for a good minute before she answered.

She turned to Murphy who was smiling. "Let me think about it."

The smile faded.

On her way back to her condo, it occurred to Lydia that there was one thing strangely absent about her conversations with the attorneys at Mayes, Murphy and McBride. Surely, they read the newspapers. They had to know about her disappearance and her escape from her kidnappers. Yet no one from Mayes, Murphy and McBride, not Reece Tanner, not Jane Halloran, had ever called and asked if she was all right. Nor did they even mention the fact that she had been kidnapped or offer any sympathy for her injuries.

When Lydia got home, she called Eric Milburn. She told him what had happened and asked his opinion. His response was that Mayes, Murphy and McBride was a highly regarded law firm who was known for their excellent work. As far as he knew, the firm did not have a criminal practice, and she was lucky to have Eamon Murphy as her attorney.

Milburn's comment about Mayes, Murphy and McBride not having a criminal practice motivated Lydia to do some research on the Internet. She went to the website for Mayes, Murphy and McBride and check the bios of every member of the firm. There were fifty-three attorneys in the firm, and not one of them handled criminal cases. She then spent two hours reading online articles about the firm and its clients. Not one of the articles dealt with a criminal matter handled by the firm.

Three hours later, she was convinced that Milburn was right, that the doubt that lingered in her mind about the trustworthiness of the firm was unfounded despite the fact that she had seen Reece Tanner talking to the person who had kidnapped her and nearly beaten Jenny Hamilton to death. She decided that maybe Reece Tanner was involved in something shady with Angela Rossi, but she felt confident that Eamon Murphy would get to the bottom of it. She would call Eamon Murphy tomorrow and accept his offer to represent her in her petition to be named as a beneficiary of Jonathan's estate.

Lydia really didn't want the property, but she needed to maintain an outward appearance that she wanted control of Jonathan Benedict's estate. She had already formulated plans for eliminating the problems associated with owning it, but she didn't want anyone thinking that what was about to happen was orchestrated by her.

Lydia met Eric Milburn and Michael Thornberry at Pacifica Bank and Trust in Santa Monica just before 5:00 p.m. They were led to the manager's office through a door that had a security lock on it.

The manager was waiting for them. He was a young man in a business suit who couldn't keep his eyes off Lydia while he was being introduced to the three of them. After the introductions were done, the manager picked up a large canvas bag with the bank's name on it. The manager opened the zipper and was preparing to dump the contents out on his desk when Lydia stopped him.

"You don't need to count it," Lydia said.

He looked at her in surprise. "I'll need you to sign a receipt."

"No problem."

"Did you bring something to carry the money?"

"I'd like to borrow your bag."

"The wrong kind of people will know what you're carrying when you walk out of here."

"I have a gun."

The manager's eyes roved over Lydia's body for a lot longer than necessary. Finally, he said, "You must be kidding."

"She's not," Milburn said. "She's a police officer."

The manager looked doubtful. After a moment he said, "Let me get the receipt."

As they were leaving the bank, Eric Milburn stopped her and said, "I hope you know what you're doing."

"You do know this transaction will come to the attention of the Feds, don't you?" Thornberry chimed in. "You may be asked questions."

"It's a legitimate business expense," Lydia replied. "All I'm doing is providing security for my shipping company."

"You need to get receipts for what you're doing with that money," Milburn added. "And make sure you have a written agreement with whoever you hired that shows what services they're providing."

Jeremy was in the corral watering his horses when Lydia drove up. She retrieved the Pacifica Bank and Trust canvas bag and a black binder from the rear seat and went over to the corral. Jeremy was pouring water from a hose into a large container. When he was finished, he poured water over his hands and wiped them off on his jeans. He met Lydia at the corral gate.

"Jeremy, before we go inside," Lydia said, "I need to run something by you."

"Okay."

"This will probably not make any sense," Lydia began. "Last night, I talked to Jenny's boyfriend. He was very handsome, and I could see why Jenny wanted to marry him. But the strangest thing happened when I was talking to him. When he started talking about getting revenge on the people who put Jenny in the hospital, his entire demeanor changed. His face became so contorted that he looked like a monster."

"Okay," Jeremy said, with a look on his face that suggested he was wondering where this conversation was going.

"Have you seen something like that before?" Lydia asked.

Jeremy nodded his head. "I've seen men, who are normally very pleasant individuals, turn into beasts when they see a friend get killed on the battlefield." He paused for a moment. "Why are you telling me this, Lydia? I'm not a psychologist. I don't have any idea why something like that would happen."

"The reason I'm telling you this, Jeremy, is that if you ever see me change like that, I want you to kick me in the ass."

The Loose Cannons were waiting for Lydia inside Jeremy's barn. They were sitting around the industrial-sized wire spool. A deck of playing cards were scattered on the spool guarded by bottles of Maker's Mark bourbon and Stolichnaya vodka.

The men rose to their feet when Lydia entered and murmured quiet greetings. They were not as exuberant as the last time Lydia had seen them.

Lydia stepped forward and examined the two bottles on the wire spool. The liquor had barely been touched.

The men were staring at the Pacifica Bank and Trust canvas bag in her right hand. They didn't seem to pay much attention to the black binder in the other.

"Pardon me," Lydia said as she stepped in between Marcum, the guy with the beard, and Tommy, the drone expert. The two men moved aside to make room for her.

Lydia unzipped the bag and dumped $800,000 in cash in bundles of hundred-dollar bills on the wire spool, scattering the playing cards and nearly knocking over the bottle of Stolichnaya.

"She just messed up our game," Tommy said in a droll tone of voice.

"That's one hell of an ante," Marcum quipped. "If you can't take an I.O.U., I think I'll fold."

Alex, the tall muscular dude with the blonde crewcut, picked up one of the packets and fanned the bills. He looked at Lydia. "What do you have in mind?"

"I've got something I want you to take care of."

The men looked at each other, and then Marcum spoke, casting a sideways glance at Jeremy. "Look, we know you're a friend of Jeremy's, but we don't offer a discount . . . even to pretty ladies."

"I wouldn't expect you to. I know you charge five million dollars for what you do. I can't come up with that amount of money without causing some people to take notice. But I can pay you six million if you're willing to sign an agreement to provide security for my shipping company and be willing to be paid a million a year."

"You own a shipping company?" Alex said in disbelief. "How many trucks do you own?"

"She's talking about freighters. Boats, big boats, not trucks," Jeremy said.

"Are you kidding me?" Alex asked.

"I'm not kidding," Jeremy said. "As far as money goes, she can deliver."

"How many boats do you own?" Marcum asked Lydia.

"The last I heard, we had twelve cargo ships."

Marcum whistled.

"I assume you're asking for protection from piracy," Rocky said.

"That's what the agreement will say. But I have something else in mind."

"You want us to sign an agreement?" Marcum asked.

"Yes. To make the transaction look legit."

There was a long pause as the men looked at each other.

Finally, Marcum spoke. "What do you want us to do that's not legit?"

"I'm being harassed by some people over property issues. I need them to stop it." She dropped the black binder on the table. "What I have in mind is laid out in there."

They spent several hours discussing the project and what Lydia wanted done. The men went through every single page contained in the black binder. They discussed the problems involved and the equipment and extra men they would need to complete the job. During that time, no one made a single joke, nor did anyone look at or touch the Maker's Mark and Stolichnaya bottles.

As Lydia listened to their conversation, she became convinced they were going to need more money based on what they were saying. They were talking about needing a lot more men as well as the purchase of at least three drones and a wide variety of explosives.

At 10:13 p.m., the men reached the last section of documents in the binder. They spent another fifteen minutes discussing ideas on how to deal with the objective described in that section.

They reached the conclusion they were going to need at least twenty additional men to do everything that Lydia wanted. Alex jumped into the conversation and said he could get them . . . even on short notice. Then they began discussing where they could get three drones before the idea was nixed because their use might get people thinking terrorism was involved.

Finally, Marcum stood up. "Okay, we know what she wants. I think we need to put it to a vote."

Jeremy touched Lydia's arm. "This is your cue to get a bit of fresh air."

Lydia nodded and started to leave.

"Wait, I have one more question," Tommy said.

Lydia stopped and turned.

"The agreement will say we're hired to provide protection for your shipping company?"

"Yes."

"Where do your ships move cargo?"

"All over the world."

"So, let me get this straight. You want us to sign an agreement to protect your ships. Is it fair to say that under this agreement, we would be expected to respond to any attempt to hijack one of your ships?"

"There won't be any hijacking. Not one of my ships will ever get within 500 miles of any region where there is a piracy threat."

"Okay. I think I understand."

"I do have a question for you," Lydia said. "If you do this, can you guarantee there will be no collateral damage? I don't want any innocent persons hurt."

Marcum stepped forward. "If we agree to take on this assignment, there will be a lot of damage, but none of it will be collateral."

Lydia waited outside the barn while the men discussed whether to take the job. It was cool outside, and there was no sign of the mountain lion that frequented Jeremy's ranch. She looked up at the night sky. It was carpeted with millions of stars. Up in the mountains, a pack of coyotes began baying, and Lydia felt goosebumps rising on her arms. Even though she knew better, she imagined the coyotes were looking at the same stars and were trying to communicate with them.

Fifteen minutes later, Jeremy opened the barn door and asked her to step inside. The men were lined up in a row behind the wire spool that made do as a table. Each of the men held a small tumbler filled with bourbon or vodka.

Jeremy handed her a glass. "It's a custom," he said. "We always pro-pose a toast to success of our new project."

Lydia took the glass. "Then, you'll do it?"

"Yes. We'll do it for what you offered."

Lydia smiled.

She raised her glass and took a sip of bourbon.

CHAPTER TWENTY-SEVEN

April 11th to the 14th, Tuesday through Friday

THE DAY after she had met with the Loose Cannons, Lydia called Jeremy's cell phone. It went to his answering machine. She then called Jeremy's gun range. One of his employees, a man called Jose, answered and told Lydia that Jeremy had gone to visit a sick mother and would not be back for a week.

Over the next few days, Lydia began buying newspapers and watching television news every day hoping to see some report about the disaster about to befall the criminal organization that had caused her so many problems.

Lydia began to get bored, so she began going out every morning to U.C.L.A. where she ran sprints at Drake Stadium. At first, she felt a little pain in her ribs, but in the following days it subsided.

On Thursday, she called her doctor and made an appointment to see him that afternoon. She saw the doctor at 3:15 p.m. After examining her and her X-rays, he signed a release allowing her to go back to work.

The first thing she did when she got home was to call the watch commander at Century Division. Lieutenant Morton answered the call. He was delighted to have her come back to work. She would be assigned to work with Hagerty the next day.

Cochise County, Arizona.

In the early morning hours of Friday, April 14, 2006, Abelino Zabatero, Lautaro Alvarez, and Matias Vicario crossed the United States border into Cochise County, Arizona. They didn't have the money to pay to use the underground tunnel, so, using a homemade ladder, they climbed to the top of the ten-foot fence and dropped over onto the other side. Abelino cried out when he fell. He had sprained his ankle. The other two men helped him to his feet. After hopping around on his foot for a moment, he told the others he was ready to go.

The three of them set off to the north. They had to get to a small village called Miracle Valley. An employee of Matias' cousin would be waiting for them in an off-road vehicle behind a shuttered restaurant. They would eventually be transferred by another vehicle after they had crossed the desert to a construction site north of Tucson where the cousin had jobs waiting for them.

They travelled due north through the scrubland, Abelino struggling to keep up with the others. After ten minutes of trudging through a landscape of tall grass concealing bruising rocks, they came to a small rise. In the distance, they could see the faded lights of a small village to the northwest.

When Matias turned to tell his two friends that the lights were from the village where someone would be waiting for them, he noticed a large building about a quarter mile to the east. It had a large hangar-like door that was open. The lights were on inside.

Abelino and Lautaro turned to look.

"Are there men working there this early?" Lautaro asked.

Matias shrugged and was about to set off in the direction they were heading when he saw four men running out of the building and disappear into the darkness. Seconds later, Matias and his friends heard an engine starting up. A vehicle, its lights out, emerged from the darkness alongside the building and began speeding north toward the main highway that paralleled the border.

The three men looked at each other.

And then, in the distance near the border was a large booming sound, followed by another, and then another, as a series of violent explosions walked across the desert floor from the border towards the building.

At first, the three men saw no visible sign of the explosions. But then, the ground began shaking with each detonation and the desert began heaving, throwing tons of dirt into the air, as the blasts followed a line directly toward the building. It looked as if an angry fire breathing dragon was forcing its way underground toward the building.

The last explosion was the biggest, and the only one that the three men saw with their own eyes. The building exploded into a giant fireball, lighting up the desert, throwing large sheets of metal into the air. A wave of heat followed by a gust of wind swept over the men.

The three Mexicans dropped to the ground, flattened themselves, and waited for the roar to subside. When they thought it was safe, they raised their heads.

The building no longer existed. There were small fires around the area where the building once stood, some of them not more than a hundred yards away.

When Matias got to his feet, he heard a fluttering sound in the sky. Thinking it might be a drone, he looked up.

A sheet of metal, about the size of a car hood, was sailing down on them. He yelled a warning at the men. They ran a hundred yards to the west before they thought it safe enough to stop and look back.

They watched the fires caused by the explosion for at least five minutes before they decided to move on. But they didn't head northeast to the closed restaurant where a man would be waiting for them. They headed towards the border, hoping to find some way to get back through the fence and return to their wives and children.

Beauford County, North Carolina.

Benedict Armory was located in North Carolina on the outskirts of a small town called Chocowenty. The factory consisted of a large building approximately one hundred yards long surrounded by a ten-foot-high security fence that was wired to detect intruders. The factory manufactured semi-automatic pistols in three different calibers, all of them match grade, which meant they were extremely accurate and designed for competition. The plant also manufactured a specialty line of semi-automatics without serial numbers that were not available to the public but designed for certain types of people who needed to throw them away after they were used.

It was after 1:00 a.m. The only people on the plant grounds were two security guards. Andy Lambert was in a guard shack at the entrance just inside the gate that had been locked for the night. The other guard named Travis Jones was inside the plant in the security office. His job was to monitor the CCTV system that covered the fence line. Every hour, Travis would leave the security office, walk around the plant, and check in at the time clocks mounted at the five different entrances to the plant.

At 1:15 a.m., a black van drove into the well in front of the main gate. Andy stepped out of the shack and waved it away. The van didn't move, so Andy walked up to the gate to see who was inside.

A man wearing a black watch cap and sunglasses stepped out of the van. His black denim jacket had the name Ray embroidered on it. He held up a badge in the light so Andy could see it. "A.T.F. Open the gate."

Andy examined the badge and looked up at the man holding it. "I'm sorry, officer. I'm under orders not to let anyone in."

Another man got out of the van. He was also wearing a black watch cap and sunglasses. "What's the problem?" he asked Ray.

"He won't let us in," Ray said.

"No problem. We ram the gate and arrest the sonovabitch."

Both men moved to get back into the van.

Andy noticed that the van had a heavy-duty bumper guard on it. These men weren't kidding.

"Wait a minute," Andy said. "I'll open the gate."

He opened the gate, and the van pulled up to the guard station. Three men got out of the van, removed Andy's gun, and tied his hands behind his back with plastic handcuffs.

"Wait a minute," Andy said. "Why are you handcuffing me? I didn't do anything wrong. I just work here."

"What is your name?" Ray asked.

"Andy Lambert."

"Is the front door to the plant locked, Andy?" Ray said.

"Yes."

"Do you have a key to get in?"

Before he could respond. another man had reached into the guard's pocket and retrieved a set of keys.

"Okay, Andy, listen up," Ray said. "We know there's another guard in the plant. Is he armed?"

"Yes."

"With what?"

"A Benedict 45."

The man named Ray walked the security guard to the main entrance of the plant while the van followed. Almost immediately, a large box truck appeared at the gate and followed the van into the lot.

"Who are you guys?" Andy asked, nervously looking back at the truck.

Ray said nothing. When he got to the main entrance, he began trying the keys to the lock.

The truck had turned and was now backing up towards the entrance. The invaders got out. There were eight of them, all dressed alike, wearing sunglasses, black watch caps, and black coveralls.

Two minutes later, Ray escorted Andy into the security office. The lights were on, but no one was present.

Ray turned to Andy. "Where is the other guard?"

Andy looked up at a clock on the wall. "He's making his rounds."

Ray went to the windows and looked out onto the floor of the plant. There were at least twelve lathing machines placed in three rows across a large open space. The machines were finished in a light gray metallic color. They were at least ten feet in length, and all of them had large control panels. Behind them were drill presses and other metal working machines whose functions could not be determined by sight alone.

Three teams of the invaders entered the open space and spread out. It didn't take long for them to find the second guard named Travis. They brought him to the security office with his hands tied behind him with plastic cuffs.

Ray approached the guards with a Springfield 1911 semi-automatic in his hand. The guards stumbled back when they saw the gun. "Relax," he said. "I'm not going to shoot you. You can either sit down in one of the chairs, or you can stand by the windows and watch."

The men choose to watch.

The invaders were well-organized. They brought in cannisters about the size of one-gallon paint cans that had little square boxes attached to the lids. The teams set two of these devices on each machine, one on the control panel and another on the machine itself. Four other men brought in small barrels about the size of beer kegs and placed them at different positions throughout the plant.

The guards watched as two men placed one of the barrels in the center aisle of the factory floor and bent over it for a moment before going to help others doing the same thing.

Andy turned to Travis. "They're going to blow the plant up."

"No way," Travis said.

"Shut up!" Ray said. "No talking!"

The men on the factory floor finished what they were doing and returned to the security office. One of the men was holding a small computer. He sat down at a desk and began typing into it.

"Are you going to let us go?" Andy asked.

Ray pointed to the factory floor. "Watch!"

The security guards turned to look in the direction he was pointing.

Five seconds later, the first set of thermite bombs on one of the lathes ignited, sending up a brilliant shower of white sparks. A second later, another set of thermite bombs were ignited on another machine, followed by another, and then another, until the entire factory floor was ablaze with a shower of white sparks.

The mouths of the security guards gaped in astonishment.

"All right now," Ray said, as he approached the security guards with a large knife. "Turn around!"

"I'm not going to turn around," Travis said. "If you're going to kill me, you need to do it looking me in the face."

Ray grabbed Travis by the shoulder and spun him around so fast that he nearly fell. "If I were you," Ray said as he cut off the plastic cuffs, "I would follow us out the door and run like hell. Don't even try and get in your cars. You won't have time to start them. Ninety seconds from now, this plant will cease to exist. Do you understand me?"

The two security guards did what they were told. They ran as fast as they could toward the front gate. By the time they got out to the road, the taillights of the van and the box truck were disappearing around a curve a quarter mile away. The guards were a hundred yards away from the main gate to the plant and still running when it was blown to smithereens.

That same morning, Rod Mallory called Lydia and told her that he had checked every hospital north of Marin County and was unable to find any hospital that had Jenny Hamilton as a patient. He speculated that she had possibly been checked in under another name.

Disappointed, Lydia turned on her computer and checked the news that had been posted overnight. There was no report of anything unusual concerning any of the properties in Jonathan's estate. When she turned on the television at noon, there was a brief mention of an explosion of a warehouse in Cochise County in southern Arizona. A video taken from a news helicopter showed a massive hole centered in the middle of an open area. Numerous emergency vehicles were parked around the site.

But the big news was a lengthy report about the murder/robberies occurring in Century Division. A highly agitated reporter interviewed five residents and business owners who railed against the Police Department and its management. Lydia was amazed at the way the reporter conducted the interviews. She asked questions that were designed to elicit a negative response, and then after getting the sound bite she wanted, she asked each of them what they thought should be done about the men who were in charge of Century Division. She emphasized the word 'men'. In each case, the response was that the men should be replaced with more aggressive commanders.

Lydia was so upset at the coverage that she wanted to turn the television off but thought better of it. She wanted to see if the reporter mentioned that every officer in Tactical Operations Division was assigned to Century Division. She wasn't surprised when that fact was never mentioned.

There were no women in the locker room when Lydia reported for work. That was unusual. Normally there were six to eight women in the locker room getting ready for work.

She realized that something was up when she saw no one in the hallways. The big surprise came when she entered the roll call room and found it filled with over a hundred officers and detectives who began applauding when she walked through the rear door. Standing on the platform in front of the assembled officers and detectives were Captain Kemper, recently promoted Captain Hardeman, and Lieutenant Morton.

Lydia blushed as she walked down the aisle to take her seat in the front row. Halfway down the aisle, Hagerty leaned over and whispered, "Welcome back, partner."

She smiled in return. She took her seat next to another officer on probation, thinking about how different her entrance was from the days when she had to walk past several officers who believed she had killed her partner.

Captain Kemper welcomed her back after her ordeal in a speech that was less than ninety seconds. After another round of applause, the brass and visitors left the roll call room. Lieutenant Morton sat down and began calling out the assignments. As expected, Lydia was assigned to work Five-Adam-99 with Hagerty.

Once they were out on the street, Hagerty updated her with what had been happening. Tactical Operations was still flooding the Division with every officer at its disposal, including another twenty that had been loaned from other divisions. In the meantime, the streets were quiet, the area crime rate was at its lowest since World War II, and the two killers had not struck again.

"I expect we will not hear from them until Tactical Operations has left the area," Hagerty said. "Vernor has been trying to persuade Kemper to call off the Task Force."

"Why would he want to do something like that?" Lydia asked.

Hagerty chuckled. "I asked him the same thing. He just smiled and walked away. He's got something up his sleeve."

"Do you think he picked up information from one of his informants?"

"Maybe. I don't know for sure. But whatever Billy's thinking, it's going to involve us. He asked Morton for permission to use us at a moment's notice. When Morton asked him why, Vernor told him he needed back-up on a major bust. Morton agreed without asking what he was talking about."

CHAPTER TWENTY-EIGHT

April 15-16th, Saturday through Sunday

AT NOON on Saturday, Lydia turned on the television news. The same video of the demolished building near the southern border showed up in a report. This time, the coverage focused on what it called a breaking story. The Cochise County Sheriff's Office had found a massive grave site on the property. The Sheriff reported six bodies had been recovered, and they expected to find at least another dozen.

The coverage switched to a lady who lived in Miracle Valley a few miles away who stated that she always suspected that the people who owned the property were up to no good. When asked why, she said, "They's always sneaking around the place like they's hidin' something." When asked who they were, the woman said, "I don't know."

This comment prompted the coverage to switch to the television anchor in the studio who was trying to hold back a smile. "She might not know who those people were, but we found out who the property owner is," the anchor said. He introduced another reporter who was standing in front of the Cochise County Courthouse.

The smiling young lady said that a search of the property records showed that the property was owned by an alleged member of a crime syndicate named Jonathan Benedict who was found burned to death in his California estate a month ago. The reporter further stated that she had been informed by a confidential source that the murder of Benedict and the destruction of his property had all of the earmarks of the beginning of a power struggle between rivals for control of the drug trade into the United States.

Lydia turned off the television and sat back in her sofa, thinking about what was said. It had to be the biggest piece of bullshit she had heard in a long time, although she liked what the reporter had said about a power struggle between rival gangs. It provided good cover for the Loose Cannons.

Her telephone rang and she answered it. It was Billy Vernor.

"Have you seen the news?"

"About what happened in Arizona?"

"Just to warn you. Prepare yourself for a lot of attention coming your way."

"From the press?"

"The press is the least of your worries. A whole host of law enforcement agencies will want to know what your take on this is. Be prepared."

"Thank you, Billy."

"Did you hear about Kemper?"

"What about him?"

"He's being transferred to Personnel. Hardemann will be taking over as C.O. of Century. A lieutenant by the name of Maria Borders is being brought in to take over detectives. Rumor is that she's a real go-getter."

"Is Kemper being blamed for what's happening in the Division?"

"Not really. The Chief is just trying to show the public that he is doing something about the problem. Think about it for a second. You put an up-and-coming woman in charge of detectives. What broadcaster in their right mind is going to criticize the Department when a woman is in charge?"

"Do you really believe that?"

Vernor hesitated for a moment. "Not really. I'm just pissed off at what's being done."

Lydia was assigned to work the car with Kenny Ferris that evening. The most interesting thing that happened at roll call was the announcement of the changes in management. There were a few grumbles from some of the male officers even though none of them would be directly affected by a woman being in charge of the detective division. They just didn't like the idea that the Department could do something so stupid as assigning a woman to command a detective division.

Nothing much happened in the way of police work that night either, but all hell broke loose after Lydia's shift had ended.

Culver City, California

Just after 1:00 a.m. on the morning of April 16, a tractor trailer pulled up alongside the guard shack of the Red Dog Trucking and Shipping Company. The guard had never seen the truck before, so he came out of the shack to question the truck driver, not noticing that a black van had pulled in behind the trailer. He was quickly taken prisoner and placed in the screened area in the back of the van.

The driver of the tractor trailer drove onto the lot and backed it up to the loading dock. Nearby, two dock workers were unloading a trailer using a forklift. They were also taken into custody without incident and joined the security guard in the back of the van.

The invaders, five men in all, began unloading fifty-gallon drums from the trailer. Instead of stacking them in one place, they used the forklift to space them evenly throughout the warehouse. Once they were finished, they got into their vehicles and drove off the premises with their prisoners.

The three prisoners were released in a residential area. They began walking back to the warehouse.

One of the dock workers spoke up first. "What in the hell do you think they were doing?"

"Well, they weren't stealing, that's for sure," the security guard said. "They were unloading barrels. And they were nice enough to lock up after they were done."

"One of Jake's midnight special deliveries, I suspect," the dock worker said.

"Probably. He's connected with some dirty people."

"They were from Chicago," the other worker said.

"How in hell do you know that?"

"One of them said they had to get back to Chicago as soon as possible."

The men were one block away from the warehouse when they heard the first of ten explosions.

The estate of Jonathan Benedict had a seventy-five percent interest in the partnership of the shipping company. The remaining twenty-five percent was owned by Jake Nilsson, the former fiancé of Lydia Harte. When the warehouse blew up, they had a percentage of nothing.

Culver City, California

The Pacific Coast Car Conversion Company, owned by Jonathan Benedict, deceased, and formerly run by his also dead son Milo was located just two miles from where the warehouse exploded. A gasoline leak from one of the cars managed to flow across the garage floor. Somehow, the gasoline found what it was looking for, a gas water heater in a small cabinet. Nothing happened at first until the water in the heater reached a certain temperature. The electronic igniter snapped on to light the burner. When that happened at 1:14 a.m., the entire facility containing twenty-three exotic cars went up in flames.

When the facility was inspected by arson investigators later that day, they could not understand how so much gasoline could have leaked out of the tank of one car.

Stateline, Nevada

Primm, Nevada had several small casino hotels on the border with California that had a customer base that just couldn't wait to drive forty more miles to Las Vegas before gambling. The smallest casino happened to be owned by Jonathan Benedict and had just been reopened after being shut down by the Nevada Gaming Commission.

Around 1:30 a.m., a casino employee smelled a gas leak and reported it to the manager who ordered the casino evacuated. The manager notified the Clark County Fire Department and was told a unit would be out in thirty minutes, which was not unusual since the nearest fire station was thirty miles away.

No one seemed surprised, least of all the casino manager who was eager to get back into the business of robbing customers blind, when two men wearing blue coveralls with the words 'Nevada State Fire Marshal' emblazoned on their backs appeared at the scene ten minutes later and ordered everyone to back off a hundred yards from the casino.

They proceeded to open the back door of their van and pulled out a large tank mounted on a dolly. They wheeled the tank inside the casino. The casino manager fumed as most of his customers got into their cars and began heading in the direction of Las Vegas. A minute later, the two men came back outside, loaded another tank on their dolly and wheeled it inside.

Ten minutes after the fire marshals entered the casino for the fourth time with the fourth dolly and tank, they came running out of the building, yelling, "Get back, get back!"

Some of the customers tried to go to their cars which were located close to the building, but the two men from the fire marshal's office told them that the casino was about to blow. The customers fled across the street, along with the casino manager who was wondering why in hell didn't he order his employees to put the money in the vault before evacuating the building.

The explosion blew off the entire roof of the casino and sent pieces of it soaring across the desert. When the dust settled, the casino manager walked back across the street. What was left of the casino was on fire. He looked around for the fire marshals.

They were gone and so was their van.

The phone began ringing in Lydia's apartment at 8:00 a.m. She picked it up. A woman on the line asked her to hold the line for Mr. Murphy. Lydia had to shake off the fog of sleep before she realized the call was from her attorney, Eamon Murphy.

When Murphy came on the line, he didn't waste any time getting down to business.

"Have you seen the news this morning?"

Lydia paused before answering. "No. What's happening?"

"Nearly every valuable piece of property owned by Mr. Benedict has been destroyed. Last night, somebody firebombed his trucking company and conversion facility in Culver City. About the same time, two men posing as fire marshals set off a propane explosion in a casino owned by Mr. Benedict in Nevada."

Lydia smiled. When she didn't say anything, Murphy went on.

"A few days ago, somebody blew up a factory owned by Mr. Benedict in North Carolina and a warehouse in Arizona."

"But why . . .?" Lydia said. "I mean, who would do something like that?"

There was a long pause before Murphy answered.

"Well, the press is speculating it might be the start of a turf war between gangs. You know, of course, about the allegations that have been made about Mr. Benedict's involvement with organized crime."

"But he's dead," Lydia said. "Why would someone want to destroy property he owned? His associates wanted it in the worst way. They kidnapped me and tried to force me to turn it over."

"Well, it obviously wasn't his business associates who did this. It was someone else."

Lydia bit her lip to keep the smile on her face from becoming a permanent fixture. "So, what does this mean? Do I drop the petition?"

"Oh no. Don't do that." Eamon Murphy was clearly alarmed. "Some of the property is valuable. Particularly, the two parcels of land in Culver City. Most of what Mr. Benedict owned is probably insured. There might be insurance money involved. I would advise you not to drop the petition."

"Okay," Lydia said. She was disappointed. She thought that the destruction of Jonathan Benedict's assets would make the problem go away and that she would be rid of Robert Moreno, Angela Rossi, and Eduardo Santini forever.

"Shall we go ahead with the petition?" Murphy asked.

"Of course."

After Lydia hung up, she spent a good part of the morning on the Internet looking for news regarding the destruction of Jonathan's properties. Some of the articles ignorantly suggested terrorists were involved. But most of them had made the connection with organized crime and Jonathan Benedict.

Not one of them mentioned that a certain Lydia Harte had an interest in the properties. Once that connection was made, Lydia was sure she would be bombarded by the press for interviews. She spent the rest of the morning trying to determine if she needed to find another place to stay for a while. A short-term rental of an apartment on the beach would be just perfect.

All was quiet at Jeremy Morgan's rustic ranch off San Francisco Canyon Drive at the edge of the Sierra Pelona mountains. Despite the fact it was approaching noon, Jeremy was asleep in his cabin, the five members of his team were asleep in tents across from the barn, and the mountain lion was dozing on the dirt road under the morning sun when a convoy of five vans belonging to the FBI drove onto the premises.

The lead van pulled up alongside the tents. Agents began piling out of the vans. All were wearing body armor emblazoned with FBI markings in print large enough to see from a hundred yards away. All had their guns drawn. Four agents carried Colt M4 carbines, the others were armed with semi-automatic pistols.

The agent in charge, a man in his thirties with a shaven head named Frederick Pinzler, signaled four of his men to check out the cabin up the road. They began trotting up the dirt road.

Pinzler turned his attention to the tents where Alex was the first of the Loose Cannons to emerge.

"Well, I'll be damned," Alex said. "It's the fucking FBI."

"Are any of you armed?" Pinzler asked.

"We got guns." Beard said. "Lots of them. Ammo, too."

"Where are they?"

"Boss!" It was one of the men Pinzler had sent up the road.

"I'm busy, Forrester. I told you to check the cabin."

"We can't. There's a fucking mountain lion in the road."

Pinzler looked up the road. The mountain lion was now on its feet staring at them. Pinzler made a decision. "Shoot it!"

"I wouldn't do that if I were you, sir," Marcum said. "The California mountain lion is an endangered species. If you shoot it, you're likely to get fired."

"Is there anybody up at the cabin?"

"Jeremy Morgan," Marcum said. "He owns the place. What do you guys want?"

"Are you armed?" Pinzler asked.

"Does it look like we're armed?" Marcum asked. "You got us out of our fucking sleeping bags. But, let me ask you a question, sir. Do you have a warrant?"

Pinzler stepped forward. "Listen, I don't know who you are, buster. But this is an emergency. Do any of you have weapons?"

Alex stepped forward. "We got lots of weapons!"

"Where are they?"

"Most of them are in the barn," Alex said,

"I've got a Sig Sauer in my tent," Beard said.

"I got one too," Alex said. "In the tent."

"I got an M-1 carbine in my tent," Tommy said.

"And we got a whole bunch of weapons in the barn, sir," Marcum added.

"What's going on here?" It was Jeremy Morgan. He was walking toward them.

Forrester looked at Morgan and then at the mountain lion who seemed to be glaring at them. "Are you Jeremy Morgan?"

"I am."

"We have information that you and your friends were involved in destroying several businesses over the past few days."

"Who told you that?"

"It doesn't matter who told us, Mr. Morgan. We come up here, and we find you and your friends sleeping and it's almost noon. Why is that?"

"We were up most of the night."

"Where were you?"

"Fishing. We were on a three-day fishing trip out of Ventura."

"Can you prove it?"

"Of course, I can prove it. Do you want to see the fish we caught? They're in my freezer. You can check any of our phones. Most of us were taking pictures of fish we caught. And if you want further proof, call Sally Reese in Ventura. She'll be able to confirm where we were."

Pinzler made the call to Ventura and talked to Sally Reese at Marve's Fishing Charters. Sally not only confirmed what Jeremy had said but told Pinzler that she would never book those idiots on a fishing trip again.

272 · TED KOZAK

Frustrated, Pinzler ordered his men to search Jeremy's barn and cabins. They found nothing that would tie the six men to what had happened over the past few days. They did find an invoice for the charter, cell phone photos that were date-stamped, and a freezer half full of fish that confirmed what Jeremy Morgan had said was true.

Pinzler drove to Ventura and talked to Marvin Reese, the owner of the charter service. Reese confirmed that Jeremy and his friends had been with him on a boat for the past three days. What Marvin Reese didn't tell Pinzler was that he and Jeremy were Army buddies, and that he and Jeremy were part of the team that destroyed the Red Dog Trucking and Shipping Company earlier that morning.

The main topic of discussion at roll call that afternoon was the destruction of two businesses in Culver City. Lieutenant Morton stated that the pundits in the press were talking about the possibility of terrorism. Morton cautioned the officers that they should avoid discussing their opinions about who was responsible for the attacks with anyone outside the Department, because the press was going so ballistic over what happened that they would thrust a microphone in front of anyone who had an opinion.

Near the end of roll call, Lieutenant Morton introduced the new Commanding Officer of Detectives. Her name was Maria Borders and she had just been promoted to lieutenant after a successful career at Robbery-Homicide. To Lydia's surprise, Borders had been seated right across the aisle from where Lydia sat, and she had never noticed her. When Borders got up to take the platform alongside Lieutenant Morton, Lydia smelled a whiff of lemon-scented perfume.

Just what the detectives needed, Lydia thought, a new leader who smells like lemon pie with meringue.

But Lydia quickly discovered that this woman was no piece of fluff. Lieutenant Borders was wearing a women's business suit in dark blue without a jacket and a white silk blouse decorated with a string of pearls. Although she was only five feet tall, Borders exuded power and confidence.

Borders announced that she would continue the policy that her predecessor had instituted, a policy that Lydia was not aware of. One third of the detective unit consisted of detectives at the police officer rank, and

Borders promised that any vacancy that came up in detectives would be filled by police officers in Century Division. She emphasized that she would read every arrest report written by officers in the Division and would keep copies of the reports that showed energy, dedication, knowledge of the Division, and enthusiasm for the job. Whenever a vacancy came up, she would review these reports to find a suitable replacement.

When she had finished speaking, she looked out at the officers, paused for a moment, and then said, "That's my promise to you. And while I'm at it, I can promise you that we're going to find the thugs who are killing innocent people in our business community. These men are the most sadistic bastards I have ever run across in my ten years with the Department. They do not deserve a trial. If you run across them, be careful. Don't take any chances by trying to take them into custody. If you find them and they resist, gut and skin them."

It was silent for a minute in the roll call room after Borders left.

Finally, Morton said, "You heard the lady. Let's go to work."

Out in the hallway, Lydia told Hagerty that she needed a moment to speak with Billy Vernor. When she arrived in the detective squad room, she found that Vernor was not at his desk. The other burglary team, Finlayson and Gordon, was there, so she asked them if they had seen Vernor. Finlayson looked up from the report he was writing and jerked his head in the direction of Borders' office.

Borders' office had a plate glass window that allowed the Commanding Officer of Century Detectives to look out onto the squad bay. Lydia could see Vernor standing in front of Borders' desk. The two of them were having a serious conversation.

Two hours into the shift, Five-Adam-99 received a message to call the station. Hagerty pulled over to the curb to phone in, but Lydia already had her cell phone out and was making the call. She listened for a moment and then said, "Okay," and then hung up. She looked at Hagerty.

"What did they want?" Hagerty asked.

Lydia looked at him, her mouth was open for a moment or two before she answered. "I've been ordered to report immediately to the Chief's office."

"Are you in trouble?"

Lydia shook her head. "Hell if I know."

"If you need a rep to . . ."

"I'll let you know."

Lydia was escorted to the conference room by the Chief's adjutant, Lieutenant Kirby. She was assured she didn't need a representative, so Kirby suggested that Hagerty take a seat in the outer office.

Nearly every chair around the conference table was occupied. Most of the men in the room wore business suits, but one giant of a man sitting close to the Chief of Police was wearing an unfamiliar uniform with four stars on his collar. His shoulder patches indicated he was from the Culver City Police Department.

Kirby took Lydia to a seat to the right of the Chief of Police who sat at the head of the table. He smiled at her as she sat down. Directly opposite her was Captain Malcolm Smith from the Intelligence Division. To his left was Sergeant Hector Maldonado.

She didn't know the man seated to her right, but she would never forget him. He was wearing cologne that smelled of spiced rum. It was not pleasant.

Lydia looked down the length of the table. Everyone was staring at her.

"Officer Harte," the Chief began, "as you may already be aware, two businesses were destroyed by fire in Culver City last night. You might not know this, but we have also learned that seven gentlemen's clubs, and I use the term gentlemen very loosely, have been torched in the past few days. We have with us today representatives from the Mayor's office, the Culver City Police Department, the FBI, and the Los Angeles Sheriff's Office. It has been noted by Sergeant Maldonado that you have a fledgling interest in every one of these properties that were destroyed in that they were owned by your stepfather, Jonathan Benedict. We don't know who is responsible for the destruction of these properties, but we seemed to have reached a consensus that a turf war has broken out between rival gangs for control of California. The reason we have invited you to take part in our discussion is that we believe you may be able to help us."

Lydia started to protest that she didn't know anything about a turf war, but the Chief held up his hand. "We have agreed that we will not bombard you with a thousand questions as a group. Captain Smith on my left will take the lead."

"We'll try and get you back out into the field as soon as possible," Captain Smith said. "Jonathan Benedict was your stepfather, is that correct?"

"He was married to my mother."

"Do you know anything about his business interests?"

Lydia shook her head.

"Do you know if he had any enemies?"

"My mother."

"How so?" asked the man sitting next to her.

Lydia turned to look at him. She wished there was a switch that would turn off her nose. "I don't know everything that happened, but he killed her."

"He killed your mother?" the man said, incredulously.

"I'm pretty sure he did."

Captain Smith intervened. "Look, I thought we had an agreement that I would conduct the interview."

"We did," the Chief said. "You may continue, Malcom."

"First of all, let me say that what Officer Harte just said is correct," Captain Smith said. "We have reason to believe that Jonathan's Benedict killed Officer Harte's mother."

The man next to Lydia held up his hand to speak, but Captain Smith waved him off and turned his attention back to Lydia. "To your knowledge, did Jonathan Benedict have any other enemies?"

"Maybe I can cut this short. I know very little about what Jonathan has been doing in the past seven years. When I was sixteen, my mother sent me to a prep school near Napa. When I graduated, I spent four years at UCLA. I kept a room at Jonathan's place to keep some of my stuff, but I haven't lived there since I was sixteen. I know he had poker parties with his friends every Friday night, but I don't know who attended them. I was never there when he had them. The only other person I know who visited his place after my mother died was his girlfriend, Victoria."

"What was her last name?"

Lydia paused for a moment. She didn't want to open a can of worms and spend the rest of the night in the Chief's conference room. She decided she would tell Maldonado if only she could get him out into the hallway.

"You don't remember, or you don't know her last name?" Smith said.

"I don't know."

"Do you have any ideas why someone would destroy the properties owned by Jonathan Benedict?"

"I don't."

"None at all?"

Lydia shook her head.

"Well," interjected the Chief of Police. "I think we're done here."

When Lydia was told she could go, she stood up and looked at Maldonado. When she had his attention, she blinked her eyes.

She met Hagerty in the outer office, and they went out into the hallway.

A few minutes later, Maldonado came out. "Do you have something for me?"

"I do," Lydia said. "But only if you can tell me what's going on in there?"

Maldonado glanced at Hagerty who was glaring at him. "Maybe, we should talk in private."

"He stays," Lydia said firmly. "What's going on?"

"Well, nearly everyone in there thinks that it's a turf war. For a while, there was speculation it might be terrorism. Don't ask me why they believed that. It doesn't make sense. Then they thought it might be a direct action by a group of shadow military who had been hired to carry out the attacks. They know about your friendship with Jeremy Morgan and his buddies. They thought he might have done it, but they cleared him this morning."

Lydia felt like someone had clenched a fist inside her gut when Maldonado mentioned Jeremy's name. "How did they clear him?"

"Morgan proved that he and his buddies were on a fishing charter the past few days."

"Are you kidding me?"

"Not at all. They were on a fishing boat out of Ventura. Now, why did you want to see me?"

"Two things. Jonathan's girlfriend's real name is Angela Rossi. She is either married to or related to Roberto Moreno. I'm sure you already know that. You could have told me, but you didn't. Those two were the ones who kidnapped me. If you want proof, go to their house on Stone Canyon. You will find a Humvee parked in front of their garage that has paint from my BMW on its bumper."

Maldonado looked away, a pained expression on his face. "Okay. You're right, Lydia. I knew Victoria was Angela Rossi." He turned back to her. "I hope you understand why I can't share that kind of information with you."

"Don't feed me any more bullshit, Sergeant. I have had enough handed to me in the past few weeks that I could fertilize a small farm. There's something else you need to know. There is a guy who calls himself Jamie who works as a waiter at Schroeder's Deutsche Hofbraumarkt out on Santa Monica. He is wanted by the Feds. I know he is connected to Rossi and Moreno, but I don't know his real name. I have a water glass with his fingerprints on it. If you're interested, I'll have it wrapped up in a package waiting for you with the security officer in my condo."

When Hagerty got into the police car, he turned to Lydia. "You lead a complicated life, don't you, Harte?"

"I'm not the only one," Lydia replied. "You also lead a complicated life."

"I do," Hagerty admitted. "But it's usually only for eight hours a day. Then I go home to my wife and kids. But with you, it's complicated twenty-four hours a day. You should really spend more time with Jeremy. Have some fun. Maybe, even go fishing."

Lydia nodded. That would be wonderful, she thought, but that would not solve anything. A lot of problems facing her needed to be dealt with. She remembered what a fellow athlete at U.C.L.A. said about a persistent groin injury that was plaguing her. It's like having a dead stinking cat tied onto your ankle that followed you wherever you go.

Chapter Twenty-Nine

April 17th and the following week.

LYDIA WAS about to call Jeremy the next morning when her phone rang. She hesitated for a moment when she saw the call was coming from a number in Northern California. She decided to answer it.

"It's me," the voice said.

Lydia found herself pushing the phone back and looking at it before she could think of anything to say. "Jenny? Is that you?"

"It's me. I've escaped and I need a favor."

"Are you all right? Where are you? What do you mean you escaped?"

"Listen, I don't have much time. I borrowed this phone from some guy I promised to fuck. I've got to get away from my parents. Can you send me some money? I need five hundred dollars."

"What's going on with your parents?"

"I'd rather have my tongue pulled out with a pair of hot tongs than spend another minute with my mother. Can you wire me the money? I'll pay you back."

"Where do I send it?"

"I'm in the Big Truck Travel Plaza on the interstate not far from Ukiah. It has a Western Union office."

"Are you coming home?"

"Yes. As soon as I get rid of this guy who brought me here."

"Are you all right?"

"I'm fine. There's nothing wrong with me that a bottle of vodka couldn't make better. I got no complaints."

"Aren't you going to ask me about what happened? About why they grabbed both of us?"

"Sweetie, I'm doing my best to forget what happened. I don't want to end up like a lunatic in a straitjacket. Hurry up with the money. Please. I have got to get rid of this guy before he slobbers all over me."

It took Lydia less than an hour to arrange for the wire to the Western Union office in the truck plaza. Except, she didn't wire five hundred dollars. She wired a thousand dollars. She owed Jenny that much and more.

Before reporting to work, Lydia called Jeremy.

"How was the fishing?" Lydia asked.

"How do you know I've been fishing? I forgot to tell you where we were going."

"Word gets around. I have two days off starting tomorrow. I'd like to try some of that fish."

"Come on up. I'll be home by six."

"I'll be there. Tomorrow. By six."

Lydia found Sergeant Hector Maldonado waiting in the hallway outside the women's locker room. He was smiling.

"I hope you can account for your whereabouts for the past twenty-four hours," Maldonado said.

"What are you talking about?"

"Do you remember those railroad tracks up in Palmdale? Next to the orchard where they found your friend, Jenny?"

Lydia nodded.

"They found three bodies out there this morning who weren't so lucky. A train ran over them. We have tentative identifications. They were three of Jonathan's old friends, Rossi, Moreno, and Santini. I thought you would want to know."

Lydia stepped back and stared at Maldonado. Could this be the work of Rod Mallory? He wouldn't do something like that. Would he?

"But why?"

"Who the hell knows," Maldonado said. "My gut tells me it's because they screwed up. They couldn't even get you to sign that document."

"Maybe my problems are over," Lydia said.

"I seriously doubt that. There's somebody out there that we don't know about. Somebody who killed them and wanted to make a statement."

Maldonado stepped aside to let Lydia enter the locker room. "By the way, that guy Jamie you told me about. He's in the wind. You wouldn't happen to know where I could find him, would you?"

Two days later, Lieutenant Maria Borders stepped out of her office and announced to the detectives that tonight would be the last night Tactical Operations would be working in Century Division.

Vernor immediately got up and left for the day. It was he who convinced Captain Hardemann and Lieutenant Borders to call off Tactical Operations. Now, he had work to do. A lot of work, and there were only a few people in the station he trusted to help with it.

Later in the afternoon, Assistant Watch Commander Joanna Watson also announced in roll call that tonight was the last night Tactical Operations was going to be working Century Division, and that it was up to the officers in roll call to keep the two thugs from striking again.

At 6:00 p.m., Hagerty called Lydia's cellphone and left a message. He told her that they were going to be working plainclothes tomorrow night and to meet him at Stubb's Restaurant in Culver City at 6:00 p.m. He also told her they were going to be doing some rough work and to dress appropriately in dark colors.

Lydia didn't notice the message on her cell phone until she got back to the apartment that she had rented on the beach in Santa Monica. She swore under her breath. She would have to go back to her condo tomorrow and pick up some old clothes before reporting for work.

A day later, Lydia parked her BMW in the street in front of Stubb's Restaurant. She was wearing a dark gray, long-sleeved shirt with a mock collar and dark gray jeans. A .45 Springfield XDS semi-automatic pistol was under the polo on her right hip, and two loaded magazines in a pouch were on her left hip. Just as she was about to enter the restaurant, she heard a voice calling her name.

It was Hagerty. "Have you eaten?"

"No."

"Then we better grab something. It's going to be a long night."

They took a booth as far away as they could from any other customers in the restaurant and ordered. Lydia stared at Hagerty expecting him to explain what in the hell was going on.

Finally, he spoke. "You've been involved in a shooting on the job, haven't you?" He held up a hand to stop her from saying anything. "You don't have to answer. I know you have. If Billy Vernor is right, we could very well get involved in one hell of a gunfight tonight. So, get ready. When we get out of here, check to make sure your gun has a round in the chamber. Put your mind in the right frame. This is not going to be an easy job."

Thirty minutes later, Hagerty was driving south on a nondescript street in the southern end of Century Division with Lydia at his side. They were in one of several dark gray vans that the Department used for surveillance work.

Hagerty turned south onto a street consisting of small shops and slowed down almost to a stop. "Everything is in place," he said.

"What's in place?"

"That!" He pointed to the right.

Lydia had no idea of what he was talking about. There was a line of five cars parked at the curb, but then there were no cars parked on that side of the road all the way down to the next intersection. The street was posted with temporary 'No Parking' signs. She looked at the other side of the street. There were no cars parked there either.

"We're trying to control the flow of traffic on this street," Hagerty said.

He resumed driving at a normal speed. At the next intersection, a barricade blocked half of the northbound lanes. Hagerty turned right, drove sixty yards, and then turned right again into an alleyway.

A beat-up Ford Taurus was parked about halfway down the alley. Hagerty pulled in behind it. Two men wearing coveralls emerged from the back door of a business.

Hagerty got out of the car and approached them, Lydia not far behind.

"It's ready," the taller of the two men said. "Are we supposed to take your vehicle?"

"You are," Hagerty said, "but we need to get our guns out of the back."

Two minutes later, Lydia walked into the backroom of an abandoned business. It was dark and dusty inside. She was followed by Hagerty. They were both carrying Ithaca shotguns. Lydia also carried two hand-held radios tuned to Century Division's frequency. Hagerty carried a small cooler.

The front part of the store was a large empty room that had full length mirrors on either side. There were a few empty clothing racks pushed against the walls. The only light coming into the abandoned shop was through two large plate glass windows on either side of the front door. The windows were covered with a darkened film.

Hagerty checked the handle on the front door to make sure it was unlocked. He then pulled up a metal chair and placed it in front of one of the windows. Lydia grabbed a metal chair and placed it in front of the window on the other side of the entrance to the store.

They sat down and waited.

Across the street, one door down, was a small convenience store. The windows were plastered with cigarette and beer signs. A sign suggested that it catered to Koreans.

"I assume that's the target," Lydia said.

"It is," Hagerty replied. He looked at his watch. "I don't expect much will happened until later so we might as well relax." He opened the cooler, pulled out two bottles of water and set them on the floor.

Lydia looked at the bottles. "I hope this place has a bathroom."

"It does," Hagerty said. "But no water. If you need to go, there should be one-gallon containers of water that you can use to flush. I hope they remembered to bring toilet paper."

"Who were the guys that took our van?"

"They're the support team from the Surveillance Unit. They work out of Robbery-Homicide."

Lydia watched the convenience store for a few minutes. It didn't seem to have many customers. She also noticed that there was little traffic coming from the south, but there was a lot coming from the north. The barricade at the intersection to the south was working, but what about the traffic coming from the north?

Hagerty sensed what she was thinking. "When it gets dark, a truck will double park up at the next intersection. The driver will turn on his emergency lights and leave it there as long as we need it. It should minimize traffic on this block."

"What about the parked cars that it blocks? What if the owner comes and calls the police?"

"No one will call the police. The cars that you saw parked belong to the City. They're used by Narcotics for undercover work."

When it got dark, Lydia noticed that the traffic coming from the north was no longer as busy. It occurred to her this was a well-planned operation.

She turned to Hagerty. "This was all Billy's idea, wasn't it?"

"Yes."

Lydia thought for a moment. There was no way Billy Vernor would set up something like this without him being actively involved. She turned to Hagerty. "So, where is he?"

"Who?"

"Billy!"

"He's in the store. He's working the cash register."

Lydia was incredulous. "Working the cash register? By himself? Are you kidding me?"

"The owners spent the afternoon showing him how to do it."

"Who in the hell approved this?"

"Hardemann and Borders. Billy spent a lot of time telling them how he wanted to set this up, and they agreed. That's why they asked Tactical Operations to leave the area."

"But what if these guys begin shooting when they enter the store. Billy could get killed."

"The plan is that we take these guys out before they enter the store."

"Is Billy sure they're going to hit this place?"

"Yes."

Billy Vernor was one of the most amazing persons that Lydia had ever met on the Police Department. Hardemann had once told her that Billy Vernor arrested more people in one week than the entire detective unit combined. From an outsider, it looked like Vernor was omniscient, but Lydia knew better. Vernor had developed and maintained a list of snitches that kept him informed of what was happening in the street. Vernor would use the information from his informants to make an arrest, and at the same time make it look like he did it on his own.

"Listen Lydia, I need to tell you something," Hagerty said. "At the Academy, they teach you that when you confront a gunman that you yell, 'Police officer. Drop your gun'. We're not going to do that tonight. If we see these thugs and they have guns, we yell, "Hey" to get their attention and then blast the shit out of them when they turn toward us."

Watch changeover at Century Division began at 11:30 p.m. That's when the P.M. Watch crew headed to the station and A.M. Watch took over. Unfortunately, it was just then that Lydia's cell phone message system pinged. She took the cell phone out of her pocket and looked at it.

She didn't get a chance to find the message because the next thing she heard was Hagerty who yelled, "Jesus Christ!"

Lydia looked out the window. A blue compact was parked at the curb directly opposite their position.

Two figures wearing ski masks and dark clothing got out of the car and began moving quickly toward the entrance of the convenience store. A third person behind the wheel of the car immediately drove off.

Lydia threw down her phone, grabbed the shotgun, and ran toward the door. Hagerty followed her.

Once they were outside, they saw that the two men had already entered the store. Seconds later, they heard gunfire coming from inside the store. It sounded like someone had set off a string of firecrackers.

Hagerty and Lydia were halfway across the street when the first of the two men came limping out of the store. He was holding his left thigh with his hand while frantically looking up and down the street. The second man backed out of the store while firing a handgun at someone inside.

Lydia raised the shotgun to her shoulder and waited for him to turn. When he did, he saw her and raised his gun. Lydia didn't hesitate. She pulled the trigger and the blast ripped apart the man's chest.

She jacked in a fresh round and swung the gun around toward the other man. Before she could line up the sights, Hagerty shot him.

Lydia looked at Hagerty and said, "My God! What did they do to Billy?"

"Get inside and check on him. I've got to get a broadcast out on that blue car before it gets to the freeway."

Lydia sighed in relief when she found Billy Vernor behind the counter, wiping the side of his bloody face with a handkerchief.

"Are you all right?" Lydia asked, thinking he had been shot.

"Did you get the assholes?"

"Are you all right?"

"Flying glass. Did you get them?"

"Both of them are down. I'll get you an ambulance."

Once outside, Lydia heard the rising sirens of police cars coming from two different directions. Hagerty was on the radio asking for cars to block either end of the street.

Vernor came out of the store. His left cheek was streaked with blood. He bent down and pulled off the mask of the taller of the two killers.

Lydia stared at the face. It wasn't a man; it was a teenager. He was also someone she had seen before.

"Billy, who is that boy?"

Vernor didn't answer right away. He turned the body over and began rifling through his pockets.

A car slid to a stop in the middle of the street. It was a police car. Hagerty began issuing instructions to the officers to keep people away from the scene. At the north end of the street, a police car was now blocking the intersection.

Vernor found a wallet in the boy's pocket and pulled out a driver's license. He showed it to Lydia.

"He lives with his aunt," Vernor said. "The getaway driver will go there."

Hagerty came alongside. "Billy, who are these guys?"

"This one is Akim Bahri." Vernor reached over and pulled the mask off the other one. Another youthful face, this one with open eyes that could no longer see. "This is Jamal Chandra. They're student volunteers. They worked for me."

"How did you know they were going to hit this place?" Lydia asked.

"Because they're stupid. I heard them talking while they were fucking around with the map board." Vernor looked at Hagerty. "How in hell did you let these guys get in the store? That wasn't supposed to happen." There was no anger in voice.

"They didn't walk up like you said they would. The driver dropped them off."

Vernor handed the driver's license he had taken out of Bakri's pocket and gave it to Hagerty. "You'll find the driver there."

Sergeant Johanna Watson pulled up to the curb. She looked around, saw Hagerty and Lydia with shotguns in their hands, saw the blood on Vernor's face, and said. "Billy, we need to get you an ambulance. Hagerty and Harte, we need to get you to the station."

"What we need," Hagerty said, "is to borrow your car."

Hagerty pulled the car to the curb about a half block away from the address that was on the driver's license Vernor had given him. Hagerty and Lydia retrieved shotguns from the trunk of the car and began walking toward the house.

A blue Toyota compact was parked at the curb a few doors away from the house. Lydia raised a hand to point it out to Hagerty, but he had already seen it.

Hagerty put his hand on the hood. He looked at Lydia and nodded. It was still warm.

The house they were looking for was a small bungalow. Lights were on in the front windows. They heard sound of laughter coming from a television.

Hagerty went to one of the windows and looked inside. He signaled Lydia to take a position on the right side of the door. Lydia was sure that Hagerty was going to kick the door in, but he surprised her. He gently knocked on the door instead.

A diminutive woman with dark features answered the door. She looked to her left and saw Lydia and then to the right and saw Hagerty. Despite the fact they were carrying shotguns, she didn't seem surprised. She put the fingertips of one hand to her mouth and then stepped back and pointed to a staircase and then to the ceiling above.

Before Lydia followed Hagerty up the stairs, she looked back to make sure the woman stayed behind. The woman had shut her eyes and was covering both ears with her hands.

A short hallway at the top of the stairs led to the rear where light spilled out onto the carpet from an open doorway. The sound of a twenty-four-hour news station was coming from inside the room.

Jimmy Spahn was sitting on the bed, his head down, listening to the radio when Lydia followed Hagerty into the room. He looked up, surprised at seeing two shotguns trained on his chest. He unexpectedly slid off the bed and dropped to his knees, putting his hands above his head.

Hagerty covered him while Lydia pushed Spahn face down on the floor and handcuffed him.

"How did you find me?" Spahn asked.

"You can thank your friend Akim for that."

Spahn wiggled around to look at Lydia. "I'll kill that bastard when I find him."

"It's too late for that now, you little shit. He's already dead."

AUTHOR'S BIO

Ted Kozak is a proud veteran of the United States Marine Corps. He served for nearly twenty-six years with the Los Angeles Police Department where he once had a tour of duty as the Commanding Officer of the 77th Street Detective Division. On retiring from the Department, he worked for ten years as an attorney in California and another ten years in Kentucky. He lives in rural Kentucky with his wife and two dogs.

He is the author of Charlie Wolf's Revenge, Charlie Wolf's Justice, The Messiah's Spy, Alex and Christina–Saving Lumenaria, Teresa–The Snake Witch, and Lydia Harte.

His seventh novel, Lydia Harte—Loose Cannons, is a sequel to Lydia Harte

Lydia Harte has a supporting role in Charlie Wolf's Justice as the leader of Apache Platoon making a forcible entry into a building occupied by armed felony suspects.

Printed in the U.S.
 MIDNIGHT
STARPRESS.

www.ingramcontent.com/pod-product-compliance
Lightning Source LLC
Chambersburg PA
CBHW060855250626
47159CB00008B/2743